USA TODAY bestselling author **Janice Maynard** loved books and writing even as a child. After multiple rejections, she finally sold her first manuscript! Since then, she has written sixty books and novellas. Janice lives in Tennessee with her husband, Charles. They love hiking, travelling and family time. You can connect with Janice at

www.janicemaynard.com
www.Twitter.com/janicemaynard
www.Facebook.com/janicemaynardauthor
www.Facebook.com/janicesmaynard
www.Instagram.com/therealjanicemaynard

Adriana Herrera was born and raised in the Caribbean, but for the last fifteen years has let her job (and her spouse) take her all over the world. She loves writing stories about people who look and sound like her people, getting unapologetic happy endings. Her Dreamers series has received starred reviews from *Publishers Weekly* and *Booklist* and has been featured by the *Today* show on NBC, *Entertainment Weekly*, *O Magazine*, NPR, *Library Journal*, the *New York Times* and the *Washington Post*. She's a trauma therapist in New York City, working with survivors of domestic and sexual violence.

Also by Janice Maynard

Southern Secrets
Blame It On Christmas
A Contract Seduction
Bombshell for the Black Sheep

The Men of Stone River
After Hours Seduction
Upstairs Downstairs Temptation
Secrets of a Playboy

Discover more at millsandboon.co.uk

TEXAS TOUGH

JANICE MAYNARD

ONE WEEK TO
CLAIM IT ALL

ADRIANA HERRERA

MILLS & BOON

First Published in Great Britain 2021
by Mills & Boon, an imprint of HarperCollins*Publishers* Ltd
1 London Bridge Street, London, SE1 9GF

www.harpercollins.co.uk

HarperCollins*Publishers*
1st Floor, Watermarque Building,
Ringsend Road, Dublin 4, Ireland

Texas Tough © 2021 Harlequin Books S.A.
One Week to Claim It All © 2021 Adriana Herrera

Special thanks and acknowledgement are given to Janice Maynard for her contribution to the *Texas Cattleman's Club: Heir Apparent* series .

ISBN: 978-0-263-28292-4

0521

MIX
Paper from
responsible sources
FSC™ C007454

This book is produced from independently certified FSC™ paper to ensure responsible forest management.

For more information visit: www.harpercollins.co.uk/green

Printed and bound in Spain
by CPI, Barcelona

TEXAS TOUGH

JANICE MAYNARD

To 'romance lovers' everywhere.
You help keep the human spirit alive.
Thanks for your support of the genre and
your dedication to characters and stories.
There would be no books with you!

One

Abby Carmichael was a Starbucks and bright-city-lights kind of girl. What was she doing out here in this godforsaken section of Texas? Maverick County was flat. So flat. And the town of Royal, though charming enough with its wealthy ranchers and rough-edged cowboys, didn't even *have* a storefront for her usual caffeine fix.

So far, she'd been in Royal less than a day, and already she was regretting her current life choice. That was the trouble with being a documentary filmmaker. You had to go where the stories took you. Unfortunately, this particular assignment was smack-dab in the middle of the old Western movies her grandpa used to make her watch.

She pulled off onto a small gravel side road, dazzled by the glorious sunset despite her cranky mood. Flying did that to her. Not to mention having to drive a rental car where all the buttons and knobs were in different places.

Taking a deep breath, she concentrated on losing herself

in the moment. All she needed was a hot bath and a good night's sleep. Then she'd be good as new.

Grudgingly, she admired the stunning display of colors painting the evening sky. The orangey reds and golds caught the tips of prairie grasses and made them flame with faux fire. New York City *had* sunsets, but not like this.

While she watched the show, she lowered the car windows. It was June, and plenty humid. The air felt like a blanket, dampening the back of her neck.

At least the heat didn't bother her. Gradually, the peaceful scene smoothed her ragged edges. She'd left her cameras back at the hotel. This excursion was about relaxation and mental health, not work.

Suddenly, she noticed a lone figure far-off on the horizon, silhouetted against the glow of the quickly plummeting sun. The phantom drew closer, taking on shape and form, moving fast, paralleling the road. It was a rider, a horseman. With the sun in her eyes, Abby could make out nothing about the cowboy's features, but she was struck by the grace of man and beast and by the beauty of day's end.

As the horse drew closer, Abby could hear the distinctive *thud, ka-thud* of hooves striking the raw dirt. Something inside her quivered in anticipation.

Grabbing her phone, she jumped out of the car, ran down the road to get closer and began videoing with her cell. That was often how she processed information. Give her a lens, even a phone lens, and she was happy.

The man's posture was regal, yet easy in the saddle. As if he and the animal were one. Soon, they would be past her.

But without warning, the rider pulled on the reins abruptly. The horse whinnied in protest, reared on its hind legs and settled into a restless halt.

A deep, masculine voice called out across the distance, "You're on private property. Can I help you?"

For the first time, it occurred to Abby that she was entirely alone and far from civilization. *Vulnerable.* A frisson of caution slid down her spine, and some atavistic instinct told her to run. "I have Mace," she warned over her shoulder as she walked rapidly back toward her car.

The man's laugh, a sexy amused chuckle, carried on the breeze. "Mace is good, but it's no match for a Texas shotgun."

Her heart bobbled in her chest, her breath hitching as she moved faster and faster away from him. She had come farther than she realized. Surely, the man was joking. But she didn't plan on finding out.

She jumped into her car, executed a flawless U-turn and gunned the engine, heading back toward town.

Two hours later, Abby was still a bit shaky. Her room felt claustrophobic, so she grabbed her billfold, pocketed her key card and went downstairs. Maybe a drink would calm her nerves. She wasn't normally so skittish, but everything about this place felt alien.

Not the hotel. The Miramar was lovely. Comfortable. Just the right amount of pampered luxury. And still in her budget. She *could* have stayed at the lavish Bellamy, but Royal's premier five-star resort was too high-profile for her needs.

At the entrance to the bar, she paused and took a breath, soothed by the dim lights and the traditional furnishings. The room was filled with lots of brass and candles and fresh flowers. And almost *no* people. The bartender looked up when she walked in. He was an older man with graying hair and a craggy face. "Plenty of room at the bar," he said. "As you can see. But feel free to take a booth if you'd prefer."

"Thanks." Abby debated briefly, then sat down at the booth in the corner. It was private, and she felt the need to regroup. She was well able to handle herself in public, or even wave off the occasional pushy male. After all, she was a New Yorker. But tonight, she just wanted to unwind.

The bartender came around to her table, pad in hand. "What can I get you, young lady? The appetizers are on that card right there."

She smiled at him. "No food for me, thanks. But a glass of zinfandel, please. Beringer if you have it."

"Yes, ma'am," he said, walking away to fill her order.

When the man returned with her drink, Abby took the glass with a muttered thanks. "I needed this," she confessed. "I was driving outside of town, and some macho cowboy on a horse threatened me with a shotgun. It was scary."

The bartender raised a skeptical eyebrow. "Doesn't sound like Royal. Folks around here are pretty hospitable as a rule."

"Maybe," Abby said, unconvinced.

When the man frowned and walked away, she realized belatedly that either she had insulted his fellow Texans, or maybe he thought she was an interloper dressed a tad too casually for the Miramar. Whenever she flew, she liked to be comfortable. Today, she had worn a thin flannel shirt over a silky camisole with her oldest, softest jeans and ankle boots.

Oh, well, it was late, and the bar was almost empty. She hoped no one would even notice her…

Carter Crane yawned and stretched as he sauntered into the Miramar and headed for the bar. He should be on his way home for a good night's sleep, but he had just finished a late evening meeting with a breeder, and he was feeling restless for no good reason he could pinpoint.

At thirty-four, he'd thought he would have a wife and

maybe a kid by now. But he had gambled on the wrong woman and lost. His fault. He should have seen it coming.

The gorgeous summer weather made him feel more alone than usual. Maybe because this was the time of year for socializing. Carter hadn't *socialized* with a woman in far too long. A year—or maybe a year and a half?

He worked hard enough to keep his reckless impulses in check. Mostly.

Tonight, he felt the sting.

There were other more popular watering holes in Royal, but he liked the private, laid-back ambience at the Mira-mar.

He grinned at the bartender. "Hey, Sam. I'll have a beer, please. The usual." Carter's dad had known Sam since the two men were boys. Now his father was enjoying the good life in a fancy condo on Miami Beach.

Sam brought the frothy beer and set it on a napkin. "Food?"

"Nope. I'm good."

"How's the herd?" the older man asked.

"Best one yet. Barring tornadoes or droughts, we should have a banner year."

"Your dad says you work too hard."

"It's all I know how to do," Carter said. "Besides, he was the same way."

Sam nodded as he rinsed glasses and hung them over-head. "True. But not now. He misses you."

"I didn't realize you kept in touch."

"Now and then," Sam said.

Carter changed the subject. "You won't believe what happened to me earlier tonight. Some crazy tourist lady threatened me with Mace. On my own property."

"How do you know she was a tourist?"

"Who else would carry Mace?" Carter scoffed. "Royal is a safe town."

"Maybe she didn't know that. And the way *I* heard it, you threatened her with a shotgun."

He gaped. "Say what?"

Sam pointed. "Little gal's over there. You probably should apologize. It rattled her."

Carter glanced over his shoulder. "Looks like she enjoys being alone."

The bartender shook his head, eyes dancing. "Come on. I'll introduce you, so she won't think you're hitting on her."

Sam didn't wait. He poured a glass of wine, swung around the end of the bar and went to where the woman sat, half shielded by the high wooden back of the banquette. "This one's on the house, ma'am. And I'd like to introduce you to Carter Crane. He's one of Royal's fine, upstanding citizens. I think he has something to say to you."

Carter felt his neck get hot. The woman eyeing him warily was visibly skeptical of Sam's assessment. "May I sit for a moment?" he asked.

After a long hesitation, the woman nodded. "Help yourself."

He eased into the booth, beer in hand, and cut to the chase. "I was the one you saw on the road outside of town. I was kidding about the shotgun," he said quickly as her eyes rounded. "It was a joke."

The woman looked him over, not saying a word. Though her perusal wasn't entirely comfortable, Carter seized on the excuse to do his own inventory. She was slim and young, almost too young to be drinking alcohol, but maybe her looks were deceptive.

Her hair was long and brown and wavy, her eyes a rich brown to match. She wasn't wearing a speck of makeup, except possibly mascara. Even then, her lush lashes *could* be real, he supposed.

It was her complexion, however, that elevated her from

merely pretty to gorgeous. Light brown with a hint of sunlight, her skin was glowing and perfect.

Carter felt a stirring of lust and was taken aback. Ordi-
narily, he preferred his women sophisticated and worldly.
This artless, unadorned female was the rose that didn't
need gilding. She was *stunning*.

He cleared his throat. "As Sam said, I'm Carter Crane.
I own the Sunset Acres ranch. Most days I'm proud of it.
Others, I curse it. What's your name?"

The tiniest of smiles tilted her lips. "Abby Carmichael.
And I knew you were kidding about the shotgun."

"No, you didn't." He chuckled. "I've never seen a woman
move so fast."

She lifted her chin. "I was in a hurry to get back to the
hotel, because I needed to pee. It had nothing to do with
you."

He laughed again, letting the blatant lie go unchallenged,
charmed by her voice and her wide-eyed appeal. "I think
I recognize the accent," he said. "You're from back East,
right? New York? My college roommate was born and bred
in Manhattan."

"I don't have an accent," she insisted. "You're the one
with the drawl."

Carter shook his head slowly. "I never argue with a lady,"
he said.

"Why do I not believe that?"

Her wry sarcasm made him grin all over again. She
might be young, but she was no naive kid. "What brings
you to Royal?" he asked.

"I'm doing a documentary on the festival—Soiree on
the Bay."

He grimaced. "Ah."

She cocked her head. "You don't approve?"

"I don't *not* approve," he answered carefully. "But events

like that bring hordes of outsiders into town. I like my space and my privacy."

"The festival takes place on Appaloosa Island."

"Doesn't matter. People have to sleep and eat and shop. Royal will be a madhouse."

"You're awfully young to be a curmudgeon. How old are you, forty?"

He sat up straighter, affronted. "I'm thirty-four, for your information. And even a *young* man can have strong opinions."

"True…"

From the twinkle in her eye, he saw that she had been baiting him. "Very funny," he muttered. "But since we've broached the subject, how old are you? I guessed seventeen at first, but you're drinking wine, so I don't know."

"Didn't your mother tell you never to ask a woman her age?"

"Seventeen it is."

"Don't be insulting. I'm twenty-four. Plenty old enough to recognize a man with an agenda."

"Hey," he protested, holding up his hands. "I only came over to say hello. And to assure you that you're in no danger here in Royal."

"I can handle myself, Mr. Crane."

"Carter," he insisted.

"Carter. And because I'm a nice person, I'll forgive you for the shotgun incident, if you'll do me a favor."

He bristled. "There *was* no shotgun incident, woman." Was she flirting with him? Surely not.

She smiled broadly now. The wattage of that smile kicked him in the chest like a mule. "If you say so…"

"What kind of favor?" He wasn't born yesterday and wasn't going to give her carte blanche.

"A simple one. I'd like to see your ranch. Film it. And interview you. On camera."

"Why?" He was naturally suspicious. Life had taught him that things weren't always what they seemed. "I have nothing at all to do with the festival. I don't even care about it. Period."

She shrugged. When she did, one shoulder of her shirt slipped, revealing the strap of her camisole and more of her smooth skin. His chest tightened as did parts south.

The fact that her expression was matter-of-fact didn't jibe with his racing pulse.

"My documentary about the festival will be punctuated by scenes from around Royal. To provide local color. Since Royal is home to the famed Texas Cattleman's Club, it only makes sense for me to include ranching. You're the only rancher I know, so here we are."

"My days are busy," he muttered, sounding pedantic, even to his own ears. "I don't have time for futzing around with movie stuff."

Her jaw dropped. "Do you have any idea how patronizing you sound? My job is no less important than yours, Mr. Carter Crane. But don't worry. I'm sure I can find another rancher to show me the ropes."

Like hell you will. The visceral response told him he was wading into deep water. "Fine. I'll do it," he said, trying not to sound as grumpy as he felt. This artless, beautiful young woman was throwing him off his game. "Give me your contact info."

Abby reached into her wallet and extracted a business card. It was stylish, but casual. Much like the gal with her hand extended. He reached out and took the small rectangle, perusing it. "I'll call you," he said.

"That's what they all say," she deadpanned.

"I said I would, and I will."

"I appreciate it, Carter."

The way she said his name, two distinct syllables with

a feminine nuance, made him itchy. Suddenly, he was in no great hurry to head home.

"I could stay a little longer," he said. "Since you're new in town."

The rosy tint on her cheekbones deepened. "How chivalrous."

"May I buy you another glass of wine?"

The woman shook her head. "I'm a lightweight. But I wouldn't say no to a Coke and nachos. Though this place might be too upscale for comfort food."

"I'm sure Sam will rustle some up for us," he told her.

"I love how you do that."

Carter frowned. "Do what?"

"Talk like a cowboy. *Rustle some up.*"

He leaned back in the booth, feeling some of the day's stress melt away. This unexpected encounter was the most fun he'd had in ages. Though he was likely destined for a cold shower and a restless night. "Are you making fun of me, Ms. Carmichael?"

"You can call me Abby," she said.

"Don't move…" He went to the bar, gave Sam their order and came back. "I told him we wanted fried pickles, too."

His companion wrinkled her nose. "Ew, gross. Don't you care about your health?"

Carter hid a smile as he took off the noose around his neck. He removed his jacket, too, and stretched his arms over his head, yawning. "Do I look unhealthy to you?"

Two

Not fair, Carter Crane. Abby would have choked on her pickle... If she'd been eating one. Which she wasn't. Her face heated and her pulse stumbled as she drank him in from head to toe. The man was eye candy, leading man material, drop-dead *gorgeous*.

Carter Crane was a lot of male. In every way. When she had seen him earlier on horseback, she'd barely had the time to digest what he looked like, much less what he was wearing. But she was pretty sure it hadn't been this expensive navy sport coat, pristine white button-down and tailored dress pants. Not to mention the patterned crimson necktie that he had shed so quickly.

The fact that he managed to wear cowboy boots without looking even a smidge ridiculous told her he was the real deal.

Underneath the soft cotton fabric of his shirt was a chest that went on for miles. Hard, with ripped abs. She'd bet her gym membership on it.

Summer-morning blue eyes were bracketed with tiny lines from squinting into the sun. His hair was brown and tousled, as if he had just tumbled out of bed and run his hands through the silky strands.

She downed a gulp of the Coke that Sam had just set on the table. "I have no medical training," she said primly. "You might be at death's door for all I know." When she thought her expression wouldn't give her away, she sat back and gave him an even stare. "I'm not a doctor, but you look fine to me."

He raised an eyebrow. "*Fine?* That's the best you can do?"

Humor lifted the corners of her lips, despite her best efforts to take him down a peg or two. "You know what you look like, rancher man. You don't need me to stroke your ego or anything else."

Carter blinked and quirked a brow. "Umm…"

Suddenly, she heard the blatantly suggestive comment she had made. Unwittingly, but still… "Moving on," she said briskly, trying to pretend she was not embarrassed. Or interested. Or *turned on*.

Her companion didn't call her out on her faux pas. Instead, he leaned forward on his elbows and offered her a pickle. "You're a filmmaker. Surely you sample the local cuisine when you travel. Come on, Abby. At least try one."

Against her better judgment, she opened her lips and let him tuck the crispy slice in between. She bit down automatically and felt the flavors explode on her tongue. The sharp bite of the pickle and the tangy seasoning of the outer layer were utterly divine. "Oh, my…this is good."

Carter sprawled in the corner of the booth and scooped up two for his own pleasure. "Told you," he said as he chewed and swallowed.

Abby was mesmerized by the ripples in his tanned throat. She turned to the nachos in desperation. Apparently, New York wasn't the only place in the world with good food. "These are amazing, too."

Carter offered her a napkin, his gaze intense. "You have cheese on your chin," he told her quietly.

Abby quaked inside. This was getting way too personal, way too fast. She needed to put on the brakes. "Tell me about your family." She blurted out the request.

Carter ran a hand across the back of his neck, eyeing her with undisguised male interest. Abby was interested, too, but they had just met, and she certainly wasn't going to invite him upstairs to her hotel room.

Finally, he sighed. "Not much to tell. I'm the older of two kids. One sister. My parents retired to Florida, leaving me in charge of the ranch. It's been in our family for five generations. Sunset Acres is not only in my blood, it's part of me."

A squiggle of disappointment settled in Abby's stomach. The last thing she needed was to get involved with a man who was wedded to a plot of dirt in this remote, flat, rural landscape. "Did you always want to be a rancher?"

He shook his head slowly. "When I was ten, I wanted to be an astronaut."

"Seriously? Wow. That's cool. Why didn't you go that route?"

"Several reasons. Turns out, I'm claustrophobic. But more to the point, one of my ancestors fought with Davy Crockett at the Alamo. Walking away from a couple centuries of family history wasn't an option." He signaled Sam for another round of drinks.

They were the only customers in the bar now. Abby glanced at her watch. "Should we go? Maybe Sam wants to shut down."

Carter shook his head slowly, his gaze still focused on her mouth. "We have another hour," he said.

Those four words were innocuous, but the handsome

rancher's tone was not. Suddenly, Abby wanted to take off her shirt. She was far too hot. The camisole was not indecent. But such a move might signal something she wasn't ready to signal.

"What shall we talk about?" she asked in desperation, her hormones melting into a puddle of heated sexual attraction. "Politics? Religion. Something easy?"

Carter leaned forward and touched the fingernail on her pinkie, barely any contact at all. "I want to talk about you."

Carter wasn't the kind of man to press a female who wasn't interested. He'd been taught by his daddy to respect the fairer sex. And truth be told, women usually came on to him, not the other way around.

If Abby had been uninterested, he would have paid the check and walked out of the bar. But she *was* interested. He'd bet his prize stallion on it.

Still, he gave her an out. "Should I go now?" he asked gruffly. "Am I making you uncomfortable?"

She stared at him, pupils dilated slightly, as he rubbed her fingernail. He'd never done such a thing before. Ever. In fact, in the cold light of day, this move on his part would probably look dorky and dumb.

But right now, they were connected.

Her chest rose and fell. "No," she whispered. "Don't go."

His hand shook. So much so, that he pulled it back and tucked it under the table out of sight. It wouldn't be good for her to realize how close he was to begging for a night in her bed.

One-night stands were indulgences he had given up long ago—about the time his father began handing over more and more responsibility for the ranch. Carter was not a selfish twentysomething anymore. He was a landowner, a wealthy rancher and a respected member of the community.

For Abby Carmichael, though, he might make an exception.

He cleared his throat, trying to focus on anything other than the fantasy swirling in his head. "As I recall, you never answered my question about where you're from."

"You were right about that. New York City. I went to film school at New York University, and I still live with my mom when I'm in town. Apartments are ridiculously expensive."

"So I've heard. NYU. I'm impressed. Isn't it hard to get accepted?"

She grimaced. "Definitely. But I had two things going in my favor. My father is Black, and my mom is white, so I ticked the biracial box."

"And the other?" he asked.

"Daddy is a filmmaker out on the West Coast. He and my mom are divorced. I spent summers with him growing up and got the movie bug. He asked a couple of his influential friends to write recommendation letters for me. So here I am," she explained.

"Why documentaries?"

"We're a visual society. As much as I love books and believe in the power of the written word, there's no faster way to touch someone's heart or change someone's opinion than with a well-framed documentary." She spoke with intensity.

"What piqued your interest about Soiree on the Bay?"

"Well, you talked about family legacy—" She smiled, her face lighting up. "I can claim one, as well, though not so long-lived. My grandmother was at Woodstock. In fact, she supposedly got pregnant with my mother there. Gave birth to her when she was barely eighteen. Music is in my blood, and in any big gathering like that, there are fascinating stories to tell. Lots of stories. I want to capture this festival from beginning to end."

Carter had lost his appetite for nachos and fried pickles. What he wanted now, *needed* now, was far more visceral. "I love your passion," he said slowly. "I'm sure that comes across in your work."

Pink stained her cheeks again. "I hope so. And you'll let me film you? Please?"

With Abby's big brown eyes staring at him hopefully, he felt churlish for turning her down. But he sensed that a yes from him right now would ensnare him in something he wasn't sure he was prepared for, neither the movie project nor the woman who wasn't going to stick around.

"I'll think about it. I promise."

He saw her disappointment, but he held firm.

"Well, thank you then," she said. "For the nachos and Cokes. And the conversation. But I should get some sleep. The time change is hitting me." She yawned, proving her point.

They both slid out of the booth at the same time, suddenly standing far too close. Carter's throat constricted. He wanted to grab her up and kiss her until her body went limp with pleasure.

He shoved his hands in his pockets. "Welcome to Royal, Abby Carmichael. I hope you enjoy all we have to offer…"

Abby left the cowboy standing in the bar, his hot gaze giving her second and third thoughts about being reckless. It wasn't vanity on her part to think he would have accompanied her upstairs. There were enough sparks arcing between them to pretty much guarantee the sex would be explosive.

But once she was in her room, she knew she had done the right thing. She was really tired, and she had a meeting tomorrow that was very important. Lila Jones, from Royal's

Chamber of Commerce, was going to welcome her to town and even give her a tour of Appaloosa Island.

Abby hoped she would also be able to do some preliminary filming.

As she showered and crawled into bed, however, it was hard to keep her mind on work. When she closed her eyes, Carter Crane was there with her, laughing, flirting, teasing. It had been a long time since she had met someone so intriguing, so different from the men she knew in New York. Or even California for that matter.

Carter was his own man. A Texas rancher. That meant something in this part of the world. Still, even aside from his ranching expertise and land holdings, she knew he would stand out anywhere in the country. Carter had a commanding presence, an innate confidence that was very appealing and sexy. And though his intense masculinity was flavored with a tinge of arrogance, the arrogance wasn't off-putting.

After the *interesting* evening she'd had with him—starting out on a deserted stretch of highway and ending in a dimly lit bar—she might have tossed and turned. Fortunately, exhaustion claimed her, and she slept long and deeply.

When she awoke the next morning at 6:00 a.m., her batteries were recharged, and she was eager to jump-start her day. After heading out for a run and then taking a quick shower, she couldn't deny feeling bummed when she glanced at her phone. Not a single text or missed call. Would Carter agree to let her film him? He had promised to think about it. But without a time frame. He might keep her dangling indefinitely.

She would give him forty-eight hours. After that, she would assume his answer was no. Which meant she would have to find someone else. Handsome ranchers might be a dime a dozen in this part of the world. Who knew?

When she stood at the window for a moment and looked out over the heart of Royal, she had to admit it wasn't so bad after all. Though it wasn't quite big enough to be called a city by her standards, it was definitely a very nice, large town. The broad main thoroughfare was landscaped with flowers and ornamental trees, and in the distance, she could make out the shape of the venerable Texas Cattleman's Club.

There were clothing stores and restaurants, bars and banks—even an intentionally retro country emporium. In her research, she had learned that the schools were rated highly, and in addition to all the wealthy cattle barons, the town was home to artists and potters and other creative types.

It wasn't New York City or Malibu, but she could see the appeal.

A tiny alarm beeped on her watch.

Grabbing up her roomy leather tote, a water bottle and a rain jacket just in case, she headed out to meet her tour guide.

Lila was right on time, waiting at the curb in front of the hotel. She jumped out of her car. "It's wonderful to see you again, Abby. Welcome to Royal."

Abby shook the other woman's hand. "Thanks. I'm happy to be here." As they got settled, she took stock of her companion. She had met the other woman in LA and knew she was about her age, maybe a little older. She reminded Abby of the actress Zooey Deschanel.

Lila waved at the back seat. "I have snacks when you get hungry."

"Thanks. I appreciate your taking me out to the island today. But tell me again why I can't just stay there for the length of my project?" This was going to be a heck of a commute. Three hours each way.

Lila chuckled. "Well, first of all, you have to get used

to Texas. Everything is big out here in the Lone Star State. Big ranches, big egos, big open spaces. It's fairly common to travel by helicopter or small plane. You'll find landing strips just about anywhere you want to go."

"But I can't stay on the island?"

"Not realistically. It doesn't have everyday amenities. There are some huge mansions out on the western end, but the rest of it is undeveloped. That's why the Edmond family decided it would be the perfect spot for Soiree on the Bay."

"And Mustang Point?"

"Mostly private residences for the super wealthy. Mustang has a ton of water sports, but I promise you, living in Royal while you do this project will be far more reasonable. Not to mention the fact that all the people you'll need to interview for your documentary live in Royal or just outside of town."

They had been driving for twenty minutes when Lila pulled the car into a gravel parking lot. Abby's stomach pitched. She was a frequent flier on coast-to-coast routes. But the tiny prop plane sitting on the narrow strip of tarmac looked flimsy and unimpressive.

Lila didn't seem at all concerned. She hopped out and greeted the young pilot. "Hi, Danny. Thanks for running us out to the Point."

The freckled kid ducked his head bashfully. "Happy to do it, Miss Lila. I need flying hours to keep my license up-to-date, and Daddy said not to charge you a dime."

"I'll add my thanks, too," Abby said.

Soon, they were airborne. Abby took out her camera and aimed through the tiny plane window. The result was not great, but it helped her get a feel for the landscape.

Lila watched with interest. "What kind of camera are you using? It looks fairly portable and light."

Abby sat back in her seat. "Twelve pounds. It's a Panasonic DVX200. Pricey, but it shoots great 4K resolution and has up to twelve stops of dynamic range."

"I'll pretend I know what you're talking about," Lila said, laughing.

"The camera was a gift from my dad when I graduated. He was really hoping I would follow in his footsteps."

"And now here you are."

"Yes. After you invited me to film the festival, Dad hooked me up with somebody at Netflix who might be interested in a documentary about Soiree on the Bay, but I'll have to find a strong human interest angle."

"A hook as they say?"

"Exactly." Abby tucked her camera back in her bag. Incorporating Carter's story would add depth and local color, but she wasn't holding her breath. "What's on our schedule for today?"

Lila tapped her phone and perused what was clearly a calendar. "We'll catch the ferry out to Appaloosa Island. It's a quick, fifteen-minute ride. On the island, Jerome will meet us. He acts as a groundskeeper for several of the landowners, and he's arranged for me—and by extension you—to have the use of a golf cart anytime you come out to the island. You'll just call him in advance, and it will be waiting. Today, we'll do an informal tour and answer any questions you might have."

"I really appreciate you giving up a huge part of your morning and afternoon to do this."

"No problem. It's my job, of course. And besides, any chance to get out of the office is a plus."

As the small plane touched down, Abby glanced at her watch. The trip had taken an hour and a half. So, better than the three-hour drive she'd been expecting, but still not quick. She was going to have to be very disciplined about planning her shooting schedule. Much of the groundwork would have to be done in Royal.

She grabbed her things, thanked the young pilot and followed the other woman out of the plane. The ferry dock was a quarter-mile walk. Though a small line of cars sat waiting to cross, foot traffic was almost nonexistent. Abby and Lila boarded and made their way inside the air-conditioned cabin.

Abby frowned as she thought about the logistics. "How is this going to work during the actual festival?"

Lila uncapped her water bottle and took a sip. "It won't be easy. The organizers are planning to add four more ferries. And parking on the island will be limited. Festivalgoers who want to have their personal vehicles on-site will pay a hefty premium in addition to their ticket price."

"So part of the cachet of the festival will be that it's hard to access…it's *exclusive*."

"Exactly."

At the end of the brief ferry ride, Lila waved at an older man with deeply tanned skin and grizzled salt-and-pepper hair. *That must be Jerome*, Abby guessed. He sat in one golf cart alongside a second cart with a much younger driver.

The younger man jumped down and slid onto the seat beside Jerome. The groundskeeper tipped his hat. "That one's all yours, Ms. Lila. When you ladies are done for the day, just park it right here and leave the keys under the seat."

Abby's eyes widened. "Isn't that dangerous?"

The other three chuckled. "Safe as going to church," Jerome said. "You little gals have fun."

Lila motioned toward the back of the golf cart. "Toss your things in there and hang on. Not everything has been paved yet."

The sun was hot and directly overhead, but a breeze danced off the water. Trinity Bay was idyllic, deep blue, touched with whitecaps. No wonder the Edmonds had acquired this private island. It was exquisite.

Abby looked around with interest as the small vehicle

lurched into motion. The festival grounds were larger than she had imagined. And far more upscale. This would be no Woodstock with music lovers lounging on the grass.

Lila narrated as they wound among the structures that smelled of new wood and excitement. "The two main stages will anchor the event with headliners. Big names. Crowd-pleasers. The scattering of smaller venues you see will be home to quirkier bands. The kind of musical groups that in five years might become household names."

"And over there across the main pathway?" Abby curled her fingers around the top edge of the golf cart. Some areas had been prepped for sod, but others were covered in wood chips. The golf cart bumped and jolted.

"Those are the wine bars and pop-up restaurants. Each will have a celebrity chef."

"Wow." The logistics of putting on an enormous music festival—on an *island*—boggled the mind. There was so much to coordinate: food shipments, the sound equipment, a medical presence, seating—presumably chairs and benches. The portable toilets… Abby definitely wouldn't want to be the person in charge. The whole thing could be a smashing success or a raging headache fraught with disaster.

Lila eased the golf cart onto a small point surrounded by water on two sides. "I brought fruit and cheese. And a bottle of wine. You hungry?"

"Actually, I am."

Lila wasn't a huge talker, which Abby liked. It was peaceful to sit in silence, watch the water and enjoy the simple pleasures of an alfresco meal.

Without warning, a vision of Carter Crane popped into her head. The handsome rancher was no doubt neck-deep in cattle ranch business in the middle of a busy workday. Maybe Abby could convince him that his routine was exactly what she found fascinating. There was only so much video she could take here on the island before the festival got underway. But to immerse the viewer in the flavor of Texas, she would need solid footage of what it meant to be from Royal.

Lila yawned. "Do you want to get some preliminary shots? I can check email on my phone or maybe grab a quick nap. Take your time."

"That would be great." Abby finished her light lunch and slid out of the golf cart, going around to the back to retrieve her camera. For the actual festival she would need her tripods. Today, though, she wanted to shoot the mood of the unoccupied island.

The bay was an obvious star. Out in the distance, sailboats glided along, pushed by the wind. Abby was sure she saw a dolphin break the surface in a carefree arc. When she had what she wanted from the water, she turned to the land.

Some of the empty structures would be dramatic in black and white. She paused for a moment, listening. Trying to envision what the energy of the crowd would sound like... Imagining the steady thump of the bass. The sharp twang of an electric guitar.

Steadying the camera on her shoulder, she panned from left to right. And caught a cowboy dead in the middle of her viewfinder.

Three

Carter enjoyed catching Abby Carmichael off guard. She had incredible confidence and self-possession for someone so young, but he had managed to rattle her. He saw it in her eyes when she lowered the camera.

"Carter," she said, her gaze wary. "What are you doing here?"

He hid a grin by rubbing his chin. "I was in the neighborhood and thought I'd drop by." He took a moment to enjoy the picture she made. Being a filmmaker was a physically demanding job at times. Abby must have dressed for comfort and professionalism, but her choice of clothing flattered her.

She wore an ankle-length, halter-neck sundress of a thin gauzy material that hinted at the shape of her body. The colorful fabric made him think of Caribbean islands and cold drinks with tiny umbrellas. Abby's beautiful wavy hair was down, despite the heat. The breeze fanned strands out across her golden-skinned shoulders.

She chewed her bottom lip, clearly convinced he was up to no good. Maybe she was right. "We're miles from Royal," she said. "And I have it on good authority that your little cows are a demanding lot."

He laughed softly, suddenly very glad he had come. "None of my cows are little, city girl. Besides, I told them I wanted the day off."

She frowned. "Your cattle?"

"Nope. My staff."

"Oh…" She glanced back over her shoulder. "I should go. Lila will be waiting for me."

He reached for the camera. "Here. I'll carry that. I'd like to say hello."

Abby surrendered the video equipment with obvious reluctance, but she fell into step beside him. "You know Lila?"

"Everybody knows *everybody* in Royal. Besides, Lila is big news lately. She enticed a celebrity Instagram influencer—whatever the hell that is—to come to Royal and promote the music festival. Next thing I knew, the gossip was flying, and Lila was engaged to Zach Benning."

"I've heard about Zach, and I did notice the gorgeous ring on her finger. Sounds like a fairy tale."

Carter grimaced. "Don't tell me you're one of those."

Abby stopped abruptly. "What does that mean?"

He faced her with the camera tucked under his arm. "A dewy-eyed romantic. I thought documentary makers were more realistic." Though he had to admit that her soft brown irises were pretty damn gorgeous. A man could dive into those eyes and get lost.

"You think romantic love is fiction?"

"Yes," he said baldly. Perhaps his response was harsh, but he knew better than most men that romance was little more than a charade.

Abby continued walking, her expression thoughtful.

When they approached a golf cart parked by the water, Lila Jones got out and waved. "Hey there, Carter. What brings you to Appaloosa Island? You're several weeks early for the festival."

He kissed her cheek. "You know I'm not a festival kind of guy. But I haven't had a chance to congratulate you on your engagement."

Lila blushed. "Thanks."

Abby studied them both. "How long have you two known each other?"

Carter shrugged. "Forever... Folks in Royal tend to put down roots."

Lila's brows drew together. "I might ask you two the same question. Abby, I thought you only got into town last night."

"That's true. But I went for a drive, and on a dusty secluded road, Carter here threatened to shoot me."

"No, no, *no*," Carter protested. "The truth is, Abby isn't as innocent as she looks. The woman tried to Mace me."

Abby's eyes danced. "I don't think that's a verb."

Lila put her hands on her hips. "I'm missing something."

Carter lifted his face toward the sun, feeling more carefree than he had in a long time. "Let's just say that our first meeting was dramatic and our second far more cordial."

"I need to hear the whole story," Lila insisted.

"I'll fill you in on the way back." Abby took her camera from Carter and tucked it into a cushioned bag. Then she climbed into the cart and glanced over her shoulder at him. "We have to go. Our ride is picking us up in twenty minutes."

Carter lifted a brow, looking at Lila. "Danny getting in practice miles?"

"You bet."

"Abby?" He touched her arm briefly, feeling the insistent *zing* of attraction. "I was hoping I might persuade you to drive back with me. When we get to town, I'll take you to dinner."

"I came with Lila," she said, her face giving nothing away.

Lila shook her head slowly. "Carter has a gorgeous black Porsche. It's by far the better offer."

He smiled at the woman in the passenger seat. "You said you wanted to interview me. Now's your chance."

"I said I wanted to *film* you."

"Yes, but the interview should come first. I've been reading up on how to make a documentary. I wanted to be ready."

Abby's lips parted, almost as if she felt the same magnetic sexual pull and wasn't sure what to do about it. "I don't want to abandon Lila."

Lila pooh-poohed that idea. "Go with Carter. You and I will have plenty of time together. I don't mind at all. Honestly."

Carter gave both women his most innocent smile. "Abby?"

"Okay, fine." She exited the golf cart with a graceful swish of skirt and a flash of toned thigh. "Let me grab my stuff."

Lila intervened. "Better yet, why don't we just give Carter a ride back to the dock? It's too hot to walk around with no shade."

"I'll take that offer," he said. The golf cart had two rows of seating, so he slid in behind the women. Abby reclaimed her spot in the front. If he leaned forward, he could kiss one of her bare shoulders. That thought had him shifting uncomfortably on the seat. Maybe spending three hours in the car with the delectable filmmaker wasn't such a good idea after all.

He had parked the convertible adjacent to the dock. The

ferry was moments away from pulling out. Because there was no room in his small sports car for a second passenger, Lila and Abby exchanged goodbyes, and Lila boarded on foot.

Carter helped Abby in, started the engine and, when instructed, eased his vehicle onto the ramp and into the ferry. Because the ride was so short, they stayed in the car with the windows down. Abby had her camera out shooting the seagulls chasing the boat. He suspected it was a ploy not to have to converse with him.

Was she nervous? Carter wasn't. Well, not exactly. He would describe it as being *on edge*. His senses were heightened, and truth be told, he rarely reacted this strongly to a woman he had just met.

When they reached Mustang Point, Carter and Abby greeted Danny and said goodbye to Lila. Then they wound their way back to the highway. Carter still had the top up. The blistering heat was too much right now.

He adjusted the air and glanced at his silent companion. "You okay?"

Abby smiled, playing with her large hoop earring. "Yes. This is a very nice car."

"I'm glad you like it. When we get closer to Royal, there's a two-lane road that turns off the main drag but still leads into town. It's the old highway actually. I thought we could put the top down then and enjoy the view."

"Sounds good."

Carter gripped the wheel, wondering why he had taken the day off. He never played hooky in the middle of the week. In fact, he had been known to work six and seven days in a row. The pace wasn't healthy, but ranching took up most of his life.

It was just him. All day every day. Carrying the weight of a family legacy. He wasn't complaining. He knew he was lucky beyond measure.

But Abby Carmichael was the best kind of interruption.

"How old were you when your parents divorced?" he asked quietly. His own mom and dad were heading for their forty-seventh anniversary.

Abby sighed. She had kicked off her sandals and was sitting with one leg tucked beneath her. "I was five. So I don't remember a lot. But as an adult, I finally understood why the marriage unraveled."

"Oh?"

"My mother was an Upper East Side society princess," she explained. "My grandparents owned tons of real estate, and Mom had the best of everything growing up. She met my father during a spring break trip to Jamaica."

"Her parents didn't approve because he wasn't in their social circle?" he mused.

"They probably didn't, but that wasn't the tack they took in opposing the relationship. My father's family was wealthy, too. They were bankers and lawyers in Jamaica. Daddy was a musician when he and Mom met, but he was studying to be a filmmaker. Mom says her parents weren't impressed with the odds of success in that career."

Carter looked over at her before returning his eyes to the road. "Were they right?"

"Yes and no. It took my dad years to break into the industry. And it meant going where the jobs were. If he'd had a wife and kid in tow, it might never have happened."

"Did your grandparents give in?"

"Sadly, no." She sighed. "My mother wanted a cathedral wedding with all the frills. In the end, she had to settle for a Vegas chapel."

"Did her parents ever come around?"

"When she got pregnant with me…yes. But maybe my mom and dad were too different from the beginning. Even sharing a child couldn't keep them together."

"I'm sorry, Abby," he said quietly. "It must be hard to have them on opposite coasts."

When he glanced at her again, she was staring straight ahead, as if the road held answers. Her expression—what he could see of it in a quick glance—was pensive. "I've learned to be happy anywhere. I love both of them, and whatever animosity there might have been during the divorce evaporated over the years."

"Have you thought about where you'll settle? For the long haul?"

She shot him a look of surprise. "I don't know that I *will* settle. Living out of a suitcase doesn't bother me."

"But surely you see yourself putting down roots eventually."

"Maybe."

"Don't you want kids someday?"

"Do *you*?" Her question was sharp. "Why do people ask women that? I bet never once has anyone tried to pin you down on the fatherhood question."

"Well, you'd be wrong then," he said wryly. "My mother brings it up regularly. I'm a terrible disappointment to her. And I have ten years on you, so the pressure is mounting."

"I guess you're glad they don't live here anymore."

"Not really," he said. "I miss them. But they deserve this time to spread their wings. The ranch always tied them down."

Abby heard the clear affection in his voice and experienced the oddest moment of jealousy. She loved her parents—of course she did. And she got along well with both of them. But the three of them weren't a family unit. Not like the close bond Carter evidently had with his mom and dad. Abby and her parents were two halves of a family that somehow didn't add up to a whole.

She let the conversation drop. Carter didn't seem to mind. It was a beautiful day for a drive. In a strange way, she felt very comfortable with him. Well, that was true as long as she ignored the palpable sexual undertones.

Without meaning to, she dozed. When she jerked awake and ran her hands over her face, she was embarrassed. "Sorry," she muttered. "I was sleep-deprived coming into this trip. I guess I'm still catching up."

"No worries. You're cute when you snore."

"I *don't* snore," she retorted, mildly offended, and also worried that he wasn't joking. Carter didn't answer. He kept his eyes on the road, but she could see the smile that curved his lips. The man had great lips. World-class. Perfect for kissing.

To keep herself from fixating on his mouth and his jaw and all the other yummy parts of him, she looked at the view beyond the car windows. Fields and more fields. Cows and more cows. It was all she could see in any direction.

Carter shot her a sideways glance. "What?"

Abby frowned. "I didn't say anything."

"No. But you were thinking really loud. You can say it. You don't like Texas."

It seemed churlish to agree. "That's an overstatement."

"Is it? You're missing the skyscrapers and the world-class ethnic food and the museums and Broadway."

"Maybe. But that doesn't mean I'm criticizing your home. You love it here."

"I do. But I've traveled, Abby. I know what the world has to offer."

"May I ask you a question?"

She saw him frown slightly. "Of course."

"Why did you come to Appaloosa Island today?"

His chest rose and fell as he sighed deeply. "The truth?"

"Yes, please."

"You intrigue me, Abby. My personal life has been pretty boring for the last year and a half. The pool of available romantic partners in Royal—for someone like me who has always lived here—is finite. You're new and different, and I wanted to spend time with you."

Her stomach flipped. Here was an übermasculine man, not a boy, stating unequivocally that he was interested. What was she going to do about that?

"Does this mean you're willing to let me film you at your ranch?"

He winced. "I'm still debating."

"So, what you're dangling is carte blanche as a videographer if I consent to get better acquainted with you?"

He grimaced. "This isn't a negotiation. One has nothing to do with the other."

"Well, if you let me film you, we'll be spending *lots* of time together."

"I'm not interested in being cast as some token rancher for your viewers. I am who I am. It's nothing exotic."

"For a city dweller, this lifestyle you've chosen has a certain je ne sais quoi."

"That's what I'm talking about," he grumbled. "There's nothing romantic and exciting about sweat and dirt and cows."

"Familiarity breeds contempt. You don't see yourself as an outsider would."

He shot her a look. "I thought you were doing a documentary about Soiree on the Bay."

"I am. But I'm beginning to realize that the town of Royal and the Texas Cattleman's Club may be as much or more interesting than a music festival that hasn't even happened yet. You see, I've picked up a lot from Lila about how things work around Maverick County. I'm still after the human interest angle."

"Well, good luck with that."

Carter pulled off onto the side of the road. He reached across her lap and opened the glove box. "Here. If I'm putting the top down, you'll need this."

This was a narrow silk scarf, clearly expensive. It was deep amber scattered with tiny navy fleur-de-lis. When he leaned close, Abby inhaled his scent. Probably whatever he had shaved with that morning. Lime… And a hint of something else.

Her pulse beat faster. It was a relief when he straightened.

She pulled her hair to the nape of her neck and secured the ponytail with the scarf, knotting it tightly. The wind would still do a number on the loose ends, but she didn't mind that.

She watched as Carter hit the button and made sure the top retracted slowly. Then he climbed back into the driver's seat and gave her a grin that caused her knees to quiver. "Ready?"

Abby nodded, her heart beating more quickly than the moment warranted. "Hit the pedal, cowboy."

The next hour took on a surreal quality. The open road. The wind in her face. The man beside her. With a sigh, Abby leaned against the headrest and closed her eyes. Clearly, there was more to Carter than she'd first thought. This busy, successful rancher who was willing to blow a whole day chasing down a woman who might or might not sleep with him had layers. Interesting layers. *Irresistible* layers.

Texas roads were straight and flat, and Carter drove with confidence. Never once did Abby have any qualms about her safety. For the first time, she understood the appeal of a fast, sexy car and an adventurous man behind the wheel.

When they arrived in Royal, she was windblown but content. She touched Carter lightly, her fingertips registering his muscular forearm and warm skin. "I'm hungry," she admitted. "So dinner sounds great. But I should change first."

He eased into a parking spot and turned to face her. His blue eyes reflected the sky. "Only if you want to. Your dress is beautiful." He paused. "And so are you." His gaze roved from her face to her breasts and back up to her eyes, making her shiver despite the heat.

Her throat tightened. Were all cowboys so direct? She licked her lips, telling herself they were dry from the hot summer breeze. "Um…thank you. But I'd feel more comfortable if I could shower and change."

"Whatever you want. It's still early. An hour and a half? I'll make a reservation at Sheen. It's a newer restaurant. I think you'll like it."

"How dressy?"

"Anything similar to what you're wearing."

At the hotel, Carter pulled up under the portico and they both got out of the car. He retrieved her belongings from the back seat. "I'll run out to the ranch and be back to pick you up around six thirty." Casually, he kissed her cheek. "See you soon, Abby."

She stood and watched as he gunned the engine and sped away around the corner.

In the elevator, she barely recognized her reflection in the mirrored glass. Her cheeks glowed with a deep rosy hue. Slowly, her smile faded.

She was getting off track. She had come to Royal to make a documentary and get her career on solid footing. Flirting with a sexy rancher wasn't on the list.

Even so, as she showered, washed her hair and changed into another dress, nothing could block Carter from her thoughts. Or erase the feel of his hot lips burning against her skin.

He was dangerous. Why would she get involved with

a man, even temporarily, whose worldview was so different from hers?

She would have to tread carefully. Needing him for her documentary was one thing. Tumbling into his bed was another entirely.

Four

Going home to the ranch was a mistake. Too many people needed to ask Carter too many questions. By the time he escaped the inquisition, showered and changed, he barely had enough time to make it back into town to pick up Abby at her hotel at the appointed hour.

As he drove to get her, he thought about the day. He'd had fun. Honestly, that was never high on his list these days. Responsibility, yes. Hard work, definitely. But fun? Not really.

Abby made him want things. Lots of things. Sex, of course. She was real and beautiful, and he couldn't deny the powerful attraction. But it was more than that. She represented a time in his life when he still had choices. At her age, he'd been actively working on the ranch, but had still entertained the idea that he might ultimately do something other than be a rancher.

Unfortunately, his dad had suffered a heart attack when Carter was twenty-five, and soon after, his life was mapped out for him. He hadn't minded. He loved the ranch. But it had been a shock to go from his carefree postcollege days to being the top dog.

And then there was the whole thing with Madeline. His gut clenched. He'd been wrong about her. *So wrong.* Was Abby too much like his ex-fiancée? Did he have a type? Was he setting himself up for embarrassment and hurt again?

The unpleasant thought was one he didn't want to dwell on, especially since his libido was firmly in the driver's seat. He shoved the past into a locked box where it belonged and concentrated on the evening ahead.

Abby met him in the lobby. She had changed into another sexy outfit, this one more sophisticated, but no less flattering. The sleeveless, knee-length dress was white jersey knit. It clung to her body in ways that probably should be outlawed in the presence of red-blooded males. The bodice plunged in a deep vee, where a gold necklace dangled. Again, her shoulders were bare, her hair was loose and she wore white espadrilles with three-inch cork heels. The laces crisscrossed around her ankles.

He closed the distance between them. "You look amazing," he said. When he kissed her cheek lightly, she seemed flustered.

The restaurant wasn't far away. Over dinner, they spoke of less personal topics. Abby was funny and smart and well-informed. He should have expected that from a woman who spent time on both coasts. She might only be twenty-four, but she had grown up in a privileged atmosphere with a top-notch education.

Carter liked the fact that she challenged him. The conversation was stimulating and wide-ranging. She kept him on his toes. And underneath their back-and-forth was a slow, molten sexual awareness.

He knew it was too soon to sleep with her. He thought

she wanted him, but a man needed to be sure. On the other hand, maybe he could speed things along with a little co-operation.

Over dessert, he played his best card. "I've decided I'm willing to let you do some filming at the ranch, within reason. How about coming over for lunch tomorrow?"

Abby wrinkled her nose. "I'm glad to hear that, but I already have plans. Lila has arranged for me to sit in on a meeting of the advisory board for the festival. I think we'll be at the Texas Cattleman's Club."

"Ah." Now he was really frustrated.

"I could come the next day," she said, perhaps reading his mood. Big brown eyes focused on him intently. She reached across the table and patted his hand. "I appreciate the invitation, Carter. Really, I do. But this meeting is important."

"Of course it is," he replied. "I understand."

"May I make a personal observation?" she asked quietly.

He stared at her, trying to read her thoughts. His fingers itched to tangle in her hair, to pull her closer and press his lips to hers. To hold her and trace the curves of her body beneath that soft, clingy dress. "Personal?" The word came out a little hoarse.

Abby nodded. "If you don't mind."

So polite. So incredibly enticing.

"Sure," he said. "I have no secrets."

When she swallowed, the muscles in her slender throat moved visibly. For the first time, he realized she was not as calm as he had imagined. "I get the feeling," she said, "that you want to sleep with me. Am I way off base?"

After nearly choking on his tongue, he found his voice. "Are you always so direct?" Her question rattled him.

"I don't play games, if that's what you mean. Most men and women make things too complicated."

"What happens if I say yes?"

"Well…" She stared at her hands clasped on the white linen tablecloth. "I'd probably explain that it's too soon." She looked up at him from beneath her lashes.

His breathing hitched. "So, you're saying there *is* a hypothetical date that might *not* be too soon?"

Her smile was slow and mysterious. "Precisely. I like you, Carter. A lot. But there are things to consider."

"Such as?" He would bat them all down one by one.

"I've never in my life slept with a man I've known only two days. Or two weeks for that matter."

He felt his advantage slipping. "Is there a *but* in there?"

"Not really. The problem is, you and I have nothing in common, and I'm only going to be in Royal for a limited time. I don't know if I'm willing to do short-term with you. It might be better to settle for flirting and friendship."

"Nope," he said, scowling. "Not a choice. I have friends, Abby. You don't fall into that category."

"Acquaintances then? Or business associates?"

Was she taunting him? The fact that he wasn't sure frustrated him. Or maybe it was the need pulsing in his gut. "I don't have to label anything, Abby. We'll be who we are. If that leads to sex, I'm all for it."

Abby trembled. Had she ever met a man who was so earthy and civilized at the same time? Carter wasn't rude or crass, but he took no pains to hide his sexual desire. For *her*. She was both flattered and intimidated. Could she hold her own with so much testosterone? Carter was a man who knew what he wanted and wasn't shy about going for it.

She suspected that a woman in his bed would find incredible pleasure. And she wanted him. No question. Still, sex and men had been tripping up women for millennia.

In her adult life, she had been disappointed by a few guys. She'd misjudged a couple of others. Not once had she faced heartbreak. Maybe that said something about her tolerance for risk. She always calculated the odds for success in any situation.

Carter Crane might turn out to be her weak spot. The strength of her desire for him was enough to make her put on the brakes. It would be dangerous and indulgent to embark on an affair when she was in the midst of a possibly career-changing project.

"Fair enough," she said. "No labels. No clock. No expectations."

His grin was tight. "I'm expecting plenty, gorgeous. But you'll have to make the call. Agreed?"

She nodded, her stomach fluttery. "Agreed."

"Dessert?"

"Yes, please."

Because looking at Carter was making her rethink her sensible approach, she scanned the restaurant. It was beautiful, made almost entirely of glass. An interested patron could observe a chef at work or track the sunset.

Sheen was hugely popular, not only because it was new, but because the food was spectacular. Every table was full. Over strawberry crepes slathered in real whipped cream, she eyed her dinner companion. Although earlier he had tried to convince her she didn't need to change for the evening, she was glad she had.

It was true that some diners had come in casual attire, but at least three-quarters of the men and women around them were dressed in what Abby would call special occasion clothes. The clientele ranged from the occasional high school couple on a date, to clusters of business associates, to folks like Carter and Abby enjoying a night out.

She was sad to see the evening end. Being with the ruggedly handsome rancher made her feel alive and intensely feminine in a way that was novel and exciting. Still, she was cautious. He could coax her into bed with little effort on his part. That knowledge was sobering.

If she wasn't ready for such a rash decision, she needed to limit her exposure to him.

She licked the last dab of whipped cream off her spoon and set it on her plate with an inward sigh of appreciation for the pastry chef's expertise. "I should probably get back to the hotel. I still have some prep work to do for my lunch meeting tomorrow."

Carter's face was oddly expressionless. "Of course." He dealt with the check and then escorted her between tables to the front door.

The night was perfect. A summer moon. A light breeze. Unfortunately, the trip back to the hotel was quick. Carter parked the convertible just around the corner from the main entrance beneath a dim streetlight. He'd kept the top up this time.

She jumped out, bent on escaping her own wants and needs. Carter met her on the sidewalk and put a hand on her wrist. "A good-night kiss? Or is that too much to ask…"

Her legs trembled. "I'd like that," she said.

When his lips covered hers, it was like jumping off a cliff into unknown waters. Her stomach shot to her throat and dropped again, leaving her woozy and breathless.

He held her with confidence. One big male hand settled on the curve of her ass. She made a small noise, somewhere between a whimper and a moan, when he pulled her more tightly into his embrace. Her arms curled around his neck.

His body was hard everywhere hers was soft. She smelled the scent of his skin, trying to memorize it. How had she known from almost the first moment that he was the one? Not *the* one as in gold rings and white picket fences, but the one who could reveal everything she had kept tightly furled inside her.

Carter's reckless passion burned through her inhibitions, her ironclad caution. They were on a public street just off the central thoroughfare, somewhat secluded this time of night, but in plain view of anyone who might happen by. Truthfully, he could have taken her against the hood of the car, and she might not have protested.

When she felt the urgent press of his erection against her abdomen, she knew one of them had to keep a clear head.

Though it pained her to do so, she put a hand against his chest and pushed. "Carter…"

To his credit, he released her immediately.

They faced each other in the shadowy illumination from overhead.

"Do I need to apologize?" he asked gruffly.

It was impossible to read his expression. "No. Not at all. Thank you for dinner. I enjoyed our evening. And thank you for driving me home this afternoon from the island. I'm touched that you gave up an entire day for me."

He shook his head slowly, his jawline grim. "I'm beginning to think I'd do just about anything for you. Which makes you a dangerous woman."

She traced his chin with a fingertip, feeling the late-day stubble. "I like that. No one's ever called me dangerous before."

"You don't have a clue…"

Was he feeding her a line? Spinning a tale of a man made vulnerable by sex? How could she believe that?

She knew she was attractive in a casual, understated way. The male sex responded to her. But she was no femme fatale, luring unsuspecting men into reckless behavior. That was a ludicrous notion.

Still, she wanted to trust his words, wanted to believe that he felt the same urgent pull she did. Pheromones were a powerful thing. That didn't mean she and Carter were kindred spirits. It only meant they wanted to jump each other's bones.

With reluctance, she made herself step back. "Good night, Carter."

His eyes glittered. "Good night, Abby."

Turning her back on him as she walked away felt risky, but she had to get inside.

"I'll make sure you get to the door," he said, following her at a short distance.

"It's only a few steps." She picked up the pace.

"A gentleman doesn't drop a lady on a street corner."

By the time Abby made it to the portico where the doorman stood, her heart was pounding. Carter had lingered on the sidewalk. She felt his gaze on her back as she headed for the double glass doors.

She wanted badly to turn around. But she kept on walking...

After a remarkably peaceful night, given her jumbled thoughts and feelings, Abby awoke ready to meet the day. She was determined to focus on her job and not the enigmatic Carter Crane.

Lila had offered to pick her up again, but Abby waved her off. It was time to get acquainted with the town of Royal. Besides, the Texas Cattleman's Club was only a few blocks away. Even with her camera and tote, it was easily within walking distance.

Today, she dressed in black dress pants and a cream blazer over a cinnamon silk tank. The jacket had large, quirky black buttons. When she was ready, she glanced at herself in the mirror. The only jewelry she wore was a pair of onyx studs she had purchased from an artisan in Sedona. Her black espadrilles were comfortable enough for the stroll, but nice enough to complement her outfit.

She debated what to do with her hair. Her preference

was to leave it loose, but it was going to be very hot today. In the end, she twined it in a loose French braid.

When she had grabbed what she would need for the morning and then exited the hotel, she realized she was nervous. The people who would attend this meeting today were key players in Royal's high-powered business scene. It took a lot of money and influence to pull off an event like Soiree on the Bay.

Seeing the famed Texas Cattleman's Club in person was fascinating. The imposing edifice dated back to 1910, though it had been updated over the years. The large, rambling single-story building was constructed of dark stone and wood with a tall slate roof. Though once an all-male enclave, the onetime "old boys' club" now welcomed females into the membership.

Inside was even more impressive. Super high ceilings, large windows and, of course, the ubiquitous hunting trophies and historical artifacts displayed on paneled walls. Abby liked history as much as the next person, but dead animal heads weren't her thing.

The meeting was to start at ten. She had arrived at nine thirty. After gawking in the spacious foyer, she spoke with the receptionist and showed her credentials. The woman directed her to a conference room down a broad hallway.

Lila was already there, setting out water glasses and pens and paper. She looked up when Abby walked in. "Hey, Abby. I'm glad you're early. I made up a cheat sheet for you."

"A cheat sheet?" she asked.

"Yeah, I thought you could use a head start. It's confusing when they all start talking at once. Do you want me to introduce you formally?"

"Whatever you think. Honestly, I wouldn't mind being the proverbial fly on the wall. At least until I get my bearings."

"Then we'll do that," Lila said cheerily. She handed Abby a sheet of paper. "This isn't everyone, but it's the core of the group. I copied their pictures in color and gave you a brief bio of each."

"Excellent." While Lila finished her prep work, Abby took a seat at the back of the room against the wall. The main participants would be seated around the large, beautifully polished conference table.

She had studied up on the main players already. Russell Edmond—Rusty—was the oft-married patriarch of the überwealthy family. His money came from oil, and he owned a massive, luxurious ranch outside of town. It was his three children, Russell Jr., known as Ross, Gina Edmond and Asher Edmond, who were spearheading the festival.

When the door opened and the principals began arriving, she put aside her cheat sheet and concentrated on learning about the actors involved. Ross Edmond—tall and lanky with dirty blond hair and blue eyes—was impossible to miss. He had the innate confidence that comes with wealth.

His sister, Gina, had gorgeous dark hair and eyes and was super stylish. She looked to be close to Abby's age. That left the other Edmond sibling, Asher, who, according to Lila's cheat sheet, was actually a stepbrother. Odd, because his close-cropped brown hair and brown eyes resembled Gina's. Even at first glance, he seemed the most intense of the trio.

There were a few other people entering the room in a trickle, but it was soon clear they were either assistants or people like Lila who represented the town of Royal in various capacities.

That left only one unidentified player. According to Lila's info, his name was Billy Holmes. Somehow, he was involved with the Edmonds in planning the festival.

Abby had to admit he was gorgeous. Black hair, pale

green eyes and scruffy facial hair gave him a roguish presence. He smiled. A lot. At *everyone*. Who was he, and how did he fit into this scenario?

Ross Edmond convened the meeting. Apparently, all the heavy lifting had been accomplished in earlier gatherings. Today was about tying up loose ends and making sure everyone was on the same page.

Abby listened carefully, making notes about anything she thought might have a bearing on her film.

At a lull in the conversation, Lila stood and motioned toward Abby. "I want you all to meet Abby Carmichael. She's the documentary filmmaker I've told you about. If the festival goes well, Abby's work will help lift our visibility to the next level and ensure that the festival continues for years to come."

Abby smiled and nodded, well aware that no one was particularly interested in what she had to offer. Except perhaps Billy Holmes. His grin seemed personal, and he looked her over carefully. The perusal fell just shy of being inappropriate. She had met men like him. If any female appeared on their radar, they *had* to make a good impression.

Eventually, the meeting wound to a close. There was a sense of urgency, given that the festival was only weeks away. After months of planning, everything was finally falling into place.

As Lila did her job, chatting with everyone and gathering up the materials she had brought with her, Abby was disconcerted to realize that Billy Holmes had lingered and was making a beeline in her direction.

She stood and smiled politely. "Hello, Mr. Holmes. I wonder if I might interview you in a few days. I'm sure you're a very busy man."

He reached out to shake her hand. "I always have time for anyone who wants to promote the festival."

Abby hesitated. "Well, I'm not *promoting* the festival per

se. I'm a visual storyteller. Soiree on the Bay—along with the town of Royal—promises to be an interesting project. But of course, my film won't be out anytime soon."

"Doesn't matter. We want the festival to be such a big hit it will go on for years."

"You sound like a man with a vision."

"I like to think so." He glanced at his watch. "I've gotta run. How about Thursday at eleven for your interview? Would you like to see the Elegance Ranch? I live in a guest-house on the Edmonds' property. I'll get my housekeeper to feed us."

"Sure," Abby said, wondering if she might be getting in over her head. Billy Holmes seemed nice enough, but she couldn't figure out where he fit in with the Edmond clan and the festival. Until she did, she would be on her guard.

As Billy walked out of the room, Lila joined Abby. "Well, what did you think?"

"I think people with a lot of money are a different breed."

Lila cocked her head, smiling gently. "Your father owns a Malibu beach house and your mom is a Manhattan socialite. You're hardly scraping by."

Abby grimaced. "Fair point. But you know what I mean. The Edmond family has buckets of cash. Not to mention land and influence. Here in Texas, they're practically royalty. Now that I've met several of them, I'm seeing a new direction for my film. Maybe the documentary will be less about the festival and more about the people who can pull off such a feat. What do you think?"

Lila held up her hands. "Not my area of expertise. But the Edmonds *are* fascinating, that's for sure. What's next on your schedule?"

"I've asked Carter Crane to let me do some filming on his ranch. You know, for local color."

The other woman grinned. "How was the drive yesterday? You must have made a big impression on the man."

Abby felt her face get hot. "It was a fun afternoon. I like him. And I think the camera will *love* him…those sharp cut features and strong chin."

"I'm surprised he's agreed to that. Carter likes to keep a low profile."

"I'm not sure how much latitude he'll give me. But I'm hopeful."

Lila sobered without warning, her expression serious. "Be careful, Abby. I wouldn't want you to get hurt."

Five

Abby's stomach curled with anxiety. "What's wrong with Carter? He's been a perfect gentleman as far as I can tell."

"I feel bad gossiping, but you need to know the truth. Carter keeps women at a distance, particularly women like you."

"Women like *me*? What in the heck does that mean?" She was mildly insulted. And worried.

Lila perched on the edge of the table, one leg swinging. "Carter was engaged to a woman from Chicago a few years ago. Madeline moved to Royal, and they began planning a wedding. But the next thing I knew, the festivities were canceled and the two of them were officially over. Apparently, Madeline hated life 'in the sticks' as she called it. She missed her big-city life, and she detested cows and horses and dust."

"Oh." Abby felt stupid and small. Maybe Carter was just playing with her. "Thank you for telling me," she muttered.

"I hope I haven't stepped over the line," Lila said, her

expression conveying both worry and concern. "But if I weren't a happily engaged woman, Carter Crane might give *me* a few heart palpitations. He's macho and sexy and aloof. The trifecta when it comes to attracting the female sex."

"He *is* handsome."

"Maybe I shouldn't have said anything," Lila fretted.

Abby summoned a light tone. "I barely know the man. But I appreciate the information." She picked up her bag. "I'd better head out. Plenty to do. Thanks for letting me sit in on this meeting. It helped a lot."

"Sure," Lila said. "And let me know if there's anything else you need."

As Abby walked down Main Street, she tried to absorb the feel of the place. It's true that the town wasn't huge. Maverick County was mostly rural. But still, there was an upscale feel to the buildings and the businesses. Perhaps because oil money and cattle money had a far reach. Good schools. Great roads. This was no backwoods holler.

Her stomach growled, reminding her that lunch was next on the agenda. On a whim, she popped into the Royal Diner. Its 1950s retro decor and red, white and black color scheme were charming. When Abby had asked her hotel concierge for recommendations, he told her the diner was top-notch, and that the owner, Amanda Battle, was the sheriff's wife.

Now Abby slid into a red faux leather booth and tucked her things on the seat beside her. The menu offerings made her mouth water. When the pleasant older waitress stopped by the table, Abby ordered a vanilla milkshake, a tuna melt with fries and a glass of water. It had been a long time since she had indulged in such comfort food. Her mother was always dieting, and her father was a vegan.

When the meal arrived, Abby dug in with enthusiasm. Often while eating alone, she used the time to "people watch" or to get ideas down on paper. Today, she did both.

With a sandwich in one hand and a pen in the other, she began filling a small notebook with her observations from today's meeting.

The Edmond siblings each had distinct personalities. She didn't know what to make of Billy Holmes. Perhaps her interview with him would uncover interesting layers. Often, people were more at ease in their home settings, so she wasn't averse to meeting him out at the ranch. He might even give her access to the Edmond family members if she decided to explore that route.

She had finished her sandwich and was nibbling on the last of her fries when she realized two women had taken the booth right behind hers—the one that had been vacant when she arrived. Abby tried not to eavesdrop, but the hushed conversation turned interesting quickly.

Though the women were conversing in lowered voices, Abby was only inches away. The words *festival* and *money* caught her attention immediately. Unfortunately, she couldn't hear every single phrase. But the gist of the topic was clear: the women seemed to be discussing the possibility that someone had taken a large sum of money from the festival coffers.

Abby's eyes widened. Not a hint about finances had come up during the advisory board meeting, nor a whiff of a problem. Were the members of the board hiding something, or was she overhearing idle gossip?

Unfortunately, the waitress brought Abby's check. There were customers waiting to be seated, so it seemed rude to linger. As she stood and picked up her belongings, she glanced at the women in the booth behind her. Neither of them was remarkable.

But what she heard stuck with her.

She spent the next couple of hours exploring Royal, filming anything that caught her fancy. Historic buildings. Quirky shop signs. Kids playing in a park. Though the town definitely possessed an almost palpable energy, that feeling was balanced by a sense that life was comfortable here. Predictable. *Enjoyable.*

Despite the fact that she was definitely out of her element, she had to acknowledge that Royal was interesting and charming. People were friendly. More than once, she found herself embroiled in a sidewalk conversation. In a community where everybody knew everybody, Abby apparently stood out.

She didn't mind the attention, not really. But after a few hours of walking the streets, she was more than ready to head back to the hotel. Getting clean, donning comfy pajamas and watching TV sounded like the perfect way to unwind.

The only irritant marring her peaceful afternoon was knowing that Carter hadn't called or texted. When he invited her to his ranch, she'd had to wave him off because of the advisory board meeting. Unfortunately, he hadn't said a word about tomorrow or the next day or the day after that.

When she got back to her room, she decided to be proactive…

Hi, Carter. Is it okay if I come out to the ranch in the morning? Seven-ish? I'd love to do some filming with the morning light. If there are no gates to unlock, I won't even have to bother you.

After a moment's hesitation, she hit Send. Then she turned her phone facedown and headed for the shower.

Carter rolled over in bed and glanced at the clock—5:00 a.m. He had no reason to be up at this hour, but he'd been dreaming. Hot, sensual, disturbing dreams.

And all because Abby Carmichael was coming out to his

ranch. He slung an arm over his head and stretched, feeling the brush of cool sheets against his hot skin.

Already he knew the shape of her body, the sound of her voice, the scent of her skin. At this particular moment, he felt like a hormonal teenager about to catch a glimpse of his high school crush.

The difference was, he and Abby were consenting adults, fully capable of making rash decisions.

By the time he showered and dressed and gobbled down some breakfast, he was jittery as hell. He didn't want to be interviewed, and he didn't want to be filmed. But he *did* want more time with Abby, so he was stuck.

In their text exchange last night, she had offered to stay away from the house. Abby claimed to want ethereal shots of the stables and the pastures and the corrals bathed in warm light. She promised not to get in the way of any ranch operations.

Did she really think he would ignore her presence? Surely, she wasn't that naive or clueless. That one kiss they shared had been incendiary and left him wanting more.

He walked out back to the barn and saddled up his horse. As a teenager, he had sometimes slept until noon. Now he had come to appreciate the mystical purity of the early morning. A man could think and plan and contemplate taking risks at this time of day. The slight chill in the air was invigorating—even more so because it was fleeting.

Carter galloped along the gravel and dirt road that bisected the ranch, squinting into the strengthening rays of the sun. It was after eight now. Where was she?

And then he spotted her. She had parked her rental car at the edge of the road and was climbing the fence to get a shot of sunflowers. Carter hadn't planted them. They were his mother's legacy. But he had to admit, they made his heart swell with happiness and pride every time he passed them.

Sunset Acres had been passed into his keeping. Carter had a duty to perform. And he was working his ass off to make sure the ranch remained healthy and viable.

As he approached his visitor, he slowed the horse to a trot. Abby seemed to not notice his presence yet. She was intent on her task. With the camera balanced on her shoulder and one leg wrapped around the fence, she was perched precariously.

He didn't want to startle her.

Instead, he tied off the horse and covered the last few yards on foot.

"Abby," he said quietly. "Good morning."

After a split second, she half turned and looked over her free shoulder at him. "Carter. I didn't hear you."

"I could tell." Then he noticed her earbuds. "Ah. You're listening to music."

She shook her head, grimacing. "No." She lowered the camera. "It's a podcast."

"About?"

She shrugged. "Learning to take chances. Building self-confidence. Stuff like that."

"All set?" he asked.

"Yes."

"Then let me help you down. Camera first."

She handed it over without argument and watched him as he placed it carefully on the seat of her car. Then he lifted his arms. "Come off that fence, Ms. Photographer. Before you break your neck."

When he settled his hands on her waist, she leaned forward and let him take her weight. She was thin. Maybe too thin. But she was really tall for a woman, so perhaps that accounted for it. In the split second when he held her completely with her slender body pressed to his, his heart punched hard.

Carefully, he let her slide to her feet. She stumbled, but he steadied her.

"Thanks, Carter," she murmured.

There it was again. That odd and disarming way she pronounced his name.

"I thought you might stop by the house to say hello," he muttered, swamped by a wave of need so intense it made him tremble.

Abby swept her hands through her hair. "I didn't want to wake you. Or catch you in the shower."

"Perhaps you could have joined me."

Her eyes opened wide. A tinge of pink darkened her cheeks. "Still too soon," she muttered. But her body language was not as negative as her words. She had plenty of room to step away, to put distance between them. Yet she was so close he could feel the brush of her breath against his ear.

He had to get a grip. Clearing his throat, he focused his gaze just past her shoulder, telling himself he was imagining the strength of his arousal. It was deprivation. That's all. He needed a woman. *Any* woman. Abby Carmichael was nothing special.

"Did you get the early morning shots you wanted?" The words came out husky and slow as if he were seducing her, not asking a mundane question.

Abby nodded. "Most of them. With your permission, I'd like to come back at sunset to shoot some more."

"You could stay all day," he said, brushing his thumb across her cheekbone. "You know, shadow me. See how things work."

Her smile was rueful. "You're a man used to getting what he wants."

"Not always. But yes, frequently."

"I suppose it doesn't help my case if I admit that I want what you want."

He sucked in a sharp breath. "Not fair, Abby. Not when you're asking to take things slowly."

She toyed with a button on his shirt, one right near his heart. "I didn't expect a complication like you when I came to Royal. You're perfect for my documentary. Beyond that, I'm not so sure."

He lifted her chin with his fingertip and brushed a light kiss over her soft lips. "Why don't we let things unfold and see what happens?"

At last, she backed away. Big brown eyes stared at him. "I suppose I could do that."

"Do you ride? Horses," he clarified, since she seemed dazed.

"No."

"I could put you up on Foxtrot with me. Show you the ranch. You won't have to do a thing but hold on."

"Foxtrot?" Abby raised an eyebrow.

"He's been known to do some fancy footwork when he doesn't want to be ridden."

"Sounds dangerous."

"I won't let you fall," he reassured her.

"What about my car?"

"Leave it here. No one will bother it."

"Do you think I could film on horseback?" she wondered aloud.

"I have no idea, but you're welcome to try." He watched as she glanced from him to his horse and back again.

"Okay," she said. "It might be fun."

He ignored the jolt of jubilation that fizzed in his veins. Abby was wearing a thin, orangey-red cotton shirt over a white camisole and a pair of pale denim skinny jeans with artful holes at the knees. Her sneakers were white Keds, already stained by the Texas soil. It wasn't exactly riding attire, but he supposed it would have to do...

He held out a hand. "Shall we?"

* * *

Abby was no dummy. She knew what kind of trouble she was courting. But she couldn't stop herself. Ignoring Carter's outstretched arm, she sidled around him and headed for her car. Fortunately, the enormous horse was tethered in the opposite direction.

In the end, she decided it would be too awkward to hold her video camera and cling to Carter at the same time. For the record, she knew there would be plenty of clinging. By the time she put her camera away, locked the car and pocketed her keys, Carter had already mounted the beautiful glossy black stallion.

As she walked back to meet him, he stared at her. The intensity of his gaze was as intimate as a caress. Beneath her top, her nipples beaded. The day was heating up, but she couldn't blame her rapid heartbeat on the rising temperatures.

When she was six feet away, Carter leaned down and held out his hand, smiling as if this was no big deal. "Put your left foot on the heel of my boot to steady yourself," he said. "I'll pull you up, and you swing your right leg over."

"You make it sound so easy." She hesitated, trying to remember every movie she had ever seen where the heroine joined the hero on horseback. There weren't that many. Especially not ones filmed in the twenty-first century. "I don't want to be responsible for pulling your arm out of its socket or tearing your rotator cuff."

"You're stalling, Abby. Don't overthink it."

"Couldn't I climb on top of the fence and do it from there?"

"Where's the romance in that?" His broad grin taunted her.

Still, she paused. In the course of her dating life, she had been acquainted with a few very wealthy men. But they were generally ensconced behind corporate desks and wore suits. She had also known surfers and ballplayers and gym rats who prided themselves on their hard bodies and athletic prowess.

Carter was a disturbing mix of both wealthy confidence and masculine strength. He didn't posture or preen. He was who he was. The whole package.

Stifling her doubts, she reached out and took his hand. His grip was firm and sure. As soon as he saw that she had situated her foot as he had instructed, he tugged her up behind him. The entire maneuver took mere seconds. She landed in the saddle with a startled exhalation.

And then she looked at the ground. Her arms clenched around his waist as her knees quivered. She hadn't realized how high off terra firma she would be.

With her cheek pressed against Carter's back and her fingers in a death grip on the front of his belt, she tried to calm down.

"You okay back there?" he asked.

She wanted to hate the amused chuckle in his voice, but she was too busy relying on him to keep her from a painful death. "Just peachy," she bit out, rounding up all the sarcasm she could find and stuffing it into those two words.

Carter set the horse in motion and laughed harder. "Is it a fear of heights that's getting you, or the horse?"

The breeze whipped her hair in her face. "The horse is fine. And it's not a fear of heights. It's a fear of hitting the ground in a bloody, broken mess."

Carter laid his free hand over both of hers, stroking her knuckles in a move that shouldn't have been particularly erotic, but did in fact send arousal pulsing from her scalp to her toes.

"You're safe, Abby. I swear. Now, how do you feel about speed?"

Six

Carter was enjoying himself immensely. Abby was plastered against his back as if he could protect her from every source of harm. He didn't want her to be scared, but he liked having her close.

He gave Foxtrot free rein as Carter took Abby from one end of the ranch to the other, looking at it through her eyes, pointing out every spot that had meaning for him. From the small corral where he learned to ride as a five-year-old to the copse of cottonwood trees where he had his first kiss a decade later, this ranch was home.

Occasionally, they stopped, and he lifted Abby down, taking advantage of the situation to flirt with her while he showed her a new barn or an old steer—the saddle shop or the historic bunkhouse. Abby was enthusiastic, but always in the context of her documentary. Never once did he get the impression that she saw things through *his* eyes.

A Texas ranch was a novelty to her, perhaps even beau-

tiful in a certain context. But Abby was a city girl. It was
a truth he'd do well to remember.

Eventually, they both gave in to hunger—for food. He
dropped her off at her car, and then rode ahead to show her
the way to his house.

When they went inside, Abby's genuine praise soothed
some of his disgruntlement.

"This is gorgeous, Carter! I love it."

As she wandered from room to room, he followed her,
remembering the choices he had made with a designer.
Comfort had always been his first priority. And natural
light. Lots of windows. Furniture made for sitting.

Abby skittered past the door to his bedroom with comi-
cal haste and went on down the hall to explore the laundry room, the workout room and the small in-ground pool
outside, just past the breezeway. When they doubled back
to the living room, she smiled at him. "This is the perfect
house for you. I see your stamp on every bit of it."

"When my parents moved, and I took over, they gave
me their blessing to remodel extensively. At the same time,
we all went in together to design a large guesthouse about
a half mile from here. We're a close-knit family, but they
didn't want to cramp my style when they came to visit."

She sobered. "Lila told me about your fiancée…or ex-
fiancée, I should say. I'm sorry. I wasn't prying."

His jaw tightened. "You're saying she volunteered the
information? And why would she do that?"

Abby chewed her bottom lip, visibly uncomfortable.
"She warned me that you were not in the market for a relationship. That you'd been burned."

He slammed his fist against one of the chiseled wooden
support beams. "This whole damn town needs to mind its
own business."

"But they won't. Not according to you."

He exhaled, not really sure why he was so pissed. "No,"

he said curtly. "They won't." He turned toward the kitchen. "How do you feel about turkey and mayo sandwiches with bacon? My housekeeper comes in three time a week and keeps my fridge stocked."

"Lucky you." Abby seemed as glad as he was to move on to other topics. "And yeah, a sandwich sounds good," she said.

They ate their lunch in the small breakfast nook, enjoying the view from the large bay window. Carter was extremely aware of the woman at his side. Her scent. The sound of her voice. The enthusiastic way she devoured her meal.

She seemed to be a woman unafraid of indulging her appetites.

He shifted on his seat, realizing that he needed to focus his attention on something other than Abby's slender, toned arm, her hand almost touching his. "So, have you nailed down a theme for your documentary, an angle? You were hoping yesterday's meeting of the advisory board would help."

Abby stood and carried her plate to the sink. Then she refilled her lemonade and returned. "It was just business, unfortunately. I did get to meet the Edmond family and see them in action."

"And?" he prodded.

"They were nice. I like them. Tell me what you know about this Billy Holmes guy. I can't figure out how he fits into all of this."

"I've only met him a handful of times," Carter told her. "He moved to Royal a few years ago. Has plenty of money. People seem to like him."

"And he lives on the Edmond estate?"

"That's what I've heard," he replied.

"I wonder why?"

Carter shrugged. "No idea. You'd have to ask him."

"I will. He and I have an interview set up for tomorrow."

Carter tensed. He had nothing concrete against Holmes, but the other man struck Carter as a womanizer. "Are you going alone?"

"Yes. Is there a problem?"

"No. But women are vulnerable. Sometimes when you don't know a person, it's better to meet on neutral ground."

"I'm having lunch at *your* house at this very moment," Abby pointed out with a mischievous grin.

"Touché."

"It will be fine. I've taken self-defense classes since I was sixteen. I can handle myself."

Carter didn't argue, but he remained mildly concerned. Maybe he could wrangle an invitation to go along as Abby's sidekick. Even as the thought formed in his head, he dismissed it. Abby would never admit she needed a bodyguard.

He let the subject drop. "So, what now? My sister always leaves a few swimsuits here. She's close to your size. Do you fancy a dip in the pool?"

"It sounds lovely, but I really want to start interviewing you on camera."

"That again?" He groaned. "I was hoping you'd moved on from that idea. Ranchers are a dime a dozen around here. The job is nothing special."

"Maybe so. But you don't see the big picture, pardon the pun. What you do here at Sunset Acres echoes the frontier cowboys of the olden days. There's poetry in it. And tradition. This probably won't be the central focus of my film, but it could serve as a powerful backdrop. Please, Carter. It won't be so bad. I promise."

He had boxed himself into a corner. By inviting her to stay the entire day, he'd all but guaranteed that she would not give up. "Fine," he grumbled. "Let's get it over with, so we can move on to something that's actually fun. Where do we do this?"

"The great room, I think."

Instead of having a traditional living room or den, Carter had designed a large, open space that could be configured in a number of ways. Despite the ample square footage, he liked to think the cozy furniture and the artwork and large windows worked together to create a welcoming atmosphere.

Abby went out to her car and returned five minutes later with the camera, a tripod and a large tote bag. "It won't take me long to set up," she assured him, practically bouncing on her feet with enthusiasm.

"I could have helped carry something," he said. "I didn't know you had so much gear."

"Well," she replied, dumping everything on the sofa, "often it's just me and the video camera, but when I'm doing serious work, I want to have all my options available." She put her hands on her hips and surveyed the room. "I think that big leather chair will be good. Can we build a fire in the fireplace?"

His brows shot to his hairline, his reaction incredulous. "It's June. In Texas."

Abby faced him, smiling sweetly. "Please, Carter. It will make the scene perfect. We can run up the AC...all right?"

His muttered response was not entirely polite. "Sure. No problem."

As he pulled together a pile of kindling, small logs and fire starter, he was conscious of Abby flitting around the room. Once she had the camera attached to the tripod, she began unfolding filters and screens to get the light exactly as she wanted it.

It was obvious she was a pro at what she did. There was no fumbling, no second-guessing. She worked with purpose, her slender hands moving at lightning speed as she manipulated settings and angles and equipment.

At last, she was satisfied. "Will you take a seat in the chair, so I can take a look?"

He sat down, feeling stiff and ridiculous. "I don't want to be turned into some romanticized stereotype. That's insulting."

"Quit being grumpy. I would never do that to you."

She touched his leg, rearranged his arm, smoothed the collar of his blue button-down shirt. With every moment that passed, he grew more and more uneasy. And more horny.

At last, Abby was satisfied.

Almost.

She peered through the camera and wrinkled her nose. "Would you mind grabbing your Stetson? We can place it artfully on the arm of the chair or on the back near your shoulder."

He glowered, ready to end this before it started. "I don't wear a hat inside the house."

"I'm not asking you to wear it. I just want it for the ambience."

"No," he said firmly. "*This*—" he waved a hand at the ridiculous fire "—is plenty."

"Fine." Abby sulked, but it was a cute sulk.

His fingers dug into the supple leather of the chair arm. "Can we please get started? This fire is making me sweat…"

Abby could tell she was losing her reluctant subject. Carter was visibly fidgety. Was it weird that his irritability made him more attractive to her? She must be seriously messed up. Or maybe she was tired of slick guys who thought they could fast-talk a woman out of her clothes. Carter was rougher around the edges. More real.

She took a sip from her water bottle and ignored her jumpy pulse. "I'm going to ask you a series of questions.

Talk as long as you want on each topic. None of this will be included word for word, but during the editing process, I'll pull out bits that complement the documentary as a whole. Does that make sense?"

"Sure."

She checked the camera once again to make sure Carter was still framed nicely, and then hit the record button. "Tell me more about how you came to run the ranch," she began, giving him an encouraging smile. She had learned that many people were not comfortable on camera, but if she got them talking, they loosened up. "You're a wealthy man. Couldn't you simply hire a manager?"

Carter grinned. "I'm pretty hands-on."

"And why is that?"

"I suppose it's what I learned growing up. My sister and I ran wild. Very few rules except for being home in time for dinner. My father worked long hours. He and my mother had a very traditional marriage. He'd come home tired and dirty at six, sometimes later."

"And why didn't *he* hire a manager?"

"It goes back a couple of generations. My dad's grandfather died in a riding accident when Dad was only seven years old. So my grandfather groomed *my* father from a very early age. Dad was used to working sunup to sundown. Those were the years when the ranch really boomed. The money was pouring in, and my father loved what he did. When my grandfather passed on, he left the entire ranch to my dad."

"That's a lot of responsibility," she remarked.

"Definitely. But my dad never questioned his role. Unfortunately, my grandfather wasn't a fan of organized education. Dad never had the opportunity to go to college. But Sunset Acres was his consolation prize."

"Some prize."

"Yes," he acknowledged. "My mom is from Royal, too.

They were schoolmates. She fit right in with the ranching lifestyle, because she'd had a similar upbringing. After they got married, they spent the next two decades and more building the ranch into an even bigger operation."

"But you mentioned health issues?"

"He had a massive heart attack when I was a year older than you are. We almost lost him." A shadow crossed Carter's face. "The doctor said it was imperative that Dad cut back on both the physical labor and the stress, but my mother knew Dad too well. She realized he couldn't *play* at being a rancher. So she convinced him to retire and hand over the reins and the keys and the headaches to me. They moved to Florida and threw themselves into fishing and boating and everything else that comes with a carefree lifestyle."

"How did you cope in the beginning?" she asked.

"It was scary as hell, I'll admit it. I had a good roster of men working under me, but knowing that the decisions were all mine was terrifying."

"Did you resent having to shoulder so much responsibility?"

His jaw tightened, his gaze stormy. "Is this a documentary or a therapy session?"

"It was just a question, Carter. You don't have to answer."

"Yes," he said, the single word flat. "I did have some negative feelings at first. I was a young male adult, intent on pursuing my own agenda. I'd finished a degree in business management, but I wasn't particularly interested in settling down."

"I'm sorry. That must have been hard."

He shrugged. "I've made my father proud. That was reason enough to put aside my personal goals. And as the years have passed, I haven't regretted that decision. This ranch is thriving. It provides jobs."

"And the legacy is unbroken," she murmured softly.

"That, too."

"I assume you'll want to pass Sunset Acres on to your own children someday?"

"Next question."

Okay. Touchy issue. She checked the viewfinder again and shifted the tripod to get a new angle. "So tell me about Madeline, your ex-fiancée."

Carter rose to his feet, glowering. "Turn off the camera." The words were curt. "I don't see how that question pertains to your documentary. If you want to ask me for personal info, Abby, please have the guts to admit that you're interested."

His sharp criticism stung, particularly because it was on point.

Flushing uncomfortably, she shut off the recording. "Sorry," she muttered. "Lila told me the bare bones. I guess I wondered how your girlfriend fit into your legacy."

"She didn't. That's why we broke up."

"How did you meet?"

He prowled, his hands shoved into his pockets. "I was in Chicago with my whole family to attend the wedding of one of my cousins. Madeline was a guest. We hit it off. There was sexual chemistry. I think both of us were looking for something and had convinced ourselves we found it."

"That must have sucked when you realized otherwise."

"Yeah, it did," he admitted gruffly. "Partly because I disappointed my mom. She was over the moon that her boy was finally settling down."

"You were running a huge ranch. That seems pretty settled to me."

"It's different. I told you…she wants grandchildren."

"Ah, yes," Abby murmured.

"Are we done with this now?" He scowled at her.

"Sure. I'd like to ask you some more questions," she

said. "Not personal. More about what your days are like. The actual running of a ranching operation."

He glanced at his watch. "I have a few things I need to take care of. Why don't you make yourself at home, and I'll be back in an hour or so…"

"Do you have internet?" she asked.

"Of course I do. What kind of question is that?"

"A valid one. We're in the middle of nowhere."

His expression cooled. "Only in your eyes."

When Carter strode out of the room, Abby realized that she had let her prejudices show. No matter how rural the landscape, Royal and the surrounding environs were home to an upscale roster of citizens. Money flowed like water apparently. These people were worldly and powerful.

She'd heard somewhere that Maverick County had more cows than people. That might not be true, but it was certainly possible. Still, the people themselves were the furthest thing from unsophisticated.

Even in the short time she had been in town, she had been forced to confront her expectations. It was becoming clear that her documentary would include entrepreneurs and politicians, society mavens and trendsetters. Blue bloods and old money. Not to mention the occasional upstart.

How was she going to capture all that and still frame Soiree on the Bay in an interesting way? The footage with Carter was a start, but she needed more.

With him gone for an hour, she was free to explore his house on her own, this time more carefully. She didn't open drawers or closets. *Duh.* She wasn't a weirdo. Instead, she walked room to room, soaking up the ambience.

She stopped at the threshold to Carter's bedroom. Even alone, she wouldn't trespass. It didn't take a psychologist to tell her that she was fascinated with his personal space. The man was intensely masculine, but he lived alone. What did he do with all that pent-up sexual energy? A little flutter low in her belly told her she wanted to find out.

It took considerable effort, but she made herself go back to the great room and deal with email. Her mother wanted to know how things were going, as did her dad. She gave them each a slightly different version of her time in Royal. After that, she watched the raw footage of Carter that she had just shot.

Holy heck, he looked good on camera. Broad shoulders, brooding good looks. And his occasional smiles were pure gold. Plus, when he talked, there was an authenticity about him, a sense of integrity. In the old days, people would have called him a straight shooter.

She ran out of things to do about the time she heard the back door slam. Carter appeared in the doorway, looking hot and windblown. "Any chance you'd be interested in that swim now?"

"Sure. As long as one of the suits fits. I'm not skinny-dipping with you, ranch man. At least not in broad daylight," she said, giving him a taunting grin.

The heat in his laser-blue gaze seared her. "Then I suppose I'll have to keep you here until dark. I grill a mean steak."

She swallowed, feeling out of her depth. She'd been teasing about the skinny-dipping, but Carter appeared to take her words at face value. "I don't want to drive back to Royal in the dark," she said, entirely serious. "I don't know these roads. I might hit an armadillo."

His face lit up with humor. "I'll take you home. One of my guys can return your car in the morning."

Well, she had run out of excuses. What did she really want? And was she brave enough to take the risk?

Seven

Carter wondered if Abby knew how expressive her face was. He swore he could read every emotion. She was flattered. And probably interested. But she was cautious, too. He could hardly blame her.

"I won't pressure you, Abby. All you have to do is say the word, and we can part as friends."

"Is there another category than friends?" Her smile was a little on the shaky side.

"You know there is. I want you. But only if you feel the same way. And beyond that, there's no timetable… Is there?"

She lifted one slender shoulder and let it fall. "Actually, yes. I won't be here more than a few weeks. That's not much time to decide whether I can trust you."

He cocked his head. "Trust me how? I'm no threat to you, Abs." He held up his hands, palms out. "There's no quid pro quo. I'll let you interview me some more even if you and I never knock boots. You have my word."

"*Knock boots?* Are you kidding me? Is that a Texas expression? Besides, it's easy for you to be magnanimous. You know how sexy you are. I'm not sure I can keep this professional. I'm not even sure I want to…"

"So, where does that leave us?" It wouldn't do for her to know how tightly wound he was as he awaited her answer.

She grimaced. "Let's swim," she said. "After that, I don't know…"

Fifteen minutes later, when Abby exited the house and joined him in the pool, he was damn glad the water concealed his instant boner. She was the most beautiful thing he had ever seen.

And he was wrong about her being skinny. Now that she was wearing a remarkably modest, but nevertheless provocative, black two-piece swimsuit, it was painfully clear that Abby had all the curves a man could want. Long, toned legs to wrap around his waist. A flat stomach with a diamond belly button piercing that caught the sun, and breasts that were just the right size to fill a man's hands.

His fists clenched at his sides. "I see the suit fit you."

"Quit staring," she said sharply.

With no apparent self-consciousness, she walked to the end of the diving board, bounced once and made a clean dive into the pool. When she surfaced, she lifted her face to the sun and slicked back her hair, laughing.

"The water is perfect," she said. "Do you swim every day?"

"Not always." And why was that? There was no good reason other than the fact that his waking hours were busy.

Abby began doing laps, her long legs and strong arms propelling her through the water easily. Carter followed suit, careful to keep to his side of the pool. They were completely alone. None of his staff would dare seek him out without an okay ahead of time. And since he had his phone on silent, this little bubble of intimacy was intact.

At last, Abby tired. She stayed in the deep end, treading water. Finally, she clung to the metal ladder, one arm curled around the bottom step. "This is nice."

An invisible cord drew him across the pool to where she lazily kicked her legs. He stopped a few feet away, his heart pounding. Water clung to her beautiful skin in droplets that refracted the sunlight. Her eyelashes were spiky. Brown eyes stared at him as if assessing his intent.

"I'm gonna kiss you, Abs," he said hoarsely. "Unless you object."

Her eyes widened. But she didn't speak. She didn't move.

He was tall enough to touch bottom. Moving closer still, he brushed her arm. "Hang on, Abby."

Without hesitation, she released the ladder and curled her arms around his neck. Now their bodies were pressed together so closely he could feel the rapid rise and fall of her chest. All the blood left his head, rushing south.

Maybe he had heat stroke. His brain felt muzzy, and his hands tingled. "Abby…" With one arm around her back and the other hand gripping the ladder, he stared into her eyes. Deep in the midst of those chocolate irises he found tiny flecks of gold.

"Car…ter…" She caressed his name, infusing it with sensuality. Her lips curled in a smile. "This feels naughty."

"Hell, yeah…" He tried to laugh, but he didn't have enough oxygen.

She nipped his bottom lip with a tiny, stinging bite, then soothed the pain with her tongue. "You taste like chlorine," she whispered.

He yanked her closer and slammed his mouth down on hers. No smooth moves, no practiced technique. Only sheer desperation.

She met him kiss for kiss, not submitting, but battling. He wondered in some far distant corner of his brain if the heat they were conjuring would turn the pool water to steam.

If two people could devour each other, this was how it would happen. She was strong and feminine, her skin and muscles soft and smooth everywhere he was hard. Lust roared through his veins. He wanted her. But his conscience said, *too soon...*

After what seemed like an eternity, he made himself pull back. Abby's lips were swollen and puffy from his kisses. Strands of her wet hair that had dried in the sun danced around her face.

He stared at her. "We should probably find some shade," he said. "How about a lounge chair with an umbrella and a cold drink?"

Abby's expression was dazed. "Sure. Water is fine for me. But you go up the ladder first. I don't want you staring at my ass."

"Too late."

That finally made her smile.

He did as she asked, lifting himself out of the pool and deliberately shaking water at her. When Abby screeched, he chuckled. The small fridge in the pool house held chilled water bottles. He grabbed a couple of those along with some dry towels that he spread on the two chaises. Abby hovered nearby, her arms wrapped around her waist. Long, beautiful hair cascaded down her back.

"Ladies first," he said.

Abby widened the gap between the two chairs by about a foot, and then settled onto the lounger gracefully, raising her arms over her head and bending one knee.

Carter took the remaining seat and lay back with a sigh. Despite his arousal, the sensation of hot sun on his wet skin was a familiar, soothing taste of summer. Behind his sunglasses, he managed to sneak a sideways glance.

Was she asleep? Awake? He couldn't decide but chose

to assume the latter. "You want to tell me more about yesterday's advisory board meeting?"

She turned her face in his direction, a half smile lifting the corners of her mouth. "Business talk?"

"It's either that or carry you to my bedroom. Seemed premature."

He witnessed her startled breath, a gasp really, quickly disguised. "I think I covered everything."

"Then let's talk about *you*."

She slung an arm over her eyes, shutting him out. But he wasn't so easily dissuaded. "Seriously, Abs, you've grilled me nonstop. And if that weren't enough, Lila blabbed about my personal life. I think it's only fair that I get to delve into your psyche."

Moving her arm, she scowled at him. "Couldn't we just have sex?"

He laughed. "You don't like being interviewed any more than I do."

"Why do you think I chose to be on this side of the camera?"

"You're only twenty-four," Carter reminded her. "How bad could your secrets be?"

"Who said I have secrets?"

He exhaled, emptying his lungs so he could inhale the scent of her again. "Everybody has secrets, Abby. But you can start with your childhood. What were you like in school?"

Her profile made him ache. Vulnerability etched her features. "I was lonely mostly. That whole mean girl stereotype is based on reality. I was a biracial kid in a sea of white faces. I was an oddity. So that put me on the outside looking in. I didn't understand why until I was seven or eight. But the first day someone said a nasty thing about my father, I was done trying to fit in. My mother went to see the principal over and over, begging for adult intervention. That only made things worse."

His stomach twisted. "I'm sorry, Abby."

"It got better in high school. There was a more diverse population. Supersmart kids whose parents had immigrated to New York as children, grown up there. I gradually built a circle of intimates, classmates with whom I could be myself." She released a breath. "In fact, my very best friend is a Pakistani woman who's now a doctor at Lenox Hill Hospital in New York. She's doing a residency in geriatric medicine. We've brainstormed about me maybe doing a documentary about the social and emotional costs of increased life span."

"Wow." Carter stared at her, for the first time understanding how complex she was, how passionate and talented. "I'm impressed, Abby. You've made an amazing life for yourself."

"It suits me. I love to travel, and I don't mind traveling alone. My parents have always given me a lot of freedom. I tried never to abuse their trust."

Silence fell between them, but it wasn't awkward. They were sizing each other up, wondering about the differences in their lives and whether there was even the tiniest bit of overlap.

He honestly didn't know. A decade separated them, though that age gap was hardly a novelty. Abby was city mouse; he was country mouse. She was happiest crisscrossing the country, whereas he had deep roots in this Texas soil.

"Do you still want to film me talking about the ranch?" he asked gruffly.

Her eyes flew open, and she turned on her side. "You don't mind?"

He tried not to notice the way her breasts nearly spilled out of her swimsuit top in that position. "It wouldn't be my first choice, but if it will help you with your project, I'll do it."

Her smile blinded him. "Thank you, Carter. That's awesome." She jumped up. "I'll go change, and we'll get started."

After she left, he stared glumly at the water. Was he stupid? If he'd kept his mouth shut, Abby would still be beside him, sunbathing like a beautiful goddess, at arm's length.

Maybe his subconscious was trying to point out how self-destructive it would be to initiate a physical relationship under these circumstances. Even so, his libido demanded equal time. It was hours yet until sundown. Anything could happen.

Abby was thrilled and surprised that Carter had agreed to more on-camera time. She changed back into her clothes, twisted her damp hair into a loose knot on the back of her head and rushed to the great room to prepare for this next session. The fire, of course, had long since burned out.

Since she didn't have the heart to ask Carter to build another, she shifted his chair in front of some beautiful cherry bookcases. And she tossed a Native American blanket over the back corner of the chair.

By the time she had the scene prepared to her liking, Carter was back.

He had showered. Her twitching nose told her that. The scent of a very expensive aftershave emanated from him. Why would a man shave midafternoon? To be ready for a rendezvous later in the evening?

Her heart skipped a beat, but she focused on her work. "I'm all set," she said. "Why don't you take your seat, and we'll get started."

Carter was dressed a little less casually this time. His dark dress pants and gray knit polo shirt showcased his impressive physique. It was clear that the owner of Sunset Acres was a hands-on boss, one who spent plenty of time doing heavy chores and building up the strength to bench-press a car. Or woo a woman.

When she noticed he had chosen to go without shoes, she melted a little. Something about those large, tanned feet struck her as both masculine and boyish.

He smiled at her as he sprawled in the chair and ran his hands across his head. "I threw some potatoes in the oven. If we can wrap this up in forty-five minutes, I'll get the steaks on the grill. There's stuff in the fridge to make a salad, if you don't mind doing that."

"I'd be happy to." She peered through the camera and frowned. "I like you relaxed, but you've messed up your hair." Without overthinking it, she went to him and used her fingers to comb the thick, damp strands until she was happy with how he looked.

Carter took her arm and kissed the inside of her wrist. "I like it when you groom me, Abs."

She pursed her lips, refusing to let him see that one ach-ingly tender kiss had her undone. "You mean like a gorilla mom with her baby?"

His jaw jutted. "I'm a full-grown man, Abby. You can count on that."

"Duly noted." She took her spot behind the camera. "Start with staff," she said calmly. "How many full-time employees do you have? What do they do? And what about seasonal and part-time?"

The camera started rolling, and Carter began talking. Despite Abby's total unfamiliarity with the topic, he man-aged to make it interesting. She quizzed him on herd sizes and breeds and what constituted a "good" year. She asked about weather disasters like tornadoes and hailstorms and fires, and then lesser crises like drought and floods.

The more Carter talked, the more Abby realized how

deeply devoted he was to his heritage. He had to be. No one else loved it like he did.

Lastly, she touched on his family.

"They're actually coming for a visit this weekend," Carter said. "My parents, my sister and brother-in-law, and my niece, Beebee."

"Beebee?"

"They named her Beatrice, but that might stick when she's ten or eleven. At eight months, Beebee works."

Abby turned off the camera and stretched. "I have one last question, but I don't want it on camera."

He raised an eyebrow. "Oh? Should I be worried?"

"It's not about you. It's about the festival."

"Sounds serious from the tone of your voice."

Abby curled up on one end of the sofa and picked at a loose thread on the knee of her jeans. "I stumbled on something yesterday…something that might make a huge jumping-off point for my documentary. But I wanted to get your opinion."

"Go on…"

"When I was in the diner eating lunch, I overheard a conversation in the booth behind me. I wasn't eavesdropping on purpose, but it was hard not to listen. One woman was saying she heard someone stole a ton of money from the Soiree on the Bay checking account. Could that possibly be true? Nothing was mentioned in the meeting yesterday."

Carter scowled. "That's a dead end, Abby. We've talked about this. Royal thrives on innuendo and gossip. It grows as fast as kudzu. But ninety percent of the time, there's nothing to it. People don't like outsiders poking their noses in our business. You need to drop it. Find another angle. Otherwise, you'll end up alienating the very people who could help you with your project."

Abby was stunned by his vehemence. And hurt. The

careless way he referred to her as an *outsider*, gave his warning a personal slant. Was that what he thought of her?

When Carter left to go put the steaks on the grill, she carried all her gear to the car and then wandered into the kitchen and began fixing a salad. As promised, she had everything at hand in the oversize, cutting-edge refrigerator. Finding a large bowl and a small pitcher for the dressing gave her an excuse to snoop through his cabinets.

As she worked, her pride still stung from his harsh rebuke. And her heart. Soiree on the Bay wouldn't be the first festival to be rocked by graft and greed. Local sponsors, both individual and corporate, had fronted an enormous amount of money to move the event forward.

Carter might not like it. In fact, she wouldn't bring it up again. But on her own, she was determined to explore this lead, tenuous though it was. Almost all gossip contained a grain of truth, no matter how tiny. She would follow this road until it petered out—or gave her the impetus she needed to put her documentary on a strong footing.

Abby didn't eat much red meat as a rule, but the steaks were extraordinary. She supposed a man who owned an enormous ranch learned early how to prepare beef. It was tender and subtly flavored. With the loaded baked potatoes and salad, it was the perfect meal.

Though Abby offered to help with cleanup, he refused. "There's not that much. And my housekeeper comes at ten in the morning."

"In that case, I should be getting back to town," she said.

Carter stilled, his back to her as he put things in the fridge. He shot her a look over his shoulder. "Or you could stay." The gleam in his beautiful blue eyes was temptation, pure and simple.

Here it was. Decision time. It would be much easier to get caught up in the moment, but Carter wasn't taking that tack. He was asking flat out. Offering her a clear choice. Be intimate with him, or choose to walk away.

He had given her everything she could ask for in terms of the interview. It was going to make incredibly good footage. But she felt no compunction to stay based on that. Whatever happened between the two of them was not going to be business.

The positives were clear. He was an honorable man, a conscientious son. A reputable landowner. Beyond that, he was sexy as hell. She knew without hesitation that he would be good to a woman in bed. Or *bad*, if she desired.

Up until this visit to Royal, Texas, she had been cautious in her love life. Her few relationships had been based on shared interests and a mutual desire for sexual satisfaction. But in every case, she had felt relief when the weeks or months were over, and she was *single* again. She'd told herself that she wasn't good at giving and receiving intimacy. Mostly, because she was too self-sufficient, too private.

Yet now, here was Carter. The man who burned away every last one of her reservations with a single look. Her body recognized him as a potential lover. But there was nothing simple about it. In fact, the urgency she felt was both astonishing and intimidating.

"Is that a good idea?" she asked, stalling for time to answer her own doubts.

"I could be convinced to come to the hotel with you." He leaned his hips against the counter and folded his arms across his chest. His face was hard to read.

She forced a laugh. "After you lectured me about Royal's gossipy grapevine? No, thanks. I don't want the whole town knowing what we do."

His expression softened. "It's your call, Abs. I won't be accused of pressuring you."

"I know that, dammit." She put her hands to her hot cheeks, mortified. "I'm sorry." Perhaps this was where his extra decade gave him the edge. He'd probably lived this scene half a dozen more times than she had. She took a deep breath to steady her nerves. "I liked riding with you this morning. Could we take Foxtrot out for an evening cruise? I want to chase the sunset, hard and fast."

A flush rode high on his cheekbones. His eyes darkened. "We can do that. Meet me in the stable in fifteen minutes."

And then he was gone. Abby sought out the guest bathroom again and tidied her hair, securing it more tightly in its knot. As she stared at herself in the mirror, she wondered what Carter saw when he looked at her. Some men had called her exotic. It was a description she didn't really enjoy.

She didn't want to be different, at least not in that way. Though she had no hard data to back it up, her gut feeling was that Carter saw her as a woman first. A sexual being. A human with hopes and dreams.

She was okay with that. Because she recognized those same aspects in him. And something about him drew her like no one she had ever met.

It struck her suddenly, that not once had she entertained the idea of taking her camera on this outing. The professional Abby was done for the day. Tonight was all about *pleasure*.

As she walked through the house and out to the barn, she listed all the reasons not to stay with Carter. She had no clothes, no suitcase, nothing but a tube of ChapStick in her purse. Would she wake up in the morning feeling awkward and embarrassed? The answer was almost surely yes.

But even as she tried to talk herself out of tumbling into his bed, she knew the decision had been made.

The barn smelled amazing. As a city girl, she saw it as an anomaly, but one she liked. The atmosphere was earthy and real. When she saw the man waiting for her, her heart

88 TEXAS TOUGH

stumbled. He was wearing the Stetson this time. And riding boots.

The horse whinnied softly when Abby approached.

Carter smiled at her, an uncomplicated, straightforward look that encompassed welcome and desire and forbidden promises.

"I'm putting you in front his time," he said.

Unlike before, there were no instructions. He simply put his hands on her waist and hefted her up into the saddle. His easy strength gave her a little thrill.

Moments later, he settled in behind her, his arms coming around her to hold the reins. His lips brushed the back of her neck. "You ready?"

It was a question with layers of meaning. "Yes," she answered, her response firm and unequivocal. "I can't wait."

Eight

Carter knew the exact moment Abby unwound. Like a rag doll, all the stiffness left her body, and her spine relaxed against his chest. He held the reins with one hand, so he could curl his arm around her waist.

The large saddle accommodated both of them comfortably. Foxtrot was a strong stallion, easily capable of bearing their weight and more. As the horse ambled away from the house toward the road, Carter told himself he had to concentrate. He had precious cargo. But all he wanted to do was bury his face in Abby's hair and hope she had stayed for more than an evening excursion on the ranch.

The sunset was particularly beautiful. Just enough clouds to make striking patterns of orange and pink and gold, much like the night he and Abby had first met. Already, that moment seemed like eons ago. But it wasn't, and he'd do well to remember that.

He nuzzled her ear. "You still want speed?"

She nodded. "Definitely."

He gave Foxtrot a nudge with his knees and felt the jolt of adrenaline as the powerful animal reached his stride. They were streaking down the road that bisected the ranch at a dizzying speed. It was a safe enough course.

Abby's delighted squeal made Carter smile. He pushed the horse faster and harder. Foxtrot loved the free rein. Even though it had been a hot day, at this hour and this speed, the wind felt chilly. He held Abby close, his posture protective.

Carter knew she was strong and independent, but she was young and new to Texas. He wouldn't let any*thing* or any*one* harm her, not even himself.

At last, they reached the far boundary of his acreage and turned around to head for home. Now Foxtrot's gallop was more sedate. Eventually, Carter slowed him further still. No point in ending the night too soon.

"Are you cold?" he asked.

"A little. But it's okay. I wouldn't have missed this."

"What would you be doing back in New York about now?"

He felt her shrug. "Maybe seeing a play. I adore Broadway. Always have. I actually thought about pursuing acting at one point."

"You'd have been good at it, I think. You have a very expressive face. And a beautiful voice."

She turned her head and rested her cheek over his heart for a moment. "Thank you, Carter. That's a sweet thing to say."

"But true."

He held her close, steering the horse in the gathering gloom.

As they neared the house, Abby whispered something he didn't quite catch.

"What was that, Abs?"

Still facing straight ahead, she reached behind her and

cupped his cheek with a slender, long-fingered hand. "I don't have any clean clothes with me. Or anything for that matter."

The insinuation went straight to his head and his groin. "I can hook you up," he said gruffly. "The guest bathroom has everything you'll need. And we can throw your clothes in the washer. I'll give you one of my shirts in the meantime."

She nodded. "Then I'd like to stay the night."

Things got fuzzy for Carter after that. He had wanted her for hours. The day had been one long and wonderful—but frustrating—dance of foreplay.

Now Abby was in his arms and committed to his bed. He'd won the lottery, though he would have sworn he wasn't a gambling man.

At the stable, he dismounted and helped her down. "I have to deal with the horse. If you'll wait for me, we can take a shower together."

In the illumination from the light inside the barn, her expression was bashful. "I think this first time I'd feel more comfortable getting ready on my own. Okay?"

He kissed her forehead. "Whatever you want." He was still fixated on that one important phrase *this first time*. How many would there be? Abby had a job to do in Royal. She wouldn't be at his beck and call. And his days were plenty busy, too.

It was pointless to overanalyze things. He removed Foxtrot's saddle and rubbed him down before checking his food and water. Then he lowered the lights and closed up the barn. As he walked back to the house, he felt jittery. A shot of whiskey might be nice. But even that couldn't dull the hunger he felt.

When he reached his suite, the walk-in closet door stood open. Abby had clearly helped herself to an item of his clothing. That image kept him hard all during his shower. And when he returned to the bedroom and found her sitting cross-legged in the center of his bed, his erection grew.

She had picked out a plain white cotton button-down and had rolled the long sleeves to her elbows. Her dark, wavy hair fell around her shoulders. The shirttails covered her modestly.

But not for long…

Carter wore only a damp towel tucked around his hips. He had a hard time catching his breath. "Did you find everything you need?"

She tilted her head to one side and gave him a mischievous grin. "Not yet."

That was the thing that kept tripping him up. Abby Carmichael looked young and innocent, but she wasn't. She was an adult, with a woman's wants and needs. Luckily for him, she had found her way into his bed.

When he tossed the towel on a nearby chair, Abby lost her smile. Her gaze settled on his sex. He saw the muscles in her throat move when she swallowed.

"Scoot over," he said, pulling the covers back and joining her. He sprawled on his side, propping his head on his hand. "You look beautiful, Ms. Carmichael. And you smell delicious."

Abby didn't move. He thought she might be holding her breath. Finally, she exhaled a little puff of air. "Your guest bathroom is stocked with lovely toiletries."

"I'm glad you approve." He ran his thumb across her exposed knee. "Are you scared of me, Abby?"

She wrinkled her nose. "No. My birth control pills are at the hotel. You'll have to wear a condom."

"That's not a problem." He slid his hand from her knee to her thigh, under the shirt. "Talk to me, Abs."

Her hands were clasped in her lap. She looked either

nervous or uncertain, or both. "I haven't slept with a lot of men," she admitted. "And you're not like any of them."

"Meaning what?"

"What if this doesn't work? I've known you four days. That's not me, Carter. I'm not an impulsive kind of woman. But this chemistry between us…it's…"

"Undeniable? Explosive? Breath-stealing?"

She nodded. "All those things."

He sat up and leaned against the headboard, pulling her into a loose embrace, combing his fingers through her hair. "We'll take it slow. You tell me if I do something you don't like."

She pulled back and stared at him with those deep brown eyes framed in thick lashes. "I don't think that's going to be a problem."

With unsteady hands, he unbuttoned the shirt Abby wore, *his* shirt, gradually revealing pale brown skin that was soft and smooth and begging for his kisses. Her breasts were high and full, the tips a lighter shade than her eyes.

When he managed the final button, he slid the garment off her slender body and cast it aside. Abby watched him with a rapt expression that stoked the flame burning inside him. When he palmed her breast, she gasped.

He thumbed the nipple, watching in fascination as it furled tightly. When he leaned down to take that bud into his mouth, Abby's choked moan ignited him. He dragged her onto the mattress and lifted himself over her, giving the other breast equal attention.

Her hands fisted in his hair painfully. He suspected they were both too primed to make this last as long as he wanted, but he was going to try.

She moved restlessly as he kissed her forehead, her eyelids, her nose and finally, her soft lips. The taste of her was like a drug, clouding his brain. "Abby," he groaned.

They kissed wildly, like they had in the pool. Only now, they were in a big soft bed made for a man and a woman. And pleasure. *Endless* pleasure.

He lost himself in the kissing, his hands equally occupied learning the hills and valleys of her lithe, long-limbed body. She was soft and strong, a seductive combo.

In some dim, conscious corner of his brain, he remembered protection. Rolling away from her, he snatched open a drawer and found what he wanted. After ripping open the package, he sheathed himself, knowing he couldn't hold out very long this first time.

When he delicately stroked Abby's center, she was warm and wet and ready for him. He entered her with two fingers, feeling her body tighten against his intrusion. "I need you, Abs. I'll make it up to you, I swear."

Even then, he waited, stroking that tiny bundle of nerves that controlled her pleasure until she arched off the bed and cried out.

He entered her then with one forceful push, feeling her inner muscles contract around him, her body still in the throes of sweet release. The sensation was indescribable. He was consumed with lust and racked with the need to give her tenderness and passion in equal measure.

As he moved in her slowly, Abby squirmed beneath him, locking her legs around his waist and angling her lower body so they fit together perfectly. She was dreamy-eyed, flushed, her skin damp and hot.

"Don't hold back, Carter. I want it all."

Her words were a demand, one he was happy to meet. His world narrowed to her face. Each time he pumped his hips, he saw her react. The flutter of long-lashed eyelids, the small gasps of breath, the way her chin lifted toward the ceiling and her lips parted as she reached for a second climax.

She found it as he found his. He came for eons, it seemed,

shuddering against her and whispering her name. When it was over, he slumped on top of her, barely managing to brace most of his weight on his elbows.

He might have dozed.

When reality finally intruded, it was because Abby squirmed out from under him to go to the bathroom. Carter rolled to his back and slung one arm over his face. He felt blissfully sated, but oddly unsettled.

Some things were too good to be true, and this might be one of them. Madeline hadn't been the woman for him. He could see that now with the benefit of hindsight. Losing her had wounded his pride and his dignity. The broken relationship left him lonely and afraid to trust.

Abby wasn't Madeline. Carter knew that. But she was no more likely to hang around, so he needed to keep his head out of his ass and be smart about this.

While his lover was still occupied, he crawled out of bed and retrieved her clothes from the guest bathroom. As he turned on the washing machine and added soap, he stared at the bra and panties in his hands. They looked alien.

This was a male household.

He'd had a handful of one-night stands since his aborted engagement. Mostly out of town. Almost exclusively with sophisticated women who took what they wanted and asked for nothing in return.

Abby was different. Honestly, he couldn't say exactly how or why, but he felt it in his gut. The fact that confusion swirled in his brain warned him to take a step back.

He tossed the few items of laundry into the water and closed the lid. She was spending the night. There was nothing he could do about that. So, he might as well enjoy himself.

Abby was tucked up in his bed, snug beneath the covers when he returned to his room. The sight of her constricted his chest.

She raised up on her elbow. "Where did you go?"

"I promised to wash your clothes, remember?"

"Oh. Right. I was thinking about leaving in a little bit, but I guess I won't."

He frowned. "Leaving? Why?"

Abby shoved the hair from her face, some of it still damp. Her gaze was guarded. "You'll need to be up early in the morning. And I've already taken a lot of your time this week. I don't want to overstay my welcome."

Was there a note of hurt in that explanation? Had she picked up on his unease? Guilt swamped him. He climbed back into bed, pulling her close. "I'll let you know if you're in the way, Abs. For now, we're right where we should be."

They slept for an hour, or maybe two. Then he made love to her again. This time was less frantic, but no less stunning. He wasn't a teenager anymore. Sex was an important part of life, but it hadn't been the driving force in the last few years.

Now he craved her with a fiery intensity that took his breath away. What was he going to do about that?

When he roused the next time, he stumbled down the hall to put her clothes in the dryer. He contemplated *forgetting*, so she would have to stay longer. But he knew she had an interview lined up with Billy Holmes, and Carter couldn't be the one to sabotage her project, even if he wasn't keen on knowing Abby would be alone with Holmes.

Sometime before dawn, he awakened to the pleasant sensation of female fingers wrapped around his erection.

Abby nuzzled her face in the crook of his neck. "It will be morning soon. Are you up for one more round before I go?"

He cleared his throat, feeling like a sailor lost at sea. The only thing he could hang on to was Abby. "I think you know the answer to that."

He took care of protection once again, and Abby climbed on top with no apparent self-consciousness. Cupping her firm, rounded ass in his hands, he thrust into her warmth, feeling his certainty slip away.

Were there some things a man could make exceptions for? Some prizes worth any price? His life was all mapped out. It was a *good* life. But there was no room for self-indulgence. Abby was cotton candy at the fair, a brilliant display of fireworks on a hot summer night. But she wasn't the mundane day-to-day of responsibility.

When she leaned down to steal a kiss—her hair cocooning them in intimacy—he quickly lost the desire for self-reflection. Her breasts danced in front of him, ripe for the tasting. He took every advantage.

Her body was a mystery and a wonder of divine engineering. This was the third time he'd taken her tonight. He should have been sated and tired. Instead, he felt invincible.

When she cried out and came, he rolled her to her back and pounded his way to the finish line, shocked even now at the effect she had on him. Was it some kind of sorcery? Or was he simply sex deprived?

Maybe there was yet another explanation he didn't want to acknowledge.

He had slept only in snatches the entire night. This time, he fell hard and deep into unconsciousness. When his alarm went off at seven, one side of the bed was cool and empty, and his lover was gone.

Abby yawned her way through a hotel breakfast in the dining room. The eggs and bacon, fresh fruit and croissants were delightful, but she didn't enjoy the meal as much as she should have. She felt disheveled and gloomy, and she didn't have the luxury of going to her room and crashing.

Billy Holmes was expecting her at eleven.

She refused to think about Carter at all. He confused her. That was the last thing she needed right now. Her documentary was still an unfocused blob. She *had* to find a sound angle if she hoped to make any progress at all.

By the time she had showered and changed into a melon-colored pantsuit with a jaunty aqua and coral scarf around her throat, she felt a renewed determination. The fashionable clothes were intentional. This documentary was her big shot. She had someone at a major studio willing to take a chance on her. The film she produced had to be rock-solid. And it didn't hurt to dress for success.

Driving out to the Edmonds' property steadied her. As she passed an ornate sign that read Elegance Ranch, she wrinkled her nose. The name was pretentious, at least to her. Billy had texted her a set of directions. That was a good thing, because the sprawling private dynasty included a pool and stables and several guesthouses in addition to the massive, luxurious main house.

She recalled from the meeting at the Texas Cattleman's Club that Rusty Edmond, the oft-married but now-single patriarch, lived there along with his son, Ross, daughter, Gina, and stepson, Asher. And for a reason yet to be discovered, Billy Holmes lived in one of the guest cottages.

The property was completely private, surrounded by miles of ranch land. Abby stopped several times to get out and photograph interesting spots. Once she was cleared at the gatehouse, there were no other impediments. She had allowed herself plenty of extra time. Being prompt was one of her personal mantras.

By the time she located Billy's guesthouse, her nerves returned. His home was beautiful, lushly landscaped and neither huge nor tiny. How had he ended up here? And why had the family accepted him as one of their own?

When Abby rang the doorbell, a uniformed older woman

with gray hair answered. "You must be Ms. Carmichael," she said. "Please come in. Mr. Holmes is expecting you."

Abby followed the woman through the house to a pleasant sunroom overlooking a grassy, well-manicured lawn.

Billy Holmes stood. "Abby. Right on time. So glad you could join me. Would you like a drink?"

"Water for me, please."

He offered her a comfortable seat and took an adjoining chair. "How are you liking Royal, so far?"

"I'm getting my bearings," she said diplomatically. "The people are friendly. And I enjoyed the advisory council meeting." She set her glass of water aside. "Would you mind if I go ahead and get set up to film our conversation? I don't want to miss anything. Unless the camera makes you uncomfortable."

"The camera doesn't bother me at all," he said, giving her a smile that was almost too charming.

Fortunately for Abby, Holmes's phone dinged. He stood and dealt with the text, leaving her a few moments to frame a backdrop and get her equipment where she wanted it. By the time she was ready, Billy returned.

She motioned to where she had situated a chair adjacent to a large-paned window. "May we get started?"

"Of course." He put his phone in the breast pocket of his jacket and unbuttoned the coat before sitting down. With the sun gilding his dark hair and his deliberately scruffy five-o'clock shadow, Billy Holmes looked every inch the bad boy.

Abby sighted her subject through the viewfinder one last time and then stepped back. "How long have you lived in Royal, Mr. Holmes?"

"Call me Billy, please. I guess it's been two and a half years now. Time flies."

"And what is your connection to the Edmond family?" she asked.

"Ross and I were college buddies. He always talked about Royal and how much he loved it. When I decided to relocate and get settled for good, I thought about Maverick County as an option. Ross offered me one of the guest-houses, and here I am."

"He sounds like a very good friend," Abby remarked.

"Indeed."

"Who came up with the festival idea originally? Was it you?"

His smile was modest. "Hard to say. Ross and Gina and Asher and I were talking one day about ways to put Royal on the map. It was a brainstorming session, a group project."

"What do you hope to achieve? The actual festival site is a long way from here."

He shrugged. "Distance is nothing in Texas. Royal will be the jumping-off point for the festival. Our main focus is luxury, whether it's food or wine or music or art. We're marketing to a particular clientele. No empty beer bottles and smelly port-a-johns. Beyond that, we want to bring people together, and also raise significant money for charity." He cleared his throat. "To that end, we're sparing no expense. We want Soiree on the Bay to be talked about for years to come."

Abby kept asking him questions for another half hour and then began winding down the narrative. Billy Holmes was good on camera, charismatic, easy to listen to… This footage would be excellent.

Before she wrapped up, she decided to take a risk. "I heard a rumor in town," she murmured, keeping her tone light. "Something about money missing from the festival account. Could you comment on that?"

Billy's expression changed from affable to calculating. He seemed tense. "Turn off the camera."

"Of course."

After she did as he demanded, Billy stood and paced, his face flushed. "Off the record? Yes, that's true. Ross discovered the discrepancy. But it's a family matter. We're handling it."

Yet Billy Holmes *wasn't* family. "I see." She didn't see at all, but she was stalling. "Is the festival in danger?"

"Of course not," he snapped. "We're full steam ahead. It's going to be epic."

Abby realized she wasn't going to get anything further out of Billy Holmes. If he had slipped before, now he was covering his tracks.

In the end, she was forced to put her equipment away and sit through a long and one-sided lunch conversation. Holmes liked talking about himself. That much was clear.

But he was being closemouthed on the topic that interested her most.

Only the housekeeper's culinary skills made the meal memorable. The quiche lorraine was amazing, as was the caprese salad.

Eventually, Abby decided she had stayed long enough not to seem rude if she bolted. "I should get back to town," she said. "Thanks so much for lunch and the interview."

Holmes stood when she did. "My pleasure." His expression was guarded now, as if he was aware he had overstepped some boundary and now regretted his candor.

He walked her to the front door and out to her car, helping carry one of her bags. Abby had left her sunglasses in the glove box. She shielded her eyes with her hand. "One other thing. I'd love to speak with a few of the charities who will benefit from the Soiree. Could you make that happen?" She was deliberately playing to his vanity.

"Of course." He preened. "You should start with Valencia Donovan at Donovan Horse Rescue. You'll like her. She has an interesting story to tell."

"Perfect," Abby said. "You'll give her my number? See if she's willing to be interviewed? I don't want to assume…"

"I'll deal with it this afternoon. If you're lucky, she might be able to see you tomorrow."

Nine

Abby was thrilled that the wheels were beginning to turn more quickly with regard to her documentary, but even so, she couldn't stop thinking about Carter. She'd written him a polite but brief note that morning, explaining that she had a busy day ahead.

What did he think when he found her gone? Was he disappointed?

Maybe he was glad. Some men didn't like complications.

When she got back to the hotel, she forced herself to concentrate on work. Between the brief footage she had shot during the advisory board meeting and the personal interviews with Carter Crane and Billy Holmes, she already had a great start. Now came the hard part of scrolling through frames and editing the sequences she knew would serve her purpose.

Billy Holmes was as good as his word, apparently. Abby got a text midafternoon from Valencia Donovan inviting her to meet Valencia and see her charity at ten tomorrow morning. That should work. After responding in the affirmative, Abby was soon deep into her storyboard. What was the hook going to be? More and more, she was convinced it was the money trail.

When her stomach growled, she was surprised to realize it was after seven. Sitting in the restaurant didn't appeal, so she ordered room service. That way she could continue working while she ate.

Two hours later, she stood and stretched. She'd made good progress. Now she could goof off and watch TV or add some new shots to her Instagram account. As a budding filmmaker, social media was essential.

She was just about to get in the shower when her phone dinged. It was Carter. Her pulse skittered. What did he want? She snatched up her cell and read the text.

Abby—Hope you had a good day. How about coming out to the ranch for dinner tomorrow night? I know my family would love to meet you. Let me know...

In the bathroom mirror, her expression was startled. Meet his *family*? Why? She scowled at her reflection, parsing his words for hidden meanings. Maybe the invitation was no more or less than it seemed. After all, not all families got along perfectly. Maybe Carter thought an outsider would cushion any squabbles.

She didn't answer right away. During her shower, she tried not to think about Carter's offer to *shower* together at his house. She had turned him down. Maybe now she regretted that. Would he have made love to her then? And again in the bed?

Thinking about sex with Carter made her hot and bothered. By the time she dried off and put on a clean T-shirt and sleep pants, she was no closer to knowing what to do.

She liked Carter Crane. A lot. He was funny and smart,

and so sexy she had let him coax her into bed with embarrassing ease.

That was what worried her. If she had so little self-control around the man, wouldn't it be safer to keep her distance? This town wasn't for her. Neither was this lifestyle. She liked being free and able to go wherever the wind took her.

If she embarked on a relationship with one of Royal's premier bachelors, wasn't it possible she could end up getting hurt?

In the end, she chickened out. Her text was a monument to indecision.

Carter—I'm not sure about my schedule tomorrow. I should be able to let you know by noon. Okay???

She hit Send and tucked her phone under a pillow, too anxious to wait for his answer. Although she was finished with work for the evening, she couldn't resist taking another look at the interview with Carter. She uploaded some of the raw footage to her laptop and unmuted the sound.

Like most people, she didn't enjoy hearing her own voice. But Carter's made up for it. The timbre of his speech was intensely masculine. He looked straight at the lens, unflinching. Though he claimed to have no experience being on camera, he came across as natural and appealing. Even someone with no interest in cattle and horses would find his enthusiasm compelling.

It didn't hurt that his rugged good looks played well.

Finally, she shut off the electronics and did a few half-hearted yoga stretches. Her usual routine had been shot to heck. She was supposed to be finding a revelation or two. About Soiree on the Bay. Or ranchers in general. Or the Texas Cattleman's Club way of life.

Instead, Texas was showing her a few truths about herself.

* * *

The next morning, she hopped out of bed, refusing to think about hot, sexy ranchers and wild, incredible sex. She grabbed a croissant and coffee downstairs before bolting to her rental car. Valencia Donovan's property was a few miles outside of town, but Abby wasn't sure how far out.

In the end, she made it with ten minutes to spare. Valencia met her at the gate with a friendly smile. "Hi, Abby," she said. "Billy filled me in about your work. How exciting. I'd love to have my organization featured in your documentary."

Valencia was gorgeous. Her eyes were the same brown as Abby's, but the comparison ended there. She was tall and leggy with a mane of wavy, golden blond hair. Her skinny jeans and multicolored peasant blouse painted a picture of free-spirited warmth.

Abby felt a little dowdy in comparison, which was dumb, because she had been perfectly satisfied with her appearance when she left the hotel. Perhaps something about Valencia was an unpleasant reminder of all the blond and perfect girls who had at times made her life a misery growing up.

In reality, Valencia was nothing but welcoming and complimentary of Abby's chosen profession and everything else. She was patient while Abby filmed various aspects of the horse rescue. After they toured the barn and met a few of the horses, the other woman sighed. "I'm in the mood for some of Amanda Battle's lemon meringue pie. What if we head back to town and finish our conversation at the diner?"

"I'm game," Abby said.

Over lunch, the two of them bonded. Valencia was funny and unpretentious. Abby learned that she had left a successful corporate career to rescue horses.

Abby took a sip of her tea. "From boardroom to horse ranch? What was the appeal?"

"I love horses, always have," Valencia said. "I had saved up enough money to buy the land, and I've begun locating horses in peril. You'd be shocked how many people think they want to own a horse and then find out how much hard work it is."

"But not Royal ranchers."

"Oh, no. The horses I rescue come from all over. I sometimes drive five or six hours to pick up an animal."

"Impressive. I don't mean to be rude, but are there enough people who care about mistreated horses to donate to a charity? Billy Holmes told me that Donovan Horse Rescue is one of the beneficiaries of Soiree on the Bay."

"I'm hoping to make the focus of my work equine therapy, in particular for children. You see, I'm very interested in providing immersive summer camp opportunities, and kids who have experienced tragedy respond well to horses. Particularly when part of their activities include learning how to care for an animal. Feeding, brushing, that sort of thing… I filled out an application and submitted it to the festival board. They must have liked my pitch."

"Do you mind if I ask how much you're going to receive?"

"Not at all." Valencia named a number in the high five figures.

"Wow! You must be very excited."

"I definitely am. I've been working on my business plan. Of course, I won't receive any money until all the ticket sales are in. But in the meantime, I'm getting everything ready on paper, so I don't miss a single moment. I'm thrilled that I was chosen."

"I see why." Abby flashed her a warm smile. "You're passionate about this project, and I'm sure that came across in your proposal. Good for you. I think it's wonderful that the money from the festival will get you started. And to know that children will benefit? You must be very proud."

Back at the hotel, Abby studied the notes she'd made during lunch. She had filmed Valencia speaking in the barn. But the footage of the horse rescue operation would be excellent B-roll. No one wanted to see a documentary that was only talking heads. Abby's narration would flesh out the woman's vision.

At one thirty, she stared at her phone, wishing she could pretend she had never seen last night's communication from Carter. If he'd sent a simple "let's hook up" text, it might have been easier to answer. She could have responded from the standpoint of purely physical gratification, nothing more. But if she went out to Sunset Acres this afternoon, she would have to interact with his family.

It didn't make sense. She knew without a doubt that Carter wasn't making a grand meet-the-parents gesture. Abby had known him less than a week. So why had he invited her at all?

The clock was ticking. To wait any longer would be unforgivably rude.

Gnawing her lip, she tapped out a long-overdue reply.

Is the offer still good? I finished up a couple of things earlier than expected.

One minute passed. Then two. When the phone finally dinged, she exhaled all the breath she had been holding. Carter's reply was not nuanced at all, darn it. No lines to read between.

Sure. Why don't you show up around five? We'll eat at six. Or I can pick you up, if you don't want to drive.

Abby was alarmed to realize how much relief she experienced.

I'll see you then...happy to drive. Can I bring anything?

Carter posted a smiley face.

You're staying in a hotel. I think that gives you a free pass. See you soon...

Abby clicked out of the text screen. Now her next question was very personal. Should she pack a bag? If she *didn't*, she'd be giving her libido a clear signal. That this was dinner. Nothing more.

On the other hand, if Carter was interested in a repeat performance of *Abby and Carter's Greatest Hits*, she would be much more comfortable with her own toiletries and a change of clothes.

Did a grown man invite his lover to spend the night when his parents were in residence? Of course, Carter *had* made a point of mentioning a guesthouse and his privacy.

On the other hand, was Abby really his lover? That sounded like a far more formal relationship than what she had with him.

They had slept together. True. But that was it. Or was it?

She changed her mind about what to wear half a dozen times. It was hot today, scorching really. In this weather, she always preferred a light, loose-fitting dress. Fortunately she had one she hadn't worn yet. The double layer of white gauzy fabric and halter neck meant she wouldn't even have to wear a bra.

That seemed like a prudent choice when the temps were nearing the hundred-degree mark. The dress had its own woven, gold leather belt. She had sandals to match. And a pair of unabashedly over-the-top dangly gold earrings.

Because she was antsy, she got ready far too early. She decided to leave anyway and drive around town before heading out to the ranch. Her camera would be in the trunk, just in case.

Friday night in Royal meant a lot of people in town. Restaurants and bars were hopping, even at this early hour. Teenagers thronged the streets, doing all the silly things adolescents do when it's summertime, and hormones are raging.

Abby had to smile. Some behaviors were universal. She hadn't dated much in high school, but she'd suffered through a couple of unrequited crushes. It had been college before she had really come out of her shell. She'd been shy by nature and inclined to stay out of the spotlight.

That was one reason filmmaking appealed to her. She could control the narrative. No one would be staring at her as long as she stayed behind the camera.

Finally, she turned the car in the direction of Carter's ranch, smiling as she recalled their first encounter. Even now, the memory of him on horseback—silhouetted against the sun—caused her heart to beat faster.

This evening's visit to Sunset Acres made her uneasy, and she wasn't even there yet. Despite their night of unbridled sex, much of her contact with Carter up until now had been couched in terms of her project. Nothing about this latest invitation was business related.

It felt *personal*.

The last time she had seen him, he'd been asleep— his big, tanned body sprawled against white sheets, his hair mussed and his face unshaven. She had tiptoed out at the first hint of dawn, not wanting a confrontation. Cowardly? Sure. But an action and a choice predicated on self-preservation.

This time, she didn't linger anywhere on the property. She drove straight to Carter's house and parked. As she stepped out of the car, a curvy brunette with a baby on her hip came down the steps. "Hey there. You must be Abby. I'm Denise, Carter's younger sister. And this is Beebee."

Abby gazed at the infant with something like awe. Beebee was solid, her legs bracketed in rolls of baby fat. "Hi, Beebee."

The kid babbled a few nonsense syllables, but she didn't smile. Maybe she didn't approve of women who wanted to travel the world instead of getting pregnant.

Denise retrieved a plastic booster seat from her car, the kind that could be strapped to a chair. "Come on in, Abby. I want you to meet my husband and my mother. Dad is out back grilling with Carter."

Abby fell into step. "That must be a macho Texas guy thing. Grilling? I guess it's a requirement?"

Abby held open the door as Denise replied, "Not gonna lie. It's in their DNA. After all, this is beef country. At least Mom and I have convinced them to branch out over the years. There will be steaks, always, but chicken breasts, too, and fresh veggies."

"Sounds delicious." Abby's stomach growled. She'd gone easy at lunch, but now the smells wafting from the grill teased her taste buds.

Mrs. Crane was in the dining room. She was in her midfifties, attractive and fit. Carter's mom seemed pleasant enough, but Abby had the feeling that she was being assessed by her de facto hostess and maybe falling short.

The older woman grilled Abby right away. "So how long has my son known you, Ms. Carmichael?"

"Call me Abby, please. Not long at all. I've come to Royal to do a documentary on the Soiree on the Bay festival."

"Ah. But Carter has no interest in the festival."

"No, ma'am. None. But he's allowing me to film here at the ranch, so that I can showcase Royal and the ranching industry as a backdrop to my story."

"I see."

"Mama." Denise raised an eyebrow. "Behave."

Her mother gave her an innocent look. "I'm just getting to know Abby."

"Right." Denise shook her head, apparently used to her mother's tactics. She handed Beebee to the only other person in the room. "This is my husband, Ernie. Ernie, Abby."

Abby shook the man's free hand. "Nice to meet you. Your daughter is a sweetheart."

Ernie was quiet and seemed not to mind when his little one yanked handfuls of his hair. "She keeps us on our toes," he said ruefully.

Mrs. Crane's given name was Cynthia, as Abby learned when the father-son duo came in bearing a platter of shrimp, the ubiquitous steak and chicken breasts.

When Carter's gaze met hers across the room, the jolt of heat was so profound, she looked around to see if anyone had noticed. Apparently not.

Carter smiled at the room in general, though his introduction was more personal. "Abby, this is my dad, Lamar. I see you've met the rest of the clan."

"I did," she said, taking the seat Denise offered her. Cynthia had set the table earlier while her son-in-law poured drinks. Abby was surprised to see that the menu was free of any alcoholic beverages. Only tea and iced coffee and lemonade were offered.

Denise whispered an explanation. "Daddy's a teetotaler now. Doctor's orders. He's supposed to be avoiding red meat, too, but that won't happen tonight."

There were no formalities observed, though everyone was dressed nicely, and nary a paper plate in sight.

Cynthia had used china and crystal and a heavy, ornate silver service adorned with the letter *C*.

Abby wondered if the Cranes always dined so elegantly or if this show was for her benefit. No one seemed to think it odd that she was in attendance. But the longer the dinner lasted, the more she wondered why she had been included.

Conversation flowed freely. Abby was questioned at length about her job and her background and whether or not she watched college sports.

Cynthia pressed delicately at times, but finally with a vein of determination. "Tell us about your family, dear."

All eyes shifted to Abby. She set down her glass of iced tea and managed a smile, even though she might as well have been on the witness stand. "I'm an only child," she said. "My parents have been divorced for a very long time, though they are on good terms. Daddy is a filmmaker out in California. My mother works at Sotheby's in New York. Her specialty is appraising twentieth-century paintings."

"Impressive." Cynthia's gaze was assessing, as though trying to read between the lines. "And is this your first trip to Texas?"

"Yes, ma'am." Abby fell into old habits. Carter's mother was a force to be reckoned with, even though his father was a big ole teddy bear.

Denise chimed in. "And what do you think of Maverick County?"

A hushed silence fell over the room. Abby frowned inwardly. This was weird. "Um, it's very different from what I'm used to. But it has a beauty all its own, I suppose."

Ernie laughed, his kind eyes dancing. "Good for you, Abby. Stand up for yourself. This family is a bit much. Diplomacy is a required skill."

There was a momentary lull in the conversation. Denise and Cynthia left the table to serve dessert. Carter's sister had made two apple pies. Apparently, both Crane women were homemakers extraordinaire.

The remainder of the meal passed without incident.

Abby noticed that Carter didn't have a whole lot to say in the midst of his boisterous family. Of course, the baby kept things lively, but even so, Carter's quiet presence was notable. He smiled a lot. And he answered when spoken to. Still, he seemed more watchful than anything else.

At last, Beebee fell asleep on her father's shoulder. Denise smiled. "We should head for the guesthouse soon. Mom, Dad…you stay as long as you want."

Cynthia gave her son a pointed look. "May I speak with you in the kitchen, Carter?"

Abby breathed a sigh of relief. The other members of his family were far less frightening.

But Denise unwittingly put a confrontation in motion. She scooped up Beebee and glanced at Abby. "Would you mind helping me change her into pajamas? Daddy and Ernie are dying to have another slice of pie without Mom noticing."

"Of course." Abby stood and followed the other woman down the hallway. They were heading away from the kitchen. But apparently, Carter and his mother had chosen to go to the sunroom instead.

Suddenly, Denise held up her hand and backed up. But it was too late. The conversation was impossible to ignore.

Cynthia's voice carried. "Why did you invite that girl tonight, Carter? What are you up to? Is this another doomed romantic alliance?"

Carter's tone was perfectly calm. "Abby is not a prospective fiancée. We're friends. I thought she might enjoy meeting my family. That's all."

"Bull testicles," his mother snapped. "You're playing games. But I must say that this one is better than your wretched *Madeline*."

Carter's reply was less conciliatory now. "At least you're being honest. It might have been nice if *one* of you told me you didn't like Madeline. I didn't find out until it was all over that my nearest and dearest had reservations about her."

"We didn't want to meddle."

"Since when?"

Abby's whole body was one big blush. She touched Denise on the arm. "I'm going to step outside for a few minutes. Please make my excuses."

Before Carter's sister could reply, Abby darted back the way she had come. She dodged the dining room and sneaked out onto the veranda and down to the driveway. In the dark, she put her hands to her hot cheeks. What had Carter been thinking? She was humiliated and confused.

After fifteen minutes, she knew she couldn't stay outside any longer without causing comment. She grabbed a thin sweater from the front seat of her car as an excuse and started to walk back inside.

As she hit the top step and took a breath for courage, the door opened suddenly. A familiar voice spoke out of the darkness.

"There you are," Carter said. "I was starting to worry about you."

Ten

Carter was pissed and frustrated. He loved his parents, but his mother could be a handful. Thankfully, Denise had whispered a heads-up to him, warning that she and Abby had unwittingly overheard the conversation between mother and son.

He turned on the porch light and saw Abby freeze when she realized it was him. "I just came to get my sweater out of the car," she said.

"No. You overheard my conversation with my mother, and you were embarrassed. I'm sorry, Abby."

He couldn't read her expression, but her body language spoke volumes. Her arms were wrapped tightly around her waist, and she had backed up as far as humanly possible without falling off the porch.

She placed her sweater with exaggerated care on the railing. "Why did you invite me to come here tonight, Carter?" she asked.

The slight tremor in her voice made him feel like scum.

"Two reasons. First of all, I wanted to see you."

"And the second?"

"I haven't socialized much since Madeline called off the wedding," he admitted. "My mother is constantly on my case to *get back out there*. So I thought if she met you, I'd get credit for dating but she wouldn't pressure me, because she wouldn't approve of our relationship."

Abby's shock was visible. "Why not? I'm delightful."

He chuckled, charmed by her candor. "I won't argue with that. You definitely are. My mother, though, doesn't see you as ranch wife material. Sunset Acres means everything to my parents, even though they've handed it over to me. They know the kinds of sacrifices that are required, because they've made those very same sacrifices."

After a few beats of silence, Abby took a step toward him and exhaled audibly. "Not that I have any interest in marrying you or having your babies, Carter Crane, but why am I not ranch wife material?"

He stepped closer, as well, reaching out to brush his thumb over her cheek. "You don't even *like* Texas, Abs. There's nothing wrong with that, but it means my mother won't start making wedding plans. That's a good thing."

"Ah."

"I didn't think she would react so strongly tonight." He grimaced. "Usually there's a honeymoon period before she starts vetting my female companions."

"Aren't you kind of old to have your mommy picking out your lovers?"

He pressed the heel of his hand to his forehead where a headache hammered. "You would think so, yes."

Abby cocked her head and gave him a steady stare that made him want to fidget. "I'm sure we should get back inside," she said. "I don't want to be rude."

"Why not? My family certainly hasn't been kind to *you* this evening."

"That's not entirely true. Denise and Ernie and the baby were pleasant. Your dad's a peach. And to be honest, your mother wasn't technically rude to me. In fact, you're the one who set this train wreck in motion."

He curled a strand of her hair around his finger. "I'll make it up to you, Abs, I swear. You look beautiful tonight by the way." His throat tightened as his body hardened. Her scent, something light and floral, teased his nostrils. "Are you wearing anything under that spectacular dress? I've been wondering all evening."

When she rested her cheek against his chest, his heart bumped against his rib cage. "That's on a need-to-know basis."

He held Abby close, linking both arms around her bare back, resting his chin on top of her head, feeling her slender body and feminine curves nestled against his flatter, harder frame. "I need to know," he said huskily. "Really, I do."

"Feel free to explore," she whispered.

It was a dangerous game they played. But he was counting on his family's guilt to give him a few moments of privacy.

Slowly, he gathered Abby's skirt in two hands, pulling it upward until his fingers brushed her bare ass. Well, not entirely bare. She wore a tiny, lacy pair of panties that barely merited a mention.

His mouth went dry. He stroked her butt cheeks, feeling the smooth skin and taut flesh. As caresses went, it was mostly innocent. He didn't trespass anywhere he shouldn't. "That answers half the question," he groaned, wondering why the hell he had started this adventure with his whole damn family close at hand.

Abby slid her arms around his neck and looked up at him with a tiny smile on her face, one that mocked his handling of the evening. "You could kiss me," she said.

The last time they were together, he had been driven by

hunger and adrenaline. Tonight, he was no less hungry, but he had more control. He kissed her deeply, holding her chin with two fingers and tracing the seam of her lips with his tongue, giving her passion wrapped in tenderness.

The kiss could have stayed that way, but Abby groaned and went up on her tiptoes to take what she wanted, reminding him that she was no shrinking violet waiting for him to direct her. She was passionate and needy and generous with her kisses.

His head swam. Though the hour was late, the humid air made his body damp and hot. He wanted to strip her naked and swim with her nude.

That image broke the last ounce of control he had over his baser impulses. "God, Abby." He dragged her closer still and ravaged her mouth. Sliding one hand beneath the top of her dress, he found a bare breast. The soft skin and pert tip were a fascinating contrast.

He was rapidly reaching a point of no return. With a muttered curse, he released her and stepped back. "Did I ruin your lipstick?"

"I'm not wearing any." She reached in her pocket and pulled out a clear lip gloss, using it to soothe lips that were puffy from his kisses.

Carter winnowed his fingers through her hair, tidying away the look of passion. "We have to go back in. They won't leave until we do."

"Okay."

He couldn't blame her for the lack of enthusiasm. "I'm sorry I made you uncomfortable tonight. It won't happen again, I swear."

She wrinkled her nose. "Don't make promises you can't keep."

As he started to open the door, she tugged on his arm. "One more thing. I haven't talked to you since I interviewed Billy Holmes."

His hackles went up. "What did he do?" Something in her voice made him wonder if there had been an incident.

"Not a thing. He was a perfect gentleman. But at the end of our meeting, I told him the rumor I had overheard… about the missing money."

"Oh, geez, Abby. I told you not to poke around in that. Was he angry?"

"Actually, he said it was true."

The smug look on her face didn't even bother Carter. He was too stunned. "You can't be serious."

"The camera was off. He lowered his voice and said it was a family matter, and that it was being handled."

Carter shook his head slowly. "I have a bad feeling about this. Who on the committee is handling the actual money part of the festival?"

"Asher, I think. But he's rich. Why would he need to skim funds?"

"I don't like you messing around in this, Abby. People get squirrelly when money is involved. You could be getting yourself into a dangerous situation."

"Or," she said, excitement lighting her face, "I could have found the focus for my documentary. An exposé. It doesn't get better than that!"

He ground his jaw. "Promise me you will let this go." He didn't want to quarrel with her, but he was certain his fears were well-founded.

Abby frowned at him. "Why are you so angry?"

"I'm not angry," he bit out. "I'm aggravated." And it was true. His feelings about Abby and his family and the festival coalesced into a fiery ball of sexual frustration that churned in his gut.

Carter yanked her close, lifting her off her feet and kissing her again. He held her tightly, relieved when she wrapped her legs around his thighs. "You drive me nuts, Abby." Didn't she know how vulnerable she was?

He wanted her in his bed. Now. Naked and needy. He wanted that more than anything in the whole world.

Abby patted his cheek and kissed his forehead. "We have to go inside. Remember? Your family?"

"Hell." She was right. "Tell me you brought an overnight bag."

"That wasn't part of the invitation."

"Abby…" He was at the end of whatever stores of patience he had accumulated.

She slid down his body and stepped away, gathering her sweater and smoothing her hair again. "I did," she said quietly. "But I'm not sure why."

"Don't lie to me, Abs. Or to yourself. We may not be a match made in heaven, but between the sheets we're dynamite."

He took her by the hand and dragged her inside. They found his family gathered in the room where Abby had interviewed Carter earlier that week.

The four adults were seated around a card table playing a game. Denise and Ernie had apparently decided to linger, given the drama that had transpired. The baby snoozed on a pallet on the floor.

Denise was the first to notice them. "There you are," she said, smiling. "Would you like us to deal you in?"

Carter managed not to cringe, though he could think of nothing more dreadful. "No, thanks," he said, his tone mild. "You guys finish your game. Abby and I will hang out. Or maybe have more dessert."

Cynthia Crane stood and approached them with a contrite expression on her face. "I'm sorry you overheard our conversation, dear."

Abby didn't smile. "But you're not sorry you questioned my presence here tonight."

Wow. Carter wanted to high-five somebody. Abby Carmichael had just put his mother in her place.

The older woman narrowed her eyes. "I love my son. It's normal for a mother to want the best for her children. That said, Carter is free to invite whomever he likes to his home. I'm glad I met you, Abby. You are a very interesting woman."

There was a collective exhale in the room when Cynthia returned to the game and left Carter and Abby to entertain themselves.

Half an hour later, the house was finally quiet. Carter shot Abby a wry glance. "Now you see why we built the guest cottage."

"I do," Abby said. But her laugh sounded forced.

"You okay?" He lifted her chin with a finger, looking deep into those dark brown eyes surrounded by thick inky lashes.

Abby stepped away, breaking the small contact. "I'm fine, Carter. Really. But I think I'll head back to town. Your family wants to spend time with you. It feels weird to be sneaking around."

"We're not *sneaking*," he protested. "We're two grown adults. I want you to stay the night." Her reluctance dented his mood.

She flipped her hair over her shoulder, unwittingly drawing his attention to the spot where her throat met her collarbone, a spot he would like to nibble. Soon.

"They'll be coming over for breakfast, right?"

"Not if I tell Denise to keep them away."

"Oh, Carter. This is complicated. I don't want to get in the way of you enjoying your family. You told me they don't visit all that often."

He shoved his hands in his pockets and leaned against the door frame. "If you don't want to stay, just say so."

"I *do* want to stay." She played with her earring, pacing the confines of his living room. "But I don't want *them* to know I stayed."

"Well, that's easy. I'll set an alarm for seven. You can be on your way, and I'll pretend I slept alone. Although it's really nobody's damn business."

Humor lit her face. "As weird as this evening was, I do like your family."

He ducked and looked over his shoulder.

She frowned. "What are you doing?"

"Waiting for the lightning to strike. That's usually what I do when somebody tells a whopper. You can't honestly say you *like* my mother."

She scrunched up her face. "Maybe *like* is the wrong word. But she brought you into this world, so she can't be all bad."

His shoulders loosened, and he crossed the room to take her hands in his. "I've been wanting to get you out of this dress for hours. Swim first? Or straight to the main event?"

Abby realized that the window for changing her mind was over. Actually, as soon as she admitted she had an overnight case in her car, the course of the evening was set. Carter wanted her here, and she wanted to be here. In the end, nothing else mattered.

She snuggled up to his chest, sliding her arms around his waist. "We can swim later. Isn't there a full moon tonight? For now, I'm more than happy to see your bedroom again."

Abby realized a couple of things in the next hour. First, Carter was far less serious than the face he showed to the world. Beneath that mantle of responsibility was a man who liked to play.

And second, he knew way too much about how to pleasure a woman. The man made an art form out of removing her dress. He did it so slowly and with so much sensual heat, she was ready to dissolve into a puddle of lust by the time he had stripped her down to her panties.

They took a quick shower together, one that involved

lots of soap and teasing. Then they dried off and returned to the bedroom.

Abby was less self-conscious now, more willing to let her gaze linger on Carter's aroused sex. He was a stud. No question. A very masculine man with the body of someone who did physical labor. If she were a sculptor, she would carve him, every sinew and muscle.

He scooped her up in his arms and nuzzled his nose against hers. "You cold?"

Her heart beat faster. "Not at all. Make love to me, Carter."

His face flushed with heat. "Whatever the lady wants."

For a split second, she wished she had used a different phrase. There was no love between them. How *could* there be? She didn't believe in love at first sight, and besides, these feelings she had were physical, not emotional. Carter made her body sing.

He didn't give her time for second-guessing. Soon, he worshipped her, kissing from earlobes and eyelids to the throbbing spot at her center, making her squirm. She was close to coming already. She'd been aching for him since that moment when she had slipped out of this bed like a thief in the night.

"Now..." she begged.

He left her for mere seconds to take care of protection and came back to shift her thighs apart and thrust deep. The noise he made was half groan, half curse.

She understood what he didn't say. This was beyond words. He filled her completely, his hard sex claiming everything she offered willingly. Their joining was something more than the two of them slaking a sexual thirst. Rather, it was the kind of chemical reaction that fizzed and sparked and boiled over.

Because it was hot and urgent and not to be denied, Abby

was swept up in a wave of sheer bliss. How insanely wonderful could a moment be? How *perfect*...

Carter surrounded her, aroused her and, paradoxically, protected her.

When her orgasm yanked her up and threw her into the abyss, she felt limp with joy, sated with pleasure.

In the aftermath, he pulled her against his side. She stretched one leg across his thighs and pillowed her cheek on his chest.

Abby wasn't asleep, and she wasn't 100 percent awake. She floated, wallowing in the seductive feeling of invincibility.

Carter played with her hair, his breath warm on the top of her head. "I can't feel my legs," he complained.

She pinched his upper thigh, hard enough to bruise. "I can."

"Brat."

"Bossy, arrogant rancher."

His raspy chuckle made her feel happy and warm. In Carter's embrace, she felt like herself. With the few other men she had let into her life on a sexual basis, she had always held something back, wary of being judged.

In this bed, with this man, her world was complete.

And that was scary as hell.

Finally, she lifted up on one elbow and smiled at him. "I'm not sleepy. Can we take a glass of wine out by the pool and enjoy the moonlight?"

His gaze was hooded, his hair mussed. "Of course, beautiful. But don't get dressed. We might take a dip. There's no one around to peek."

He gave her a robe out of his closet, a hotel-style garment that was soft and plush and smelled faintly of Carter's aftershave. For himself, he grabbed a towel and tucked it around his waist.

In the kitchen, he didn't bother with the overhead light

as he gathered glasses and a corkscrew. Abby was glad. These minutes felt precious and private. She wanted to pre-serve this bubble of intimacy, to savor every moment of it.

Outside, the moon shone down serenely, illuminating the pool and chasing away shadows. They settled onto cush-ioned lounge chairs. Carter opened the wine and poured. When he clinked his glass against hers, he smiled. "To new friends. And beautiful cinematographers. I'm glad you stayed."

Abby wanted to say something nice in return, but her throat was tight, and her thoughts were all jumbled. Instead, she sipped her wine and wiggled her toes, feeling the peace of the summer night wash over her.

Beside her, Carter resembled a large, lazy jungle cat. His body was completely relaxed. So much so that it took her by surprise when he spoke.

"I want to see you again, Abby."

He laid it out there. No games.

"Your family is here all week, right?"

"Yes," he said. "But they don't bite."

"I'm not your girlfriend, Carter. It would be different if I were. You need to spend quality time with them. Be-sides, I have several more interviews lined up this week. I'll be busy."

Turning toward her, he pinned her with his blue gaze. "The weekend, then?"

"I'm flying out to LA on Friday. My father is going to help me begin to piece together my story. He's great at ed-iting."

"When will you be back?" he asked.

"Midweek probably," she replied. "I'm bringing some camping gear then. Since there isn't any public lodging on Appaloosa Island, I have to find a way to spend the night and get those magical early morning shots. Camping is the best solution. If I can get permission."

"And after that?"

"I'll probably go home to New York, regroup and come back to Royal right before the festival starts."

"I see." He paused. "It sounds like you consider New York home, and not California. Is that true?"

"Yes. My mother wanted my school years to be uninterrupted. But summers and holidays were a roll of the dice." Abby raised the wineglass to her lips and took a sip. "Neither she nor my father meant to make me feel bad, but there was always an unspoken tug-of-war. I think that's when travel started to appeal to me. I could go where I wanted, when I wanted, without having to answer to anyone."

"Makes sense."

"I haven't told you much about my parents," she said quietly. "They still care about each other, even after all these years apart."

"Why did they split in the first place?" he asked curiously.

"Because their lives were too different. Once they got past the wild rush of falling in love and having me, the reality of day-to-day life didn't work." She shrugged. "My mom couldn't conceive of leaving New York. But my dad dreamed of becoming a filmmaker and needed the flexibility to go where the opportunities arose. Having a wife and a little baby held him back. Ultimately, my mother set him free to be who he was meant to be. And she found happiness and fulfillment on her own."

"Is this the part where I'm supposed to see the parallels? If so, I'm not convinced." A muscle ticked in his jaw. "I don't give a damn about the future right now. But I want to be with you, Abby."

The lump in her throat grew painfully. "I want to be with you, too."

A light breeze danced around them, ruffling the water,

diluting the moon's reflection. The wine bottle was empty now. Abby felt mellow, but melancholy.

When Carter said nothing for long minutes, she blurted out the truth that had struck her tonight. "I envy you, you know."

He set his glass on the table. "How so?"

"Your family. I love my mom and dad, and they love me, but I've never had the kind of family unit the Cranes have. Even your brother-in-law is an integral part of that tight circle. I can tell that each of you would do anything for the others."

"Like taking over a huge ranch far too young?" Carter sighed. "I'm handling things now, though the first few years were tough. I grew up here, but suddenly sitting in the owner's seat was terrifying."

"Your father is proud of you."

"I hope so."

Abby was drenched in sadness suddenly. To come close to something so perfect and yet know it was out of reach shredded her emotions.

"I think I'll swim now," she said.

Eleven

Carter stayed where he was, his hands fisted on his thighs. Watching Abby shed his robe and dive gracefully into the water was an experience he couldn't describe. Her beauty in the moonlight made his heart ache.

When she surfaced, laughing, he felt something crack inside his chest, some wall of self-protection that had begun to crumble without his knowledge. Since Madeline's defection, he had put his emotions on hold, denying his needs, focusing on the ranch.

Tonight, beneath a full moon, sated sexually and slightly drunk on a bottle of very good wine, he felt reborn. Yet, at the same time, he knew nothing for certain.

Was he feeling lust and gratitude, or something more?

Abby swam and played like a creature familiar with the sea. He supposed she really was. With one home base in Malibu, she must have spent long hours on the beach, or frolicking in the Pacific.

Carter was jealous suddenly of every teenage boy and

young man who had lain at her side, flirted with her, wallowed on a sandy blanket and kissed those perfect lips.

His breath sawed in and out of his lungs as if he was running full tilt. His heart pounded. He didn't know what to do. That very uncertainty was so novel, he was stunned.

At thirty-four, the world was his oyster. He had money and power and unlimited opportunity.

What he didn't have was a mate, a lover, a life partner.

With Madeline, he had seen her as he wanted her to be. His blindness had cost him greatly in terms of his pride and his confidence. Thankfully, he had ultimately realized that while she had treated him shabbily, she hadn't broken his heart.

He didn't want to make another impulsive mistake. Especially with so little time. He and Abby weren't ships passing in the night. They were high-speed trains on opposite tracks. This moment with her was nothing more than a blip.

She came to the side of the pool and waved at him. "Come join me."

He noticed that she was careful not to expose her naked breasts. The show of modesty amused him. "How's the water?"

"Somewhere between chilly and almost perfect."

"You'd better not be kidding." He dropped his towel and walked down the steps into the shallow end.

Abby stayed near the rope that marked deeper water. "It's your pool. You should know by now. Or do you never go skinny-dipping when you're alone?"

He strode through the water, stalking her, grinning when she ran out of her depth. "Stay put, little mermaid. Don't be scared."

She lifted her chin. "I'm not scared of you. But I'm not accustomed to being stark naked in public."

He glanced around the pool. "It's just us, Abs."

Finally, he was within touching distance—close enough

to see the droplets of water beading on her arms, each one reflecting a tiny moon. Her dark hair floated around her, partially obscuring her bare breasts.

Was that intentional?

"Do you know how beautiful you are?" he whispered hoarsely.

She didn't respond. But a blink of her eyes could have meant anything.

He shook his head slowly. "I know you're smart and competent and career focused, and all those things strong women aspire to be. But damn, Abby, you're also incredibly lovely. The kind of lovely that makes a man wish he could paint you exactly the way you look right now."

"You're embarrassing me," she whispered.

"Oh? Does that mean you want me to stop talking?"

She nodded slowly. Even with the moon, he couldn't read the secrets hidden in her dark eyes. Carefully, he took a piece of her hair and tugged. She came to him willingly, her smile striking him dead in the chest, stealing his breath.

When their bodies met, they groaned in unison. Naked flesh to naked flesh. The water made them buoyant. He coaxed her legs around his waist.

"I like your…pool," she said, with a naughty grin.

He fondled her butt, feeling his sex flex and stir. "I like the way you're all wet and slick. Like a sea otter."

Her head fell back, and she laughed so hard one breast popped up above the water. "That's awful, Carter. No wonder you don't have a girlfriend."

He took them a few steps closer to the side of the pool. Then he kissed her long and slow. "If you're auditioning for the part, it's going really well," he muttered.

She clung to his shoulders as her smile dimmed. "I'm not an actress," she said. "What you see is what you get. Just a girl who's a friend."

The moon dipped behind a cloud, plunging them into darkness. "I want you again, Abby. Now."

"We can't, Carter. It's too dangerous."

Beneath the water he stroked her sex, entering her with two fingers. "Did I ever tell you I was a Boy Scout years ago? Always prepared?"

He leaned toward the side of the pool briefly and reached for the robe she had discarded, finding what he wanted.

Abby stared at him, mouth agape. "You hid a condom in my pocket? That's sneaky, Mr. Crane."

"Sneaky? Or very, very smart?"

He set her on her feet and tugged her by the hand. "Come toward the steps for a minute."

When he ripped open the packet and dealt with the latex, Abby watched. He liked that. A *lot*. Men had a tendency to show off for the opposite sex. He was no different.

He took her hand. "I'm ready. Are you?"

She ran her hand down his chest, stopping to toy with his navel. "I was born ready, cowboy."

They moved into deeper water. Carter scooped his hands under her hair and cupped her neck. "I'm glad you stopped to film the sunset that first night. Otherwise, we might never have met."

Now that she couldn't touch bottom, she clung to his shoulders. "I'll tell you a secret. The sunset was gorgeous, but I was filming *you*. Riding flat out. Horse and man moving as one. It was poetry in motion. I liked what I saw."

He kissed her slowly, intimately. "And now?"

"I'm super glad you dumped that skank Madeline."

This time he was the one to laugh uproariously. "Hell, Abby. If I'd been *married* to her, I'd probably have dumped her for you."

Abby smiled softly, running her thumb over his lower lip. "No," she said. "If you'd been married, you never would have looked at another female. I've learned a lot about you since I've come to Royal. You're a man of honor. A gentleman. The kind of guy all women want. But when they don't find him, they settle for less."

"You're buttering me up, Abs. I'm as flawed as anyone. For instance, right now I'd like to beg you to forget about your documentary and stay with me for a while."

She rested her head on his shoulder, her legs tangling with his. "It sounds like fun. But I know you're not serious, not really. We both see the bigger picture. Sometimes doing the sensible, mature thing sucks."

"Yeah," he said gruffly. "It does." He was done with talking. Nothing Abby had to say made him feel any better about their situation. His erection hadn't flagged, not even in the midst of a semiserious moment. In fact, holding her like this was pure torture. The moonlight. The silky water. The way Abby's body felt against his... His sex throbbed with urgency, even as his brain tried to draw out the pleasure.

Abby kissed his chin. "Take me, Carter. I want you so much I'm shaking."

It was true. He could feel the tremors in her body, could hear her fractured breathing. "Hang on, sweetheart."

He lifted her, aided by the water, and positioned her to slide down onto his swollen sex. The muscles in his arms quivered as he supported her weight. When they were joined, male to female, yin to yang, he cursed. "Damn, woman. You're killing me."

His knees were embarrassingly weak. Abby's body accepted his as if they had been designed for this exact joining. Her sex took him in and wrapped him tightly in blissful heat. The sensation was one he couldn't have imagined.

"I've never done this in the water," he said, the words breathless.

Abby pulled back so she could see his face. "Really?"

"Really."

He wasn't sure she believed him, but he was beyond talking. He'd gone into this without overthinking the logistics. Now his body was driving him to seal the deal. "Abs?"

"Hmm?" She pressed kisses along his jawline.

"I need the wall."

Her lips curved. "I can handle that."

He lurched toward the metal stairs and gently pressed Abby to the right of them against the slightly rough surface of pool. The water was up to her chin. "Does this hurt?" He thrust into her while he asked the question, obviously not under control.

"I'm good," she said.

It was weird, weirder than he had anticipated. The water made his movements clumsy. Carter drove into her once, shifted, and then went deep again. He was close to coming, but what about the mermaid in his arms?

She had one hand wrapped around the metal steps. Her breasts pillowed against his chest. Leaning back, he reached between their bodies and found her most sensitive spot. As he thumbed it, Abby climaxed, a little cry echoing on the breeze.

Her inner contractions were all it took to set him off. He moaned and came hard. The pleasure was mind-blowing, yet at the same time, he found himself mentally cursing the way the water made it difficult to move like he wanted to…

Abby was limp in his embrace. He peeled her fingers from the step railing and put her hands behind his neck. "It looks more romantic in the movies, doesn't it?"

She rested her cheek against him. "I've got no complaints. Except that my fingers are getting pruney."

"Well, we can't have that."

With no small amount of regret, he separated their bodies. "Time to get out."

Abby refused to go first, so he dragged himself up the steps, dealt with the condom and reached down to take her hand. "Up you come."

It felt strange to be on firm ground. The night air seemed colder suddenly. Abby's arms were covered in gooseflesh. He fetched her a towel and grabbed the one on the lounger for himself.

She didn't say anything. Neither did he.

They walked back inside the house and down the hall to his room. "Do you want to shower again?" he asked, trying to be the gentleman she proclaimed him to be.

Abby yawned. "Nope. I just want to sleep."

They tumbled beneath the covers. He twined his arms and legs with hers and turned out the light.

His lover was asleep in seconds, her damp hair spread across his pillow.

Carter was not so lucky. He lay awake, staring into the darkness. An odd memory floated across his brain. Something from when he was six or seven years old. He'd heard a tale about a pearl that was so valuable, a man sold everything he had to purchase it.

At the time, he'd thought it was a stupid story. His Sunday school teacher had been a stern, no-nonsense woman who—as Carter remembered it—had little patience for wiggly boys who only wanted to be let loose outside.

He turned his head and watched Abby sleep. Unable to resist, he kissed her forehead and gently stroked her hair. Even if the merchant's actions made more sense now, Carter couldn't follow suit. The ranch belonged to him on paper, but its legacy was a joint venture, a family bond.

Even worse, he couldn't repeat the mistakes he made with Madeline. He'd met her at that damned wedding and proposed to her far too soon, without even knowing her. His impulsive behavior had doomed the relationship from the start.

But Abby was different, wasn't she? There was no artifice in her, no selfishness. And Carter was older and wiser.

The more he thought about his situation, the more trapped he felt. In that moment, he felt the sting of loss.

Abby was right there beside him, but he knew their time was short.

Sometimes life was a bitch.

Abby didn't leave a note this time. They had come too far for that. She'd set her alarm for six thirty. When it buzzed, she silenced it quickly. Carter never moved.

After she showered and dressed, she sat down on the bed at his hip. "Carter," she whispered.

He grunted and rolled onto his back, scrubbing his hands over his face. "What time is it?"

"Barely seven. I wanted to say goodbye before I left."

He sat up and frowned. "What's the rush?"

"We talked about this," she said quietly. "Your family will be over for breakfast soon. I'm heading back to the hotel."

"And did we agree on anything for when you return?"

Her smile cost her. Leaving Carter like this was a physical pain in her chest. If she'd had her wish, she would have lingered to play all day. "I'll let you know when I get back from New York." She leaned down to kiss him. The cheek seemed too casual for what they had shared. But the mouth was dangerous.

She chose the mouth anyway, her lips melding with his. Carter was warm. His big arms wrapped around her and held her close.

He nuzzled her forehead with his. "You sure you don't want to stay a few more minutes?"

"No. It wouldn't be a few minutes, and you know it. Tell your family I enjoyed meeting them. Bye, Carter."

She fled the house, perilously close to letting him sweet-talk her into staying. But she knew what was right. Family was important.

* * *

Every moment of the week that followed, she worked herself hard, researching, filming, interviewing. She had thought that she and Carter might text back and forth casually. But neither of them initiated a virtual conversation. After all, what was there to say?

She missed him terribly.

Though her personal life was a mess, her professional life flourished. Most notably, Lila arranged for Abby to have access to the Texas Cattleman's Club to shoot interior montages after hours. With patrons on-site, the permissions involved would have been too complicated.

Abby began working on a voice-over script that would narrate this particular section, touching on the history, but also pointing out how the club was central to life in Royal even in the twenty-first century.

Carter was a member. No surprise there.

When Abby had first sat in on the meeting of the advisory board, she had seen part of the club, of course. Now, with no one in residence but the night watchman, she was free to roam the halls and peek into the various rooms.

She was surprised to see a state-of-the-art day care on the premises. The center was a bright, cheerful place with murals on the walls and everything a young child could possibly want.

Lila had given her a roster of current members and oddly, Billy Holmes was included. He'd only lived in Royal a few years, and he didn't own a ranch. But other people of influence in the community were recognized for their accomplishments, so maybe Billy had been inducted based on merits Abby wasn't privy to during her short visit with him.

The night watchman himself had related how an F4 tornado a few years before had destroyed part of the town and even damaged this fine old building. The community had pulled together to rebuild Royal stronger and better than before.

At last, Abby had all the footage she needed, in truth, far more than she would ever be able to use. But she was fascinated by what seemed like a vestige of the Old West. Money talked. Here in Royal, it talked louder in this building than almost anywhere else.

When she packed up her gear and wandered back to the front lobby, she found the night watchman talking to someone familiar. Carter.

Her pulse jumped. She approached the two men calmly. "What brings you here, Carter? I thought I was the only after-hours visitor."

They made their goodbyes to the guard and stepped outside. Carter took two of her bags and carried them to the car. "I wanted to see you before you left," he said.

"Oh." She didn't know how to respond to that. "Is your family still in town?"

"They're leaving in the morning, too. Maybe you'll see them at the airport."

I hope not, she thought wryly. "Did you have a good visit?"

"Actually, yes. It was great. My brother-in-law helped me around the ranch. Dad's health is doing well, so he joined us occasionally. It was especially fun to spend time with the baby. She's changing every day."

"And your mom and sister?"

"My mother was extremely well-behaved. I think she feels guilty about what happened with you. My sister, on the other hand, told me not to let you get away."

Abby winced. "But you told her we weren't a thing?"

He shoved his hands in his pockets and leaned against the car. "I did."

"Good."

Her stomach curled with regret. She had always hated

goodbyes. "I should go," she said softly. "Thanks for stopping by."

"I was hoping you might invite me up to your room."

And there it was again. The insidious temptation that made a mockery of all her grown-up plans.

What could it hurt, the devil on her shoulder whispered. *He'll break your heart*, said her conscience.

Five seconds passed. Then ten. "I have a very early flight, Carter. And I haven't finished packing. I'm sorry."

He didn't react visibly to her polite refusal, but he straightened and took her hand, reeling her in with ease, since she had no intention of protesting.

His mouth settled on hers, his lips firm and masculine. She breathed in his scent, trying to memorize it. He tasted of cinnamon and coffee.

"Don't forget about me, Abs, while you're gone," he muttered. "I'll miss you."

Her eyes stung with tears. "I'll miss you, too."

He kissed her again. This one almost took her down. It wasn't him she was resisting; it was her own yearning. At last, he let her go. "Keep in touch, Abby. I want to know how you're doing."

"I will," she promised.

He opened her car doors, put her gear in the back seat and then leaned down to watch her fasten her seat belt as he closed her in. "Do you need a ride to the airport?"

"No, thanks. I'll be turning in the rental car."

"Ah, yes."

Her window was lowered, letting out the heat that accumulated even at this hour. He had a hand on the sill. She put her fingers over his. "Bye, Carter. Thanks for everything."

Then she put the car in gear and drove away, looking in the rearview mirror only once to see him standing tall and alone in the club parking lot.

Twelve

Abby's father met her at the airport. He was a tall, barrel-chested Black man with kind eyes and a gentle sense of humor. Though they had lived on opposite coasts for most of her life, she had always known that he would drop everything and come to her if she ever needed him.

Her dad negotiated the horrible traffic without flinching. He truly was a Californian after all these years. They stopped at Abby's favorite seafood restaurant before heading on to the house. Over lunch, she brought up a subject that had been occupying her mind recently.

"Daddy, when you and Mom first separated, did you know you were doing the right thing?"

He seemed surprised, but he answered readily enough. "Yes. We both did. The hard part was how much I adored you. We wanted to stay together for your sake, but we knew it couldn't work. Sometimes people come into our lives for a season, Abby. Your mother and I were very happy for a time, but life shifted us onto different paths."

"I understand." She didn't. Not really. It was hard for her to imagine loving someone and then *not* loving them.

That was the last of the personal conversation, even during the drive to the coast. She sensed the introspection made him uncomfortable. After she was settled into her old bedroom, they met out on the back veranda overlooking the Pacific. Her father had done very well in his career. His neighbors up and down this stretch of Malibu were actors and producers and other luminaries.

Though the land had increased in value over the years, her father's house was relatively modest. He had no interest in redecorating or following fashion trends. Right now, Abby was grateful. It was comforting to know that some things stayed the same.

They watched the sun go down.

She worked up her courage and took the plunge. "Daddy?"

"Hmm?"

"What would you think if Mom and I came out for Labor Day and stayed with you? Just the three of us."

He'd been watching the water; now he turned to face her. "I have no problem with that, baby girl. I've always told you that your mother is welcome here. Is something going on with you?"

"No. Not really. I just thought it would be nice for the three of us to get together. Now that I'm an adult, too."

"It will depend on your mother," he said with a wistful smile. "You know how stubborn she is. I'm sure she'd rather do a get-together like that on her turf."

"True. Well, I'll ask her, and let you know."

Afterward, her father excused himself to go make a work-related phone call. His state-of-the-art studio was upstairs. For the next couple of days, she knew that the two of them would bond over her fledgling movie.

For now, she lingered to enjoy the stars and the sultry ocean breeze.

What was Carter doing tonight? She regretted not letting him stay with her the evening before, but it would only have made things harder. He was wrapping himself around her heartstrings without even trying.

Her father rarely asked about her personal life. Maybe because he didn't want any questions in return. They loved each other, but certain lines were never crossed.

In many ways, her relationship with her mother was the same. Abby loved her parents and had always known that she was loved unconditionally in return. But her family was different than Carter's. *Very* different.

However, as much as Abby had yearned for a "normal" family while growing up, she knew how lucky she was.

The long weekend passed in a blur. Her father had a keen eye for visual storytelling. Though he was always quick to point out that it was her project, *her baby*, the suggestions he made for her documentary were spot-on.

By the time he put her on a plane for New York, she was ecstatic at how the film was coming together. And more confident, too. If this project turned out as well as she was expecting it to, she would be on her way to a promising career.

She was already almost regretting the flight to New York. It wouldn't have been a big deal to simply fly from LA to Royal. Still, even though this would be a super short visit, she wanted to swap out some of her clothes, and she also hoped to talk to her mother about Carter. If the right moment arose.

Her flight landed on time Monday afternoon. Abby took a cab from LaGuardia to Manhattan. She and her mother lived in a high rise on a quiet block of East 77th Street. Abby had never questioned her mother's finances. There was money from Abby's grandparents. And she was certain her father had paid child support. Beyond that, she only knew that she and her mother lived a very comfortable life.

When she took the elevator to the tenth floor and unlocked the door, her mother wasn't home. No real surprise. But for the first time, the apartment's quiet emptiness struck her as a little sad.

What would it be like when Abby moved out for good? Did her mother have any desire for grandchildren? Some women didn't.

Abby did some laundry and rifled through her closet to repack her suitcase. On a whim, she folded a beautiful, fire-engine red evening dress and added it to the pile. Lila had mentioned the possibility of some special events surrounding the festival kickoff. Abby wanted to be ready.

It was hard to admit that in the back of her mind, she was already picturing herself wearing that sexy dress for Carter. Days ago, he had asked her to stay in touch. But she hadn't known what to say. When he didn't text either during their time apart, she had assumed he was busy or distracted or both.

Or maybe he had decided a clean break was the best.

Abby picked up her phone and stared at the screen. She had lots of emails and texts, but not the one she so desperately wanted.

Her fingers had a mind of their own. Quickly, she composed a message before she could change her mind.

Hey, Carter... I'm in New York now. My dad was super helpful with my film. We enjoyed catching up. Hope things are good at Sunset Acres...

It was a breezy, nonpersonal text. She almost deleted it, but then she sucked in a breath and hit Send.

Now that she was far away from Royal, it seemed almost

ludicrous that she had indulged in an exhilarating, short-lived affair with a sexy, rugged Texan. The list of things they *didn't* have in common was depressingly long.

Had he already forgotten about her? Had she been an easy mark to him?

It was painful to consider. She honestly thought he was as caught up in the magic as she was. But maybe she was kidding herself.

Her beautiful, stylish, blond-haired mother made it home at six and brought food from Abby's favorite Chinese restaurant. Both her parents spoiled her when she was around. It was nice, but despite being twenty-four years old, Abby was in that odd stage between being a college student and a fully grown adult.

In any other place in the country, she might already have her own apartment by now. New York's cost of living was exorbitant, though, and her mother had often said Abby was welcome to use this apartment as home base for as long as she needed it.

Over a combo meal of various chicken and rice dishes, Abby mentally rehearsed how she was going to present the Labor Day idea. Something about the prospect of having her mom and dad together in Malibu, with her, excited Abby. Was she re-creating a childhood fantasy? A time she barely remembered?

Her motives were murky.

Before she could make her pitch, her mother set down her glass of wine and gave Abby a nervous smile. "I'm glad you're here, sweetheart. I have something I need to tell you, and I didn't want to do it over the phone."

Abby was alarmed. "Are you sick?"

"Oh, no. Nothing like that." Her mother fiddled with her chopsticks. "The thing is… I've met someone. A nice man who works in the financial district. He came in to have a painting appraised, and we hit it off. He asked me out to dinner, and well…things snowballed. He's asked me to move in with him."

"Mom!" Abby gaped, her brain swirling. "How long ago was this?"

"Back in February. You've been traveling a lot, and I didn't want to say anything until I knew if it was going anywhere."

Abby was shocked to the core. She didn't remember her mother ever dating anyone, which now that she thought about it was highly unlikely. Maybe her mom had been discreet for Abby's sake. Or maybe she had put her personal life on hold until her daughter was old enough to fend for herself.

"I'm happy for you, Mom. Really."

Her mother beamed. "I'd love for you to meet him, but I suppose it will have to be when you're finished with that festival project. August, maybe?"

"I'd like that."

"And about this apartment…"

"You should sell it," Abby told her. "I'll find a place. Don't worry about me."

Her mother grimaced. "I'm not going to rush into marriage. I'd rather you keep the apartment for now. That way, if things don't work out for me, I won't end up looking for some place to live."

"Are you unsure about this relationship? Is that it?"

Her mother's face glowed. "Oh, no. Not at all. Bradley is a wonderful man. We have fun together. And we laugh a lot. But I failed at marriage once. It's made me gun-shy, I guess. For now, I just want to enjoy his company and see what happens."

Half a dozen emotions buffeted Abby. Time never stood still. Her parents had been divorced for almost two decades, but this new development felt like a threat. That was dumb.

After all, Abby wasn't a child anymore. Her mother deserved to be happy.

Clearly, there would be no mini family reunion in Malibu.

Her eyes burned. "Tell this Bradley person that he's found a jewel. I love you, Mom. This is wonderful news."

They both stood. Hugged tightly.

A few moments later, Abby put her dishes in the dishwasher and threw away the take-out cartons. "I need some exercise after sitting on a plane forever. You want to come with me? A walk in the park, maybe? It's too hot to run."

Her mother shook her head. "Thanks, sweetie. But I have some work to do, and Bradley will probably call in a bit. Will you be okay on your own?"

"Of course."

Abby changed clothes and went downstairs. Out on the pavement, the heat was oppressive. Instead of her usual three-mile run, she decided to walk the streets.

New York was *home*. She loved the hustle and bustle and even the crowds in Times Square. The city was huge and vibrant, and always *open*. Where else could you get a doughnut and coffee at 2:00 a.m.? Or a pizza.

The clothes shopping and the bookstores energized her. She found entertainment in the trendy boutiques and the high-end fashion empires that might not have what she wanted or needed, but were fun to explore anyway. Everything about the city of her birth was part of her DNA.

Yet, for the first time, she felt something was missing. Sex with Carter was great, but she yearned to hear his laugh. To enjoy his droll sense of humor. Her day felt empty and flat without him.

What did that mean? Was she in too deep?

She lost track of how far she walked. Surrounded by

strangers, she nevertheless felt completely at home. Alone, but not lonely.

When it was time to head back, she was no closer to making a decision. Truthfully, there was no decision to make. If she wanted to sleep with Carter Crane a few more times, she could do that. He'd be happy to oblige. She was sure of it.

Why did she have to get swept off her feet by a man who lived several hundred miles away? As much as she cared for him, why indulge in something that had no future?

It was a question with no answer. Or at least not one she wanted to hear.

Even worse, Carter had never responded to her text. What did that mean? Was he done with her?

Tuesday flew by. Abby had lunch with a couple of friends. They had known each other since the beginning of high school and always managed to pick up right where they left off. Abby wanted to tell them about Carter, but she felt self-conscious. She wasn't in a relationship with him. Just because he had seen her naked, and she was crazy about him didn't mean anything was going to come of it. Carter was Carter, and Abby was Abby.

They were great in bed, but morning always came.

After lunch, she stopped in at a high-end outdoor adventure store and picked out a small tent and the most basic of camping supplies. Her family had never done the camping thing, but Abby was certain she could make it through one night in the relative wilds of Appaloosa Island. Shooting at dawn was one of her passions. The morning light made cinema magic.

She plunked down her credit card and paid an ouchworthy premium for two-day delivery to Texas. As the day passed, she grew more anxious about returning to Royal. Would Carter expect to see her again? And could *she* handle seeing him again now that she was at least being honest with herself about her feelings?

Abby and her mother went out for dinner that evening. They even dressed up and made a celebration of it. The meal was fun and delicious and just like old times.

But the world was turning, and life was changing. Abby had to change along with it whether she wanted to or not.

Wednesday morning, her mother gave her a tight hug before heading off to work. "We'll make a date for August," she said. "Whenever you know your plans and your schedule for coming home. I'm glad the documentary is going so well."

"Thanks, Mama." Abby hugged her again. "Bradley had better treat you right, or he'll have to answer to me."

Her mother laughed, her face alight with happiness. "I'll be sure to tell him."

After the door closed, Abby had half an hour to kill before her rideshare arrived. She stood at the living room window and looked beyond the nearest buildings to the slice of Central Park she could see.

It would be hard to find a view more different from the one in her memories of Royal, Texas.

She wasn't a weepy woman, but she felt alarmingly emotional. What had happened to her? Why was she drawn back to a Texas town with red dirt and no subway system? Lots of cows, but no Broadway.

The ostensible reason was her project about Soiree on the Bay. That much was true. But she wouldn't lie, even to herself. Her documentary had made room on the shelf for something, or someone, equally important. Carter Crane. Abby's feelings for him went far beyond the physical.

How could she be falling for a man who was so wrong for her?

At the airport, she boarded the jet, unable to ignore the undercurrent of excitement she felt. By dinnertime, she would be back on Carter's home turf. The hotel had even blocked the same room she had been in last week. Lila's recent text said everything was a go for the overnight campout on Appaloosa Island.

The festival dates were fast approaching. Abby had a lot to accomplish before then. Even if she wanted to, she couldn't afford to fool around with Carter all the time. She had to focus on her task.

Unfortunately, today's flight itinerary had two different connections, first Atlanta, then Dallas. By the time the plane finally landed in Royal, it was almost dinnertime.

Abby felt let down when there was no one at the airport to greet her. Which made no sense at all, because she hadn't told anyone her plans. Had she actually been hoping for a big, romantic scene where Carter met her at baggage claim and swore they could juggle all their differences?

She snorted inwardly as she waited for her luggage. There was a reason she produced documentaries instead of rom-coms. Her subjects were framed in truth, not romantic fiction. *She* controlled the outcome, not the notoriously capricious whims of fate.

By the time she made it to the hotel, her stomach grumbled loudly. She checked in, threw her things in the room, brushed her teeth, fluffed her hair and then headed out again. She didn't want room service, and she didn't want to eat in the hotel dining room alone. Not tonight.

Fortunately, there was a great pizza place down the street.

The elevator moved far too slowly. Or maybe Abby's patience was shot. That was the trouble with air travel. It took all day to make a little progress.

When she stepped into the beautifully appointed hotel lobby, the first person she saw was Carter. He was leaning against a column, dressed in dark slacks and wearing a snow-white dress shirt with the sleeves rolled up and cowboy boots.

His slow smile took the starch out of her knees.

He straightened and met her halfway. "Hey, Abs. I missed you."

And then he caught her up in his arms and kissed her so long and so hard that the clerk at the front desk clapped and cheered, as did a couple of guests.

Abby's face was on fire when she pulled away. "I missed you, too," she whispered.

"Where were you headed?"

"Dinner. I've been on planes all day, and little packets of peanuts don't cut it. I need real food."

"How 'bout I take you to one of my favorite hole-in-the-wall places? It's quirky, but the food is fantastic."

She looked into his blue eyes, seeing the genuine pleasure reflected there. His enthusiasm made her feel good. After two somewhat odd visits with her parents, she'd been adrift. Unsettled. Carter's presence was exactly what she needed.

As he helped her into his car, she sat back and sighed, feeling her bad mood and her gloomy outlook improve. The Caballero Cantina was just as Carter had described. The rough plaster walls inside were yellow and orange and decorated with colorful murals.

The hostess gave Carter a smile that was too flirty for Abby's peace of mind, but the young woman seated them at a nice table in a corner shielded from view by the high back of an adjacent booth.

Abby's mouth watered as she perused the Tex-Mex menu. At Carter's recommendation, she ordered a fajita bowl. While they waited, she ate far too many chips and queso. But hey—what was the point of visiting Texas and not indulging in the local cuisine? The meal, when it came, was incredible.

Carter laughed at her. "You like the food?"

"How come I've been here all this time, and you're just now telling me about this place?"

"I've been busy, I guess."

Her stomach clenched. "I'll admit, I was surprised to see you tonight."

"I thought we agreed to touch base when you returned."

She tilted her head and studied his bland expression, searching for any evidence that he was as calm as he looked. "Touch base? Or go all the way home?"

Carter leaned forward and wiped a tiny drip of cheese from her chin with his fingertip. His crooked smile was sexy and wicked. "I guess that's up to you."

Abby considered inviting him back to her hotel room, but something stopped her. She wanted him too much. Her feelings weren't so hard to decipher. She was falling in love with him, and she knew they were the least likely couple in Royal to make a go of things.

In a last-ditch nod to self-preservation, she forced herself to speak lightly. "I'm sure there will be some base touching. But I'm exhausted, Carter. Rain check? Please?"

His smile faded as his gaze narrowed. "Are you okay, Abs? What happened while you were gone?"

"Nothing really." Oh, heck. She might as well tell him. "I found out that my mother has a boyfriend. And they're moving in together."

He sat back and whistled. "That must have been a shock."

"You could say that. I didn't even know she was dating."

"Will you still feel comfortable living with her?" he asked.

Trust Carter to cut through to the basics of a situation. "Actually, she's moving in with *Bradley*. She wants me to keep our apartment, so she'll have a place to go back to if things don't work out."

"That's pretty cynical."

She sighed. "You'd have to know my mother. She's a pragmatist through and through."

"Should I say, *I'm sorry, Abby*?"

"That's just it. I don't know how to feel. When I was with my dad, I was making a fun little plan for the three of us to hang out in Malibu for Labor Day weekend. He was okay with it. He and my mom are cordial. But I didn't know about *Bradley*."

"You're gonna have to stop saying his name like that," he cautioned.

"I know."

Carter leaned back in his chair and ate another chip. "I have news that might cheer you up."

Thirteen

"Oh? Tell me." Abby was instantly intrigued, especially because Carter's smile was teasing. As if he was eager to spring his surprise on her.

He took a long swig of his drink, drawing out the suspense. "You mentioned camping out to get some shots on Appaloosa Island with the morning light…"

"Yes."

"Well, I called in a favor. A couple of my college buddies went in together five or six years back and bought one of those fancy-ass houses at the western end of the island. They share it between the families. I checked, and this weekend no one is using it. If you want to, you and I can go out there and spend a night or two. It's very private. Luxurious. What do you think?"

She thought about the camping gear she'd had shipped to the hotel. But when she balanced that against spending a romantic weekend with Carter, it was no contest. "I think it sounds great!" She knew what she was agreeing to, and why. This would be one last wonderful rendezvous with Carter. After this weekend, she had to go cold turkey.

"Good." He grinned. "I'll tell them we'd like to use the house."

"Should I offer to pay for it?"

"Nope. I'll send them each a case of their favorite whiskey, and they'll be good."

When the meal was over, Carter drove her back to the hotel. Already, she was second-guessing the fact that she had kept him at bay tonight. She had to get her head on straight. She wasn't really in love with him, was she?

The fact that she didn't know for sure made her jittery.

He pulled up under the hotel portico but didn't get out. "Sleep well, Abby."

She turned sideways in her seat. "Thank you for dinner. And thank you for working out the Appaloosa Island thing. That will be a whole lot better than sweating in a tent."

He ran a finger along her chin, his touch arousing her despite its innocence. "I'm hoping *I'll* get a chance to make you sweat, but that's up to you. We can hang out as friends. I don't expect sexual favors in exchange for our accommodations."

"I never thought you did." She reached across the console and kissed him softly on the lips. He went still but didn't react. "I want you, Carter, but I have a few things to figure out. Give me time."

"However long you need, Abs." He twined a strand of her hair around his finger. "I won't hurt you. I care about you, Abby."

The stark sincerity in his voice was exactly what she was afraid of… Carter *did* care about her. She knew that. And she felt the same way about him. But she didn't want to lose control of the situation. As long as she kept her expectations clear, everything would be okay.

She ignored those last five words he said, mostly because she didn't know how to respond.

The festival was fast approaching. After that, Abby would be spending a lot of time in LA working on the documentary. When the film was done, she would likely go back to New York. And meet *Bradley*.

"What time this weekend?" she asked.

"I'll pick you up Friday at six. We can eat a picnic in the car. Amanda Battle's diner offers that kind of thing."

"Sounds perfect. What do I need to bring?"

The uniformed hotel employee kept giving them glances, as if worried they were blocking the drive. This time it was Carter who leaned toward Abby. He put a large warm hand behind her neck and coaxed her closer for a blistering kiss that made her quiver. "The house is fully furnished," he said huskily. "All you need is a toothbrush and a swimsuit. But on second thought, maybe just the toothbrush."

When he laughed softly, Abby wanted to forget all about her rules. She wanted to drag him upstairs to her bed. Instead, she exhaled and opened her door. "Good night, Carter. Sweet dreams."

He got out of the car and rested one arm on top of the door to give her one last smoldering smile. "You, too, Abs. We can compare notes later."

And then he was gone.

The mirror on one wall of the elevator showed a woman who was weary from a long day of travel, yet also flushed with excitement. Carter did that to her. He made everything a little brighter, a little more vibrant.

That night as she showered and got ready for bed, she pondered the implications of spending the weekend with him. It was a work trip, sure. But with plenty of time for fun. She told herself this was as far as she would let things go.

They hadn't even known each other a month. Surely

this sexual attraction would burn itself out soon. She was a novelty to him.

Furthermore, she could think of at least a dozen reasons why the two of them could never be a real couple.

Bottom line? As much as she liked him, and was maybe even falling for him, she was more like her mother than she realized. Carter wasn't part of the big picture. He wasn't Abby's *future*.

Carter went into town Thursday with a list of errands his ranch foreman would have been happy to tackle. But he was hoping to bump into Abby. How pathetic was that? He had resorted to acting like a middle school boy. All hormones and no sense.

He didn't see Abby at all, but he did run into Lila at the post office. She was in line in front of him. They chatted briefly, but when he exited, she was waiting for him.

"May I speak to you for a minute, Carter?" she asked.

"Of course." They took advantage of a patch of shade beneath a large tree. "What's up?"

"It's Abby," she said. "I know it's not my business, but it sounds like the two of you are getting close."

He tensed. "Once again, Royal's grapevine is operating on all cylinders."

"Don't be mad. I'm just worried about her. She doesn't know many people here, at least not on a deeper level. And after Madeline, you haven't dated much."

"Is there a point to any of this?" he asked impatiently.

"Yes, there is." She looked him square in the eye. "What's the deal with Abby? You know she's not staying. And you know you won't leave."

His jaw tightened. "Abby and I are just having fun. And yes, it hasn't escaped me that she's too much like Madeline for any kind of long-term relationship. Abby is big-city dreams, and I'm a Royal rancher. It doesn't get much more different than that."

"She's young, Carter."

"Not that much younger than you."

"Maybe not. But beneath that big-city polish, I think she's vulnerable. You could hurt her. Why take the chance?"

"You and Zach are total opposites, too," Carter pointed out, trying not to reveal his frustration. "But you're making it work."

"Because Zach decided he wanted to stay in Royal," she said.

Lila was giving voice to every reservation Carter had about Abby. "I like her," he said slowly. "A lot. And I care about her well-being. More than I've cared about any woman in a long time. I know this thing between us is temporary. But I haven't made any promises, and neither has she. You'll have to trust me on this. Abby and I know what we're doing."

The distress on Lila's face was genuine. "I hope so, Carter. You're a good man. I know you wouldn't lie to her. But sometimes we want what we can't have."

"I'll be careful," he said. "You have nothing to worry about."

Carter carried Lila's words like a stone in his shoe for the rest of that day and into Friday. Should he call off the trip to Appaloosa Island? Let Abby go camping alone as she had originally planned? His idea about the house had seemed innocent enough, but now he didn't know. Was it wrong to take what Abby had to give, knowing it could never be anything more than this moment in time?

By the time he picked her up Friday at six, his gut was in knots. Most of that tension subsided when he saw her. The smile she gave him as she slid into the passenger seat was happy and carefree.

Lila was worrying over nothing.

Abby wasted no time digging into the wicker hamper. "I'm starving," she said. "Can you eat and drive at the same time?"

"Not a problem."

He headed out of town and onto the highway that would take them south to Mustang Point. Abby handed him a ham sandwich and opened a bag of chips. "Royal is getting really excited about the festival. People were talking about it everywhere I went today."

Carter snorted. "Wait until the shops are overrun with tourists and all the garbage cans are spilling over into the streets."

She opened a can of soda and shook her head slowly. "You really are a Scrooge, Carter Crane. New York has tons of people—tourists, too. But we get along very well."

"To each his own, I guess," he grumbled.

"Why don't we talk about something we can both agree on…books? Movies?"

The trip passed quickly. Abby seemed determined to put aside their differences. That was fine with Carter. He knew how very *unalike* they were. That was the problem.

Abby had read and reread the Harry Potter books, but also enjoyed political biographies. Carter was a Grisham fan and studied military history. They both agreed that the movie business was relying too much on blockbusters and not branching out enough.

When they finished their meal, Abby tucked the debris back in the hamper and returned it to the back seat. "I have a tiny bit of bad news," she said.

He shot her a sideways glance, seeing the apologetic look she gave him. "Oh?"

"I know you and I were planning to stay the whole weekend at your friends' house, but I got an invitation today for a black-tie reception at the Bellamy. It's a last-minute kickoff event on Saturday night for Soiree on the Bay, VIP only. They're going to hand out sample schedules, and I think one of the bands is going to play a few songs. I really need to be there."

"No problem," he said, refusing to admit he was disappointed. Having Abby naked and willing for an entire weekend had been a tantalizing prospect. "Am I invited?" he asked, tongue in cheek.

She took him seriously. "You probably are, but in any case, you're my plus-one…if you're willing."

He reached out and took her hand, lifting it to his mouth so he could kiss her fingers. "I know how important this documentary is to you. And I want to support you. So yes, I'd be happy to be your date."

"Great." Her grin was smug, as if she had talked him into something against his will. Little did she know that he would do almost anything to make her happy. It was a sobering realization for a man who walked through life alone.

He had never wanted to depend on a woman again. Yet here he was, twining his life with hers. What was that old saying? Give a man enough rope and he'll hang himself? Carter was heading for a calamity of some sort. A dramatic end-of-the-road thing. And probably sooner than later.

By the time they caught the ferry at Mustang Point, crossed the water and then drove to the inhabited western end of the island, the sun was low in the sky. He handed his phone to Abby. "Read me the directions from that text."

The instructions were simple enough. Soon, they were pulling into the driveway of what could only be described as a seafront villa. The architectural style was Italian.

Even Carter was impressed, and he was used to the immense wealth in Royal. This was over-the-top in every way.

Carter chuckled as they carried their things inside. "You pick a bedroom, Abs. Plenty to choose from."

He followed her down a hall. "This one," she said. "Look at the view."

One entire wall of the master suite was glass. Actually, there were three similar master suites, but this one was the closest to the pool.

They stood at the huge windows and used the binoculars they found on a nightstand. Dolphins gamboled fairly close to shore, probably fishing for their dinner. Sailboats streaked across the bay. Palm trees, planted by landscapers, added drama to the sunset scene.

Unselfconsciously, as if it were the most natural thing in the world, Abby rested her head on his shoulder. "What should we do first?" she asked.

His body tightened. What he *wanted* to say was crude and self-evident to any man with a pulse. But he could wait. Maybe.

"How about a swim? And then an early bedtime? Since you have to be up before dawn."

She laughed softly. "I hope *bedtime* is a euphemism for something."

"Hell, yeah…"

They changed clothes in different bathrooms. Abby still occasionally exhibited a frustrating reticence around him. As if she were guarding some part of herself. Yet the more she held back, the more he wanted to push for more.

They met out at the pool. Abby was wearing a gold bikini that made his heart slug hard in his chest. Her long, toned legs, narrow waist and high, rounded breasts were showcased to perfection.

He cleared his throat. "Nice swimsuit, Abs."

She pulled her hair into a ponytail and secured it with an elastic band. "Thanks. I picked up a few more clothes when I was in New York. I honestly didn't know what I would need when I packed the first time."

He followed her down the shallow stairs into the pool,

side by side. "What did you think Texas was going to be like?"

She shrugged as they waded deeper. "I didn't really know. Except for tales about everything being bigger in Texas." Without warning, she tweaked the front of his swim trunks. "That part turned out to be true." Laughing at his look of shock, she did a shallow dive and escaped to the deep end.

He chased her instinctively, energized by the game. But Abby was fast and nimble. Slippery, too. It was several minutes before he had her corralled against the side of the pool. He kissed her, tasting warm woman and anticipation. "You asked me to give you time, Abby. What did you mean by that? Time for what?"

"I couldn't decide what to do about you. About us."

"And now?" Her spiky eyelashes collected water droplets and let them fall, looking like tears.

Her smile was shaky. "I don't want to be serious right now. I'm like Cinderella at the ball. My time in Royal is running out. Let's have fun this weekend, Carter. That's all."

He should be happy. No-strings sex. With a beautiful woman who made him laugh. Why did her answer disturb him? "If that's what you want."

"It is," she said.

Abby curled her arms around Carter's neck and kissed him. Like every time before, the taste of him went straight to her head. Like hard liquor. She felt the strength in his gentle hold and sensed his frustration that was perhaps even more than physical. Neither of them liked the way this was playing out, but they were both trapped.

She loved the feel of his body against hers. The differences were stark and arousing. Carter was a man in his prime, his muscles the product of hard physical labor. She was rapidly becoming addicted to his flashing grin and twinkling blue eyes.

But was she really the kind of woman who would give up everything for a man?

He seemed fond of her. And yes, they were dynamite in bed. But if she even *considered* making such a huge change in her life, it would have to be for one reason only. Love.

She shuddered in his arms, relishing the way he commanded the kiss and changed it from playful and affectionate to intense and erotic. Their bodies recognized each other. Whether it was the novelty of being with someone new and different, or a deeper connection, she and Carter were made for each other when it came to sexual chemistry.

His heavy erection pulsed at her belly. "I want you," he rasped, his chest heaving against her breasts.

They hadn't been in the pool long at all. Abby didn't care. All she wanted was Carter. "Yes," she whispered back.

They took time to play in the outdoor shower, rinsing off the chlorine and stripping off their suits. There was no one to witness the moment when Carter scooped up a naked Abby in his arms and strode back to the house.

She knew suddenly that this precious moment was her swan song with Carter. The poignant knowledge was a knife to her heart, the pain searing her composure.

It took everything she had to conceal her turmoil.

In the bedroom, Carter abandoned her only long enough to grab towels from the bathroom. He dried her carefully, lingering over her breasts, kissing her again and again. She shuddered as arousal wrapped them both in a veil of need.

Carter rifled through his suitcase for protection and joined her on the big bed. He leaned over on one elbow, curling his hand in her ponytail and holding her down. "You're mine tonight, Abby."

The slight tug at her scalp made her breath come faster. He was showing her an edge to their passion that they had only skated near before. She craved his forcefulness and would give him everything in return.

When he kissed her once more, she sank her teeth into his bottom lip. "I want to push you over the edge, cowboy. What do you think of that?"

His cheekbones flushed dark red, and his pupils dilated. "I think you talk too damn much." His lips and teeth and tongue dueled with hers, establishing dominance, but with a dollop of tenderness that promised safety in a storm.

When he entered her with a guttural groan, she felt the sting of tears. Maybe love didn't come so quickly. But who was to say? What she felt for Carter was an overwhelming tide, a thrilling rush of passion. She *loved* him. Or she was *falling* in love with him. What did semantics matter when the ending of their story was so painfully clear?

He took her long and hard and then soft and slow, drawing out the pleasure until she was wild with wanting him, her fingernails marking his powerful shoulders.

"Carter…" She cried out his name when she came, lost to reason, lost in a lover's embrace.

She felt the moment when his control snapped and he let his own passion overcome him. Holding him as tightly as she could, her body absorbed the aftershocks. Her fingers tousled his hair, and her breath mingled with his.

Gradually, their heartbeats slowed. The sweat dried on their bodies.

Carter mumbled something inaudible and reached to pull up the covers.

In seconds, they were both asleep.

Abby awoke hours later, disoriented and confused. The bedroom was strange. But awareness gradually returned, and she knew whose big warm body was entwined with hers.

It was 5:00 a.m. She slipped carefully out from under the masculine arm and leg that held her pinned to the mattress. Carter never moved.

With the flashlight on her phone, Abby found clothes in her suitcase and put them on. Cotton pants with a drawstring waist, comfortable, but thick enough to protect her legs if she had to kneel on the ground. A long-sleeve T-shirt to guard against a cool morning breeze. Canvas sneakers that had seen better days.

The whole process took less than five minutes. She decided to let Carter sleep. After all, he had to drive them back to Royal later today. They'd brought no provisions for breakfast. That was an oversight. But she kept energy bars in her camera bag for just such an occasion.

She made it all the way through the house and out to the driveway before she remembered that she needed the keys to Carter's car.

Muttering under her breath, she stowed her gear in the trunk and returned to the house, stubbing her toe on a loose brick at the edge of the driveway as she moved in the dark. When she reached the top step, the door opened, and there he was, filling the space.

"Are you trying to ditch me, Abs?"

The slight hint of annoyance in his voice could have meant anything.

"No," she said. "But you were dead to the world. And you have to drive this afternoon. I'm used to being on my own."

"I'm sure you are."

Now there was no mistaking his displeasure. "Come on," he said. "I have the keys. I assume we're headed to the festival site?"

She exhaled. "Yes."

They didn't speak on the way across the island. Abby asked him to stop a time or two for a quick shot. But what she needed most, with her back to the east, was to see the sunrise bathe the upcoming Soiree on the Bay with mystical light.

The weather was perfect. Only a few high thin clouds to add punctuation to the story she was hoping to capture. Already, she could hear the commentary.

Thousands of festivalgoers will soon descend on Appaloosa Island, eager to eat and drink and rock out to the sounds of America's popular bands. But do they realize what beauty blossoms here in the sounds of silence?

Carter interrupted her mental flight of fancy. "Where do you want me to park?"

"Closer to the water, please. And you don't have to get out. I'll be ranging around."

His silence lasted two breaths, then three. "I'll go with you, Abby. I'm sure you don't need me, but it will make me feel better."

"Fine." She grabbed her camera and set up the tripod. After filming a loop of the stars cartwheeling across the heavens, she focused on the ribbon of dawn at the horizon. When she was satisfied, she put the tripod back in the trunk and shouldered the camera. "Let's go."

They walked the festival grounds for the next half hour, shooting empty stages gilded in light. Focusing on sawdust paths and eventually, beams of sunlight traveling across the water. The work was exacting and exhilarating in equal measure.

She had assumed she would feel self-conscious having Carter at her heels. But his presence was oddly comforting. She was used to being on her own, that was true. Still, he added something to her routine, something indefinable and wonderful.

By the time the sun was fully up and beginning to warm the moist air, Abby was starving. Carter still hadn't said much. He was wearing his clothes from last night as if he had dashed out of the house to catch her and not bothered with his suitcase.

"Thank you," she said stiffly. "It was nice having company."

He ruffled her hair. "You're welcome." A huge yawn seemed to take him by surprise. "Is it nap time yet?"

"I was hoping you could summon a fast-food place out of thin air. I'd kill for coffee and a bagel."

He slid into the driver's seat and turned on the AC. It was amazing how quickly the Texas heat multiplied. "I can do better than that," he said. "I asked my buddy to arrange for a few supplies in the kitchen. According to him, a local lady cooks for them and delivers whenever they request meals."

"Great setup!" Abby exclaimed. "Does this car go any faster?"

Back at the house, they found a container of homemade blueberry muffins on the counter and in the fridge, fresh-squeezed orange juice along with a sausage and egg casserole. The coffeepot soon produced a heavenly aroma.

They ate at the island, standing up.

Carter reached over to brush a crumb from her chin. "Not to be sexist," he said, "but I'm astounded how beautiful you look at this hour of the morning. You're the opposite of high-maintenance, aren't you?"

She put her hands to hair that was riotously out of control, because she had gone to bed with it wet. "I appreciate the compliment, but I'm going to need to seriously up my game before tonight. Would you mind if we headed on back to Royal?"

He stared at her even as she kept her gaze on her breakfast. "No morning *exercise*?" he drawled, his meaning impossible to misinterpret.

Her cheeks burned. What could it hurt? One last time? Of course, that's what she had told herself about last night. "Sure," she said, hoping the word was breezy and not filled with indecision. "It's still early."

He picked her up and tossed her over his shoulder, making her squeal with laughter. "What are you doing, Carter?" she said breathlessly.

His answer was succinct. "Saving time."

She thought he might suggest a shared shower. But no. Instead, he stripped her naked, undressed himself and bent her over the arm of the settee, taking her from behind.

He did pause at the last second to grab a condom, but after that, things got a little crazy. It almost seemed as if was trying to prove a point or maybe coax her into protesting.

Not a chance. She memorized every frenzied thrust, every touch of his hands on her body. Her heart was breaking, even as she climaxed sharply with his weight pressing her into the soft upholstery.

When it was over, he tugged her to her feet, cupped her neck in two hands and kissed her lazily. "Now *that's* the way to start a morning," he said.

Fourteen

Carter was sleepy on the way back to Royal. Abby had been right about that. And as soon as they left the ferry and made it over onto the highway, she was out cold, her neck bent toward the window at an awkward angle.

It was just as well. Carter needed time to think. He and Madeline had tumbled into a relationship based on sex, and that had ended in disaster. Was he doing the same thing with Abby? He honestly didn't think so. What he felt for her was different, not even in the same ballpark.

After Madeline walked out on him, he had been furious, but he had repaired his life and carried on.

If Abby left for good, he feared there would be a gaping hole in his chest, his world, his *heart*. He was in danger of loving her—or maybe he already did, but it was too soon to admit it. How could he let her go?

Could he persuade her to stay in Royal? Surely, she understood what bound him to Texas. The responsibilities he carried, the weight of his heritage and his family's expectations. But would it matter in the end?

She roused about two hours into the trip and reached instantly for one of the insulated flasks of coffee. After a long drink, she smoothed her hair and rubbed her eyes. "Sorry," she muttered. "You want me to drive now?"

"I'm fine." He squeezed her hand briefly. "Abby?" His heart pounded. "Have you thought about maybe staying in Royal longer than you first planned? You could move in with me until the festival is over and even after that. I have plenty of room to set up a studio for you."

Her silence echoed inside the car. It lasted for ten seconds. Or fifteen. Maybe an eternity. She had gone still as a bunny rabbit caught in headlights. "Well, I…"

The leaden weight of disappointment settled in his gut. "You don't have to decide right now. Just think about it."

He was glad that controlling the car gave him an excuse not to look at her.

Abby kicked off her shoes and curled her legs beneath her. She sighed. "I would love to stay longer, Carter, I really would. But as soon as the festival is over, my father has blocked off some time to help me with editing and postproduction of my documentary. And that will be in California."

He knew it was time to change the subject. "So have you settled on an angle for the film? A theme?"

Again, he experienced that unsettling lag between his seemingly benign question and her response. Abby tapped her fingers on the armrest. "I have. Dad and I looked at some of my early footage. I talked it over with him. He thinks the missing money angle could be a hard-hitting hook. Possibly even make my project more commercial."

"Abby, no. You're getting into something that could be dangerous."

"Who would hurt me, Carter?" There was a little snap in her voice.

"Money makes people do strange things. Besides, I think you're way off base. Nobody on the festival advisory board *needs* money. Billy Holmes is rich. You saw the evidence of that. The Edmond kids are each loaded, not even taking into account what they'll inherit from their father one day. I truly believe the whole missing money thing is nothing more than gossip, despite what Billy said. It's probably a few hundred bucks."

"Pull over, please," Abby said, her voice tight.

He swung the wheel immediately, steering them into a state rest area. They both got out and faced each other over the top of the car.

Abby's gaze was stormy. "You don't have any respect at all for my professional integrity, do you?"

"Of course I do, but you're—"

She made a chopping motion with her hand, cutting him off. "No. You don't. You think of this documentary as *Abby's little hobby*. I may be young, Carter, but I'm neither immature nor foolish. I have goals and dreams. Which is more than I can say for you."

His temper lit. "You don't know me. Don't pretend like you do. Sunset Acres is *my* ranch now, not my parents'. It's a huge part of who I am."

"Ah, yes. A Texas rancher. An esteemed member of the Texas Cattleman's Club. There's more to life than cattle, Carter. Maybe that's why your precious Madeline left you."

Though the flash of regret on Abby's face said she regretted her harsh words, Carter sucked in a deep breath and counted to ten. They were both exhausted, and if he read the situation correctly, they were each fighting an attraction that was bound to hurt them both. Why keep pushing?

His fists were clenched on the roof of the car. He relaxed them and stepped back. "Do you need to use the restroom?"

Abby glanced at the squatty brick building baking under the afternoon sun. "Yes. I'll make it quick."

Carter didn't move. As he waited for her to return, he tried to find a way out. But every idea he pursued mentally ended up a dead end.

Besides, he had no proof that Abby was as caught up in him as he was in her.

As she walked across the sidewalk in his direction, he studied her as a stranger would. Her graceful long legs covered the distance quickly.

When she slid into the passenger seat and closed her door, he got in, as well. Thankfully, he had left the engine running. The day was hot as hell. It might set a record.

He rested one arm on the steering wheel, tasting defeat. "I don't want to fight with you, Abs. Especially with so little time left. Maybe we should call a truce."

She half turned in her seat, her expression heartbreaking. "Yes," she said. "My father told me something recently that resonated. He said some people come into our lives for a season. I think that's you and me, Carter. As much as we l…like each other, there's no future in it."

She stumbled over the word *like*. Had there been another word on her tongue? Had Abby been considering *love*?

He turned the radio on, covering the awkwardness. The last thirty minutes of the trip felt like an eternity. At the hotel, he got out to help Abby with her bags. Although she protested, he carried the two heaviest items upstairs, waited while she unlocked the door and then dumped everything on the extra bed.

She shifted from one foot to the other. "You can skip the reception tonight. I'm fine on my own."

Her words seemed prophetic. She didn't need him. "No back-sies," he said, hoping his smile was more genuine than it felt. "You invited me, and I said yes. What time should I pick you up?"

"Six thirty will work. Remember, it's black tie."

"Got it."

They stared at each other across what seemed like an acre of thick carpet. Her bed was mere steps away. He wanted her with a raw ache that didn't let up.

Abby was visibly nervous. Did she want him gone? Was that it?

"I should go," he said, hoping she would try to change his mind.

She nodded. "I'll see you at six thirty."

He carried the memory of her with him as he said a terse goodbye and made his way back downstairs. A woman of secrets, a woman of mystery. What thoughts raced behind those dark brown eyes?

He crashed hard when he got back to the ranch. The way he counted it, he'd barely managed four hours of sleep last night. Weaving on his feet, he knocked the AC down a few degrees and climbed into bed. But the hell of it was, Abby had taken up residence in that bed. He couldn't forget the taste of her skin, or the faint scent that was uniquely hers.

When he awoke, it was almost five. He scrounged in the fridge and found a couple of chicken legs and some potato salad. Standing in the kitchen wearing nothing but his boxers, he pondered his options. At the end of the party tonight, he could take Abby somewhere private. The Bellamy had lots of luxurious nooks and crannies. He could find a spot and lay out his argument.

The two of them had something. Sexual chemistry. And feelings. Strong feelings. If he admitted that to her and asked her to stay for him, for *them*, he figured there was a fifty-fifty chance Abby would agree.

Later, when he strode into the lobby of her hotel right on time, she was waiting for him. Was that by design? To keep him out of her room?

He was so caught up in analyzing her motives, it took him a few seconds to register what she was wearing.

When he did absorb the full picture, all he could do was shake his head. "Wow. You look incredible."

"Thank you," she said, her smile guarded.

Gone was the young woman who didn't mind getting dirty in pursuit of her career. In her place was a female who would draw the eye of every man at the Bellamy tonight. Abby's beautiful, wavy dark hair fell down around her shoulders. Her dress was red. *Sin* red. Fire-engine red. If his physical response to her had a color, it would be exactly this shade of red.

The dress was made of a thin, silky fabric in several layers that shifted and moved, drawing attention to her tall, alluring body. Tiny spaghetti straps supported a bodice that plunged deeply in front.

Abby's breasts curved in that opening, suggesting lush, unapologetic femininity. The dress clung to her form, defining her narrow waist and hugging her hips. The floor-length hem swished as she moved, revealing silver stiletto sandals and toenails painted to match the dress. The only jewelry Abby wore was a pair of dangly crystal and silver earrings.

Carter struggled to find his breath. "I should have taken you to a party sooner," he said, only half kidding.

She kissed his cheek casually. "*I'm* taking you, cowboy. You're my plus-one…remember?"

"I stand corrected." Outside, he helped her into the car and carefully tucked her skirt out of the way. When he slid behind the wheel, he shot her a glance. "If you were hoping to keep a low profile while you investigate possible fraud, that dress isn't going to do it."

She shrugged, toying with the small beaded purse in her lap. "I've decided not to discuss business with you anymore. It only makes us quarrel."

His lips twitched. "Understood. We're keeping things

personal." He reached for her arm and rested his thumb where a pulse beat at the back of her wrist. She seemed so fragile, and yet he knew differently. Abby Carmichael was strong and resilient.

She tugged away, folding her hands primly in her lap. "Behave, Carter. I need to focus tonight."

"Is it possible you're a little obsessed with this movie you're doing? If you'd relax, we could eat and dance and mingle. You know…fun, normal people stuff."

"Don't pick a fight with me," she said. "I'll dance with you. But I'm also going to network the heck out of this party."

Abby realized that she wasn't at all bothered by Carter's gibes. She sensed the two of them were sustaining a fake argument for no other reason than to keep from jumping each other's bones.

The man was seriously hot. As a rich, rugged rancher, he always looked sexy, but tonight in his tux, he could make a girl swoon. His aftershave alone made her dizzy.

When they entered the Bellamy and headed for the ballroom where the Soiree on the Bay event was taking place, the whole place hummed with excitement. At a long table just outside the ballroom entrance, Abby surrendered her invitation.

No one was wearing name tags. This was too fancy a party for that. Besides, almost everyone present was a resident of Royal. They all knew each other.

Abby tucked her tiny purse in Carter's jacket pocket. As they made their way around the outer edge of the room toward the hors d'oeuvres, she spotted a number of people she recognized. The charismatic Rusty Edmond held court in one corner of the room, surrounded by beautiful women. He'd been married four times, but was currently single, hence the crowd.

All of the Edmond offspring were in attendance, though none of them were in the same vicinity. Ross was with his fiancée, Charlotte. Asher was deep in conversation with a cluster of men who all held cocktails and ignored the crowd that ebbed and flowed around them. Gina flitted from group to group, talking up the festival and laughing with friends.

Billy Holmes stood off by himself, surveying the chaos with a pleased smile.

Then suddenly, there was Lila Jones wearing a lavender gown that flattered her pale complexion. She flashed a smile at Carter and Abby. "Hey, you two. I want you to meet my fiancé, Zachary. Zach, this is Abby Carmichael, who's doing the documentary, and Carter Crane owns the Sunset Acres ranch just outside of town."

After greetings were exchanged, Abby whistled inwardly. Sweet little Lila Jones had hooked up with a blond, gorgeous guy like this? Good for her.

When someone else demanded Lila's and Zach's attention, Carter leaned down and whispered in Abby's ear, "Quit drooling. He's taken."

She grinned. "I can appreciate a fine work of art."

Carter brushed a strand of hair from her cheek and gave her an intimate smile, his body close to hers in the press of the crowd. "Is he your type? Blond and hunky?"

"I think you know that's not true." She searched his gaze. But it was as opaque and unreadable as the ocean at night. What was he thinking?

A few moments later, Carter was drawn into a conversation with a trio of fellow ranchers, something about alarm over the falling price of beef.

Abby was happy to escape that discussion. She finally made it to the food table and snagged a couple of shrimp and a bacon-wrapped scallop. Though this was cattle country, there wasn't much beef on the spread—only a tray of candied beef jerky.

The room was sweltering. Her forehead was damp. She spotted Valencia Donovan on the opposite side of the floor. Abby made her way through the throng. "Hey, Valencia. How are you?"

Valencia fanned her face with a napkin. "Hot. And you?"

"The same. I realized after I left you the other day that I had one more question I wanted to ask."

"Go for it," the other woman said.

"After your proposal was approved, who has been your contact on the committee? Who will be the one to disburse the funds to you?"

"Ah, yes. That would be Asher Edmond. He's been so helpful along the way. And very encouraging about how soon I might have the money. I owe him and the committee a great deal."

Before Abby could respond, another guest snagged Valencia's attention. Abby was alone for the moment. She wished fervently that she had thought to bring her video camera. Shots of this event, even if she only used snippets, would have been helpful. But in any case, she didn't have permission, so maybe it was a moot point.

Gradually, the room filled with glitz and glamour and excited chatter. The tuxedo-clad men were foils for the fashionable female plumage. Abby had grown up in an elite cross section of New York society. Her mother's family had deep connections in the city.

But here, she didn't belong. Just as she had never completely belonged back at home. The ache in her chest made her wonder if she would ever feel comfortable anywhere. Or maybe her destiny was to be what the Greeks referred to as *planetes*, wanderers.

Carter's life was anchored by the ranch. He had a purpose, a fixed spot in the universe.

Abby was a planet, always orbiting. Never finding home.

Suddenly, a large hand landed on her shoulder. She flinched and backed away instinctively. When she spun around, Billy Holmes stared at her.

"We need to talk," he said.

Was she imagining a hint of menace in his words? "Why?" she asked.

"I don't think I stressed enough how much I want you to drop the missing money idea. As I said before, it's a family matter. We're dealing with it. The festival doesn't need any bad publicity. Back off, Abby."

Before she could respond to his extraordinary remarks, Carter was back at her side. Scowling. He glared at Billy. "I hope I didn't hear you threatening my date."

Billy shrugged. "She's been poking her nose in a lot of places. If I were you, I'd convince her to stick to sweet stories with happy endings. Nothing like a libel charge to ruin a budding filmmaker's career."

Abby was stunned. This was a very different man than the one who had entertained her at his home. "But is it true?" she asked. "Is some of the money gone?"

Carter took her by the arm and steered her away. He vibrated with fury. "My God, you can't let it go! There are a dozen people in this room who would be happy to give you something for your documentary, but you keep beating a dead horse. Billy Holmes can ruin you in this town. I think it would be best if you go back to New York until the festival starts."

Abby felt as though someone had punched her in the stomach. There was not enough oxygen to breathe. "I was just doing my job," she whispered, conscious of eyes watching them.

"No," Carter said. "You were endangering your health and your reputation. *If* there is a significant amount of money missing—and I'm not saying there is—then all hell will break loose when the truth comes out. If Billy knows who the culprit is and he's protecting someone, you need to stay far, far away from this story."

"It's not your call," she hissed, angry and hurt.

"Maybe not. But I won't stand by and let you get caught in the cross fire. Come on," he said. "The band is starting to play."

The last thing Abby wanted to do was dance with the infuriating, dictatorial Carter Crane. But short of making a scene, she had little choice.

He pulled her into his arms and held her close. The music and the other dancers swirled around them. Abby felt her heart break clean through when she laid her cheek against Carter's shoulder and finally admitted to herself that she was deeply in love with him.

His body was big and hard and warm against hers. When they moved too quickly, her skirt tangled with his legs, binding them close. She felt the steady beat of his heart, heard the ragged tenor of his breath. He smelled of orange and clove and soap.

For a moment, she debated telling him how she felt. Offering to move to Royal permanently. After all, he had broached the subject, at least on a temporary basis. A few weeks ago, such an idea would have been laughable. But that was before she met the man who made her want to put down roots. Royal might not feel like home, but Carter did.

Even when he was being an overbearing pain in the ass, she knew he was the man for her, the man she wanted. But it was so quick. Could such intense feelings be trusted?

Carter had already suffered through one broken relationship. He wouldn't be eager to rush into another. She knew he had feelings for her. Lust. Affection. But anything more? How could she take that gamble?

And what about her life and her career? Why did it always have to be the woman who made all the sacrifices?

Again, she understood bleakly that she and Carter were the worst matchup imaginable.

When the band took a break, Gina Edmond spoke briefly. As did her brother and stepbrother and Billy Holmes. Rusty Edmond looked on with a proud smile, but didn't involve himself in the speeches.

At last, the formalities were over.

Despite how much she wanted to trust that what they had was worth fighting for, Abby couldn't get over the fact that Carter had said he wanted her to leave town. Which meant he couldn't be as emotionally involved as she was if he could so easily say goodbye. If she was looking for a sign, she had found one.

Her chest hurt so badly she wondered if she was having a heart attack. She reached in Carter's jacket pocket for her small clutch purse. "I'm leaving," she said brokenly. "I—I don't want to see you anymore. Goodbye, Carter."

His face went blank with shock. Before he could say anything, Rusty Edmond took him by the arm, demanding his attention. Abby used Carter's momentary distraction to flee. She was counting on the fact that it would take him a few moments to break free.

Thankfully, she found a Lyft driver waiting at the front entrance. She flagged him down, climbed in and gave the hotel address.

But she didn't cry until she was in her room with the door locked and the dead bolt turned.

Carter felt like he was living in an alternate universe. How could Abby simply disappear? They'd been having a fight, sure, but he thought their dance had smoothed over the rough patch. He loved holding her, moving to the music.

I don't want to see you anymore. Goodbye, Carter. It was only when he heard those words that the blinders had fallen. Yes, it was quick. And yes, such emotion was suspect. But dammit, he loved Abby Carmichael.

If he'd had doubts about that, the sick feeling in his gut spelled out the truth. He had held something fragile and beautiful in his grasp, but he had let it slip away.

For three hours he called her cell, and then the hotel room landline. Eventually, he resorted to storming the Miramar and banging on Abby's door. When the night manager politely asked that he leave, Carter drove to the ranch, momentarily defeated, but not deterred. He paced the floor until 3:00 a.m. After that, he finally slept.

The following morning was Sunday. There was nothing he *had* to do. Nothing but find Abby and tell her the truth. He loved her.

But as it turned out, he had missed his chance. She was gone. Checked out of the hotel. And he'd been the one to send her away. In fact, he had *told* her to go. He was an idiot.

His first instinct was to jump on a plane and follow her, but to what end?

The two of them had been dancing around an ugly truth for days. They had no common ground. Even so, he was a stubborn son of a bitch. He was passionate about Abby, and he refused to believe that love wasn't enough...all evidence to the contrary.

Abby returned to New York with her heart and her composure in shreds. To make matters worse, her mother was already staying at *Bradley's*. When she heard that Abby was home, she offered to come back to the apartment. But Abby declined, keeping her voice light and cheerful.

Life would go on.

The worst part was, she *had* to go back to Royal to film the festival. That was nonnegotiable. Otherwise, all the work she had done already would be wasted.

For five days, she huddled in her bed, crying, staring bleakly at the ceiling. How did anyone survive this kind of heartbreak? Carter was all she thought about.

Eventually, she got angry with herself. There was more to life than sex and love. She would go back to being the same person she had always been.

She showered and dressed and went to a museum. Had lunch at her favorite café. But it didn't help much at all. She *wasn't* the same person. Carter had changed her. He had made her want things. And she didn't know what to do.

Though she stayed out most of the day, there were no answers to be found. Late in the afternoon, she wandered into Central Park and walked the paths aimlessly. It was cloudy. A front had come through, bringing cooler temperatures and a smattering of raindrops.

A few things were clear. First, she had to return to the scene of her heartbreak. Even if she managed to avoid seeing Carter, the journey would be painful.

Second, she *would* finish her documentary. Either with or without the stolen money angle, she would do her very best work, and she would be proud of it.

And last, she had to find some closure. Did that mean confessing her love and watching Carter squirm as he searched for a way to let her down easily? The prospect was depressing. Even if she offered to move to Royal, she didn't think he loved her. How could he? They had been together such a short time.

When her legs were rubbery with exhaustion, she found a bench and sat down to watch children playing kickball on a grassy slope. All around her, the world kept marching on. Even her mother had found love.

Abby sipped her iced coffee and tried to find meaning in her rather colossal personal failure. Was she supposed to learn something from this experience? And if so, what?

People passed her occasionally, following the path. One stopped. "Abby…"

That single word, uttered in a deep masculine voice…

"Carter?" She looked up at him, wondering if she was hallucinating.

When he sat down beside her, the warmth and solidity of his presence convinced her he was real. "I've been looking for you for hours," he said, his tone terse.

She refused to apologize. "You're the one who told me to leave Royal," she said. If the words were snippy, she couldn't be blamed.

He sighed mightily. "You can't possibly know how much I regret that."

The silence between them stretched painfully. Everything she wanted was at her fingertips. But she didn't know how to reach for it…didn't know how to be true to herself and avoid her parents' mistakes.

Carter looked as handsome as ever, although perhaps there were new lines on his face, new shadows in his beautiful blue eyes. She didn't want to make him unhappy. Heck, she didn't want to make herself unhappy.

Did he expect to pull a ring out of his pocket and have her fall into his arms? Or maybe she was assuming too much. He might be here for nothing more than a booty call.

Suddenly, it was more than she could bear. She sprang to her feet. "You shouldn't have come," she said. Despair roiled inside her. She'd spent almost a week trying to forget him. How dare he stir things up all over again? It wasn't fair.

Carter reached out and took her wrist, his fingers warm as they curled against her skin. "I had to come, Abby. We weren't finished."

"Oh, yes," she said. "We were." But she couldn't find the strength to pull away from him. "There's no solution, Carter." That was the hell of it. "I can't see a way forward.

Unless I give up everything. And even then, it would be on the off chance that we might end up with more than a hot and crazy affair."

"Oh, Abs." He closed his eyes and bowed his head, his posture defeated. After long, confusing seconds, he straightened and made her sit down again. He angled his body, so she could see his face. "I love you, sweet woman. And yes, it's for real. I struggled as much as you did. We were both struck by lightning, weren't we? And it left us reeling. But even if it was quick, it wasn't fake. We have to get used to that idea, maybe. But I have time, if you do."

"I don't understand." She was afraid, too afraid to be crushed a second time.

Carter looked as if he had aged in a week. He was haggard, with dark circles beneath his eyes. The handsome cowboy was still there, but he was rough around the edges.

Now he took both of her hands. "I have never felt for any woman what I feel for you, Abby. It's as if we swapped hearts, and yours is beating inside me. When I first saw you that night, I thought you were beautiful and mysterious, and I wanted to know more. By the time we left the bar at the Miramar, you had already staked a claim."

"Love doesn't happen that fast," she whispered.

"Maybe it does." His smile was curiously sweet. "I'm thirty-four years old, Abby. I've made my share of mistakes. But I don't want this to be one of them. Tell me, Abs. Am I on my own here?"

For the first time, she saw the vulnerability deep in his blue-eyed gaze. She found her voice. "I love you, too, Carter. How could I not?"

But even then, her stomach clenched. Love wasn't the problem.

He folded her close against his chest. They had skated perilously close to disaster. He stroked her hair. "You're my heart. I'm sorry I hurt you. That was the last thing I wanted."

In his arms, she was safe. Secure. Loved. But still she felt shaky. There were questions. And hurdles. Did she have the courage to bet all her cards on this one man? What if she gave up everything, and the two of them didn't last? "I'll have to figure a few things out," she said. "But I'll do it."

Carter pulled away, his chiseled jaw hard. "No. This is all on me. And I've already put things in motion."

"In motion?" She frowned at him.

He shrugged. "I've spoken to my family. Told them I'm in love with you. And I've made it clear that Sunset Acres will no longer be my first priority."

She blinked, stunned. "What does that even mean?" Was he proposing a long-distance relationship?

Carter's eyes seemed to be sending her a message, but she was puzzled. "I'll still hold the reins if they want me to," he said. "But we're hiring a manager. My parents and my sister agreed once they understood my position. I'll still have to spend a few days in Royal once a month, but other than that, I'm yours. We'll travel the world, or you can show me New York. Whatever you want."

She put her hands to her cheeks. "But that ranch is you, Carter. You love it."

He shook his head slowly. His gaze locked on hers as if he was willing her to believe. "It's just some cows and dirt. *You*, Abby. It's you I love."

Tears leaked from her eyes. The enormity of what he was saying overwhelmed her. How could a man walk away from a legacy?

He reached in his pocket. First, he handed her an expensive linen handkerchief. It was too pretty to get wet, but she wiped her face anyway.

Then Carter held out a box. "I went to Harry Winston

before I came to find you. That was probably a mistake. I realize that now. I should have let you choose. But I wanted to give you a ring, so you would know I'm serious. We can exchange it."

Was this really happening? In a situation that was impossible, had Carter actually found a way?

Abby flipped the lid. She stopped breathing for a full three seconds. "Oh, Carter." He had bought her an enormous, flawless emerald. The setting was extremely plain, so there was nothing to detract from the magnificence of the stone. It would have cost him a fortune, even by Royal standards.

When she didn't move, he tried to take it back. "You'd rather have a diamond, wouldn't you?"

The dismay on his face galvanized her. She smacked his hand away. When she pulled the ring from the box, a ray of sunlight peeked from behind the clouds, struck the stone and flashed emerald fire in a million directions. She stared at the stone in awe. "Put it on me, please."

Gently, Carter slid the ring onto her left hand. "Marry me, Abby. When the engagement has been long enough. When you're sure."

Her heart quivered with relief and hope and love. "I'm sure, Carter." She cupped his face in her hands. "Maybe you won't believe me, but I'm sure I want to live with you in Texas. Honestly, I do. All my life I've searched for a way to fit in. But then I met you, and I realized I had found home. It doesn't matter if I don't like cows, or I miss Broadway. When I'm with you, I have everything I want."

He shook his head slowly, his expression wary. "We'll talk about this. Marriage is about compromise, or so I've been told. We don't have to make any hard-and-fast decisions today."

She beamed at him. "But you already have. You were ready to give up your family's legacy. That means more to me than you'll ever know." A man who would do that wanted more than sex. He wanted forever, it seemed. The knowledge made her dizzy.

Carter kissed her forehead. "I want you to be happy, Abs. That's the most important thing, I swear. And I'll prove it to you."

"I believe you." She held out her hand and let the sun play with the emerald.

He tucked her in the crook of his arm. "The doorman told me your mother had moved out. And that you were living up there in that apartment all alone. Though he wouldn't give me any clue where to find you, so I'm not exactly on good terms with him."

"George is a sweetie. I'll vouch for you."

Her new fiancé kissed her hard, making her pulse race. "Does that mean I can stay for breakfast?" he asked, his hot gaze locking with hers, making her shiver.

"Oh, yes." Her body heated, already imagining the long night ahead.

They stood in unison, each ready to get on with their new life. Carter tucked his arm around her waist. "I love you, Abby."

"I love you, too."

He pulled back for a moment. "One more thing. I think you may have been right about the festival money. I'm sorry I tried to steer you away."

"Tell me."

He stared at her, started to speak and then kissed her forehead. "Can it wait until tomorrow? We're going to have to go back. But we can hash it out together. Okay?"

"You're really going to keep me in suspense?"

He lifted her hand to his lips and kissed the back of it. "This thing with you and me is brand-new, Abby. And we're here in this romantic city. Let's take one night just for us. Dinner and a show? What do you think?"

She searched his face and knew he was right. The festival secrets would keep. Tonight was a celebration. As she went up on her tiptoes and kissed him, his arms came around her and held her tight. "I love you," she whispered. "And if you don't mind, I think I'd rather spend the evening in bed. It seems like an eternity since we were together."

His eyes blazed with happiness and sexual intent. "I won't argue with that, Abs. Take me to your apartment and have your way with me."

"I thought you'd never ask…"

* * * * *

ONE WEEK TO CLAIM IT ALL

ADRIANA HERRERA

To my mother and my tías: Miguelina,
Yudelka, Patria, Rebeca and Francis.
To me, you will always be the embodiment
of glamour, resilience and fierceness.

One

Esmeralda Sambrano-Peña leaned on the door to the small Washington Heights apartment she shared with her mother and took a moment to catch her breath. She could hear the excited chatter and laughter coming from inside, and the image of her mother and her three aunties holding their weekly get-together brought a tired smile to her face. Her tías and their penchant for neighborhood gossip and salacious jokes always managed to put her in a good mood. And after an extremely long and disappointing day it was comforting to hear familiar voices.

Her smile flagged when she realized she'd have to tell her mother, in front of her tías, that her project had been turned down. Again. Esmeralda sighed and tried to regroup with her body resting against the door. This rejection had hurt more than the others because she'd come so close. The TV series pilot she'd been trying to sell for almost two years had been inches away from actually getting produced. But at the last minute the producers had backed out, claiming the subject matter didn't have wide commercial appeal. Esme let out a frustrated huff as she put the key in the door and pushed it open.

"Hola, Mami!" she called tiredly from the narrow hallway leading to their small living room, while she took off her shoes and hung her jacket on the rack by the door. The apartment wasn't big, but it was enough space for them. Two bedrooms, with a living room and kitchen, on Riverside Drive was real estate gold in New York City. Esme flinched at the memory of how they'd ended up in the apartment she and her mother shared. Thinking about the reasons they'd been forced to move here in the first place still filled her with anger, even ten years later.

"Mija, the tías are here," her mother called loudly, as if Esme wasn't only a few feet away.

She shook her head, a smile tugging at her lips, as she stepped into the living room and found the four older women sprawled on the sectional couch, each with a glass of wine in hand. They were dressed to the nines, as always. To her mother and her aunts, leaving the house without a perfectly put together outfit and full makeup wasn't even an option.

"Ladies." She walked over and dutifully kissed each one on the cheek. They were supposed to be discussing self-help books. But each week the affirmations and book talk lasted about thirty minutes, and the rest of the time was dedicated to downing chilled Moscato and gossiping about the latest news in the neighborhood or back home in the Dominican Republic.

"I see the book conversation is going well," she teased, taking a seat between her mother and her aunt Rebeca.

"What did they say?" Ivelisse asked, ignoring the comment about the neglected books on the coffee table. And of course the mere mention of her production meeting had the rest of the tías perking up. As soon as Esme sat down, she noticed that her mother looked a bit tense. Her usual cheerful expression was tentative, like she was anticipating trouble. She probably suspected Esme's meeting had been a bust.

Esme closed her eyes and shook her head, feeling defeated. "They passed on it." Words of encouragement quickly followed from all directions. Her mom threw an arm around her and her tías all shuffled around so they could pat her on the leg or the arm in an effort to reassure her.

"Their loss, mija. One day those dummies will wise up to your brilliance, and when they do, it'll be too late." Esme opened her eyes to find her tía Rebeca looking thunderous. She had always been Esme's number-one fan. Even back when Esme would make short films on her phone about events in the neighborhood, Rebeca would always sit down and watch, fully focused on her creations. She never hesitated to give her serious feedback.

"Thanks, Tía," Esme said wearily. She was grateful for their love and support. But she was too exhausted to go into the nonsense reasons the producers gave her for passing. "Enough about me. What else is going on— anything exciting happen today?"

To Esme's surprise they didn't push her to share more about her meeting. Instead every one of them shifted their expectant gazes to Esme's mom, who in turn got that look she only had when she was about to hit Esme with a strong dose of the Dominican guilt trip. She braced herself. "Qué pasó, Mami?"

Ivelisse didn't answer immediately, making a show of leaning over to get something that was sitting on the table. The energy in the room changed as soon as Ivelisse grabbed the white envelope. The tías all had their eyes on the piece of paper like it was a ticking bomb. For some reason Esme noticed that the vintage Tank Française watch Ivelisse never took off glinted in the light of the small lamp on the table. The gold Cartier watch had been a gift from Esme's father. And even after everything he'd done, Ivelisse cared for it as if it was a rare treasure. "This came for you today, mija," her mother said, bringing her out of her thoughts.

Esme narrowed her eyes at the name on the upper left corner of the envelope. She recognized it as the attorney who was handling her father's estate. She took it from her mother, noticing it had been slit open. "Mami," she chastised as she pulled the paper out. Ivelisse just lifted a shoulder, not even attempting contrition.

"It's happening tomorrow, Esmeralda."

Her mother didn't have to say what. Esmeralda already knew.

There in large black font at the very top of the expensive stationery were the words FINAL NOTICE. Eleven months and twenty-seven days had passed since her estranged father's death. Since she'd learned that, to the horror of his wife and his other children, he'd left a provision in his will to make Esmeralda the president and CEO of the television studio he'd turned into a billion-dollar empire. His last wish was to leave the daughter he'd barely acknowledged for most of her life at the helm of his company. Esme could still not quite believe it herself, and had done her best to ignore it whenever her mother had tried to show her the notices that had come every month since her father's death. But she hadn't turned it down, either, and now her time to decide was almost up.

Patricio Sambrano had started small in the '70s, producing some radio dramas and news shows in Spanish for the Latinx community in New York City. The shows became an instant sensation, and with the vision that would make him a legend in the entertainment industry, he soon realized what his people wanted was to see their stories on the small screen. He hustled and harnessed old friendships on the island and across the US, and over the next fifteen years he brought Latinx life to American television. He'd been innovative, gutsy, political and unapologetic about showcasing the culture, and the end result had been Sambrano Studios, the first all-Spanish, all-color network in the United States.

Her father built something out of nothing with his ingenuity and raw talent. An Afro-Dominican man with barely a sixth-grade education had done all that. But as sharp as Patricio had been with his business, his personal life had been messy and undisciplined. Esmeralda herself was the result of one of the more chaotic times in Patricio's life. Only weeks after becoming engaged to the daughter of a Dominican financier, he married her—consolidating his ability to expand the studio's interests. It was a bold move that gave him the resources he needed to fully realize his dreams. It had been a surprise for everyone. Especially Esmeralda's mother, who had been in a relationship with Patricio for almost five years and only found out about the wedding when she heard about it on the Sambrano evening news. She'd been pregnant with Esmeralda when she realized that the man she loved had never intended to build a family with her.

When Ivelisse, devastated from his betrayal, finally told Patricio she was expecting, he told her he'd provide financially but he couldn't be a father to any child outside his marriage. And in that, at least, he'd been true to his word.

And then after twenty-nine years of treating her like she didn't exist, her father had overlooked his wife and his legitimate children to hand her the top position at Sambrano. Like that was supposed to make up for a lifetime of feeling like she didn't matter. To erase the humiliation she and her mother had suffered at his hands. The decades of being ignored or receiving messages from third parties because her father couldn't bother to pick up the phone when she called him.

Still, he *had* paid for the education that gave her the foundation to get a start in the industry and gain the experience she needed to run the studio. Because no matter how many times she'd told herself she didn't care what her father thought of her, when choosing a college she picked the University of Southern California because of their film and television program. When deciding on graduate school she went for an MBA with a focus in entertainment. Because she was a fool with daddy issues and despite being invisible to him most of her life, she still yearned for his approval.

But she'd never asked him for a job. And because she was also her mother's daughter, she'd wanted to show him that she didn't need him. She wanted to climb to the very top of his own industry without him. Not once did Esme give her father the satisfaction of hearing her ask for his help. She never thought he'd noticed and yet, his last wish was to entrust her with his legacy. She could do so much as president of Sambrano, but not at the price of selling herself out. Her pride had to be worth something.

And then again, maybe Patricio was just cashing in on the investment he'd made.

"Mi amor, where did you go?" Her mother's soft voice pierced through Esme's tumultuous thoughts. A pang of guilt and anticipation twisted in her gut as she looked at the paper again. It felt heavy in her hands: this could be the door to pursuing the vision she had for the future of Latinx television. But her father had never given her anything that didn't come at a cost, and the price had almost always been her pride. She'd learned long ago to always look for the strings whenever Patricio Sambrano was involved.

"Mami, this is a joke. Just another way for him to put me in my place. His kids and his wife won't stand for it."

Her mother and aunts responded to this with a choir of clucks and shaking heads. Her aunt Yocasta spoke before her mother could. "Mi niña, you know I've never had anything good to say about that cabrón." She didn't have to say who the cabrón was. Yocasta was never shy when it came to cursing Patricio Sambrano's name for the way he'd treated Esme and her mom. "But that baboso wouldn't risk his company to make a point. What he *would* do is go over the head of that bruja he married and put you in charge, if it's what he thought was best for the company."

Even her tía Zenaida, who usually let her three sisters opine while she silently observed, chimed in. "Patricio was always ruthless when it came to his business," she declared, while the others nodded. "If anything, I imagine he'd been keeping an eye on you and your hustle." She leaned over to tug one of Esme's curls, making her smile.

"I hated that jackass, may he rest in peace." At that they all crossed themselves in unison, as if they had not all been cursing the man's name a second ago. Esme would've smiled at their ridiculousness, but she could barely move from the warring emotions coursing through her.

"For better or worse he always put that studio first," Zenaida said, which prompted a flurry of nods from the older women. "If he picked you to be the president and CEO it's because he thought you were right for the job."

"His wife is going to make my life a living hell," Esme said, unable to hide the real wariness in her voice. Carmelina Sambrano was not above humiliating her. But that got Ivelisse's back up.

"She can try, but you can stand up to her," her mother said with a confidence Esmeralda wished she felt. "And besides, you'll be in charge."

"I don't know, Mami." She hated that even thinking of being rejected by her father's wife and children made her feel small.

Ivelisse made another clucking noise and pulled Esme closer. "Screw them. Go in there tomorrow and claim your place. Use them and this opportunity to do all the things you've been wanting to do but haven't gotten the chance to."

Esme's chest fluttered with an ember of hope and longing at her mother's words. Ivelisse was right, she'd been killing herself for the past five years—trying and failing to get her projects off the ground, but she could not get a break. Because her ideas weren't "commercial" enough, or relatable to the "mainstream" audience. She was tired of getting doors shut in her face because she refused to compromise. As head of Sambrano Studios she could make her dream come to life. Put shows out there that reflected all the faces of Latinx culture.

If she wasn't pushed out by Carmelina first.

"Mami, that woman is never going to let me stay. And I don't want to sink to her level." Ivelisse had been a wonderful mother, gentle and kind, but she was a fighter when it counted, and the mention of her old foe lit a fire behind her eyes.

"Carmelina won't know how to fight you, baby. That woman has never done a day of work in her life. When you go in there—smart, competent, full of fresh ideas— that board won't know what hit them." That ember was now a tiny flame fueled by the faith Esme's mother had in her. Still, she'd learned the hard way not to trust anything that came from her father.

"But won't the board have someone picked out already? Someone that doesn't come with the drama that I will certainly cause?"

Her mother averted her eyes at her question and *that* gave Esme pause. "Mami?" she asked wearily as she scanned the paper in her hands again, looking for whatever her mother wasn't saying. And when she got to the very last paragraph she understood. Her body flashed hot and cold, just from reading that name. There in black and white was the last push she needed to jump right into an ocean of bad decisions.

"Him?" she asked tersely, and from the corner of her eye she saw her mother flinch.

Rodrigo Almanzar, her father's protégé and the person who for years had been the only tie she had to Patricio. The man she'd given her heart and her body to only to have him betray her when she needed him most. The man whose very name could still make her ache with longing and tremble with fury. How could it still hurt so much after all this time?

She felt tired. Tired of this damn thing hanging over her head. Tired of all the complicated feelings she had about everything having to do with Sambrano Studios. Especially when it came to the tall, brawny, arrogant bastard who was probably hoping she'd do the very thing she'd been considering. Let her pride and her baggage make her decision for her.

And she might have, if *he* wasn't the one who'd end up as president and CEO. She wouldn't do it out of greed, or even to appease her mother, but she would do it out of spite. Rodrigo had betrayed her just so he could continue as her father's lapdog. Now she'd take the thing he'd sold his soul for…just when he thought he finally had it.

"Actually," she said, standing up, already feeling the fire in her gut that usually preceded her doing ill-advised things. "You're right." The four women in her living room were all looking at her with varying degrees of anticipation. "I've been saying for years that if given the chance to shoot my shot I wouldn't hesitate to take it. This isn't exactly how I'd hoped to get it, but now that I do, I'm not wasting it. Tomorrow, Sambrano will get its new president and CEO."

Her mother eyed Esme with suspicion, probably guessing what had been the deciding factor for her change of heart, while her aunt Yocasta crowed with delight, "Ay, Ivelisse, what I wouldn't give to see the look on Carmelina's face when Esme walks into that boardroom tomorrow."

Esme smiled wryly at her aunt, but her mind was already racing toward the other shocked face she was looking forward to seeing.

TWO

This is bittersweet, Rodrigo Almanzar thought as he smoothed a hand over his Hermès tie and the jacket of the slate Brioni suit he'd ordered special for this day. Finally taking the helm of the company he'd been working for since he was sixteen years old warranted splurging fifty grand. Even if this wasn't how he'd envisioned things happening.

He wished him taking the job at the head of Sambrano Studios didn't come as a result of losing Patricio. A flash of grief, and the usual tangle of emotions that his old mentor evoked in him, dulled the electric anticipation he'd been feeling all week. Patricio had been more than his mentor; he'd been his dad's best friend and his family's savior once upon a time. The man had taught Rodrigo everything he knew about the business he loved. Patricio had many shortcomings, and over the years the things Rodrigo had seen him do bordered on outright cruelty. But even when Patricio seemed to be hell-bent on alienating everyone in his life, his bond with Rodrigo had remained strong.

Well, there had been that one night. The moment when Rodrigo had bartered with everything he had, and he'd gotten what he wanted. Then lost everything anyways.

Yeah, no matter what the gossips liked to say about Rodrigo's "special treatment" from Patricio, the man had never pulled his punches. When he was in one of his moods, anyone could get the brunt of it. But Rodrigo had learned how to maneuver the older man, and even when he knew he should've quit, his loyalty had kept him working for Sambrano. Even after it had cost Rodrigo the woman he loved. *Loyal to a fault*, his mother had always said, and maybe when it came to Patricio it was true.

One night in those last days, when the once tall and powerful man had been emaciated by illness, he'd confessed that Rodrigo reminded him of himself. That he'd turned into the kind of man he'd wished he could've been. Rodrigo shook his head, dismissing that, but Patricio's eyes had been full of affection and pride. The same affection and pride that had kept Rodrigo tethered to his desk even when he'd hated the things Patricio had done. When staying in this company really felt like it had cost Rodrigo his soul.

And that line of thinking brought him right to the one person he'd been avoiding thinking about for days. For weeks, really. Since the estate executor had made the last attempt to contact Esmeralda Sambrano-Peña to ask if she would be honoring her father's last wishes and taking over Sambrano Studios. Rodrigo didn't believe in skirting the rules, even when there was good reason. But after twelve months of having the executor's calls ignored he figured that was answer enough. No matter how much he wanted to officially be named president and CEO, he'd done his due diligence. And today no one could say he had manipulated the circumstances. Hell, he'd gone out of his way to make sure Esmeralda got the chance to claim the position.

After wrangling with the likes of Carmelina Sambrano for the past year Rodrigo was more certain than ever that he needed to be in charge. Esmeralda didn't have the temperament to deal with that viper and her pack of cronies. Patricio's widow would be waiting in the wings for her to fail so she could take her late husband's life's work and sell it for pieces to the highest bidder. No, sweet and soft-spoken Esmeralda would not be up for the dogfight this was going to be.

He cleared his throat as he looked around the room. Sambrano's headquarters in Midtown Manhattan were housed in an Art Deco building from the 1920s. Patricio had all the original moldings and wood painstakingly restored, but this boardroom was the crown jewel of the executive floor. A massive space overlooking Central Park. The walls were all done in wood paneling that gave the room a warm feel, even if the meetings as of late had been anything but. The showpiece in the room was the table, a hundred-year-old behemoth that sat twenty-four people. It was a perfect solid oak oval, with an Italian rose marble top. Patricio had acquired it at an estate sale in the '70s on a whim and kept it in storage until he grew his business enough to display it. It was ostentatious now, but when Patricio had purchased it, the studio only getting off the ground, it must have seemed reck-lessly arrogant. But his mentor had made good on the promise of that table. He'd built an empire befitting its grandeur, and Rodrigo would be damned if he let it all be laid to waste by his family's greed.

The sumptuous burgundy leather chairs were occu-pied by all ten members of the Sambrano Studios ex-ecutive board, in addition to Carmelina and her two children, Perla and Onyx. As vicious as Carmelina was when it came to her husband's money, her children didn't seem to care in the slightest what happened to their fam-ily legacy. Perla seemed perennially preoccupied with her travel plans and not much else and as for Onyx…he only remembered the studio existed when he needed it to get invitations to celebrity parties.

Useless. All of them.

But that was just fine. Rodrigo would be in charge, and he knew what he needed to do, had been meticu-lously planning it for years—with Esmeralda as a no-show it seemed the one snag had been smoothed out. He got to his feet, suddenly feeling the urgency of get-ting the meeting going. In theory Patricio's heiress had another hour to claim her place, but by the time they got to that part of the agenda they would be well past the window.

"Ladies and gentlemen." He made sure to project his voice and it resounded across the room. Soon even Perla and Onyx were peeling their eyes off their phones and turning their attention to Rodrigo. "Thank you for com-ing today. I can't say that this isn't bittersweet."

Rodrigo stopped to take a breath, surprised by the wave of emotion tightening his chest. "Patricio was like a father to me…" He ignored what sounded like a scoff coming from the direction where Carmelina was sitting and focused on the people in the room that, like him, were concerned with not seeing a lifetime of work be flushed down the drain. "And he has left enormous shoes to fill. I couldn't be prouder to officially take the helm of Sambrano and hope that together we can create a future for the studio that he would be proud of."

His pulse quickened as the words he'd just uttered sank in. This was really happening. Sixteen years of working tirelessly, of sacrificing his personal life for this company, was paying off with what had always been his goal: being president and CEO of Sambrano Studios. He might not have the last name, but he'd given everything to this company, and now he would be the one to take it into the future.

Some of the people in this room—hell, people all over the industry—loved to whisper about "the forbidding" next-in-line at Sambrano. Joked that Patricio had Rodrigo's emotions surgically removed before giving him the chief content officer position. But Rodrigo let that slide right off his Brioni-clad shoulders. They talked because he'd persevered, had triumphed when so many others failed. He'd been the youngest CCO in the industry eight years ago when he got the position, and when he took over as interim CEO—after Patricio's illness had forced him to step down a year ago—he'd become one of the highest-paid Latinos in all of entertainment. He was a millionaire dozens of times over in his own right, and now was head of a billion-dollar company.

They hated him because they wanted to be where he was. And he would not apologize for how he'd gotten here.

"Sambrano has always been unique in the business

and my plan is to continue that tradition," he continued, and was pleased to hear sounds of approval from some in the room. Others remained silent. Then again this was a contentious line of conversation. The topic of what direction Sambrano would take in the next decade had been hotly contested. Some wanted to keep things as they were and others wanted to think more innovatively, to be more competitive in this new era of streaming and global programming. One more challenge he'd had to tackle immediately.

The voices around the room were interrupted when the door to the boardroom suddenly burst open. The entrance was off to the right, beyond Rodrigo's range of vision, but the varying looks of shock from those facing the door gave him an inkling of who it was before he turned around.

"Sorry I'm late. The trains uptown were a mess today." The various surprised gasps, and in Carmelina's case, something very close to a roar, went a long way to confirm the newcomer's identity. Ten years was not such a long time that he wouldn't remember the voice of the person who had meant the most to him at one time in his life. The only person that elicited regret in him. The self-confidence was new, but he'd recognize Esmeralda's raspy tone anywhere. He'd always thought she sounded like she was hoarse from laughing too hard or singing too loud. She didn't sound like she was laughing now.

By the time he turned, she was already in front of him. This was not the twenty-one-year-old girl he'd last seen the summer Patricio broke his daughter's heart— and him, too; Rodrigo had broken her heart, too. She'd been beautiful back then. Always too beautiful for him to resist. With her lavish curls that fell around her shoulders in a palette of brown and gold, and that flawless skin, like Dominican mahogany. But her eyes had always been his perdition, those big hazel orbs that always saw a little too much. He'd made mistakes with this woman that would haunt him for the rest of his life. Too many to rehash right now, especially when her arrival was about to wreak havoc on his carefully laid plans.

This was not the unsure, sensitive girl he fell for all those years ago. The one who had looked at him like he was the man of her dreams. The one whose soft body he'd lost himself in again and again. The woman standing here exuded confidence and at the moment was staring at him with open hostility. This Esmeralda was self-possessed, and she knew exactly the effect she was having on him.

"Rodrigo."

He'd never known one word could carry with it so much disdain, and that was a good reminder he had to snap out of it and get his head in the game. He had a history with Esmeralda Sambrano-Peña, but he could not let that cloud his judgment. He'd once let his feelings for her almost ruin his career, and he would not make the same mistake again. No matter how much her presence rattled him. He should have expected this. Seeing her had been a possibility hanging over his head since nearly a year ago, when the executor of Patricio's will gathered them all in this same room and dropped the bomb of the century on them.

And yet, his reaction to her still caught him by surprise. Every instinct he had incited him to get closer. But as he took her in, the defiant eyes, the determined set of her mouth, he at least saw things clearly. He could not underestimate this woman, not if he wanted to keep those three letters attached to his name.

"Started without me, I see," she said, trying to provoke him. Sarcasm dripped from her every word. Her full mouth set in a hard line. Her eyes, which in the past had looked at him with such adoration, now cool and distant. As if she could see right through him. She'd come dressed to kill today. Her black suit fit her like a glove, and even now, when he suspected her arrival was about to upend everything, he could not help but notice the luscious curves of her body.

In the past ten years Rodrigo had told himself a million times he could handle her disdain. That he'd made the right decision in letting her go. That if she hated him for it, it had been worth it, for both their sakes. But now, after just a mere moment of having her back in his space, he knew he'd been lying to himself all along. The truth was that he had a weakness for Esmeralda. And men like him could not afford to be ruled by their vulnerabilities. His father had been like that, unable to keep himself in check, undisciplined, and it had cost their family everything. Rodrigo had promised himself years ago he would never follow in those footsteps. Rodrigo did not allow his passions to rule his head, even if it meant appearing ruthless to the one person in the world he never wanted to hurt. He'd done it once before. It had almost killed him, but he'd survived, and now he'd do it again if that was what it took.

"I never took you for one for theatrics, Esmeralda." He sounded like an absolute bastard, but it had to be done. This was not a game, and if Esme wanted this position, he would treat her like he would any competitor.

Her head snapped in his direction at the sound of his

voice, and when her gaze landed on him again her expression went from cold to mutinous. Esmeralda had not let bygones be bygones, it seemed. All the better to keep himself in check. And if his stomach lurched and his blood rushed between his temples with a roar, well, that was just frustration at having his plans disrupted. Nothing more.

Rodrigo had learned the hard way not to let emotions creep into his professional life. And that was what this was for him, his job, not some family drama. Carmelina and her children, even Esmeralda, could throw tantrums now, but Rodrigo could not afford outbursts. And he certainly could not spend another second fixating on Esmeralda's mobile, generous mouth and all the ways he knew she could use it to undo him.

She waved a hand at him and turned to the seat he'd just emptied. "So testy, Rodrigo." She clicked her tongue, as derision dripped from every word out of her mouth. "You're all in your feelings because I came to ruin your coronation? I guess it didn't occur to anyone that I might actually be up for taking this job." Her tone could melt the paint off the walls, but he would not take that bait.

"That's okay," she goaded, turning to Carmelina Sambrano, who was practically vibrating in her seat at the far end of the table. "I'm happy to fill everyone in, as soon as I officially assume my position as president and CEO." With that she went to the head of the table, the very seat Rodrigo had been about to occupy, and sat down.

"Are you people going to let this travesty happen?" The widow's cry of unbridled outrage reminded Rodrigo there were other people in the room. And he'd had just about enough of the Sambranos and their need to turn *everything* into a telenovela. He stepped up to Esme, determined to get this farce under control. He'd had to put up with this for sixteen years. The Sambranos and their chaos. Their backbiting and their drama. As if this was all about them, like there weren't thousands of workers depending on the people in this room for their livelihoods. He had no idea what game Esmeralda was playing at, but he was not putting up with any of this.

"Esmeralda, what the hell do you think you're doing?"

For a second her mask slipped. For a moment shorter than the blink of an eye he saw that the way he spoke to her surprised her. And he almost hesitated, ensnared by the urge to soothe her. To fix this for Esmeralda. But he reminded himself that was not his job. "You have to know this isn't appropriate," he ground out, forcing himself to keep an even tone. "That there are timelines. There are *procedures*. You don't understand—"

"No," she said, curtly lifting herself from the seat she'd just commandeered. "*You* don't understand." She was standing so close he could see a tiny bead of perspiration gather between her breasts, and he hated himself for the throb of lust that coursed through him. "I'm taking my position as president and CEO of Sambrano and if that affects your or anyone else's plans…" That she directed at her half-siblings, who were still sitting, mouths gaping. "That's your problem, *not mine*. Now, where in the agenda were we?" With that she placidly sat down, leaving him there like a six-foot-two-inch-tall office ornament.

That arrogance, it should've incensed him. But, dammit, instead a wave of raw need almost made him stumble. His hands itched to touch her, to take that mouth and find out if it still tasted as sweet as he remembered. But he smothered that urge down to ashes. This was what he excelled at, after all. Locking down and repressing every emotion. In the last days of her illness, his mother told him he'd lost himself to this job, that she didn't recognize the man he'd become. And it would've hurt if it wasn't the truth, but Rodrigo long ago had understood that denying reality was harder work than just learning to live with it.

"I don't plan to lose this game, Esmeralda. I'm sure you've learned a lot about the industry scouting film locations." The loathing in her eyes would have made a lesser man cower, but Rodrigo thrived in moments like this. "There's a very long distance between thinking you know how to do something and actually doing it, and *I* know *everything* about this company."

He saw the moment that self-doubt crept in, when his words started edging out the confidence she'd walked in with. But like he'd told himself over and over again, that was not his problem. He'd been preparing for this moment his whole professional life and he would be damned if he let it slip away now. No matter how much Esmeralda Sambrano-Peña got under his skin.

Three

Keep it together, Esmeralda. You can handle this.

That was the mantra that had been going through her head since the moment she stepped through Sambrano Studios' front doors. She'd known what would happen in the boardroom would be intimidating. She'd even expected it to be outright confrontational. But what she hadn't expected was how unsettling it would be to be in this building and not have Rodrigo on her side. In the rare occasions over the years when Esme had been forced to come see her father, Rodrigo had always made a point of being there for her.

Arturo, Rodrigo's father, had been a good friend of Esme's mother. No, Arturo had been more than a friend—he'd stood up for Ivelisse when Carmelina made up lies about her. When Carmelina tried to push Esme out of the picture, Arturo had been her champion. And when Arturo was gone, Rodrigo took on that role. For years he was her only channel of communication to Patricio Sambrano. He'd been her rock for a long time, and then he'd been her lover. Her first everything, and he'd thrown it all away, out of his misguided loyalty to her father.

She breathed through pain that cut off the air in her lungs as she considered him. She hated that his betrayal still hurt her. And she despised that even after everything that happened between them she still wanted him. She didn't attempt to hide that she was looking at him. More than looking, she was inspecting him from head to toe. He was still heart-stoppingly handsome with that bronzed skin that seemed almost lit from within. The rough, coarse curls that he kept austerely short, and placated with exacting care. His full, generous lips were in a terse, unhappy line, and she wanted more than anything to press her mouth to them. Dark eyes to match his mood, and still she could see there was more than anger in those chocolate-brown depths, glints of desire that he couldn't hide from her. But she tamped that thought down mercilessly and focused on Rodrigo's not-so-charming attributes. Like his fastidiousness about his appearance. She could almost bet the suit he was wearing had been reserved for this day months in advance.

To all the world Rodrigo Almanzar was the unfeeling, ambitious television wunderkind. But she knew that behind all that stoic demeanor the man she'd loved was a little vain about that tall, imposing body. And she couldn't deny that he'd worked very hard for it. He'd been a point guard in high school and college. Esmeralda had gone to see him play with her mother, who had been his mom's best friend. She'd loved him then, too, but it was a different kind of love. She'd looked up to him, admired how he'd been able to balance working and going to school. That he supported his mother when Arturo gambled away everything they had. And after, when she was in college and he was fresh out of grad school and working full-time for her dad, it had turned into something different. But that happiness had been fleeting and in the end he'd broken her heart.

And that was the one thing she could not forget today—how ruthless Rodrigo could be. How on the day she'd learned her father had evicted her mother from the apartment Esme had lived in all her life, instead of helping, Rodrigo told her he could not afford distractions, and she—their relationship—was a distraction. And that was why she would never forgive him.

She opened her mouth to let him know in no uncertain terms she would not falter in taking this job from him—that she'd also learned to be merciless—when someone called her name from the other side of the room.

"Esmeralda. Turn around and look at me." She hadn't seen or heard from Carmelina Sambrano in a very long time, but the woman's voice was not one she'd ever forget. Esmeralda took a moment as she fought to keep the mask of impassive disdain she'd been wearing from slipping off. To keep from letting Carmelina's words get to her. She knew the woman was vicious and would not hesitate to humiliate her. The bastard child Carmelina had tried to erase from Patricio's life for almost thirty years was now here threatening everything she held dear. But Carmelina could rage at her, call her names and make a scene. It would not change the contents of Patricio's will.

"I'm happy to turn around," Esmeralda drawled as

she moved to face her father's widow. "I want you to take a good look at me, Carmelina. You've worked so hard at pretending I don't exist, you may have started believing it. But it's going to be a little hard to ignore me now, isn't it?"

Her father's widow inhaled sharply, her platinum updo bobbing as the woman clearly scrambled for control. "You will not get away with this," Carmelina hissed through clenched teeth.

"We'll just have to see, won't we?" She knew she was pushing the older woman, could see in her eyes she was on the verge of exploding, but Esmeralda had put up with too much over the years to back down. "Things are going to be a little different from now on."

For an instant she thought she saw a glimmer of something like pride in Rodrigo's eyes. Bolstered by the knowledge that Carmelina had no power over her, Esme ran a hand over the black tailored pantsuit she'd worn. She looked down at the Gucci stilettos on her feet, from the outlet in Peekskill, but, hey, they still made her look like a million bucks. She might have never been in the bosom of the Sambrano family, but she could play the part if she had to. Her mother had made sure of that.

She felt the weight of every eye in the room trained in her direction. "So," she said to no one in particular. "How are we going to do this?"

Despite having never been inside this boardroom before, she knew every person around the table. Not just because it was her father's company, but because Sambrano's board was made up of a who's who of the biggest Latinx names in the business. And then there were the ones sitting here because of their *last name*. Perla and Onyx Sambrano. She hadn't seen them in person since they were kids, and yet from the first glance she could see so much of herself in their faces. The same nose and thick eyebrows. Perla even had the smatter of freckles on the apple of her cheeks Esme had.

"Miss Sambrano."

Esmeralda's gaze shifted to the source of a new person trying to catch her attention. She recognized Octavio Nuñez the moment she laid eyes on him. The man had been an institution in Spanish television for decades. He'd started at the studio not long after the network began broadcasting nationally. He'd been the first Spanish-speaking evening news anchor in American television history. And now he was on the board of Sambrano—the chair of the board to be exact. He was also Carmelina's cousin and Esme had no idea what to expect from him.

"Sambrano-Peña" she clarified as she held her head up, eyes focused on the man who had stood up to address her. His expression was guarded—not friendly, but not contentious, either. She wanted to shift her gaze to Carmelina and see how *she* was looking at her cousin. Esmeralda shifted uncomfortably as the man studied her, unsure what to expect, when she heard a whisper from behind her.

"They hate each other. Octavio's on whatever side Carmelina isn't."

Rodrigo.

Esmeralda dipped her head, acknowledging what he'd said, but didn't respond. Octavio was speaking again. "Welcome. This is a surprise. After all our attempts to contact you went unanswered the board assumed you weren't interested."

Carmelina made an attempt to get up, but something

held her back. And then Esme noticed Perla's hand on her mother's arm. Octavio did not spare his cousin a glance, his attention on Esmeralda. He pointed at the chair that she'd gotten up from in a gesture that she sit down.

"Your father's wish to have you assume the role of president and CEO of the studio was a surprise to all of us." There were some sounds of agreement around the table. Some of them even sounded like encouraging ones. "You *are* young," he said, but his expression was not unkind. "However, your experience in television and film is impressive." This time Octavio did send a look toward Carmelina. A withering one. "It's hardly a secret that in the last few years Patricio didn't see eye to eye with the board on a few things, but for the most part we're all invested in doing what's best for Sambrano." Rodrigo had been right—there was no love lost between those two, not if the vicious glares they directed at each other were any indication.

"That being said…" The throat clearing from most of the people around the table told her the other shoe was about to drop. "Your father gave the board the liberty to make some stipulations around how to assess if you are the right person for the job." Esmeralda could hear the hesitation in Octavio's voice and dread sank through her like a ball of lead. Whatever those "stipulations" were, she would not enjoy them. "And there's something else. Patricio asked that his personal stake in Sambrano Studios—twenty-five percent of the total shares to be exact—be held in a trust until you decided to comply with his wishes."

"What does that mean?" she asked in confusion, no longer caring about how she sounded or looked. She was out of her depth, and everyone in this room probably realized it.

Octavio gave her a reassuring smile and picked up a folder, which he slid toward her. "That means that you are now the owner of twenty-five percent of Sambrano Studios. Fifty percent is held by your siblings and Mrs. Sambrano holds the remaining shares." Esmeralda was glad she was already sitting down because if she weren't she would've probably been knocked on her ass. This was a billion-dollar company; those shares had to be worth hundreds of millions. And right after that thought, it dawned on her that of course her father would only give those shares to her if she complied with what he wanted. Because nothing was ever free with Patricio.

Awful as that was, the shares still gave her some leverage, and she'd take it. Another round of throat clearing erupted and Esme noticed that by now, Perla was almost forcibly keeping her mother in her seat. But Carmelina's mouth was working fine.

"This is outrageous. Someone must have influenced Patricio. He was not in his right mind at the end. This is the only explanation!" she yelled, pounding her small fist on the table. "She has nothing to do with Sambrano! You can't do this. I'm trying to protect my children's rightful legacy! I will not allow this imposter to be the face of my husband's company." Carmelina's mouth was twisted into an ugly sneer as she yelled. "I'd rather see it burn to the ground than let you sit in that office."

Esme's heart hammered in her chest and her stomach churned at the loathing dripping from every word Carmelina uttered. The woman had always despised her. Even when Esmeralda was only a child she'd gone out of her way to be cruel. On the few occasions she'd been invited to her father's house, Carmelina had made her life miserable until her mother had stopped sending her altogether. But Esme was not that little girl anymore, and she was not letting her father's widow take one more thing from her. So she leaned in, both hands on the table, and spoke directly to the woman who had caused her and her mother so much pain.

"It's not up to you. They're *my* father's wishes." Carmelina twisted her mouth at the mention of Esme's parentage. "I didn't ask to be his child any more than your children did, and yet here I am. So, we're just all going to learn to live with the fact that I'm now part of Sambrano Studios. Whether you like it or not, this is *my* legacy, too." Esme didn't miss the looks of approval she saw on some of the faces in the room as she leaned back. "Mr. Nuñez, you were saying?" She made sure she sounded placid and unbothered.

Octavio seemed to appreciate her approach. "Like I was saying, we're happy to see you appointed as president and CEO if we determine you are the best person for the job." He looked to Rodrigo, who Esme noticed sat up for whatever was coming next. "Here is how it's going to go. You have one week to present a five-year strategic plan for the studio. A week from today, we will meet here again."

Esme's skin prickled with excitement even as she wondered how she'd be able to pull that off in one week. It took her months to prepare her pitch for her pilot and now she would have to deliver a strategic plan for an entire network that had dozens of programming tracks in just seven days?

She squared her shoulders at the challenge, her head

high, knowing this was part of the test. If she complained, if she asked the board for more time, it would count against her. And now she had something to prove.

"I can do that," she assured the man.

"Excellent." Octavio certainly did not seem like a foe now, and she could use a friend or two in her corner.

"I'll need a space to work and access to the archives and programming schedule. I'll also need to receive briefings from each production studio." Blood rushed to her ears as her mind raced with all the things she needed to prepare. "Including film. I know they're on the West Coast, but we'll need to set up a conference call with the different heads of departments." She pulled out her phone to make some notes and stood up, ready to get started.

"Esmeralda." Her head snapped up at the tone in Octavio's voice; something about the way he called her name made the hairs on the back of her neck stand up. "Rodrigo Almanzar, who has served as interim CEO for the past year and was our CCO for almost eight years prior to that, will be your go-to person as you prepare. He will also be consulting with you on the content we'd like to see."

No. No. *No.*

Her body ran hot and cold at that piece of news. This was it. The reason why Octavio had been all pleasant and calm about all this. They never intended her to take the position. This was all theatrics. They'd pretend they were giving her a chance while Rodrigo tripped her up every step of the way. This was the board covering their asses before they shut her out. *Of course* Rodrigo would help them do this to her; the board probably hatched this plan the moment they learned about Patricio's will.

She fisted her hands, struggling to suffuse the hurt and anger boiling within her.

This was how it was in the boardroom. Low down dirty tricks and backstabbing. They expected her to tuck her tail between their legs and thank them for setting her up to fail. Well, she would show them. "If that's what the board wishes." Her voice was as cold as she could make it, and when she turned to Rodrigo she could hardly see him through her narrowed eyes. "I'm sure Mr. Almanzar will do his duty. He always does. No matter the consequences." She infused that with as much venom as she could, but it seemed he was not taking the bait.

"You can call me Rodrigo, Esmeralda." He was next to her, so close that she could swear she felt the heat radiating from him body.

"Only my friends call me Esmeralda, and you're not my friend," she said, before turning away.

Octavio cleared his throat, looking uncomfortable. "We trust that Rodrigo will do what is best for the studio." The finality in the man's voice told her there was no point in arguing. This was what she had to work with.

She turned her gaze to her former lover. His mouth was in that mutinous line again but she could see the hurt in his eyes. Her words had put it there. She dearly wished she didn't react to that knowledge. But more than anything, she wished that Rodrigo Almanzar was not who she would need to work with on this. Because beyond anything he was planning to do, her own feelings for him were her biggest liability.

She willed herself to feel nothing as she looked around the boardroom again, her eyes never stopping, not even on Carmelina's smug face. "I'll get to work then. I will see you all here in a week."

With that she strode out of the boardroom, Rodrigo hot on her heels. But if Esmeralda had learned one lesson from her mother it was that when life gave you lemons you made lemonade. She vowed to herself the next time she walked out of this room, she would be the new president and CEO of Sambrano Studios.

Four

Rodrigo followed Esmeralda out of the boardroom, his mind reeling from what had gone down in there. He'd had no idea this was the board's plan. Octavio had not been dead set against Patricio's request, but some in the board were furious about it. They'd told him they were going to activate a contingency plan in the event she actually showed up. This was the brilliant idea they'd come up with? Forcing him to be the one to walk her through this fiasco and take the brunt of her anger when things went sideways? Because she would mostly likely fail. Having industry experience did not translate to having the know-how to manage a billion-dollar studio.

And he would not pull punches when it came down to it.

And where the hell was she going?

"Esmeralda, wait," he called as she made a beeline away from the boardroom. "We need to talk."

"I need a minute, Rodrigo." She still wasn't facing him, but he could hear the tension in her shaky voice. His protective instincts immediately kicked in, urging him to reach for her. He'd always had a hard time keeping his head in the game when it came to this woman. Which was why over the next week he'd have to remind himself as much as necessary that Esmeralda was his competition. Just from those few minutes in the boardroom he knew it would be a grave mistake to not take her seriously.

Not that he had ever thought Esmeralda was anything but brilliant. But what she'd done today, that took guts. To walk into that boardroom and claim her place had to have been terrifying, but she'd done it and held her own. He respected that. And even now, when it felt like the stress of it all was enough to make him snap in two, it was hard to ignore the pulse of desire. And this was absolutely not the moment for any of that.

"Joya, espera." As he expected, that stopped her in her tracks. She turned on him, those leonine eyes flashing with fury.

"You don't get to call me that anymore, Rodrigo Almanzar." Her mouth was pursed, nostrils flaring as she glared at him.

It had been a low blow, he knew that, to use the nickname he used to call her all those years ago, when against his better judgment he'd gotten involved with Esmeralda. No, *involved* made it seem like it had been a fling, something that had run its course after a time. When in fact it had been earth-shattering, all-consuming, the thing that brought him almost to the brink of losing everything. But that was what she'd been: his jewel.

Patricio Sambrano had named his children after precious stones. Esmeralda, Onyx, Perla. And Esme *was* the first jewel in her father's life. But Patricio never knew how to care for her the way she deserved. He'd never been able to appreciate the gem he'd been given. But Rodrigo had. He'd loved her as a kid, been protective of her. Of the child who lived in the shadows of her father's life. And then he'd loved her as a woman, who even at twenty had had a clear sense of who she was. Ten years of hustling for a dream that seemed to stay constantly out of her reach had not dimmed her light. If anything, at thirty she shone even brighter.

At the moment the light in Esme's eyes was not warm, it was mutinous. He gestured to one of the small workrooms that were scattered around the studio. Private offices where the staff who worked in cubes could have a conference call or work on more sensitive material without disrupting others. "Let's talk in here." He would've taken her to his office, but since that was the office she was here gunning for, he figured they'd stay in neutral territory.

She wasn't moving, her feet firmly planted on the ground. "I'm not going anywhere with you." She pointed in the direction they'd both come from, her face pinched with fury. "You set all that up."

He considered her for a moment. The stubborn set of her shoulders, the defiant look in her eyes. Just beyond that there was a small quiver of lips, and a brittleness to her demeanor that told him this was getting to her. And if she was anyone else, he'd go in for the kill. He'd begin listing every reason why she would fail. How unprepared she was. But this *was* Esmeralda.

"I had no idea this was what they were planning." From her expression it was clear she didn't believe him, and he wished that didn't sting as much as it did. "Despite how you or the rest of the world may feel about me, I don't actually spend my day scheming about how to steal this company."

"You have no idea how I feel about anything," she said coldly, before turning on her heel and heading into one of the offices. His eyes instantly drifted to the curve of her waist and the swell of her backside as he walked in after her and closed the door.

Her smell filled the space. The same spicy fragrance of lemongrass and ginger that she'd been using for years. This was going to be an absolute fiasco, but not in the way Esmeralda thought. He was the problem, *his reaction to her* was the issue.

"I know you're angry, but you won't win by letting your emotions get to you."

She scoffed at that, but he ignored it. "And I resent the implication that I would play dirty. I would never stab you in the back like that, Esmeralda. You know—"

"What do I know?" she demanded, her expression thunderous. "That after you promised me a thousand times that you had my back, you cut me loose in a second? That in the end you chose him?" Her voice broke just the smallest bit on the last word—*him*.

He knew this was coming, but it still felt like a blow to his solar plexus, every ounce of oxygen escaping his lungs at once. He wanted to tell her the truth, explain how things had gone so terribly wrong that weekend so long ago. How Patricio had fallen for Carmelina's lies and scheming.

"I never—"

The anger and frustration coursing through him felt

like molten lava in his veins, the need to tell her the truth almost shattering his self-control. But he couldn't. He swore he would never speak of how things went down, not even to defend himself from Esmeralda's loathing. What was the use? After all these years finally telling Esmeralda what really happened would only make things worse. Minutes, merely minutes of having her back in his life and the cold and controlled demeanor he was known for was tearing at his seams.

And yet, instead of leaving this room, going somewhere he could get himself together, he moved toward her.

His nostrils flared, body tight with the need to touch her. To see if his caress still affected her like it used to. If his hands on her hair, his mouth on hers still made her melt. But that was not what they were to each other anymore. That part of them had been irrevocably broken. He'd thrown away his chance to have her like that.

"We can keep this professional. I want to be CEO of Sambrano Studios. I've worked for it. I even think I deserve it."

She opened her mouth to speak, but whatever she saw on his face made her pause. "But despite his faults, I respected your father and I would never interfere with his wishes. If you're the best person for the job, I won't stand in your way, but I won't give it to you, either." His back molars clenched, from the need to soothe the hurt he saw in her eyes from his words. "As a matter of fact, be prepared to fight like hell, because that's what I plan to do." No matter how much Esmeralda got to him, and she clearly could still undo him, he would not back down from this.

"I don't need you to give me anything." She practically spat out the words. "And I plan to fight for this, too."

She'd come closer with every word, and now they were only inches apart. He still towered over her. She was only a few inches above five feet, but what she lacked in stature she'd always more than made up for in personality.

"Oh, that I'm very clear on," he said bitterly. She'd turned down every attempt he'd made to reach out to her over the years. Rejected every effort from her father or him to help her get ahead in the industry. She was determined to make a name for herself on her own. And now she was here, ready to claim her place and he knew she would fight to the death for it. His Joya was a warrior. And he would really need to figure out a way to stop thinking of her as his. But how was he supposed to do that when everything in him wanted to possess her? To take her in his arms and show her that he'd never stopped wanting her?

"You were always much better than I was at not letting your passions get the best of you. But I've learned," she assured him.

He couldn't contain the caustic laugh that escaped him. "Except when it came to you. I always forgot myself when I was with you."

"You have a funny way of showing it, Rodrigo." Her eyes narrowed again, and she leaned in so their bodies were practically touching and he had to fist his hands to keep from bringing her against him.

"Is that a proposition, Esmeralda?" he taunted, pressing close enough to feel her heat.

That's when he saw it— right behind the frustration

there was just a hint of desire in her eyes. He heard it in the way her breath hitched when he leaned into her. He felt it when her body reached for his even as she tried to keep some distance. When his eyes focused on her lush lips, they parted for him like he was the only water she'd seen after days in the desert. They were fools, both of them. Hadn't learned a thing in all these years, and yet he could not make himself walk away.

"Esmeralda." He said her name like it meant something all on its own. Because it did, *it always had*. He felt his pulse hammering in his chest, at once urgent and trepidatious. Once they'd done this, once this kiss happened, everything would change and Rodrigo could not bring himself to care.

He placed a hand on the back of her neck and brought her forward. "You make me crazy," he growled through gritted teeth, aching to close the last centimeter of distance between them.

"I hate that I want you this much," she muttered as her arms circled his neck.

Common sense was beyond him, need burning in him like a fever. "I could take you right here." The tension in the room pulsed around them as they stood there, poised to crash and burn before they'd even really started. The pressure of the door opening at his back sent him tumbling forward and almost knocked him on top of Esmeralda.

"Oh my goodness, I'm so sorry, Mr. Almanzar. I didn't realize anyone was here." He recognized the young woman as the executive assistant for one of the VPs. He couldn't quite remember which one, but it didn't matter. Hell, he should be thanking the woman for saving him from himself.

"That's fine. Miss Sambrano-Peña and I were just discussing some details about the five-year strategic plan." He glanced in Esme's direction and had to look away from the flush on her cheeks, because focusing on her obvious arousal would only lead to more bad decisions. "Can you give us a minute?"

The woman's eyes widened as she realized she'd interrupted something, but she quickly made a grab for the doorknob. "Of course."

The click of the door sounded like a gunshot in the quiet room, and he was sure he could hear the drumming of both their hearts. What a disaster.

"That can't happen again." Esmeralda's voice was low and husky, the heat of the past few minutes clearly still coursing through her veins. And right then, he wished he was the kind of man who could forget his responsibilities. But he was nothing if not dutiful. Hell, it was his need to always put his duty first that had cost him Esmeralda. Besides, it was all too far gone to fix any of it. This almost-kiss had been a desperate attempt to reclaim something that had long ago slipped from his fingers. The only way out was to move forward.

"It won't happen again." He looked at his watch. It was almost 7:00 p.m. and this day had been a decade. "I will show you to your office, and tomorrow first thing I will guide you through some of the material the board will want you to take into consideration."

Esmeralda nodded, but did not say a word for a long time. "I'm sure I'll be fine. Just show me where I can work and I'll take it from there." She pulled the door open and stalked off.

He followed her out, feeling off-kilter and more than a little sexually frustrated. Whether she wanted it or not, he was going to do his job, and part of that was showing her how to do hers.

That was what he was known for after all, never deviating from the task at hand. Everything else could fall by the wayside, but Rodrigo Almanzar always delivered—even when it cost him his own happiness.

Five

"I'm only here to look through some of these files. It's easier than going back and forth. I'll be out of your hair in a minute."

Rodrigo stopped short when he found Esmeralda in his office with what looked like every single one of his programming binders sprawled over his meeting table. She'd arrived yesterday morning as if the previous day's boardroom blowout—and that almost-kiss—never happened and placidly asked for him to show her around. And as the board, and the whole world, expected him to, he did his job. He'd gotten her set up, and ever since they'd given each other a wide berth.

Well, physically at least, because so far, he hadn't been able to go more than a minute without thinking about her. From where he stood in the doorway he could see she was looking through news clippings and show features from 2001, and had plastered sticky notes on a few others. It looked like she'd been at it for hours. It was barely 7:00 a.m.

"How long have you been here?" He looked at her again and noticed she was wearing different clothes than yesterday, so she must've gone home. Today she had on a pencil skirt in a deep burgundy and a heather-gray blouse. Her Gucci stilettos were off her feet and toppled over on the floor next to her. Her hair was in a top bun, smoothed back with her baby hair feathered out. He smiled when he saw the gold hoops in her ear. A Washington Heights girl through and through. Rodrigo thought to himself that Esmeralda would be good for this company, even if it was not as CEO.

"Mmm, maybe a bit over an hour," she said distractedly, as if that didn't mean she'd arrived literally at dawn. She looked up from the notes she was jotting down and took him in. Her face was bare, no makeup except for a little bit of lip gloss. She looked fresh and young, and so damn beautiful. Always so beautiful… and intense.

"There's so much to go over. I still don't have a full sense of what I'm going to do for the presentation, and the clock is ticking." She pointed at him, but the hostility wasn't there anymore, or at least it wasn't there now. "I meant what I said, Rodrigo. I'm fighting for it."

He shook his head, noticing the small smile tugging at her lips and he wished everything in him didn't react to her every word as deeply as it did. "I never expected for you to not give me a fight."

He had to watch himself very carefully with Esmeralda, because cordial was all well and good, but he could not even for a moment give her the impression this wasn't a fight to the death. "I enjoy a good competition. Here," he said, lifting up the bag in his hand. "I brought you something."

She eyed the bag suspiciously but when she saw the logo, a grin immediately appeared on her face. "You went to La Nueva?" she asked as he walked over to the table and placed the parcel in front of her on the table.

"It's in my neighborhood."

She gave him a suspicious look as she glanced at the contents. "You got me the cream cheese and guayaba Danish. How did you remember?" She sounded almost affronted he still knew what her favorite pastry was from the bakery they'd gone to as kids.

"You never ordered anything else in the thousand times we went there." Esmeralda may have forgotten that they had been in each other's lives from day one, but he never would. They were tied to each other and always would be. Their mothers had been best friends, but it had always been more than that. Hell, in those days where everything seemed to be falling apart after his father had lost everything to gambling, Ivelisse had been the one to help his mother pick up the pieces.

It had always seemed so wrong to him that Esmeralda could never be a part of Patricio's life. She lived in a small apartment and went to the neighborhood Catholic school, while her half-siblings lived in a Park Avenue penthouse and went to boarding school in Switzerland. Although for the most part that meant she was untouched by all the Sambrano drama, protected by a mother who could clearly see how that world could taint her daughter. And here she was now, a determined, strong woman, still blowing him away with that fire of hers. And he hoped that the tough exterior matched what was inside, because he would crush her hopes for that CEO position. There was no other option.

"We didn't go a thousand times," she muttered through a mouthful of pastry. He'd always enjoyed watching her eat. Esmeralda was not dainty or shy about what she loved. She took big bites and gulped things in—unapologetically ravenous for what brought her pleasure. There had been a time he'd been what pleased her the most, before he'd ruined everything with his need to do his duty despite who got hurt in the process. Before Patricio's refusal to see through Carmelina's lies.

He would never forget that day. He'd made up a story at work about scoping out some potential talent in LA and gotten on a Thursday-night redeye to spend three days with Esme. On Friday they'd driven out to Laguna Beach and eaten ceviche and drank cold beer in a restaurant on the water. Their Saturday plans to go to the Getty Villa had been completely ignored, and instead he'd kept her in bed until the afternoon. It had been all the more perfect because those moments were just theirs. They'd kept their relationship secret, because they'd both known that once their families knew it would be out of their hands. But he'd been hopeful in those few days, and foolish enough to think that the love they had for each other could endure anything. He had been so wrong.

On the Sunday morning his mother's plea for help on behalf of Ivelisse Peña shattered the joy of those few days. Gloria had delivered the news in hushed tones over the phone, telling him that on Friday Esmeralda's mother had received a notice saying she had one week to vacate the apartment she lived in. All because Carmelina had gotten in Patricio's head and he'd decided to turn the mother of his firstborn on the street.

Without telling Esmeralda why—Ivelisse had begged him not to tell her daughter what was happening until she at least had a new place to live—he'd jumped on a plane back to New York to intercede with Patricio. He'd found the man in his office, drunk off his head raving about paternity tests and Ivelisse being a liar. When Rodrigo finally got him sobered up enough to explain, Patricio showed him the "test" Carmelina had produced as evidence that Esmeralda was not his child.

Knowing Carmelina, Rodrigo had made quick work of discovering that his mentor's wife had fabricated the whole thing. He'd tried to call the laboratory that supposedly had done it, and confirmed the place didn't exist. But the damage was already done and it was twofold, because as Rodrigo worked to help Ivelisse, the truth about the nature of his relationship with Patricio's daughter came to light. And so did the price he'd have to pay to make sure Esmeralda never found out the real reason her father had forced Ivelisse out of their home.

Rodrigo had risked his job, his mother's treatment and Patricio's help getting the Almanzar family out of the debt his father had sunk them into. Once his mentor figured out he was in love with Esme, Patricio demanded that Rodrigo end it. The older man had been furious, flying into a rage about Rodrigo keeping things from him, of going behind his back.

Rodrigo had taken all the insults and humiliation; he'd had no choice. But before he fell on the sword Patricio set for him, he asked for one last thing. One final guarantee that Carmelina could never attempt to do what she'd done again, then he gave Esmeralda up.

If it had only been him, he would've walked away from everything to be able to keep her. But he couldn't do it then, and he certainly could not now. At least he'd protected her from Carmelina's vicious schemes and saved his own family.

Ten years later, knowing all the pain they'd both endured, he wondered if it had all been worth it.

"I didn't know you'd moved back Uptown." Esmeralda's voice brought Rodrigo back from his distressing trip down memory lane.

"I bought a brownstone in Sugar Hill a couple of years ago," he said as he sipped his café con leche and watched her eat. She gave him a wry look as she chewed like she couldn't quite figure out why he'd done that. Seven years ago, right after he'd taken the position of chief content officer for Sambrano, he'd bought himself an obnoxious condo in a building downtown. He'd gotten it because it seemed like the kind of place that successful people in movies about New York City seemed to live in, but it never fit him. When his mother's illness came back a couple years earlier he made the move so he could be closer to her. "It's nice to be back in the old neighborhood."

She looked at him suspiciously, still picking at her Danish. "You're only like ten blocks from Mami and me."

He wasn't sure if it was a statement of fact or a rebuke, but for the sake of his own sanity, he decided to veer off the subject of their parents and their history. It was pure survival instinct at this point. He pulled a chair from the table she was sitting at, far enough away that he wouldn't be tempted to reach over and clean the crumbs of pastry that were adorably stuck to the side of her mouth.

"Did you see Octavio's invitation for the reception tonight?" he asked, leaning back on the chair, his eyes still stuck on her mouth as her tongue lapped at the crumbs. It would be a miracle if he managed to keep his head this week. Everything about this woman was appealing. His eyes roamed over her body; her ample bosom looked downright sinful in that tailored blouse that was unbuttoned far enough he could see the plunge of her breasts. Through the fabric he caught a glimpse of the lace of her bra, and he had to cross his legs to keep from embarrassing himself.

"Eyes on my face, Rodrigo."

I'm trying, Esmeralda, but when you lick your lips like that my eyes just start roaming on their own.

The teasing tone in her voice made his face flush with heat, but how could he not stare at the embodiment of his every desire sitting only a few feet away?

"And yes, I saw the invitation. I'm not going."

Her dismissive tone annoyed Rodrigo. He could deal with pissed Esmeralda, but petulance was never something he could handle well. "It's not a suggestion. You *have* to go, Esmeralda. All of our biggest advertisers will be there." She shook her head stubbornly as he spoke and he couldn't decide if he wanted to throttle her or kiss some sense into her.

"I don't have anything suitable to wear to a formal reception at The Cloisters, Rodrigo!" Her eyes widened at the mention of the museum of medieval art in upper Manhattan where the event would take place. He could understand her feeling intimidated—as far as gala locations went, that one was definitely for the New York City A-listers crowd.

"Tantrums are not going to help you this week, Joya." He almost laughed at the way her eyes narrowed, the

Danish halfway to her mouth. But treating her with kid gloves was not going to help either of them. "Take this as the good faith advice that it is. It's not a smart move for you to miss this chance to interact with the board. It will be good for them to see how you handle yourself, how you could potentially represent the studio. You're a shareholder now and that won't change even if you're not CEO."

She opened her mouth, about to protest, but he held up his palm. "This isn't about us being competitors, it's about you assuming your place as part of the Sambrano family. You need to think of the big picture, Esmeralda. You now own a quarter of a billion-dollar company. This isn't you trying to get a job on a set or to get someone to look at your pilot. This is the big leagues, and you need to start acting like you get that." She was still glaring at him, but he could see the set of her shoulders had drooped ever so slightly. "I'm giving you good advice. Take it."

She took another sip from her mug, which from the smell wafting toward him seemed to be something spicy and aromatic—maybe Masala chai. She'd always loved that. She was staring into space, processing what he'd told her. He could see the precise moment she saw the value of his words. She was smart, smarter than any of the fools running around the building. And she'd always deserved a seat at the table.

Too bad that the seat she wanted was one he was not ready to give up. When she turned her eyes to him they were slightly less contentious.

"I see your point, but I really don't have anything to wear." She lifted a shoulder as she ran a finger over the edges of the binder in front of her. "I get that people didn't have a chance to let me know it was happening since I only showed up the day before yesterday, so it's not that I'm mad or anything. I just don't have the time to spend the entire day hunting for a designer gown."

"Leave it to me." It was out of his mouth before he could stop himself. "I'll find you a gown and you focus on your work until it's time to get ready." He could see it already. Something satiny and expensive that hugged her every curve.

"Suit yourself. I'm certainly not going shopping like a Dominican Cinderella when I have barely five days to come up with a whole strategic vision for the studio. This is no time to play games."

He laughed and she scowled. "I assure you, none of this is a game. And no one is getting a fairy-tale ending." Esmeralda wasn't sure why Rodrigo would say that, but she wasn't going to let his tough love act get in her head.

She had no intention of going to a reception or anywhere else with him. No matter how delicious he looked in the navy suit he had on. The man had no right to look that good at 7:00 a.m., especially in a blue-and-yellow shirt. The audacity. Who could even pull off that color combination? Rodrigo, that's who.

She'd almost kissed him. Ten years of telling herself she wanted nothing to do with him. That she despised him for betraying her. That if she ever saw him again she would tell him all the ways he'd hurt her. And it had literally taken *seconds* alone with him to have her swooning at his feet. Yeah, this man was not good for her, and what she needed was to pick up all the binders she'd pulled off his shelves and go to her office across the hall.

Instead she stared at him as he sipped his coffee.

"Do you still take it teeth-rottingly sweet?" What in the world? Why did she ask him that? Was she trying to *flirt* with the man?

He winked at her. The bastard. His big body was sprawled on an office chair that frankly looked a bit spindly to accommodate all that Cuban–Puerto Rican real estate. He was a beautiful man. No question about it. Brown skin, dark eyes fringed with eyelashes most women would kill for, and a broad mouth with full, fleshy lips that she could still remember on her skin.

Focus, Esmeralda. FOCUS.

The presentation. That was what she was supposed to be talking to Rodrigo about, not fixating on how his hands had gripped her two nights ago. Her belly did a somersault at the thought of how close she'd come to kissing him, and everything that moment had brought roaring back. Taking in a shaky breath, Esme willed herself to redirect her focus. Rodrigo was supposed to help her, so she could ask him some questions. Hell, she needed to.

Yesterday she'd taken the day to review some of the material she'd been given, and she had a sense of what direction she wanted to go with her presentation, but there were a few things that weren't adding up. She needed some institutional knowledge, some insight, and the only person she could get it from was Rodrigo.

"Can I ask you something?" He dipped his head in response, so she sat up. "Where did all the Afro-Latinx people go?"

He straightened in the chair as soon as she posed the question, throwing his shoulders back for good measure. It was almost like he was readying himself for them to have it out. She knew he got what she was asking, but was curious to hear what excuses he'd make. His brows dipped and the line of his mouth hardened at whatever he was thinking about.

Sambrano had begun as a studio that produced content for *all* Latinx communities. While the Spanish-language networks that came later focused on catering to a very specific kind of audience, Sambrano always embraced the many shades and sides to Latinx identity. They celebrated the Black and Indigenous communities that also wanted to see themselves reflected positively on screen, when every other outlet seemed content with erasing them. No surprise there since her father was a Black man, and for Patricio, celebrating his heritage had seemed—at least in the beginning—to be a vital part of the Sambrano brand.

In the '90s the studio had embraced the same idea as other American networks who were producing hit shows with all-Black casts. Other Spanish-language networks refused to cast Black and Indigenous casts and production staff, while Sambrano made them a central part of their programming. It had made the studio stand out to Latinx audiences, but somewhere in the past twenty years that had fallen by the wayside. Looking at the movies and TV shows Sambrano was currently producing, it seemed like they'd forgotten their roots, and Esmeralda couldn't figure out why they'd made that change. She did notice the programming had gotten a bit more diverse since Rodrigo had been chief content officer, but even with those efforts it was not even a shadow of what it had been at the start. She wanted to know why her father, who had seemed almost fervently committed to represent every face of the Latinx community, had betrayed his own vision.

Rodrigo considered her for a minute before he opened his mouth. "Depending on who you ask you will get different answers to that question."

"I want to hear *your* answer." Esmeralda didn't know too many things about who Rodrigo had become in these past ten years, but she knew there was no one more devoted to the studio than him.

He shifted in his chair again, his body tense now. He clearly wasn't sure how to answer this without pointing fingers. He wouldn't like doing that. Always the quintessential company man.

"Carmelina always had a bigger influence on Patricio than was advisable. He was a proud man, but his insecurities about his lack of education would get to him. And Carmelina knew how to prey on them. She would flaunt her Ivy League degree, her family's pedigree, and he'd end up taking her advice, even to his own detriment. That's how it started, anyway." Rodrigo shook his head distastefully at whatever he was remembering. "She always had a million ideas." He smiled then, but it was sharp, cold. "And most of them involved making Sambrano a carbon copy of American networks, to take all the Latinx culture out of it and just have the same type of programming but in Spanish." There was something in his expression, a barely restrained frustration that told her this was something he'd been seething about for a long time. "I always pushed back, reminding Patricio the core values of the studio were to make movies and television our people could see themselves in. But Carmelina was relentless. She never understood that our biggest asset was leaning into our authenticity."

Bitterness filled Esme's mouth. How had her father

let Carmelina destroy his legacy? How had Rodrigo let that happen?

"Aren't you the chief content officer? How did you let her influence things so much?" She sounded judgmental, and she knew criticizing the man would probably not help matters. But she was annoyed at all this. Annoyed that her father had gone along with his wife's greedy intentions, annoyed that she had been kept out, annoyed that Rodrigo seemed to always let people's shitty behavior slide if it meant he got to keep his multi-million-dollar salary. Yeah...she'd seen the payroll and her eyes were still watering at the figures she saw.

He gave her a long, assessing look, clearly considering what to say. "I bet it's nice to stroll in and start making judgments, but you don't know what it's been like. I'm not Onyx or Perla, or even you. I don't have 'Sambrano' attached to my name. Your father lost sight of his mission, but the man could never admit he was wrong. And that meant the rest of us could only mitigate the damage and hope he eventually saw the error of his ways. Then he got sick." With every word she could see his shoulders stiffen and his jaw tick with tension. Barely restrained frustration blended with the grief written across his face.

"If it were up to Carmelina, this place wouldn't even be a shadow of what it used to be. The only reason there's anything left is because I've fought tooth and nail to save it. And don't think she hasn't tried to bully me into being her accomplice in schemes. But contrary to what the gossips will tell you, I'm not for sale." He stood up then, dropping the empty coffee cup in the wastebasket as he moved closer to her. "And that's one of the many reasons I should be in charge of this studio," he said, all traces of the amiable conversation they'd been having completely gone. "You have no idea what you're up against, Esmeralda. This is a fight for the future of this company, and if you think I'll back down just because you're involved, then you don't know me at all."

"Oh, believe me, I'm counting on getting stabbed in the back by you."

He reared back like she'd slapped him in the face, but he recovered quickly, and soon he was leaning in across the table, face twisted in anger. "Unlike Patricio's wife and his children, I care about what happens to this place. Or maybe now that you have your shares you want to make sure to get your dividends..."

That was a low blow, but it was a good reminder that Rodrigo was not on her side. "I've never counted on a cent from Patricio Sambrano," she said, standing up to her full height. If he wanted to fight dirty and say hurtful things then she had ten years' worth of grievances to hurl at Rodrigo Almanzar. "You of all people should know that. Because if I recall correctly, you had a first-row seat to my father putting my mother out on the street on a whim. Or did you block that out of your memory together with every other thing about me you seem to have erased?"

His nostrils flared at that and she knew her words had struck true. His light brown skin flushed with red. Yeah, he *should* be ashamed of himself.

"You were the one who cut off all contact, Esmeralda," he said through gritted teeth. "I never said we couldn't be friends. Yo nunca—"

She could see the hurt in his eyes and immediately the urge to back down rose in her. But she smothered it out. She was tired of being overlooked, of being ignored.

Of the men in her life walking out on her and then expecting her to run back and forgive them. And now she was right back there, to that nightmare of a weekend.

"You would never what?" The trip had been almost a year in the making. Rodrigo had tried and failed to get out of work for months, until he finally got a few days off to come and see her. She'd been in love and sure they were starting something that could last forever, but she'd been mistaken of course. She'd been foolish about everything when it came to this man. "You would never tell me you loved me, sleep with me, only to ghost me the next morning? Or betray me for power and money? Oh, wait," she said dramatically, then pointed a finger at him. "That's exactly what you did."

His face seemed to turn to stone and her chest ached from what she was doing. She felt wretched, and yet she could not seem to stop herself. It was as if she'd had this poison sitting in her gut for ten years and now that it had started coming out she had to purge all of it.

"My father hurt me and abandoned me, but I never expected any better from him. You? You tore my heart out."

She walked out before he could respond and before he could see the tears that were rolling down her face. And as she reached her office she wondered how much of herself she was willing to lose in order to win this game.

Six

"What is this supposed to be?"

Rodrigo was still stewing over their earlier conversation —argument, fight, whatever. So Esmeralda appearing in his office looking pissed and pushing a clothing rack full of evening dresses only sank his mood further.

"It's a selection of dresses for you to pick from for the reception tonight." He didn't look up from the email he was sending off.

One more investor who had appeared out of nowhere wanting to acquire the studio. This had Carmelina's fingerprints all over it. The woman was nothing if not persistent. From the moment they'd heard about Patricio's will she'd been trying to get him on her side. That really would be a deal with the devil.

"I said I was not going," Esmeralda growled.

He kept typing. "There is also a makeup artist available if you need it." When he finally looked up, he found her fuming by his desk. "Did Marquito bring the shoes?" Rodrigo asked, ignoring her searing glare.

Her jaw actually dropped at that last part, and he would've laughed if she didn't look like she could murder him. "That's what that big box was? Wait, Marquito's here?"

He wished his chest didn't light up like the Rockefeller Center Christmas tree at the affection in Esmeralda's voice at the mention of his younger brother. Marcos was a sought-after celebrity stylist and at twenty-eight was making a name for himself in the industry. Rodrigo had asked for his help only a couple of hours ago and it seemed he'd delivered.

"Did I get the wrong size?" He doubted it. When it came to Esmeralda's body, every curve and every angle was forever etched in his memory. "Marquito's not here. He sent the dresses by messenger."

"Oh." She looked genuinely disappointed. She'd always been kind to his little brother and when Marcos had been a ball of teen angst and confusion she'd been the first person he'd come out to. Rodrigo would always be grateful to her for that, but that was neither here nor there at the moment.

"Are you listening to me, Rodrigo?" The exasperation in her voice brought him out of his thoughts. He kept going into his head. Distraction was not his friend. Not this week.

"Sorry," he muttered, as he turned back to her. "Is there a problem with the dresses?"

"No, they're perfect, which only makes this that much more irritating."

"Okay, so what's the problem then?" he asked gruffly, feeling unsettled with this woman in his space.

She threw her arms up and came closer to the desk. Her mouth pursed in an adorably irritated expression and he once again had to remind himself his instinct to reach out to her was not just stupid, it was self-destructive. No matter what happened this week there would be a falling-out. If she got the job, he knew he'd be crushed. If he got it, that would only give her another reason to hate him.

"Listen, I appreciate you trying to give me my very own *Pretty Woman* moment this week, but I already said I'm not going to this party." He dearly wished that his traitorous cock didn't pulse at that sexy huskiness of her voice. "It's not worth losing an entire evening mingling and drinking champagne when I could be working." She had both hands on her hips, her face flushed, and he wondered if this proximity was getting to her, too.

But before he could even open his mouth, the last person he wanted to see walked into his office, as if he'd conjured her up with his thoughts.

"Isn't this cozy? Rodrigo, are you spending the company's money on dresses now? I thought that big salary we paid you was to actually do work." Carmelina Sambrano knew less about television and moviemaking than a kindergartener, and yet she fancied herself an expert on what his job entailed. He was surprised it had taken this long for her to come and harass Esme.

He looked over at the younger woman and saw that she was looking at her father's widow through narrowed eyes. There was no love lost there, and that was with Esmeralda unaware of just how low Carmelina had gone to try to push her out. And as far as he was concerned she would never know. He'd promised Ivelisse he'd never tell and he didn't plan to go back on his word.

But now Esme was poised to take possession of the prize Patricio's widow had spent decades scheming to control. Carmelina wasn't stupid, but she was getting more desperate by the day. And a desperate Carmelina was very dangerous.

"What do you want?" He didn't even attempt to mask his derision for her.

Carmelina was dressed in her usual matching jacket and skirt combo, evoking old-school Jackie O. It was probably custom Chanel. But it didn't matter how much money the woman spent on designer clothes, she made everything look cheap.

"Just came to personally let you know I've forbidden any private footage of my husband from being used for this farce." She turned to Esme then. "If you don't know anything about your father, it's because he wanted it that way. You're going to have to continue your little attempt at moneygrubbing without watching his interviews."

"Carmelina," Rodrigo snapped, menace clear in his voice. "Watch your tone."

But Esmeralda didn't flinch or give any indication she was fazed by the woman's vitriol. "I never requested any footage," she said, indifferent. "I have plenty to work with."

"*I* asked that the footage be made available to you," Rodrigo retorted. "It's from a documentary we were planning as part of the studio's thirty-fifth anniversary next year. But we weren't able to finish it." That pang of dull pain he still felt whenever he thought about Patricio flared in his chest as he spoke to Esme. He could see the conflicted sadness in her eyes at the mention of her father's passing, such a contrast to Carmelina's dismissive scoff.

"Is he being very helpful, giving you guidance and advice?" The bitterness that fueled Carmelina resonated in every word she said. "The honorable Rodrigo Almanzar, who turned his back on his own family so he could steal my son's rightful place. Don't trust him, querida. This one would betray his own mother to keep this office." Her voice dripped with contempt, but he'd learned long ago to not let Carmelina's words get to him. The only thing he cared about was that she didn't get her talons into Esmeralda. *That* he would not tolerate.

Carmelina wasn't finished. "He's the one you need to be careful with, you know. I don't need Sambrano." She smiled sharply, a hyena with her prey in her sights. "I have *never* needed Sambrano Studios—Patricio married *me* for *my* money." She laughed shrilly. "I'm doing this to preserve my husband's legacy and what rightfully belongs to his *legitimate* children."

He would never lay a hand on a woman, and that was the only thing that kept him from physically removing Patricio's widow from his office.

"Carmelina, get out," he snarled, fury boiling over in an instant. The things he could throw in her face about the messes he'd had to get her son out of through the years…

"I have a right to Sambrano, too," Esmeralda said calmly, as if Carmelina's hateful words had barely registered.

"Leave." Even he could hear the menace in his voice.

The older woman shrugged, an unfriendly smile on her lips. "So testy. Don't worry. I'm going." She made for the door, but stopped again in front of the rack of dresses. "There's not couture expensive enough to hide the fact that you're Patricio's bastard."

Esmeralda took her hand off the rack and moved until she was just a few feet away from Carmelina, the smile on her lips dangerous and cold in a way he'd never seen from her.

"Well then," she said, feigning a placidness she was clearly not feeling. "If people are wagging their tongues anyway I might as well make an appearance at the reception." Esme crossed her arms and looked straight at her father's widow. "And if you think coming over here to call me names is going to distract me from wanting to take all this from you, you have another thing coming. Now, if you'll excuse me, I have dresses to try on."

"Esmeralda, stay right where you are," he demanded, making the younger woman stop in her tracks. "Carmelina, if you're done. Miss Sambrano-Peña and I have things to discuss."

"You're not winning this," Carmelina warned Esmeralda before storming out. Rodrigo's heart pounded like a drum in his chest. But it had nothing to do with Carmelina and everything to do with the hellion in front of him. Esmeralda. Time and distance had done nothing to diminish his desire for her. And now, seeing her like this, standing up proudly, unashamed. Ready to claim her place. It cracked something in him. Despite the mess he'd made of things, he was proud of her, admired her strength.

"She's really still that terrible, isn't she?" Esme asked shakily, after he closed the door to the office. She'd held her own but he could see Carmelina had gotten to her.

"She's worse," he assured her, exhausted from the exchange. "Forget her. Despite what Carmelina may think, she has no power to override the board's decisions. You and I are still in the running for CEO and she only gets one vote in that decision."

"More like three if you count my siblings," she said with distaste, and he couldn't deny that was probably true. Perla and Onyx could care less if the studio went up in flames as long as someone still covered their Amex bills.

"My hope is that it won't come down to their three votes. Carmelina has a lot of enemies on that board, and people won't just go along with her. Put her out of your mind for now. I have something to show you." He lifted his hand to take hers, but then just let it fall to his side, curbing once more the almost overwhelming need to touch her. He went to the hidden door on the wall parallel to his desk and pushed on the panel. It slid to the side to reveal the hidden bedroom suite that Patricio had built for himself. Rodrigo had no idea why he was doing this. There was no reason for him to show her this now.

"You're joking," Esme said, as she looked at the narrow hallway that led to a spacious bedroom with an en suite bathroom. "Please tell me this isn't some kind of assignation room, because I really don't think I can handle that image of my father."

A laugh burst out of him at the feigned horror in her voice, and the warmth that spread in his chest at being able to hear her make jokes again was a revelation. "I can't confirm or deny what went on in this room, but I do know that Patricio had it built a long time ago. The man always had a flair for imitating some of the telenovelas he produced, for better or worse." He frowned at the memory of the night his mentor had first shown him what was behind the secret panel. Patricio had confessed that not even six months into their marriage, he'd needed to find a way to get some distance from Carmelina. He lived for his work, so he'd built himself a suite where he could stay when he needed to focus on Sambrano.

"His marriage to Carmelina was never a happy one. It was a business arrangement that those two had, and initially I imagine it seemed mutually beneficial, but in the last ten years I saw Patricio become harder…bitter. They brought out the worst in each other. He always said that the only person who could remind him of who he was before he built all this was your mother."

"He didn't deserve her," she said quietly, still not taking a step toward the bedroom.

"No, he didn't. And I think how things ended with them was one of his biggest regrets." He extended a hand toward the bedroom. "You can change in there. Figure out which dress you want to wear." He pointed at the garment bag hanging from a hook on the wall next to his office door. "I'm changing here, too."

She didn't look too sure about it, but when he pushed the rack into the room she followed. "My assistant can get you that makeup artist."

This time her expression was hard to decipher. Not shuttered, but also not exactly open, either. "I think I can handle my hair and makeup." She paused as she looked at him again, like she was hoping to find whatever underlying motives he had to do this for her. "But thank you for the dress. I think you're right. I need to show the board *and* Carmelina that I'm not planning on scurrying away. I'm here to work, but I'm also here to claim my place. And if that means champagne and canapés at The Cloisters, then so be it."

With that she pushed the rack the rest of the way

into the suite and closed the door behind it. Rodrigo assumed she'd go back to her office until it was time to get ready. But instead she leaned against the door and turned her face up to look at him. There was something in her eyes he couldn't quite read. "Why are you being nice to me?"

And that was the two-hundred-million-dollar question, wasn't it? He could say all kinds of things, that he owed it to Patricio, that he was a professional and he would give anyone else the same courtesy, but those would all be lies. The truth felt like a dagger on his tongue, sharp and deadly.

"I'm nice to everyone," he lied.

"You're so full of it." The sly smile on her face smoothed the edges in her words. God he wanted her. The need to press her to him was a tangible force in the air. But if there was a time to live up to his supposed stoicism, it was now. He stepped away and went back to his desk.

"Let me know when you need the room to change, and I'll make sure to give you space," he said gruffly, avoiding her gaze.

"Right," she said, heading for the door. She sounded as flustered as he felt. "I need to get a few things done, before I start getting ready. Could you check the mockup I sent you? I'd like to start working on my concept tonight. Just because I'm taking a few hours to participate in this rich people show-and-tell doesn't mean I'm not coming back here to work after."

He nodded as the door slid closed behind her. Nobody needed to know that his eyes were riveted to the glorious view of her perfect ass as she walked away. He was in over his head. A lifetime of doggedly working after a singular goal was threatening to slip away. All because the one person he could see himself giving everything up for was the one standing between him and his dream.

Seven

"Dammit." Esmeralda let out another frustrated sigh as she tried and failed to zip up her dress. It was so bizarre to be in this room. A place her father escaped to when things were not going well in his home life. This was a level of intimacy she'd never had with him when he was alive. On the tall dresser—which she supposed had stored changes of clothes and personal things— were some framed photographs. Some of her. That had surprised her. One was from her second birthday—her parents on either side of her, strained smiles on their faces. She didn't remember it, but she knew in those first few years Patricio had made appearances for special occasions. There was another photo from her high school graduation. And the most recent one of her receiving an award for a short film she'd presented at the Tribeca Film Festival.

It had pierced something in her to see she'd had a place among his other children. That the picture of her and her mother was there with the rest of them. That he hadn't forgotten her, even though it had always felt that to her father she'd never existed. She'd always looked in from outside when it came to his life. And now here she was in his inner sanctum, only to realize he'd kept reminders of her around. She had no idea what to do with any of it, and worse, the only person she wanted to talk about it with was the last man she needed to be around when she was feeling this messy. Damn Rodrigo for standing up for her today. For getting her gorgeous dresses that fit her perfectly. For his sinful mouth and swoon-worthy shoulders, and most of all for making her feel this raw again.

"Ugh, crying is not the move right now," she said, frustrated as she blinked, trying to keep the tears that were threatening to escape from ruining her perfect smoky eye. And still she could not zip up her dress. She looked at the alarm clock next to the bed and saw that it was almost six. Okay, screw it, she was going to need his help with this dress. She made her way to the sliding door that led into the CEO office and opened it slowly.

Rodrigo was standing with his back to her, on the other side of the room, looking out of the enormous windows that provided a heart-stopping view of a June Manhattan sunset. He did cut a dashing figure in his suit. Everything had to be just so with Rodrigo Almanzar, everything in its place. But with her he'd been messy and free. Funny and passionate. For so many years he had meant so much to her—if she was honest with herself, he still did. But she could not walk away from this fight.

It would ruin things for them forever, she knew that.

Rodrigo would feel betrayed. He'd resent her. And wasn't that what she'd said she wanted? A chance to get back at him? Well, her taking the CEO position from him would certainly accomplish that.

"Rodrigo," she said into the quiet room, and he turned. God, but the man was a sight standing in the warm glow of the golden hour. He could always trip her up with just a look. He kept his hair very short, and his face clean-shaven. Always so formal. Tonight's dark blue tuxedo made him look like a Tom Ford model. Her eyes glommed on to him as he walked over to her and she did not miss that his eyes were burning, too.

By the time he got to her the beating of her heart was so intense she could feel it in her throat. She felt naked. Bare to him in too many ways that felt utterly dangerous. So she hid from him. She turned around and walked back into her father's secret bedroom, feeling too exposed to be in the office where anyone could see. He followed her in without a word, and she did not dare turn around. Finally, when she got to the front of the bed, she asked the question without looking up. "Can you zip me up?"

"You picked the green one," he said huskily. She'd settled on an emerald green A-line sleeveless dress by Christian Siriano. One of her goals in life had been to wear one of his creations, and even though this whole situation would probably end up blowing up in her face, she could at least have this memory.

Although now that she was the owner of a quarter of Sambrano, she supposed there could be more Siriano in her future…

She heard the quick intake of breath and felt the heat of him as he came even closer. "This color is perfect on you, Joya." There was that name again. The one she'd always told herself—and him—she hated but melted for whenever he uttered it.

He gripped her waist as his other hand traced the bare skin of her back with a finger that could've been flames licking at her skin. She didn't protest, she didn't move away, entranced by the feel of him. She'd told herself so many times this man meant nothing her. And yet just a brush of his fingers had her ready to toss out the window every self-protective instinct she had. She wanted to lean in, take those strong hands and wrap them around her waist. Let her head fall on his shoulder; but he only zipped her dress, and stepped back.

"Turn around, I want to see you."

She should be annoyed at his demanding tone. She should tell him to get out of the room, that she didn't need him anymore. She should guard her heart from someone who could so easily trample it. But instead, she turned her bare feet on the plush carpet to face him. And what she found in his eyes could easily raze them both down to ashes.

"Hermosa, mi Joya." His voice was rough with desire, and she knew in that moment, whatever he asked for she'd give him. He pressed closer, so she had to tip her head to look at his face. "Having you this close and not being able to touch you is hell." His voice was gravel and smoke as he brushed his knuckles against her cheek. She closed her eyes at the contact, her breath hitching from the effect his closeness had on her. Always overwhelming. Like he was the only person in the world.

"I want to kiss you, Esmeralda." She shook her head at the statement, even as a frustrated little whine escaped her lips.

Her arms were already circling around his neck. "If we're going to do this, just do it, Rodrigo." Without hesitation he crushed her mouth with his and the world fell away. His tongue stole in, and it was like not a single day had passed since they'd last done this. She pressed herself to him as he peppered her neck with fluttering kisses. Somewhere in the back of her mind she knew this was the height of stupidity, that they were both playing with fire. That if anyone found about this, she would probably sink her chances to get approved by the board. But it was so hard to think when he was whispering intoxicatingly delicious things in Spanish. Preciosa, amada…mia.

It was madness for him to call her his, and what was worse, she reveled in it. She wanted it so desperately that her skin prickled, her body tightening and loosening under his skilled touch.

"I can't get enough of you. I never could." He sounded bewildered. Like he couldn't quite figure out how it was that he'd gotten there.

That made two of them.

Esmeralda knew they should stop. They were supposed to head to the party soon and she'd for sure have to refresh her makeup now that she'd decided to throw all her boundaries out the window. But instead of stopping she threw her head back and let him make his way down her neck, his teeth grazing her skin as he tightened one hand on her backside and the other pulled down the strap of her dress. "Can I kiss you here?" he asked as his breath feathered over her breasts.

"Yes." She was on an express bus to Bad Decision Central and she could not be bothered to stop. He grazed his lips over her skin until he brushed the edge of the gown and flicked his tongue over her sensitive skin. She was breathless from the pleasure of it. She pressed a hand to the apex of her thighs, aching for him.

"You drive me crazy," he growled as he crushed her to him, his arousal like a fire iron against her belly. Her mouth watered at the thought of taking him in her mouth. She was about to tell him so. But she must have had some sensible angels watching over her, because right when she'd been about to burn through the last of her senses, a female voice calling for Rodrigo kept her from ruining everything.

Eight

"*Ex*-girlfriend," Rodrigo reminded Esmeralda for the fifth time since they'd arrived at The Cloisters. He should've been glad that his ex, Jimena, had shown up when she did. Saving him from himself and the utterly idiotic thing he'd been about to do. He didn't know what was going on with him. Ever since Esmeralda has stepped into that boardroom he'd been doing one stupid thing after the other. And what was worse, he could not make himself feel sorry for any of it. And didn't that make him a fool.

"She certainly seemed all cozy with you for being an ex." He returned his attention to Esmeralda, who was currently glaring at the beautifully lit courtyard where the reception was being hosted. The Cloisters were built as a replica of a medieval French abbey, with priceless tapestries and grand limestone arches everywhere. The reception was in a semi-enclosed rose garden, which was lit by what seemed like thousands of twinkling lights. It was stunning, but so far Esmeralda seemed unimpressed. She'd been in a mood on the drive over to the reception, too, as if he'd violated some kind of code by dating someone without her knowledge.

No. That primal thing pulsing in his chest was not satisfaction from seeing her jealous. Because he was not that stupid. Except, Esmeralda had always been the one place where Rodrigo forgot himself. The person who drove him to break his carefully guarded rules. She'd been the one person in his life who could always recognize the toll it took on him to hold his family together when his father lost everything they had in casinos. She had been the one to show up at the hospital while he waited for his mother to have her first round of chemo that summer they'd become more than friends. She'd been his harbor, and he'd desperately wanted to be hers. But instead he'd been one more person in her life to disappoint her.

"We're friends, Esmeralda."

She pursed her lips in a familiar expression he recognized as "stop BSing me" and his lips tugged up of their own volition. "We're grown adults who had a relationship, and then when things ran their course, we ended it amicably." He shrugged while she scowled and no matter what he did that feeling like his chest was expanding would not quit. Yes, he liked that she was being possessive. Even if he could do absolutely nothing with that.

"We're colleagues. She's one of the legal counsels for Sambrano, and honestly we're better as friends." Esme raised an eyebrow in question, apparently still too annoyed at him to talk. He couldn't help the humor in his voice when he explained. "It means we're both too committed to our jobs to be good partners."

"So you say."

Damn, but she was sexy when she got like this. He dearly wished he could drag her to a dark corner and give her a real reason to be hot and bothered. Could she really be upset about this? Or maybe Jimena said something to her. The woman could be a bit of a pit bull when it came to her loved ones, and Esme *was* technically gunning for his job. "Did she say anything untoward to you when I excused myself to use the restroom?"

He cleared his throat at the mention of the moment after Jimena had walked in on them kissing. He'd had to escape to another room before he embarrassed himself.

To his relief Esme shook her head. "No. Nothing like that. She wasn't super friendly, but she wasn't hostile, either. I didn't know that was your type," she said, before taking a sip from the flute of Moët she'd gotten off one of the servers. Again his dick was getting ideas. But it was hard not to when she was looking at him with those curious tawny eyes, her sensual mouth parted slightly as if she was waiting for his answer with bated breath.

"My type?" he asked tersely, and that brought a pink flush to her skin, and damn but he wanted to ravage her.

"Ivy League prep school, Latinx dynasty." He tried to read her expression, listened for mockery in her tone. To his surprise all he caught was a bit of discomfort there. She looked…embarrassed as her gaze roamed the crowded room. "We've been here less than ten minutes and you've already run into three people you went to Yale with." Ah, she felt out of place. Esmeralda hated feeling like an outsider. She always had. And if she'd been his, he'd make sure every person in this room knew she was a queen. That they needed to bow down to her. It was what she deserved. But she wasn't his anything. Not anymore.

"You mean pretentious asses who think they're better than everyone?" His teasing tone brought a smile to her lips.

"Yeah. Something like that." She smiled wide and again a pulse of something that felt a lot like happiness glowed in his chest. And he absolutely needed to wean himself off the need to comfort Esmeralda. Him trying to fulfill that particular role had already cost him too much.

"It's the world you're fighting to get into. Don't lose sight of that," he answered harshly and he saw the moment his words sank in. The softness in her mouth turned into a taut line and her honey-colored eyes, which had been wide and curious seconds before, narrowed in a shuttered expression.

"Oh, believe me. I'm very aware of the kind of compromises involved. I've seen it happen." She ran her eyes over him and then stormed off without another word.

His face tightened and his pulse quickened as shame coursed through him—and he welcomed it. This was what needed to happen. Pushing her away was the sane thing to do. He would give her the help she needed like he'd been tasked. But nothing between them could be like it used to. Because there was no middle ground for him when it came to Esmeralda. And at the end of this week he would have to be ruthless if he wanted to stay CEO.

"She's seen the error of her ways then." Instead of answering Jimena's taunt he took a long drink from his tumbler of Zacapa Centenario as he watched Esme storm off.

"You're not funny. And is sneaking up on people your new hobby?" he asked gruffly as he turned to face his friend.

She grinned as she reached for his glass.

"Get your own, Jimena."

"Oh, my. So moody," she muttered, looking in the direction Esmeralda had gone. "She can clearly still get under your skin. And wow, you're on her like a hawk."

"I don't know what you're talking about." He sounded pissed off and distracted because he was, tracking every step his rival for the top job at the studio made around the courtyard. He noticed he wasn't the only person aware of the fact that Esmeralda Sambrano was the most stunning woman in the room. People were turning to look at her and, yes, it was curiosity, at least at first, but plenty of them were sending her appreciative and very long glances as she made her way through the crowd. Once she got to the bar, she was barely standing there for a second when men started swarming her. She was handling them like a pro, though. Polite but keeping her distance.

"I'm just making sure she's talking to the right people."

Jimena laughed at that, because he was lying his ass off and they both knew it. "*Sure*, you're all business. She's nice, not what I expected. But she's too pure, Rodrigo. She won't be able to swim with these sharks and keep that idealism."

"She can handle them. I wasn't sure she was up for it, but she's a fighter. You should've seen her today going toe to toe with Carmelina. People underestimate her because she's not cynical and jaded. She's not what they're used to. But she's sharp and she's hungry. She's willing to bust her ass to get what she wants and that's how she can win." He meant every word, too. He knew her father's rejection hurt her, but not growing up around the likes of Carmelina Sambrano and her scheming had let Esme grow in ways she would not have been able to otherwise. She had integrity and a work ethic like only the child of immigrants could have, and that would take her far.

"Sharp, hungry and willing to work is not exactly what I'd associate with Sambrano offspring, that's for sure." Jimena was not a fan of Carmelina *or* her children. The three of them had been an ongoing headache for the entire legal department at the studio. "I know you want this job, but are you willing to see her get destroyed by the likes of Carmelina Sambrano? Because that's what she'll do under the guise of 'protecting the legacy.' Try to break her down. She's done it before. She did it to Patricio." Jimena's voice was barely over a whisper when she said that last part. And she was right, Patricio's illness had ravaged him, but his wife had accelerated the process.

Rodrigo kept his gaze on Esmeralda as he talked to Jimena. "I'll make sure Carmelina doesn't get up to any of her tricks, but this is a competition and I'm not Esmeralda's protector."

That elicited an amused laugh from Jimena. "Are you sure about that?"

"I'm serious, I—"

He never got the last of that sentence out because at the next moment Onyx Sambrano made sure every pair of eyes in the place were on him and Esmeralda.

* * *

Esmeralda let her eyes roam around the room and noticed that Carmelina and Onyx were talking in a corner, their shoulders stiff as they leaned toward each other, heads close together. It was almost like they were attempting to talk while staying as far away from each other as possible. The tension in her brother's body was noticeable even at a distance. Esmeralda sipped from her champagne as she watched them, intrigued by the discomfort in their body language. Such a striking difference from the warmth and ease she had with her own mother.

They were clearly in a heated conversation but there was no warmth there. Abruptly, Onyx backed away from his mother, his lighter complexion mottled with red. He looked angry as he stormed off, leaving Carmelina to glare at him. Whatever had passed between those two had not been a pleasant mother and son moment. Esme's eyes stayed on Carmelina's angry face for a second, but the woman stormed off in the direction of the stairs.

Esme's gaze returned to roaming the lavish garden until she found her other sibling. Unlike Esmeralda, who had gotten her coloring from their father, Perla Sambrano was fair and very slender, almost frail looking. She was beautiful, with cascading blond hair and piercing gray eyes. Tonight, she was dressed impeccably in a royal purple empire-waist gown, though she looked very small standing in a corner trying to capture the attention of a man who barely seemed to notice she was there. He was tall and commanding, dwarfing her with his height. She looked like she was pleading to him, but he barely looked at her, and after a few more attempts she gave up and walked away, swiping her fingers under her eyes.

As Perla briskly made her way to the exit she seemed to notice Esme, and for a moment she paused, hesitant. Esme's heart kicked around in her chest, curiosity and the need to feel seen by these people betraying her feigned indifference. Perla looked in her direction so intensely that for a second Esme thought she was going to walk over, to say something. But she didn't; her younger sister just lowered her gaze and left through one of the limestone arches. Esme didn't know what to make of the disappointment she felt when her sister walked away. Nothing was simple in this place, with this family. Every feeling only served to burst open another more complicated and unwanted one.

Esme stood there considering the tableau she'd just witnessed—and trying to untangle her feelings about all of it—when her phone buzzed in her clutch. She smiled sadly at the flurry of messages she had from her mother and her tías. She'd sent a selfie of herself in her green gown and their responses ranged from firework emojis to *bellísima*, *hermosa* and every other word for "beautiful" in Spanish they could come up with. It was a good reminder she had people who loved her waiting not far from here. People who had her back and would never leave her to cry alone in a corner, or speak angry words to her where everyone could see. She had something to prove to the Sambranos, but she didn't need their approval.

"Well, well, well…if it isn't my father's dirty little secret. Are you getting tired of pretending you belong here?" a very loud voice called in her direction. It took Esme a moment to react, but then she saw him. Onyx was sauntering up to her unsteadily as every eye in their vicinity turned toward her. Her face felt hot with embarrassment and she wanted to hide. She hated being a spectacle. But if Onyx thought he was going to hurl insults at her and she'd just take it, he had another thing coming.

"Nice to see you, Onyx. Did you have to take some time out from your busy schedule of photobombing celebrities to make it tonight?" She sounded like a bitch, but she didn't care.

"I hope you enjoy the free booze, because you won't be around much longer." From the slur in his words, it seemed he was enjoying the open bar enough for the both of them. "You will never be CEO of Sambrano. My mother will see to that." Her brother's mouth twisted into an ugly sneer as he looked at her with naked loathing. He really hated her, which shouldn't have been the surprise it was. On the couple of occasions her mother had sent her to spend time at their father's house, Onyx had barely acknowledged her.

He was just a couple of years younger than her and they'd both been small then—barely in elementary school—but she always remembered how he'd looked at her. Like she was something distasteful and unpleasant. Something he didn't like in his space. And it seemed like that feeling had only grown in the years since. That realization was a sucker punch. She'd expected defiance, even some territorial pettiness, but this hatred cut her. To know that people who shared her blood despised her without knowing much about her...

It hurt, but she would be damned if she let anyone see it.

"Sorry to inform you, brother, but Sambrano Studios is mine, too. That was how our father wanted it. Now you and I even own equal shares." She tipped her glass to him as if to toast the happy news, even as her stomach felt like it was trying to crawl up her throat. "Means you better get used to seeing me around." She avoided looking around, not wanting to see all the disapproving faces. She could agonize about it all later, but right now she would not give any of them the satisfaction.

Onyx looked even more furious. "You don't belong here. You're not his real daughter!" he spat, stalking closer. But before he could take another step toward her, Rodrigo yanked Onyx's arms so hard he lifted him off his feet.

"Don't even think about it!" Rodrigo whispered furiously, as he plucked her brother off his feet like a rag doll and proceeded to physically remove him from the room. She started after them as Onyx struggled in Rodrigo's grip, but it was pointless. Onyx was not a large man and he was certainly no match for six feet and two inches of solid muscle.

"Let me go." Her brother raged as Rodrigo made his way through the room, headed for the archway that led to an exit. You could hear a pin drop in the room, other than Onyx's enraged protests and the clicking of her stilettos as she followed the two men. Every single person in the room was frozen in fascination watching the drama unfold. She should've known this would happen. In the back of her mind it occurred to her that this was very much out of character for Rodrigo. The man hated messiness but here he was diving right into the fray. It was better not to dig too deeply into the why of his actions. She already had enough to deal with.

She wouldn't be surprised if a video of this shitshow wasn't on every New York City gossip website within the hour. From the corner of her eye she thought she saw Perla looking on as Rodrigo manhandled her brother. For a second she wondered if Carmelina would join this circus, and really give all these people the show of a lifetime. But Rodrigo moved fast and soon he was shoving Onyx through a door leading into a small alcove and propping the smaller man against the nearest wall.

"Rodrigo, put him down," she pleaded from a safe distance, aware that getting between the two men was not advisable.

But it was like talking to a wall. He completely ignored her and continued to get in Onyx's face. If people could only see the cool, calm and collected Mr. Almanzar now. "Are you out of your damn mind, Onyx?"

"Get your hands off me," Onyx screeched, batting furiously at the tight grip Rodrigo had on his arm to no avail. When he wasn't able to make the taller man budge, Onyx looked around as if he could find someone to help him. When his eyes landed on Esme that familiar vicious expression returned to his face.

"Oh, I see how it is. You two are scheming together." He threw his head back and laughed. "Oh, honey, have you hitched your star to the wrong wagon. This one is a cold-blooded bastard. He only looks out for himself. If he's who you're counting on then we definitely have nothing to worry about." He twisted his mouth into what she assumed was a satisfied smile.

"I guess you do have something against people who work for a living, *little brother*." Esme knew the smartest move was to keep her mouth shut and let Rodrigo handle Onyx. But it incensed her to hear her brother talk about her ex-lover like that when he'd done so much to keep their father's company going. Rodrigo shot her a surprised look, then turned his attention back to Onyx when he tried to lunge for her.

"You don't know anything about me. About any of us. You're not a part of this family." Onyx's ugly sneer disappeared when Rodrigo shook him hard, pressing him harder to the wall.

"Don't talk to her. You little shit, you're not good enough to lick her fucking boots." Onyx paled and even Esmeralda could hear the cold menace in Rodrigo's voice.

This was a freaking mess. Rodrigo was seconds from completely losing his temper and when he did this was truly going to go to hell in a handbasket. Onyx would make sure everyone knew what had happened and somehow she'd be blamed for it. She moved fast and got as close as she could without running the risk of getting elbowed in the face.

"Rodrigo, please stop," she asked with as much calm as she could manage. "He's not worth it. He's got nothing to lose. We do." She could see how the words landed by the way he ground his jaw. After a moment, he stepped back and released his grip on Onyx, who stumbled for a moment, but quickly began to run his mouth again.

"If you're sleeping with him, my advice is that you cut your losses now. He'll sell you out in a minute to stay on top."

"Are you trying to get your ass beat, Onyx?" Rodrigo growled. "I'm so fucking tired of you people and your drama." Onyx just weaved in place, that drunk smile on his face. They'd keep doing this all night until they came to blows or Onyx barfed, and she'd had enough.

You people. The loathing in Rodrigo's voice was like a slap in the face. He meant the Sambranos. He meant her, too.

"I didn't ask you to get involved in this, Rodrigo. I can take care of myself." She didn't even give him a chance to respond and moved toward the door. She was done with this. She needed to get back to what she was here to do: prove to the board she was the only one who could take the helm of the television empire.

Nine

"Why did you leave like that, Esmeralda?" Rodrigo sounded rough as he walked into Esmeralda's office, even to his own ears. He'd lost it back at the party, acted like a complete Neanderthal, and he couldn't even find it in himself to regret any of it. Well, that wasn't true. He regretted embarrassing Esmeralda. He was sorry he'd made an already bad situation worse for her, but when he'd seen that little shit coming for her, he'd gone into a rage.

"What was I supposed to stay there for, Rodrigo?" She sounded fed up, and he couldn't blame her. "As you can see, I'm working. What are you doing here? I thought you would've had enough Sambrano drama for the night." He had. He was absolutely *done* with Onyx, Carmelina and their bullshit. But instead of going home like a sensible person, he'd ended up here. He'd told himself a dozen times on the drive over that he was here to finish up some work. But he'd been lying; he'd come after her, hoping she'd be here. To make sure she was all right. She'd been magnificent. Standing up for herself when anyone else would've cowered.

"I *am* tired of Sambrano drama." He should be thanking her for the way she'd stood up for him. No one had ever done that. Usually people were only too happy to see him be dressed down. They lived to remind him he was only the help. How easily they forgot that if it weren't for him things would've fallen apart. But they still despised him. Loathed him for being the only person Patricio trusted, as if that hadn't cost him anything. "I thought after that scene you'd want to call it a night."

She scoffed at that. "And then what? Let my so-called brother's insults scare me off? Carmelina Sambrano made sure I knew what my place was my entire life, and yet I am still here," she said, leaning against the desk chair. Her tone was placid, but there was a sharpness to the way she held herself that told him that scene at The Cloisters had shaken her. "I would never give any of them the satisfaction of thinking they got to me. Sorry, Rodrigo, you're going to have to work a little harder for that corner office."

"I already have a corner office." He sounded pissed and tired, but she wasn't fazed by any of it. Her long neck and back were ramrod straight as she typed on the keyboard, her eyes darting between the three monitors in front of her. That's when he noticed she hadn't even bothered to change her clothes. She'd wiped off her makeup, put her hair up in a top bun, taken off her shoes and gotten to work.

Focused. Determined. She stayed on her path, didn't

let the drama distract her. He'd lost that somewhere along the way. The ability to let all the scheming roll off his back. To the world he looked like he was made of stone, but he felt worn down. Sometimes he could barely come up with one or two reminders of why he loved this job. Being at the helm of a television empire came with power and prestige, but when everyone thought of you as the lackey, that you got the job by kissing ass, you had to constantly prove yourself. And he was tired of having to deal with the scorn of people who could not survive one day doing what he did. And in that at least he and Esmeralda had something in common.

Patricio ignored his daughter for her entire life. And yet of all his children she was the one who'd gotten his determination and ambition. The one who had pursued a career in television. And still she was the one who had to prove herself, who had to earn the right to claim her place. "What are you working on?" he asked, taking off his jacket as he came over to look at the screen. He needed a distraction.

She glanced up at him for a moment and he did not miss that her eyes landed right at the spot where he'd unbuttoned his shirt and a sliver of skin was peeking out. His eyes locked on her lips out of their own volition and his mouth watered with the memory of how it had felt to kiss her tonight. Despite the exhaustion, a jolt of desire coursed through his body at the thought of doing it again. He'd take that smart mouth with hard, hungry kisses and then he'd pick her up, wrap her strong legs around his waist and have her right against the wall. Lose himself in the tight perfect grip of her body, until they were both spent.

Get your head in the game, Rodrigo. She's about her

business and you need to be, as well. He pulled up a chair and sat next to her as he rolled up his sleeves. Esmeralda gave him a suspicious look as he pointed at the slide she was working on. "Tell me about this."

"Are you serious?" she asked incredulously.

"The board already knows I can do the job. They want to see if you can."

She rolled her eyes at him, but something about what she saw on his face seemed to smooth the lines of tension on her forehead, and she turned to what he was asking her about.

"This is my Big Ask," she informed him, as her eyes scanned the screen. "I'm proposing we bring back some of the programming that Sambrano was known for in the early years. Remember the old comedy sketch shows they did with comedians from all over Latin America? The Afro-Latinx culture focused shows. I was also thinking that we could have a network dedicated to only Latinx food. And not just tacos and ceviche, which are the only things people seem to think we eat." Her eyes lit up as she talked, her hands everywhere as she explained, and he could not get enough of it, of her.

"I'm envisioning baking competitions, grilling showdowns. I'm talking Garifuna pastry chefs, Quechua bakers, Argentinian grill masters. I want every region, every country, *every culture* represented." With every word she said his brain woke up more, and he realized he was intrigued. He was more than intrigued. He was... energized. "There are so many Latinx chefs who have gained a huge following on Instagram and I bet would love to be on a network, you know?"

He frowned as she went through the slides, taking in some of her concepts. They were good. Innovative but still staying in line with the brand. The kind of stuff he'd pushed for in his early years at Sambrano but gave up on after getting shot down again and again.

Well, they weren't exactly like his. Her ideas were a lot bolder. Where his had been baby steps toward going back to the roots of Sambrano, she was proposing leaps. He'd suggested a cooking show; she was going in with a whole network. Then he looked down at the open folder on the desk and froze. "What's that?"

She looked down at where his finger was pointing and then up at him, beaming, all the anger and resentment from earlier in the evening forgotten. That was something he'd always loved about her. Esmeralda could never stay angry for long.

"There's no cover letter, so I don't know who drafted the memo. It's almost eleven years old, but the concept is basically a prototype of what I'd like to propose." His heart sped up again as she continued. "Listen to this," she told him as she pointed to the paper. "'We have to continue to fulfill the promise we made to our viewers, that from Patagonia to Baja California, they can go home when they tune into Sambrano networks.'" The smile on her face was radiant as she looked up at him.

"That's it. That's the mission. We have to lean into the vision that our world is wide and rich enough that we could have entire cable networks fully dedicated to us. Like a Latinx History Channel. All our histories, bringing in Indigenous producers, Afro-descendant filmmakers. Shows dedicated to LGBTQ+ Latinx communities. We can do anything, like *Project Runway*, but make it Latinx." She grinned at him and he found himself smiling back. Seeing her vision clearly. "I want every gaze represented. To make a mark in the current landscape

Sambrano has to think bigger. One channel isn't enough to carry all that we are." She was practically vibrating with excitement, her eyes on a future without limits. An artist standing in front of an empty canvas with a brush, paint and endless possibilities. And she was a force to be reckoned with.

"You were around then." She said it almost as if she'd just remembered that fact. "Do you have any idea who wrote this and if they're still here? I'd love to talk to them to find out why their ideas were never implemented."

He paused, nervous to confess this secret to her. "I wrote it." He almost laughed when she did a double take, as if she couldn't even picture it. He couldn't blame her. He could barely remember the twenty-five-year-old junior content developer who wrote that memo. When was the last time he'd felt that inspired? When he'd felt unafraid to launch himself into something just because he felt passionate about it? He couldn't recall.

"You?" she asked, her eyes wide with surprise.

He crossed his arms over his chest, feeling defensive and a little hurt at her astonishment. "Is it so hard to believe that I could've written that?"

Her eyes softened at whatever she saw in his face and tapped him on the shoulder. "Don't be such a baby. I'm just surprised, that's all. You've always seemed so... risk-averse."

"You mean boring," he said. She pointed a finger at him, clicking her tongue. "I'm a realist," he declared, doing his best to hide the peevishness in his tone.

She gave him a long look from under those thick dark lashes of hers and he could see the hint of a smile pulling up at her lips. "I meant solid, reliable. One who sticks to what works." She wasn't wrong. He'd learned to temper his ideas, to work within the confines of what was doable, and she would have to learn to, as well. He uncrossed his arms, feeling like he needed something to do with his hands, with his eyes. To keep from uttering something he shouldn't or worse, reaching out and touching her. Boundaries were his friend.

"I liked that about you," she said, almost ruefully. "Your steadiness." His chest expanded at her words, the sincerity in them. Esmeralda never said something she didn't mean. And that was what had always devastated him when it came to her. She would never lie, not even to protect her pride. He kept his mouth closed as he sensed his own onslaught of confessions coming on. No good could come of that.

They stayed with their gazes locked, and that need which seemed ever-present when he was around Esmeralda swirled like a ring of fire in his gut. Ten years of telling himself he was over her. That the entire relationship had been a mistake. That Esme had only been interested in him as a way to get back at her father. That there was nothing there. That he'd destroyed any chance of getting her back. That they were both *better off.* Each of those lies turned to dust the moment he'd seen her again and were immediately replaced by this feckless want.

"What ever happened to the guy who wrote this?" she asked, and there was a breathlessness to her voice.

"That guy learned idealism got him nowhere. That to get to the top he had to compromise." And now that he was at the top, he wondered if those compromises might have been too high of a price to pay.

"I think you're lying."

"You know me a lot less than you think you do, Esmeralda," he rebuffed, voice tight with too much feeling.

"I know that the same guy who wrote this memo was the guy I was falling in love with. I know that even though you let my father and his shitty dog-eat-dog view of the world suck you in, you're the guy who helped your family when they lost everything. You might have turned your back on that man, but he's still there." Her finger pressed right on the spot in his chest where his heart was pounding like a jackhammer.

He stood up, shaking from the way her words had struck him. "I'm heading out for the night."

"You know what else I know?" she asked, voice dripping with something that made him stop in his tracks. "That you're dying to finish what we started in that creepy bedroom suite this afternoon." He had to suppress a laugh even as his cock hardened from her words.

"And the last thing I know is that I'd let you... All you have to do is ask."

His hazel-eyed beauty bit her bottom lip, tucked a curl behind her ear as she waited for his reaction. It had been stupid to kiss her. Stupid and potentially disastrous because the floodgates were now wide open. He'd known he would do it again if she asked him. He'd been dizzy with the possibility of it. And now she had.

Hope had always come at a steep cost for Rodrigo, and he had never paid a higher price than when he'd let himself believe he could have Esmeralda Sambrano-Peña. He'd sworn he'd never again take a gamble like the one he'd taken on this woman. And yet here he was, ten years later, older but clearly not much wiser, about to plunge into the abyss again.

Ten

"If we start this, we're not stopping until I've had you, Esmeralda," he warned, already moving toward her. In an instant he'd gone from feeling a bone-deep weariness to a madness that crackled under his skin like lightning. Some things never changed, and Esmeralda had a knack for making him forget he was supposed to be measured and stoic.

"Did I stutter, Rodrigo?" He didn't say a word, he just leaned in and scooped her into his arms, and after a yelp of surprise she wrapped her legs around his waist and held on. "Why can't I keep my hands off you?" she grumbled as she worked on kissing down his neck, her hands already busy with the buttons of his shirt.

He grunted when she used her teeth on him and wished he could sprint to his office without risking ramming into a glass door. The lights of the entire floor were off except for the small lamp on Esme's desk and the ceiling light guiding him to the bedroom in his office. Patricio was probably rolling over in his grave right now, but even that thought would not stop him from doing this.

He was tired of holding back, of not letting himself have the things he wanted. The things he craved. Only with Esmeralda had he ever let go, cut loose every one of his passions, and she'd always met him each step of the way. She quenched his every thirst, and it had been so long since he'd felt this kind of urgency. He'd been walking in a desert these past ten years without her. He'd known what was missing, but his need to never step out of line, to stay on track, kept him from her. It had been unfair of Patricio to ask him to stay away from her, but none of that mattered here and now.

He reached the door to the suite in a few swift steps and slammed his hand on the button that would slide it open. Esme tried to loosen the grip of her legs around his waist and pushed off him like she was intending to walk the rest of the way. He was not having it. A sound very much like a growl escaped from his chest as he crushed her to him. "You're staying right here." He pressed the point by lowering his head and licking into her mouth.

"Why do I find this side of you so ridiculously hot?" she asked, feigning annoyance at the same time she slid a hand down to his crotch and gripped his hard cock over his pants. "Mmm, looks like someone is ready to unleash himself on me." She bit his earlobe as he reached a serviceable surface and set her down. She kept her legs around him, but now that his hands were free, he let them explore.

"Mess around and find out, Esmeralda," he warned, eliciting a wicked laugh from her.

"I'm planning to, Rodrigo." She was a brat and he loved it. He had to breathe through the need pounding inside him. He pulled back for a second. There was one small light in the bathroom, so that she was cast in shadow. But he could see her leonine eyes, like embers in the dark. Full of the heat that had always burned him down to ashes.

"I want to be right here." His voice was gravel as he cupped her heat. She writhed against him, gasping from his touch, but he wanted to see her undone. "I'm going to be so deep inside you," he told her as he nipped her earlobe, coaxing a delicious little moan from her. "But first I'm going to make you scream for me." He brought one hand to her breast, and tweaked a taut nipple, just like he remembered drove her wild. Her chest was heaving, and he could feel her need in the way she moved against him. "Once I've made you come on my tongue."

"Rodrigo." She sounded needy and the urge to give her whatever she asked for was almost overpowering. But he wanted to take this slow, savor it and do all the things he'd yearned for and could not have for so long. With agonizing gentleness he took her face in his hands, brought their faces closer, so their lips brushed against each other. He flicked out his tongue for a taste.

"Don't tease me, dammit," she protested, making him smile.

"So impatient, Joya," he teased, before going in for a rough kiss. He ate at her mouth. Their tongues tangled together in a frantic dance. He felt greedy and he already knew he would never get enough of Esmeralda. He'd been starving, taking scraps when this was the only thing that could fill him. He felt the oxygen like fizz in his lungs, every cell replenished from finally getting what he'd needed.

Her. Only her.

His hands drifted down to undo the zipper at her back, then made quick work of her bra while he grazed her throat with his teeth. "Tell me what you want," he demanded, cupping her naked breasts, his cock getting impossibly harder just from feeling the heft of them. He couldn't resist grazing the flat of his tongue against one nipple and then the other one. He could devour her and still it would not be enough.

"You," she whispered before taking his hand and placing it against her hot sex.

"Is this where you want me?" he asked while sliding his hand under her skirts, looking for her wet heat. He felt the silkiness of her skin as his palms moved over her thighs. He sucked in a breath when he reached her core and discovered what was waiting for him. "Where are your panties, Esmeralda?" He could not sound mad if he tried.

She pressed a smile to his neck and nodded. "I showered before the reception and didn't exactly have a change of clothes here." Her tone was casual, but he could hear that she was very pleased with herself for undoing him. Roughly, he picked her up again until her feet hit the floor and helped her step out of her dress. He was about to toss it to the side, but she stopped him before he balled up the fabric.

"Oh no you don't. That's Siriano. Place it on the armchair, *gently.*" It was extremely hard to focus with her completely naked in front of him. But he did as she asked, then took her by the hand and led her to the bed.

"So beautiful," he said, once she was on her back, laid out for him like an offering. He used his hands to spread her legs and admired her for a moment. He'd missed this. Ten years of making do when he knew this bounty was out there. All that flawless brown skin, for him to touch, to lick, to suck, to claim. With two fingers he parted her folds and placed his lips right at her core, tongue darting out to taste her.

"Don't stop." He'd always loved how demanding she was. That her self-consciousness flew out the window whenever he had his mouth and hands on her. That he could make her lose herself in pleasure. She groaned and fisted his hair in her hands—moving against him as he worked to pleasure her, and the little moans and gasps she made set his blood on fire. The taste of her was intoxicating, filling all his senses until she was all he could hear, taste, see and smell. Soon she was bucking against his mouth, cries of ecstasy piercing the silence of the room.

"I've missed your mouth," she whispered breathlessly, as she ran her hands over his shoulders and back, pointy nails softly grazing his sensitized skin. He shivered from the onslaught of emotions.

"I missed everything," he confessed, losing himself to her touch, mouth pressing kisses to her warm skin as he made his way up her body. He'd had relationships since her. He'd had lovers. So why did it feel like he'd gone a decade without human touch? Why did it feel like these were the first hands he'd had on him in years? His skin was parched, dry earth, and her hands were rain.

"I need you. Please, Rodrigo." Her words seemed so loud in the quiet room. He felt a tightening at his waist as she unbuttoned his trousers and unzipped them, and when he opened his eyes she was looking up at him, unrestrained hunger flashing in her eyes. Within seconds he was on her, his larger body covering hers. Skin on skin, fused together. There was nothing that could stop him from what they were about to do.

He reached for the side table where he'd left his shaving kit and plucked out a condom and rolled it on as she undulated on the bed, pleasuring herself. Her lusty moans resounded through the room and if he didn't get inside her he would combust. As soon as he was ready, he went in for another kiss, their tongues sliding together.

"More," she demanded as he placed himself right at her entrance. "Now, Rodrigo." He could not deny her or himself any longer and entered her.

"God," he gasped, heart pounding in his chest as pleasure coiled around his spine like a vise. "You're perfect. I want to be inside you forever." With one hand he moved them until her hips were canted just right and he could be seated to the hilt.

"Ah. I love this!" she cried as he pounded into her and she met him stroke for stroke. He placed a hand in between them and rubbed circles over her clit, desperate to feel her walls tighten around him. "I'm coming," she gasped, pulsing around him. And soon his orgasm was crashing over him as they shared hard, hungry kisses.

Yes, this was what he'd been missing. And as ill-advised and possibly disastrous as this was, with this woman warm and sated in his arms, he could not find it in him to regret it.

Eleven

"Hey, Mami," Esme answered the phone, her jaw cracking from a yawn.

"Mija, I never heard you get home last night, and this morning you left before I woke up!"

"I got in really late. I didn't want to wake you." Heat flooded her face as she thought of the reason why she'd gotten home at almost 2:00 a.m. "I ended up coming back to the office after the reception to um…" She cleared her throat as an image of Rodrigo with his head between her legs flashed through her mind. She closed her eyes, hoping to shut it down, but more moments from the night before came to her in a flurry of very not-safe-for-work images.

It had been supremely unwise to sleep with Rodrigo, but she could still feel the delicious aches from last night in her muscles. Yeah, that had been dumb, and so damn good. He was so strong. The way he'd taken her…his massive chest covering her as he surged into her. Over the years she'd convinced herself that being with Rodrigo had not been as earth-shattering as she'd remembered. That she'd embellished their time together because he'd been her first and she'd been in love with him for so long she created a fantasy in her head. She'd convinced herself that no one could be that good. Well, she'd been lying to herself, because the memory didn't hold a candle to the real thing.

The twenty-six-year-old gentle and attentive lover she'd been with at twenty-one was still there, but this Rodrigo was more skilled. Self-possessed like he was in every other aspect of his life. Although the restraint he carried himself with had evaporated the moment he put his hands on her. And his body, mercy. The man's chest was like sculpted, bronzed marble. Her very own flesh-and-bone lustful god who'd made her tremble in his hands.

"Esmeralda Luisa Sambrano Peña." Her mother's recitation of her full name made her jump in her seat. Her face heated again as she realized she'd been having sex daydreams while she had her mother on the phone.

"Sorry, Mami." *What was she doing?* "I just have a lot to do. I need like eight weeks and have four days, so I'm feeling the pressure to be here as much as possible."

"I hear you, but Esme, amor, don't start doubting yourself. You've been working hard for years for an opportunity like this. And you know what to do. Did that woman bother you again?"

"No. I haven't seen Carmelina." She sighed, feeling unsteady. She'd texted her mom about her father's widow showing up in Rodrigo's office. Esme wasn't planning on letting her know about the scene Onyx had made at the reception. That would only worry her. But Ivelisse's question was also a good reminder that she was on her own here. No matter how nice it had been to feel like Rodrigo was on her side, she *was* still trying to take his job. They were *not* on the same team.

She needed to get her head in the game or she would blow her chance to finally make her professional dreams come true. She had a moment with Rodrigo, and the mind-blowing sex was a way to blow off steam. A one-time thing that could not happen again and that was that. Closure. That's what it was, one last goodbye. And she hoped if she kept repeating that to herself she would eventually believe it.

"Good. If she bothers you again tell Rodrigo. He's a good boy and he'll help you." Esme rolled her eyes, because despite everything her mom still had a soft spot for him. She'd been the only one who'd known about their relationship back then, and even when Esmeralda called her mother to tell her how Rodrigo ended things, her mother had not disparaged him. She'd comforted Esmeralda and sat through many pity parties over the phone. But her mother had not spoken ill of him, not once.

"I'm trying to take his job, Mami. He's not exactly an ally. And let's not talk about how he ghosted me ten years ago."

Her mother clicked her tongue, a definite sign she did not approve of Esme's opinion of the man. "You should give him more credit. He's not a bad man. He's just loyal to a fault."

At least on that they agreed. "Yeah, and his loyalties are not with me. So, I need to keep my guard up. That means Rodrigo Almanzar is the enemy until I have the CEO position secured."

"Good morning to you, too, Ms. Sambrano-Peña."

Shit.

"Oh, hey." Yeah, there was no masking the "just got caught disparaging your name" guilt in her voice. From the look on his face he must've heard her fighting words. Dammit. Her and her big mouth. This was not the way to keep things civil. Sure, she didn't want to keep going down the path they started on last night, but she didn't want him mad at her, either. First she'd slept with him and now he'd found her talking smack about him behind his back. This was not a good development. She pointed at her earbuds. "It's Mami. Let me just end the call."

His face was back to that stony expression she could not read at all, the heat she'd seen in his eyes the night before replaced by a flinty stare. "I'm not here to chit-chat, just wanted to remind you we're meeting with the CFO in ten minutes."

A hole opened in her chest at the detached way he spoke to her. Like she was nothing to him. As if last night had never happened. But wasn't this exactly what she wanted? Some distance. She'd told herself a dozen times since they'd parted ways last night she couldn't get caught up in her old baggage about Rodrigo. That she had to keep pushing to get her presentation ready. And it seemed they were on the same page. So this was great. Exactly what needed to happen. Then why did she feel like a ball of lead had settled in the pit of her stomach?

Because Rodrigo always did this to her. He made her weak and careless then he left her alone and discarded. Was she really going to set herself up to have her heart stomped like the last time? How could she forget how it had felt when he'd dumped her? God, and she'd slept

with him. Not even 48 hours of having the man back
in her life, and she had already broken every rule she'd
set for herself with Rodrigo Almanzar. And she wanted
to be angry, she wanted to be *furious*. But the way he'd
touched her last night, the way he'd whispered in her
ear that he'd ached for her, what those words had done
to her—*that* would not be so easy to forget.

"Your office?" she asked as her mind raced.

He frowned at whatever he saw in her face, and for a
moment she thought he'd say something about last night.
That he'd mention the dozens of kisses they'd shared before they said goodbye. But instead, he uttered a clipped
"Yes," and walked out.

The meeting was brutal and not for the reasons Esme
had anticipated. Magdalena Polanco, their CFO, was
great, and gave Esmeralda the rundown on all operating costs for the studio like she'd requested. Numbers
people always intimidated her. Esmeralda's forte was
more the big picture, the overarching vision, and not so
much the intricacies of how to make that all work. But
Magdalena seemed easy to work with, and Esme thought
it would be nice to have someone like that on her team.
A strong Latina who had gotten to the top of her field
by working hard. At any other time she would've loved
to pick her brain for an hour, ask Magdalena about her
career trajectory, but Rodrigo's whole vibe was driving Esme nuts.

He'd barely acknowledged her during the meeting.
And whenever she directed a question at him, he either
answered with a monosyllable or he politely deferred to
Magdalena. It was irritating as hell.

Was he going to ice her out for the next four days because she was trying to keep things professional? What the hell was his problem? They were grown adults who'd gotten a bit carried away after a stressful day—*surely* they could be cordial. Granted, it would be so much easier if he didn't look so damn good. He'd shaved this morning, but she could still feel every spot where his scruff had scraped the sensitive skin of her thigh when he was…

"Miss Sambrano-Peña?"

Dammit, she'd done it again. "I'm sorry." She tried to smile, but it would not quite take, so she just gave up. "What were you saying?"

"Just wondering if you had any other questions for me?"

She shook her head and resisted placing her palms on her flaming cheeks. "Nope. Thank you so much. I have everything I need for now. If I have a question I can give you a call, right?"

Magdalena gave her a warm smile as she stuffed papers back into her binder. "Absolutely. You have all my contact information and Rodrigo knows how to find me if it's something urgent." The older woman smiled affectionately at the object of Esmeralda's fevered musings.

"Tell Guille I'll call him this week. We said we'd go shoot some hoops." Magdalena beamed at Rodrigo.

"My youngest son was a teammate of Rodrigo's in college." Magdalena informed Esmeralda. "He's the one who recommended me for this job, you know?" Esme wondered if Magdalena was letting her know that as a way to tell her whose side she was on. But the way she looked at Rodrigo told her that wasn't it at all. She just genuinely liked him.

As much as Esmeralda wanted to act like a jerk right

now, she only smiled. "He made a smart move then, I can tell you're great at your job."

"He's fought for a lot people in his time here," she told Esme, before walking out of the office.

"You certainly have a lot of admirers amongst the corporate team."

Rodrigo lifted his gaze from whatever he was doing on his phone and stared at her for so long she wondered if he'd heard her. Irrational possessiveness was truly not her friend. And yet here she was, acting like he was her man, never mind that Magdalena had to be pushing seventy.

"You're jealous of Magdalena now? She has grand-kids your age."

"Jealous? Please, you're so conceited." Now she sounded like a brat. His mouth twitched, but before it could turn into a smile he bit his bottom lip, and God, she wanted to lean over and suck on it. To sit astride his lap and kiss him senseless.

"You *sound* jealous, Esmeralda. I thought I was the enemy." Okay, so he *had* heard her.

She lifted a shoulder, trying very hard to feign an indifference she was not at all feeling. "You kind of are. We're at odds right now and it would do us both good not to forget that."

He arched an eyebrow at her words, and he looked so composed and controlled in that moment. Every hair in its place. His bespoke suit a perfect fit. He looked every inch the CEO. He looked like the man who should be sitting in this office. And that insidious insecurity flooded her. She wanted to lead this company. To prove—to the board, to her father's widow, to her siblings—that her father's wishes hadn't been born out of misguided guilt, but because she was the right person to run the studio.

But she wondered if she really had what it took to take the job from Rodrigo.

As she digested this fresh dose of conflicting feelings his phone buzzed, and after looking at it he stood purposefully, then waved a hand toward the door. "Go to your office and grab what you need for the rest of the day. We're going somewhere."

"What do you mean?" she asked, irritated at his attempt to order her around.

As usual he didn't give her anything. He just walked over to his desk and picked up a leather messenger bag. "I want you to see something."

She was annoyed at how vague he was being and a little hurt he hadn't brought up the night before. But she wasn't going to be a hypocrite and get mad. She had no intention of mentioning it, either.

She tried her best to give him a sincere smile when she glanced up at him. "Aren't you going to at least give me a hint? You know I hate surprises."

He stepped up to her, close enough that she could feel the heat of his body. He bent down so that his lips were almost grazing her ears. "You're just going to have to trust me, Joya."

Damn the man for being so infuriatingly enticing, and for the husky laugh he let out as she stood there shivering. She should've told him to cut it out. To stop playing games with her. But when she looked closely, she saw that he was far from unbothered. His shoulders were tense, and his eyes wary. He was holding himself as if he expected her to say she could never trust him— but that would be a lie. She thought of his easy friendship with Jimena, and Magdalena's clear affection and respect for him as evidence of the way that he carried himself personally *and* professionally. Yeah, despite everything, she still trusted Rodrigo Almanzar. And there was a simple reason for that: her mother was right; he *was* a good man.

Twelve

"The Grand Palace? Is it even open at noon on a week-day?" Rodrigo had to bite the inside of his cheek at Esmeralda's question. She'd been peppering him with them the entire thirty-minute drive uptown. She'd never liked being kept in the dark and it probably made him a jerk that he was enjoying seeing her practically vibrate from curiosity.

The driver stopped in front of the main entrance of the theater where the curator for the Latinx Diaspora Film and Television Archives was waiting for them. He turned to her and bit back the smile threatening to appear on his face. She looked so damn edible with that scowl on her face. He was so tempted to lean in and kiss all that annoyance right out of her. "It's open for us. There's something I want you to see."

He pushed open the door to the town car, but she

would not budge. "No, tell me what we're doing here first."

He crossed his arms, mirroring hers. "Terca."

"You're the stubborn one. Just tell me."

He shook his head smiling and reached for her hand. "Ven. There's someone waiting for us," he told her and pointed at the curator who was patiently waiting for them to get out of the car.

"Fine," she groused as Rodrigo stepped out of the car and helped her do the same. Once they both had their feet firmly planted on the pavement, he had to force himself to let go of her hand.

"Señor Almanzar." The curator walked over to them, a welcoming smile on his face. "And this must be Ms. Sambrano."

"Sambrano-Peña," she corrected the man in a friendly tone. Rodrigo admired that in Esmeralda— she knew who she was. And nothing would change that. Not even losing the CEO position.

Rodrigo extended his hand to the man and made introductions. "Esmeralda, this is Huchi Piera. He's the curator and archivist for the theater and he's been kind enough to prepare some footage that I think will be helpful for your presentation." He saw when his words landed and for a fleeting moment a genuinely pleased smile appeared on her face. The realization that Rodrigo had done something to help her.

And he wished he could tell her what he was really thinking. That he'd woken up wanting her. That he could not get last night out of his head even for a second. That he'd almost had to jerk off in his office, because he still had her smell on his hands. That he was desperate to know if she was thinking about it, too. He wished he could ask if what he'd overheard her tell her mother had been true, or if, like him, she was just trying and failing to keep her feelings in check. But instead, he gestured toward the entrance.

"Shall we?" His tone was a little sharper than he intended. But when she looked at him, her eyes were wide and her mouth parted just a little. She looked excited and touched by him bringing her here, and it was getting harder to not give in to his instincts. To not bring her close, or place a hand at her back, so Piera and anyone else in the theater could see she was his.

"This way, Ms. Sambrano-Peña," Piera called, breaking the spell between them. By the next second she was all business, turning to follow the curator to the private screening area he'd prepared for them.

"Have you been to a show here before?" the curator asked as they crossed the large foyer of the theater and took a set of winding stairs up to a mezzanine.

"Yes. I have, many times," she said as she looked around. The Grand Palace was a gorgeous old theater, built in 1930 by the renowned architect Thomas W. Lamb. The sumptuous filigree carvings on the walls were exquisitely done and made it one of the most beautiful theaters in Manhattan. "It's such a beautiful building. The last time I was here, I brought my mom to see Johnny Ventura," Esmeralda said, slowly taking it all in, pausing to admire the beauty of the place. She'd always been like that, an admirer of other people's craft. Reverent when she was in front of true artistry.

Piera made an approving sound at the mention of the legendary Afro-Dominican merenguero. "Those were excellent shows."

"I missed that one," Rodrigo explained. "I wanted

to come, but…" He was going to say he was working, which he had been, but he didn't want to talk about the office. "I never got around to getting tickets."

"Next time let your *novia* handle the tickets. My wife is always a lot more organized about that sort of thing than I am."

The older man calling Esme his girlfriend flustered him so much he missed the last step and almost fell flat on his face at the landing. When he got his footing back, he shook his head in her direction. "She's not my girlfriend."

As soon as the words were out of his mouth, he knew he'd made a mistake. Esmeralda stiffened at his harsh tone. "Wow, you'd think he just accused you of something." With that she turned to Piera. "We're not dating. In fact, we're barely friends."

Piera raised an eyebrow and stopped just beyond the doors to the small screening room. "Of course. My mistake." He didn't sound sorry at all. He was at that age when Latinx people said whatever they wanted with impunity and lived for getting their noses in people's business. "But you really should consider it. You make a very elegant couple."

Rodrigo swallowed down the growl in his throat and pointed at the open double doors in front of them. "Is this it?"

The curator gave him that shameless old man grin and nodded. "Yes, everything is ready for you." He winked at Rodrigo as if they were in on the same joke, then he turned to Esmeralda. "I've left copies of some old photographs that we have from when your dad did *Navidad Para el Pueblo* here at the theater." A beatific smile appeared on the old man's face at the mention of the free concerts for the Latinx community in New York City that Patricio had sponsored for decades. "Your father was a great man, and a true champion of our culture. He saved the theater in the '90s when developers wanted to tear it down. Did you know that?"

Esme gasped at Piera's revelation and turned to Rodrigo, an eyebrow raised in question. Her voice trembled ever so slightly when she finally spoke. "I had no idea."

Rodrigo felt a stinging in the back of his throat as he took in Esme's reaction. He'd been so caught up in getting through this week that he'd forgotten this was not just a competition for Esmeralda, this was her chance to finally reclaim a part of her she'd been denied her whole life.

Piera smiled kindly at Esmeralda. "Mr. Sambrano quietly did many things for a lot of groups looking to conserve and document the culture of the diaspora. That's what the footage you'll see showcases. It's a shame the documentary was never finished."

"We're watching the footage from the documentary? I thought that—" Esme asked, looking between Piera and himself.

"I'll take it from here. Thank you, Mr. Piera."

The old man dipped his head again and pointed at some doors that were visible from the balcony in the mezzanine. "My offices are down there. You can come get me once you're done. We've left everything you asked for in the screening room. You're all alone up here, so if you need anything you can call down from the phone that's inside. Just dial zero. It was a pleasure meeting you, Ms. Sambrano-Peña." With that he left them standing alone together.

"After you." Rodrigo stood awkwardly in front of

Esmeralda, gesturing toward the door. And it seemed he could not stop himself from sounding like an ass.

She narrowed her eyes at him, but her curiosity seemed to win out and she finally stepped inside.

"Is this the stuff that Carmelina swore I would not touch?" she asked mischievously.

"That's exactly what it is." He was grinning now, especially because Esme was giving him one of those "I don't want to be impressed, but I still am" looks.

"I assumed she had called anyone who could let me see the footage to warn them off."

"Carmelina thinks the only way to win is to be a bully," he said with a wave of his hand. "People do what she says not out of respect, but fear. The only way someone like me gets ahead is remembering that relationships are the biggest asset I have."

He lifted a shoulder, looking around the small room as she digested his words. "A few years ago, when the theater needed some funds to buy equipment to keep their archives in a climate-controlled space, I helped them. When Carmelina forbade the studio from giving you access to the footage, I remembered Piera had asked for copies to keep in the archives. So, I called in a favor."

"That's pretty devious, Rodrigo Almanzar," she said, a tiny conspiratorial smile forming on her lips.

"I'm not just a pretty face, Esmeralda," he joked, eliciting a laugh from her as he guided her to the front of the room. His hand pressed to the small of her back as she took everything in. The room was small, with only about a dozen large plush reclining chairs facing a large screen. There was a table at the front of the room laden with the things he'd ordered.

He knew the moment she saw it because she did a

double take. "Is that…mofongo and champagne?" she asked as a goofy grin appeared on her face.

"It's lunchtime. And El Malecón is right across the street. It used to be your favorite," he said soberly, but it was getting harder and harder not to match her delighted expression.

She clicked her tongue as she took the few steps to the table, inhaling as she reached it. It did smell amazing. "It's very hard to remember we're supposed to be archrivals when you're being this nice."

Rodrigo seriously gave her whiplash. One moment he looked horrified at the suggestion that they were a couple and the next he's walking her into a private theater with her favorite dish and champagne on a literal silver platter.

"Who pairs plantains and Moët, Rodrigo?" she asked, feigning an annoyance she didn't feel while he poured her some of the chilled bubbly.

"Bougie Dominicans, Esmeralda," he quipped as he passed her the glass, and she could see the smile tugging at the side of his own mouth.

She raised the glass to her lips and it occurred to her the fizz of the bubbles were already under her skin before the liquid touched her lips. Rodrigo always did that to her, made her body effervescent with energy. One look, one word and she could forget all the ways in which he was never a good idea. But one thing she could not deny was that he got her. Rodrigo understood what made her tick like no one else ever had. And this ridiculous and perfect lunch choice was only further evidence of that. Again the questions balled up in her throat.

Are we going to just walk away from each other

again? Are we going to let my victory steal this from us? Are you not feeling like your world got turned up-side down last night, too?

But she didn't ask a single one. She would not spill her guts just to have Rodrigo pick Sambrano Studios over her...again. "I guess it is lunchtime, we might as well eat," she said a little too brightly, reaching for one of the little white plates next to the platters of food. She placed a ball of mashed plantains and chicharron on it. Then she sat down on the stool he'd pulled out for her.

"I know what happens when you get hangry," he teased as she took a big bite.

"Jerk," she grumbled through a mouthful of mofongo, but she was too content for it to hold any real animosity. "Mmm...perfect mofongo is perfect."

He nodded, looking a bit too pleased with himself, as he watched her eat. She felt the heat from his stare warm her skin. But in the next moment he settled down with his lunch, and soon they were both tucking into the delicious food. Once she was done, she poured herself a fresh glass of bubbly and walked over to one of the plush leather armchairs in front of the gigantic screen.

Rodrigo fussed around for a moment, pushing the small table to a corner of the room. Then he turned off the lights, leaving them in total darkness for a moment before the screen lit up.

She turned around to look at him, but she could only make out his shadow as he walked over to her. "I'm ner-vous," she confessed, as conflicting emotions swirled through her. Rodrigo's eyes softened at her confession, and even if everything about these last few days felt murky and confusing, she knew he got why she was feeling that way.

"It'll be good, Joya," he said, reaching for her hand. And dammit, that was exactly what she needed. Something to ground her. And with his strong hand clutching hers she felt ready. He'd been this person for her so many times in her life. And she would be lying to herself if she didn't recognize that she'd missed his steadiness. The way he seemed to almost instinctually knew what to say or do.

"Are you ready?" he asked so gently it was barely a whisper.

She nodded as tears crawled up her throat, but the sound of her father's voice saved her from having to say anything other than a hoarse thank-you. She sat back to watch the oral history of what her father had built. It was a whirlwind of emotions, so much sadness and regret for what she never got to say to or ask him. She wished he could've been a different man, but right beside that disappointment there was admiration and an undeniable affinity.

The thirtysomething Patricio Sambrano who had set out to create something that had never been done before really was a kindred spirit. There was a fire in those brown eyes Esmeralda recognized at a bone-deep level. She may not have been the child he raised or recognized, but his ambition and drive were in her blood. He'd dreamed big and made it happen and she would do the same.

By the time the screen went dark she was dizzy with the onslaught of ideas the interviews and footage had given her. Rodrigo had been right, this was exactly what she needed to see to finally get the pieces of what she would present the board to come together. She'd known what she wanted for the future of Sambrano, and in a way it eased her to know that the Patricio from the early days would likely approve of her choices. Even though he'd let her down, he'd left her a legacy that was worth preserving. More than that, she wanted to finish what Patricio had set out to do and had not managed to achieve: make Sambrano Studios a representation of all that Latinx people were.

She turned to Rodrigo, who was still quietly sitting beside her, and all she felt was a wave of overwhelming gratitude. No one else would've done this for her. But he'd known, he understood why she needed to see these interviews. Even after a two-minute conversation last night he'd known. He'd done what was best for her, even when it meant hurting his own chances to stay on as CEO.

Rodrigo Almanzar really was a good man. Before she could talk herself out of it, she leaned over and kissed him. "Thank you," she whispered against his lips. She had too many emotions coursing through her to find the right words. Without wasting any time he brought her to his lap, deepening the kiss. And soon the soft grateful embrace turned into something torrid and urgent.

His chest rumbled with a possessive sound and his fingers gripped her waist. "Rodrigo." She gasped, already so caught up in him she could barely remember where she was. She ground herself against him, feeling his hardness against her core, just a few layers of fabric keeping her from what she needed. She was astride him now, knees on either side of his muscular thighs, rocking into him, needy and urgent.

"Unbutton your blouse," he ordered, and that commanding growl made wet heat pool at the apex of her thighs. "I want to see your breasts."

"Someone could come in," she said, hands already undoing the first button.

"No one's coming here unless I call for them. Unlike you, other people usually obey my requests," he told her with a smirk, his eyes zeroed in on her chest as he slid a hand under her flowy skirt and ran a rough palm from her knee up to the juncture of her thighs, his fingers skimming along the edge of her panties. "Do you want me here?" he asked, two fingers stroking at the seam of her pussy over the lacy material of her underwear.

"I do," she whispered.

"I can feel how hot and wet you are." His voice was dripping with sex and that edge of raw possessiveness that drove her wild. Rodrigo touched her like he owned her, and that's how he kept her coming back.

"Touch me." She gasped as the roughness of the lace grazed her clit, her hips grinding into his hand of their own volition. Without taking his gaze off her, he roughly pulled down her underwear. Two digits deftly parted her folds and soon he was circling that nub of nerves until her skin was on fire. "Pull down your bra. I want to suck on your nipples."

"Ahh…" She couldn't form words. Her body was aflame with need and pleasure. It should annoy her how he could work her into a frenzy with just a few deft touches. Instead, she slid the straps off her shoulders and pushed down her bra, just like he'd asked. She felt so exposed, but she wanted what he was giving her, *needed it*. This felt illicit and thrilling and heaven help her, she would not stop.

"Put your hands on my shoulders, lean in. Oh yeah," he said, low and dirty. "You need this bad."

She did, she really did. He turned his face up as he

worked her with his hands. He licked up the valley between her breasts, tongue flat and rough on her skin, making her shiver.

"You were always so sensitive here," he muttered, lips grazing her nipples. His tongue darted out, flicking the pebbled peaks, just like his fingers were flicking her core. He sucked on her and caressed her until her whole world reduced to the pleasure he was giving her. "Come for me, Joya," he demanded, and she did, tremors racking her body as her orgasm crashed over her.

She wrapped her arms around his neck and pressed her face to the crook of it. Esmeralda had been kidding herself earlier, telling herself this was closure, that she was over it. The only way that lie could survive was if she never saw him again. As long as Rodrigo reached for her, she would keep succumbing.

"We're a mess," she muttered, lips pressed to his skin. He circled his strong arms around her and laughed ruefully.

"I'm sure Piera would ban us for life for desecrating the sanctity of the private screening room." She could hear the smile in his voice.

"We are extremely indecent," she agreed. "These interludes are going to make it hard to enjoy taking your job." The moment the words came out of her mouth Rodrigo stiffened under her and released her from his embrace.

"Yeah. We got a bit carried away there. We really have to stop doing that," he said harshly as she worked on getting her bra back to rights and her blouse buttoned. "I'm glad you're aware none of this changes anything. I'll help you find the information you need, Esmeralda, but I have no intention of stepping down as CEO."

It was like a bucket of cold water, but she'd needed it. This was who they were now. At odds, being pulled apart even when they could not stay away from each other. In that moment she resented her father for putting her in this position, and she wished—she really wished—that for once Rodrigo could pick her. But he wouldn't; Sambrano Studios was the love of his life, the only thing that he'd sacrificed everything for again and again. He'd never give it up.

She smoothed her skirts and felt her face heat with embarrassment as she felt a wet spot right where he'd cupped her sex. She'd been so aroused she'd soaked the fabric. She was embarrassing herself. *He* was not letting his lust interfere with his plans and she had to do she same. She grabbed her purse before stepping into the aisle then turned to look at him. She hated that even after just having him, she still wanted him. That even when she despised him, she craved how he made her feel.

"My plan is to be CEO, Rodrigo. You giving me a few orgasms is not going to change that."

Thirteen

Esmeralda had stomped out of the theater after thanking Piera and got into the car without saying a word. "Could you please have the driver drop me off at my apartment? I have what I need and can work the rest of the day from home. I don't want to go back to Sambrano."

Usually someone not wanting to talk suited him just fine, but as usual, his reaction to anything and everything that had to do with Esmeralda was far from his normal. "So you're not going to acknowledge me?" He tried to keep his tone mild, but every one of his emotions was set at the maximum. He felt out of control, frustration building in him like an avalanche. He was out of sorts, regretful for ruining the moment, for reacting like he had at her words. He should just leave this alone, drop her off at home and get on with his day.

"Manny, we're taking Ms. Esmeralda home. 419 Riverside Drive."

She whipped her head back at that and he realized his mistake. "How do you know where we live?"

Shit. He was not getting into that. Him revealing how he was aware of her address when he had never set foot there—as far as she knew—would just add to the already mounting list of reasons for her to hate him.

"I must have heard it from Mami," he lied, but the words had an instant effect on Esme.

"Of course." Her eyes softened at the mention of his mother. "Gloria was able to visit before she got too weak."

When his mother had been losing her battle with cancer years earlier, Ivelisse had been there to help, sitting with his mother for days on end. And he'd heard from Marquito that Esmeralda had come to the wake for a few hours when he'd been called away to do something for Patricio. Because even at his mother's funeral he'd had to put the studio first.

"Mami misses her." Her voice was hoarse with real emotion, and seeing her hurt for his mother cracked something open in him. He never talked about his parents; he'd stopped even mentioning his father's name after he disappeared, leaving Rodrigo holding the bag for his reckless gambling. Then his mother had gotten sick. But if anyone knew what his mother had meant to him, it was Esmeralda.

His twenties were a blur, nothing but overwhelming stress and paralyzing fear that they would be destitute, that his mother would die because they could not get her decent care. But he'd done what he'd needed to. Kept his head down and made himself indispensable to Patricio

Sambrano until he was pulling in an eight-figure salary before he was thirty. Ten years of gritting his teeth, and the only moments of real happiness had been with this woman who he barely knew how to talk to anymore.

The car came to a stop and when he looked out, he saw the front of her building. He'd only been here that one other time, but everything that had to do with Esmeralda was permanently etched in his memory.

"419 Riverside Drive," Manny announced, and without saying a word to him Esmeralda pushed the car door open. He ought to let this go, to drive off and go back to his obligations, but instead he got out of the car and went after her.

"You're not even going say goodbye to me, Esmeralda?" he growled, hot on her heels.

"Goodbye," she said as she made her way to the entrance of the building. She tapped in the code for the door and soon they were inside the small but well-appointed lobby of her building. He had no idea what he was doing, but he just could not let her go.

"You're being unreasonable. This is my life," he hissed as she walked into an alcove by the door.

She came to a dead stop as his angry words resounded in the space and spun on him so quickly they almost crashed into each other. "And this is *my life*, Rodrigo. I didn't ask to be Patricio's daughter or tell him to do what he did in his will. But I *am* shooting my shot." She laughed and it sounded broken. "I want this, Rodrigo. I have ambitions. Don't you think I wish things were different? I…" Her voice broke and she lifted her eyes to the ceiling, blinking fast. "I'm sorry this is the hand we've both been dealt. And I really thought that we could, that maybe—"

But whatever she was about to say died in the space between them. "You know what, never mind what I thought."

She turned again and walked over to the elevator as he stood there rooted to the floor. Unable to go after her, but not wanting to leave without fixing what was happening between them. He wanted to know what it was she wouldn't say. But as soon as the door opened their chance to talk was drowned out by a familiar cacophony of *holas* and *mijas*. And he was screwed, because Ivelisse Peña and her three sisters all came out of the elevator, a swarm of Dominican aunties heading straight for him.

"Niña, why didn't you tell me Rodrigo was coming over?" Esme's mother cried as she engulfed him in a hug. The top of her head barely reached his shoulder, but like his mother, what she lacked in stature she more than made up for in temperament.

She put her hands on either side of his face and he bent down so she could kiss him on the cheek. "Ivelisse, it's been a minute."

She clicked her tongue, pulling back so she could get a good look at him. "Too long." She patted him on the cheek and pursed her lips in a sad expression. "You got Gloria's face. Verdad?" she asked her sisters, who promptly gave him more hugs. He felt starved for touch. But even with these women loving on him he felt cold and bereft, because the only person he wanted, the only hands he yearned for, belonged to the woman who was standing off to the side looking miserable.

He took a step back as Ivelisse asked him questions about his brother. "Marquito's good. Loves his job," he said with a smile he was certain didn't reach his eyes. He was proud of his brother, but he couldn't get excited about anything in that moment. He needed to leave. Walking in here after Esmeralda had been a terrible idea. "Listen, Ive, it was good seeing you, but I have to get going. I just came to drop off Esme."

Ivelisse was a wily woman and the mere mention of her daughter's name seemed to wake up her spidey senses. Instantly her gaze was shifting back and forth between the two of them as if she was picking up a signal from inside their heads.

"I'm not letting you out of this building until you come up and have a cafecito with us. Esmeralda, what are you doing standing there in a corner looking mad? Ven, mija." She waved over her only child, who indeed looked very unhappy to be in this tableau.

"I have my driver outside," Rodrigo pleaded, knowing Esme probably didn't want him anywhere near her.

But Ivelisse would not be dissuaded. "Rebeca, go tell the driver Rodrigo's going to come up for a visit."

And that's how he found himself sitting in Esmeralda's living room getting plied with coffee and Dominican pastries during the middle of a workday.

Fourteen

Esmeralda wanted the floor to open up and swallow her whole. Because she was pretty sure she reeked of sex and was now surrounded by her mother and all her aunts while they cooed over Rodrigo, who also probably reeked of sex. They were sitting on her mother's love seat while the older women ran around setting out food for the honored guest. Because God forbid a male visitor came to the house and they didn't serve him an elaborate feast like he was a freaking emperor.

"Esmeralda, mamita, what did those pastelitos ever do to you? Stop looking at my food like it offended you." Her mother thought she was cute. But if she didn't stop glaring Ivelisse would pick up on the fact that something was wrong. And her mother was not above asking her twenty questions in front of company.

"Sorry, Mami," she mumbled and leaned in to grab a cheese pastelito. She was annoyed but also hungry and the fried cheese-filled pastry would at least put her in a more amenable mood. When she leaned back into the couch, next to freaking Rodrigo, her hand accidentally grazed his thigh. His hard and very muscular thigh, which she'd been astride just an hour ago...before he reminded her again that he was not interested in anything other than pushing her out. She expected him to be put out, or bored, looking at his watch, desperate to leave their small apartment, but he appeared totally at ease with arms splayed over the back of the couch. He should feel out of place here in his five-thousand-dollar suit and expensive haircut. But somehow, he fit.

"I'm heading out soon," he said against her ear, and her body flooded with heat. "I just didn't want to be rude to Ive."

She exhaled and turned to him. "It's fine. It's not like they would've taken no for answer."

At that precise moment her mother walked out from their little kitchen carrying a tray laden with steaming cups of café con leche. Rodrigo sprung up from the couch as soon as he saw her, his arms extended to get the tray from her. "Ivelisse, you should've called me, I would've brought this out for you." Her mother waved him off, but happily handed him the heavy tray.

"You were always such a helpful boy." She leaned in to kiss him on the cheek as he handed cups to Esmeralda's aunts. Something about her mother's expression gave Esme pause. She looked regretful, like she always did whenever Rodrigo was in the picture.

"Rebeca, how's the teaching gig? Are you still up at Gregorio Luperón?" Esme's aunt perked up at Rodrigo's question about her beloved students. Esmeralda seriously resented the ball of warmth pulsing in her chest at the fact that he remembered the high school her aunt worked at.

"It's a roller coaster," Rebeca answered with a laugh. "Teaching those math kids that the arts are also important is always a struggle. But I keep trying."

"If anyone's going to get through to them it's you," he told Rebeca with a fond smile. By that point every one of the older women was riveted by him. And Esme couldn't blame them. The man was a walking, talking sex dream. Her hands twitched as that sculpted chest flashed in her mind. He was back to looking picture-perfect. Only an hour earlier she'd had her hands all over him. She'd kissed that generous mouth, nipped at his neck.

Yeah. She needed to calm down.

"I might be able to give you hope," Rodrigo said to Rebeca after taking a huge bite of pastelito. She really had to stop staring at his mouth. "My mentee just started his first year in the NYU film studies program and he went to Luperón."

"You still do that?" Esmeralda interrupted. "The Big Brother program, I mean." The words were out of her mouth before she could stop herself and soon four sets of eyes were on her.

Rodrigo turned his gaze to her and the intensity there was enough to make her fan herself. "Yeah, I do." He nodded, eyebrows furrowed.

"You've been in that mentoring program since college."

He dipped his head again. "Yeah, I actually started an initiative at Sambrano for people interested in being mentors. In the beginning it was just the New York offices, but it went so well we expanded it to Miami and LA, too. Altogether we have like two hundred mentors."

"That's wonderful, Rodrigo." Her mother had always been Rodrigo's number-one fan. The rest of the tías chimed in and soon he was asking each of them questions about their interests and jobs. He had them practically eating out of his hand. But that wasn't fair, either. This wasn't manipulative or fake. He cared about these women. He'd grown up around them. Because they had a history together. A history she'd forced herself to never think about—but that didn't mean it wasn't there.

And Esmeralda wished it felt like history, like something that was part of her past. But in just a matter of days Rodrigo had become a presence in her life she couldn't ignore, and worse—one she didn't know how to walk away from. Even when she was furious with him, she couldn't deny how right it felt to have him in her life. He was at home here. In her world, with her mother, with her aunts. Because he had always been a part of all of it.

"Where are all the Juanes and Keanu Reeves posters?" Rodrigo asked, eliciting a wry smile and nudge on his shoulder.

"I am a grown woman, Rodrigo. My teenage crushes are ancient history," she said, waving him over to the standing desk near the window. In reality her bedroom was sexy as hell. Dark blues and golds, a big inviting bed, and lots of art on the wall. Yeah, this was not a kid's room and the things he wanted to do to her on that bed were definitely for adults only.

"Come, let me show you something." For once Rodrigo was grateful for the diminutive spaces in New York City apartments. It gave him an excuse to get closer to her again. She'd thawed in the hour since they'd gotten to her apartment. And he couldn't deny that it had been nice to spend some time with Ivelisse and her sisters. He had to hold himself so tightly all the time at work that he forgot who he had been. Before everything had gone wrong with his parents, with Esmeralda, his life had not been only about garnering power at Sambrano. His life had been this, la familia.

Esmeralda had been the place where he always felt grounded in that, but since they'd parted, he'd changed. He'd closed himself off; he'd told himself all he needed was the job. And now in less than three days her presence had started chiseling at that barrier he'd created between himself and the world. He could feel the walls of control crumbling with every kiss. And instead of retreating, of trying to find a way to get himself back to the safety of aloofness, all he wanted was to get closer. He had no idea how he'd do it, how he would manage to keep her and the job, but with every passing second he grew more certain that finding a way was the key to everything.

He tentatively moved closer, his front only inches from her back, and instead of pulling away from him she leaned in. Almost instinctively he wrapped an arm around her waist. He pressed his lips to her neck, flicking his tongue at the warm skin there.

"I'm supposed to be showing you something," she protested as her hand skittered off the keyboard. Within seconds she'd turned around in his arms.

He trailed kisses from her mouth all the way down to the top of her breasts, lapping at her skin as she gasped with pleasure. "I have no self-control at all with you," she moaned, and despite her mother and aunts being just down the hall, his hunger for her was too fierce to stop.

"Let me see you, Joya," he urged and she quickly

obliged, revealing those gorgeous breasts for him. "Mmm, tweak them for me, show me where you want my hands, sweetheart." His hands itched to touch her, but this game of her pleasuring herself while he watched had always been a favorite of theirs.

She took his hand and guided it to an engorged peak. He worried the nipple between his thumb and index finger, and watched her gasp with pleasure. "I love seeing you like this." *I don't think I can live without it*, he almost said, but instead focused on what he had now. He moved in to kiss her and she responded with the same hunger he felt. Her tongue sliding with his, tasting and nipping until he almost regretted having started something he could not finish.

He pulled back, gasping "I need to have you again."

She nodded frantically, going in for another kiss. "I can't disappear on my mom tonight," she said regretfully. "But maybe tomorrow," she promised and a sound of pure pleasure rumbled in his chest.

"I would like that." He was about to go in for another kiss, to show her just how much he wanted her, when his phone went off. It was the ringtone he'd set for friends and family—which now were only a precious few. For it to be a call and not just a text meant it had to be urgent.

He pressed a soft kiss to her jaw and pulled back regretfully. "I'm sorry, I have to take this."

She nodded in understanding as she fixed her top. "We should stop anyway, my mother is already going to ask me a thousand questions, and I don't need to walk out there looking like you just had your way with me."

"Which I did," he teased, inciting a glare from her. A smile tugged at his lips as he tapped to accept a call from… Jimena?

"What's up?" he asked into the phone as Esmeralda gestured she was going back outside to rejoin her mother and aunts. She had barely closed the door behind her when Jimena launched into a frantic story about Carmelina.

"Slow down. I don't understand a single thing you're saying."

"Sorry," she said, sucking in a breath as if she'd just come up from being underwater. "I'm just freaking out."

He sighed, heart already galloping in his chest from whatever she was about to tell him. Jimena was the single most coolheaded person he knew. Hearing her admit she was freaking out surely meant something really bad was happening.

"Tell me."

"I just got an interesting call from one of my friends who works in the legal counsel office at Global Networks. Word is that Carmelina and her kids have a meeting with Burt Deringer tomorrow."

Rodrigo's hackles went up at the mention of the CEO of the company that had made a previous aggressive attempt to buy Sambrano. He knew Carmelina was callous, but selling out to Deringer was downright evil.

"She's selling him her shares," Jimena said, ominously. Damn the woman and her unstoppable greed. "Apparently Onyx and Perla's, too." He felt the surge of anger rise in him like a fireball. Deringer's previous bid to buy Sambrano was six years earlier, right after Rodrigo had taken over as chief content officer. The money they'd offered had been excessive, but when they presented their plans for the network, Patricio had backed out. They'd intended to gut the programming and take out all cultural nuance. They had no interest in preserving Sambrano's brand, they just wanted to own everything they could. And now, barely a year after her husband's death, Carmelina was looking to sell out to the absolute last people Patricio would have wanted in control. "How could she do this?"

"Because she's a money-hungry witch?"

"No, it's more than that. She'd rather see this place in ruins than let Esmeralda be the face of Sambrano. She hasn't wasted the chance to remind Esmeralda of that in the past few days. I really thought even if only to save face, she wouldn't sink to this, but I was wrong." He shook his head as he paced the small space between Esme's bed and her desk. The warm and easy feeling from just minutes earlier now transformed into sick dread.

Jimena sighed again, tongue clicking. "I can't believe Perla's going for this."

"She's nowhere near as bad as Onyx," Rodrigo agreed, "but she's always let Carmelina steamroll her." Patricio's youngest daughter was no match for her mother's malice. "There are still Esmeralda's shares, which she can't touch, but she technically doesn't need her to sell the rest."

"No, she's got the three votes." Jimena's voice was tight with worry as she confirmed what they both knew. Sambrano's only provision regarding selling shares to an outside party was that three out of the four majority shareholders agreed on the sale. As things stood right now, the shares were equally divided between Carmelina and Patricio's three children. With Onyx and Perla on their mother's side, Esme would not be able to stop her father's widow from essentially selling the company out from under her.

Rodrigo's fury rose as he surmised the repercussions of what Carmelina was planning. If she got her way she'd not only get rid of Esme, but would finally get him out of the picture, too. Anger burned in his gut like hot coals. Almost twenty years of this, of Carmelina scheming and destroying because of her fucked-up sense of entitlement over everything Patricio owned.

Esmeralda at least deserved the chance to have a say in the future of her father's company. That was something that had never been in question—even if he was determined to keep his job, he had never intended to see Esmeralda cast out. But if Carmelina did this, there was no saving Sambrano. He looked at the door and heard the women on the other side chattering happily and swore to himself he would do whatever it took to stop that woman from pushing Esmeralda out.

"Wait," Jimena said, bringing him out of his thoughts. "I just got a really cryptic text from Magdalena. I told her about the meeting with Deringer and she's been doing some digging around of her own." The CFO from Sambrano was a straight shooter and if there was anything amiss, she would find it.

"What did she say?" Rodrigo asked, his focus back on Jimena.

"She's asking me to come to her place in an hour," Jimena said, and Rodrigo could hear her fingers tapping on a keyboard. "She says she called in some favors and she's got some information about Carmelina's finances."

Rodrigo had heard enough. He stormed out of the room after promising to meet Jimena at Magdalena's penthouse in an hour. When he stepped into the living room he found Esme smiling as she chatted happily with her mother and aunts. He'd be damned if he let Carmelina try to break this woman again. "I have to go," he told Esme, who stood up from where she'd been sitting with her mother when he appeared.

"Are you all right?" she asked, probably noticing the tension coming off of him in waves.

For a second he considered telling her. Maybe it would be good to let her know what was going on. But then he thought of the blow that would be. To know that Carmelina had not even considered playing fair. That her siblings were colluding with their mother to end Esme's chances.

He didn't want Carmelina's machinations to mess with Esmeralda more than they already had. Besides, he was still CEO of the company and it was his job to fix this, not Esme's. No matter how much he wished for them to be able to find a way to continue to spend time together—perhaps even more than that after this was all over—he had a job to do.

"I'm fine," he lied, as he leaned in to press a kiss to her cheek. "Something came up that I need to take care of. I'll see you at the office tomorrow."

She nodded slowly, her face doubtful. She could tell something was up, but she didn't pry. "Okay, I'm going to try to finish my presentation tonight. Would you be able to take a look at it in the morning?"

"Sure," he said distractedly, his mind already racing with all the things he needed to do. Hoping it would be enough to thwart Carmelina and her kids. "I'll look at it as soon as I get in." With that he did a round of kisses and apologies for having to take off, and within minutes he was back in the town car. His phone buzzed and his stomach clenched in response when he saw Carmelina Sambrano's name flashing on the screen.

"How could you do this?" he growled into the speaker before she got a chance to get a word in.

"Wow, Rodrigo, you actually do have the ability to emote?"

He breathed through his nose, trying to manage the consuming anger this woman was inciting in him. "Are you really going to throw away your husband's life work just so Esmeralda doesn't have a chance to be the CEO?"

"I'm not really interested in talking details over the phone, querido, but I do have an offer for you."

"Why would you think I'd ever agree to do anything with you?" he asked as rage tore through him.

"Because I can make sure you can keep your job—and more importantly, that fifty-million-dollar salary you're always saying you sacrificed so much to get."

There it was. He'd known she'd do this. She thought she finally had the thing that would lure him to her side. He felt his back molars grind together at the derision in her voice. Like he hadn't earned every fucking cent he made. Like it wasn't a fraction of the money he'd brought in for Sambrano over the years. "Deringer has agreed to keep you on as CEO *if* you help facilitate the negotiations. With your support behind the sale, the board will be more amenable."

All the blood rushed to his head at once and he felt like he was going to be sick. This woman really thought she could just buy him off. That he would betray Patricio, Esmeralda and himself for money.

Then again, Carmelina didn't understand loyalty; she didn't get what it was like to stand by something because you believed in it. She only believed in one thing: herself. She only cared about winning. And that's where he would beat her at her own game.

Fifteen

"**W**here the hell *is* he?" Esmeralda was trying not to panic. But it was now a full eighteen hours since Rodrigo had stormed out of her apartment and had stopped answering her texts.

She winced, remembering what they'd been up to right before whatever he saw on his phone caused him to take off without an explanation. After he'd left, she'd shut everything out and gotten to work. She'd used the files she'd gotten from Mr. Piera and worked all night on her presentation. She was pleased with what she'd come up with, confident this was a plan the board could get behind. It was bold and it was more ambitious than anything the studio had done in decades, but she believed it was the key to taking Sambrano into the future. Except she had no one to run it by, and Rodrigo was MIA. He'd promised her he'd be here today to give her feedback, but no one had seen or heard from him all morning.

Maybe he was ignoring her because he was going to let her go into that board meeting and fall on her face. Had she been a fool for thinking that the way he'd been with her mother and aunts meant something? That it would somehow change the fact that he was still hoping she failed? Her phone buzzed and her heart practically came up her throat, but it was just her meditation app reminding her to breathe. She took the excellent advice and focused on letting air in and out of her lungs, and tried to stay grounded in facts, not feelings. She was good at her job, she knew the market, she knew the industry. *She knew she was on to something.*

"I don't need Rodrigo to do this," she told herself for the hundredth time since she'd gotten in at 8:00 a.m. "I got this," she said now, feeling stronger.

"*Do you got this?* Because it looks to me like your nerves are getting the best of you." Esmeralda snapped her head up from the slides she'd been reviewing…again, to find Onyx standing in front of her. He looked just as mean as he had at the reception.

"Why are you here?" She didn't even try to hide her animosity.

He sneered at her and lifted a shoulder as if he had all the time in the world. "Oh, just came to check if Rodrigo gave you a heads-up about the meeting with the buyers."

"Buyers?" Even though she had no clue what that even meant, her heart still pounded in her chest, apprehension pooling in her stomach. "What are you talking about?" She didn't know her brother very well, but she did recognize a smug jackass when she saw one. Esmeralda had a feeling that whatever Onyx was here to tell her would almost certainly ruin her day.

"Oh, he didn't tell you? He's on his way to a meeting with Global Networks. They've made an offer to buy the studio. He's going there with my mother." Bile churned in her stomach as Onyx walked in a little closer, for the last piece of gossip he had to share. Esme braced for it. "They want him to stay on as CEO, so he's all in."

"You're lying," she said, even as her mind reeled.

"Am I?" Onyx asked, showing her rows of perfectly white teeth. "Has anyone even heard from him today?" He was speaking so casually, like they were just chatting about the weather. God, he was cruel. "Mr. Workaholic is usually at his desk at 7:00 a.m. sharp, but no one's heard from him since yesterday. Ask his assistant."

He was right.

All the wind went out of her lungs at once, the pain of Rodrigo's betrayal like a knife in her gut. But she would be damned if she let Onyx get the satisfaction of seeing her undone. She quickly regrouped and tried her best to send a withering look toward her brother. She gathered as much strength as she could, even as she reeled from the bomb that he'd had just detonated.

How could Rodrigo do this? Had he been in cahoots with Carmelina even as he told her that the woman was a snake? Even as he assured her again and again that he would not interfere with her presentation, that he wanted the CEO position only if he got it fair and square? But maybe that was the problem, that he thought Esmeralda didn't deserve it. Maybe the way he saw it was that she'd sauntered in and tried to claim the position unfairly. And she'd let him distract her with sex and her messiness. He was probably using her unprofessional behavior as an excuse to push her out at this very moment.

"Get out of my office, Onyx," she demanded. "Unlike you, I have work to do. If Rodrigo is scheming with your mother then good luck to him. Just two days ago she was telling him he was a nobody, and today she's doing business with him. Sounds like they deserve each other."

With that she turned her attention to the monitor in front of her in an attempt to ignore Onyx's ugly sneer.

"I'd start cleaning out my stuff if I were you," he said in an awful singsong voice.

"In case you forgot, I still own twenty-five percent of the shares in this company." To her surprise, the comment seemed to make him even more smug. If that melodramatic laugh was anything to go by anyways.

"You're in for all kinds of surprises today," he gloated maliciously before rushing off.

Esmeralda felt a sob closing her throat, and she savagely pushed it down. She would be damned if anyone in this place saw her shed a single tear. She had vowed to never cry over Rodrigo Almanzar again. And she would not break that promise to herself today. Esme had really thought her heart was done breaking for that man.

She'd been so wrong.

He'd literally left her apartment, after kissing her mother and tías, to go meet with Carmelina Sambrano and concoct a way to push her out. She counted to fifty after Onyx was out of her office before she stood up and hurried to shut the door. Not that it gave her much privacy since all the office walls were made of glass, but at least no one would be able to hear her. She grabbed her phone and quickly dialed the only person she knew who would help her figure out what to do.

* * *

"Mami." She could barely choke the word out at the relief of hearing her mother's loving and familiar voice.

"Mija, what's wrong?"

Esmeralda let out a shaky breath, relief coursing through her. She could always count on her mother's unfailing steadiness. Even when nothing else worked, her mother was always there for her. Her rock, the person who always stood by her no matter what. For a time she'd believed that Rodrigo could be that for her, too. But he'd proven again and again that his only loyalties were to himself and to the Sambranos.

"I'm not sure what's going on, but Onyx was just here and told me that Rodrigo and Carmelina are meeting with an outside buyer. That he's working with her to stay on as CEO and get rid of me." Saying that last part out loud almost broke her. She could not believe she'd trusted him again. Was she so desperate for acceptance that she'd put herself in this position again with a man who had proven to her she was expendable to him? "I can't believe I let Rodrigo play me again."

She was pathetic.

"Esmeralda, take a breath, mi amor. What are you talking about? What happened?" Her mother's voice was taut with tension. She hated worrying Ivelisse, but this felt too familiar. Like those times when her mother had reluctantly let Esmeralda go spend time with her father only to see her return in tears after being humiliated by Carmelina's venomous words.

"Rodrigo's going to help Carmelina sell the studio so he can stay on as CEO."

Esme squeezed her eyes shut when she heard her

mother's shocked gasp. "Ay, mija. Are you sure? I can't believe he would do that."

"He *is*, Mami," she cried, sick to her stomach with regret. "I get that *she's* scheming against me, hell, I even expected it." She fought to keep her voice low. "But to know that Rodrigo is in on it with her... I should've known he hadn't changed." She scoffed, shaking her head as her belly roiled with nausea and uneasiness. "I don't even know why I'm surprised. He's done this to me before."

Esme heard her mother suck in a breath, as she sat there steeped in misery. For a moment she wondered if she should just leave. Grab her purse and her laptop and leave these people and their drama behind. "Maybe this is for the best. Maybe I just need to walk away from all this."

"Esmeralda, I'm going to tell you something right now and I need you to understand that I kept this from you because I thought it was for the best."

"Mami, what are you talking about?" Esmeralda had never heard her mother sounding so serious. Ivelisse Peña was one of those people who managed to maintain a positive outlook even in the darkest of moments, but right now she sounded subdued. Scared even, and that, more than anything that had occurred in the past hour, terrified Esmeralda.

"I need to tell you the truth about the reason why your father evicted us from that apartment and why Rodrigo disappeared on you that weekend."

Esmeralda felt the skin on her face tighten at her mother's words, sickening dread roiling in her gut. "He left you because his mother called him and told him what Patricio was doing and he jumped on a plane to come help me."

"What?" Esmeralda's voice sounded distant to her own ears, like she was speaking from somewhere far away. "Why didn't he tell me that, Mami?"

"He was so careful back then, Esmeralda. He had so much to lose." Ivelisse sighed tiredly. "I still don't know how he managed, but within twenty-four hours that boy found me this apartment, figured out the down payment and had movers coming to the house to pack me up and take our stuff the two blocks down from our old place." Her mother clicked her tongue, a sound Esme knew she made only when she was thinking hard. "I swore I would never tell you this, but I think it's important for you to know what you're up against there.

"Your father sent me that eviction notice after Carmelina showed him a fake paternity test. One that said you weren't his." Her mother's voice broke as Esmeralda sat there in stunned silence. She knew Carmelina was vicious, but this was monstrous.

"She did what!" she shouted on the phone, hardly able to believe what she was hearing.

"She forged a paternity test," her mother said numbly. "That was after Patricio agreed to pay for your master's at NYU. She knew you were getting an education that could put you in a position to take over the company someday, and like the vicious bitch she is, she tried to sabotage you." Esme sank into one of the armchairs in the office, reeling from what her mother had just told her.

"I don't even understand. My father just took her word for it?" She was fighting to get the words out at this point.

"I'm not going to make up excuses for Patricio, because he should've known better, but apparently she had papers. Rodrigo was the one who discovered she'd faked it all." And there went her heart, trying to gallop out of her chest again. "I still don't know how he figured it all out. He dug around and discovered the laboratories that supposedly ran the test didn't exist. And your father, who hated nothing more than looking foolish, was furious with Carmelina." Ivelisse laughed bitterly at that. "He was mad at everybody. He did walk back the eviction, though. But by then Rodrigo had helped me get into this building and that was that." Esmeralda heard another long and heavy sigh, as she tried to process what her mother had just told her.

"Mija, Rodrigo ensured Carmelina could never pull something like that again. That boy stood up to your father, and risked losing his job to make sure your place as Patricio's daughter was never questioned again. Rodrigo's not perfect, but I don't believe the man who did that for us could ever betray you like that. And especially not with that woman."

Esmeralda felt like she was floating, her mind almost unable to take in everything she'd learned in the past five minutes. The resentment and the hurt she'd held on to for ten years had been based on a lie. Rodrigo had not been on her father's side, he'd been helping her mother. He'd been looking out for her.

"Why did no one tell me? Why did he break up with me?" she asked, a real sob escaping her lips.

Her mother sighed. "He begged me not to tell you he helped, and about the break-up, I don't know, honey. He was in such a tough spot. You have to remember he was just starting to get ahead at the studio. He was fresh out of graduate school, had loans. His mother was sick and

Patricio was still helping him get out from under all the debt that bum Arturo had racked up. Who knows what all went down between the two of them? Patricio was not a man to take people standing up to him well, and he would've seen Rodrigo dating you behind his back and helping me as an affront. Maybe he distanced himself from you to appease your father. I just don't know."

"Even if that's true, why didn't he tell me? It would've hurt to lose him, but at least I would've understood!"

Her mother made a comforting sound. "It will be all right, mija. I know you two will figure this out."

She was openly crying now, her mind like a tornado, thoughts swirling so fast she felt light-headed. "I have to figure out what's going on then. I have to find Rodrigo." Esmeralda felt numb, like her emotions had shut down.

"I think that's a good idea. And remember, sweetheart, you have a right to be there and you have people on your side. Never forget that."

She felt completely alone in that building, like there wasn't a single person on her side, but hearing her mother's words was a small comfort. A call came in right as she was about say goodbye and when she looked at the screen she frowned at the unknown number. "Someone's calling me, Mami."

"Call me as soon as you hear something." After promising she would, she picked up the other line.

"Esmeralda Sambrano-Peña," she said briskly.

"Talk to Jimena Cuevas." The voice on the phone sounded female, but they were obviously trying to muffle it to avoid being recognized.

"Who is this?" Esme asked tersely. "Why do I need to talk to Jimena?"

"She'll tell you what you need to know," the muffled voice said, but offered nothing else.

"Please, who am I talking to?" she asked urgently, but after a few seconds she realized there was no one on the other end. Without pausing to consider if this was just someone else trying to mess with her, she took the elevator to the legal counsel's office. Jimena's executive assistant tried to stop her, but Esmeralda barreled right into the woman's office.

"Esmeralda." If Jimena was surprised to see Esme crashing into her office unannounced, she did not show it. "Come in, please." Her tone was friendly, and she almost seemed glad to see her. Esme would just add it to the growing list of bizarre occurrences of the day.

"Do you know where Rodrigo is right now?"

"Close the door," Jimena said. This time her tone was more serious.

Once Esme did, she launched right into it. "Rodrigo's trying to stop Carmelina from selling her and her children's shares to an outside party."

"Stopping? But Onyx said—"

Jimena shook her head, her mouth twisting sourly at the mention of Esme's sibling. "Rodrigo had to make them think he was in on it. They're meeting with the buyers in less than an hour at the Peninsula. Hopefully Rodrigo will have what he needs to stop her in time.

"Here," she said, jotting something on a sticky note and handed it to Esme. "They're meeting in this conference room."

"I'm going over there."

"Good," Jimena said approvingly. "I'll have my assistant arrange a car for you,"

Esmeralda shook her head. "It's only a few blocks

from here, it'll take longer to drive. Besides, it'll give me a chance to calm down."

Rodrigo's friend canted her head to the side, as if she were only now really looking at Esmeralda. "You have guts, but you're not a hothead," she stated, approval in her voice. "You'll be good for him."

Esme was not going to answer that, and made a move to walk out, but Jimena's voice stopped her. "He'll be pissed I told you, but it's about time Rodrigo learned he can't do everything on his own."

Sixteen

"I knew you'd come. I told that girl you're only loyal to yourself."

Rodrigo took one deep breath and then another as he walked into the small conference room Carmelina had arranged to sell out her husband's legacy. He looked at her and could barely keep the bile from rising in his throat. Carmelina had been a beautiful woman when she was young, with her pale skin and striking blue eyes. But she had not aged gracefully. Her face was twisted and swollen from too many procedures. She wore one of her signature Chanel suits in a navy blue with cream on the neck and cuffs. It was expensive and elegant, but on her it looked shabby, ill-fitting.

"So you've taken it upon yourself to sell the studio," he stated, barely able to contain his anger.

"Yes, I have." She looked smug as hell sitting at the

head of the conference room table waiting for him. She really thought she had him. After years of trying to manipulate him, she thought she'd managed to find the one thing he would betray Sambrano over. But that had always been Carmelina's problem—she was too self-interested to ever notice that not everyone was motivated by the same things she was. She'd invited him here thinking she had him in her clutches. She had no idea how badly she'd miscalculated.

"You didn't think it was appropriate to consult the board on your plan to sell three-quarters of the company out from under them?" he asked, too incensed at this woman to not demand answers.

Carmelina lifted a shoulder as she poured packet after packet of sweetener into her iced tea. "I don't need to consult the board. All I needed was three out of the four majority shareholders on board. I have that," she said triumphantly. She smiled that cutting, menacing smile and a wave of disgust ran down Rodrigo's spine. "This isn't about money. This is about preserving the respectability of our name."

"Stop, Carmelina. We both know what this is about— spite and money. You can't get rid of Esmeralda, so you'd rather see Patricio's company destroyed." He didn't know if he was expecting remorse or even a flicker of emotion, but it was like talking to a wall.

"I guess you *are* smarter than you look, Rodrigo."

He ignored the jab as he fought for control. "Do you not care at all about the ramifications of this?"

"The only thing I care about is making sure I never have to hear or see that girl's name again."

He couldn't take it anymore. "Esmeralda being a part of the studio was Patricio's decision. It was his final wish, for goodness sake. Are you so dead inside that you don't care about your husband's legacy?"

"Patricio was always too sentimental. I'm the only one who's willing to do what's necessary. This is for the best." That's how Carmelina had done it all these years. The woman was so good at persuading people because the truth wasn't even a concept to her. She sounded convincing because to her, if she said it, *it was* the truth.

She looked Rodrigo up and down, her eyes roaming from his face all the way to his shoes, and the expression on her face told him that as always she found him thoroughly lacking. "But that's something someone like you would never understand."

Ten, hell, even five years ago those words would've stung. The reminder of his family's shame, of what his father had done slicing across his pride. Because she was right—there were not enough Brioni or Zegna suits in the world to cover up the fact that if it wasn't for Patricio's help his family would've ended up on the street. But he was not ashamed of who he was, and his conscience was clean. He'd never taken advantage of anyone to get to where he was. And now he had amassed enough wealth to never have to worry about money again. Rodrigo knew exactly what it took to stay on top when everyone around you wanted to see you fall. And what Carmelina didn't know was that he was about to beat her at her own game.

"That must be Deringer and his people." Carmelina jumped to her feet as the door opened. "And try not to look like you're about to go to the gallows, Rodrigo, would you?"

In that moment three men walked into the room—one he recognized as Deringer, the other men he assumed were his attorneys. Deringer's face was constantly all over the news. The online retail magnate who had turned his interests to television and film, and in the past few years had amassed multiple networks, streaming services and film studios. The disturbing part was that he seemed to transform the programming into nothing but advertisements for his other companies. If Deringer acquired Sambrano he would turn it into a whitewashed Spanish language infomercial.

"Gentlemen, come in," Carmelina crowed, all smiles. The introductions were being made when a harried Onyx walked into the room.

"Ah, my children are here, we can finally get started." The frown on the younger man's face and the worry lines bracketing his mouth were a sharp contrast to Carmelina's overly genial tone. Carmelina kept her eyes on the door to the conference room while Onyx whispered in her ear, as if waiting for someone else to walk in.

Rodrigo smiled to himself, well aware of what was coming. He caught the exact moment she understood what was unfolding. Her shoulders stiffened and her mouth twisted into a snarl. He could tell she was battling to control herself. That she didn't want Deringer to figure out there was a problem. And Rodrigo went in for the kill.

"Perla's not coming, Carmelina," he said in her same sickly sweet tone. She pivoted her head up, looking at him suspiciously.

"Of course she is," she snapped, and then stopped herself, probably remembering she had an audience.

"Is there an issue?" asked one of the two men flanking Deringer. The magnate had not looked up from whatever he was doing on his phone, seemingly only there to sign the paperwork and go on with his day. The fact that Carmelina was willing to hand over everything her husband had worked so hard for to someone who only saw it as another pawn in his chessboard galvanized Rodrigo's anger.

"Just a little hiccup with my daughter. But we'll get her over here right away," Carmelina assured the man as Onyx looked at his mother with a terrified expression.

"Oh, I'd say there's more than a little hiccup," Rodrigo told her. "You no longer have seventy-five percent of the shares to sell."

Carmelina laughed hysterically, her eyes wide as she rushed to talk over Rodrigo. "What are you talking about? My children and I are ready to sell to Global Networks. We have three out of four votes as majority shareholders."

"No, you don't," Rodrigo corrected her as he pulled out the papers from his briefcase. "This morning Perla sold me her shares, and thus her vote, for the sum of two hundred million dollars." Liquidating practically everything he owned, calling in every favor he'd garnered over the past sixteen years, was worth getting to see the realization dawn on Carmelina's face that he'd beaten her at her own game. "You don't have the votes to sell anything to Global Networks," he told her, eliciting a scream of absolute fury.

"You can't do this! You're nobody, you're a paid employee. This company belongs to my children!" She looked at Deringer, who was already standing up and packing up his stuff as if he was about to walk out of the room.

Rodrigo held up a hand to stop her lies. "You're selling the company because you're broke. Your father's investments in the last ten years have completely depleted your family's fortune, and you've been funneling all of Patricio's money to keep him afloat. And now you're going to sell what's left to keep sinking money into a bottomless pit."

The door burst open again and Esmeralda walked in with Octavio Nuñez, both of them looking like they were walking into battle. And even if her arrival would only make Carmelina even more vicious, he was glad to see her.

"You, this is all your fault." Carmelina lunged for Esme as Deringer and his people stood up, clearly done with the Sambrano drama. "I won't let you take what belongs to me. I won't let you have it! I'd rather sell the studio for parts than let you win. Patricio was only too happy to believe that gold digger when she told him she was pregnant with his brat. I can prove you're not Patricio's child," she screamed frantically, rifling through papers, and he was ready for this, too.

"Stop lying, Carmelina. It's over!" Rodrigo roared as he got between Carmelina and Esmeralda. "Here." He handed the other piece of paper he'd brought with him to one of Deringer's attorneys. "This is an affidavit signed by Patricio Sambrano confirming that he is in fact Esmeralda's father."

He felt Esmeralda's legs give out, but he held her up, as he tried to end this farce with Carmelina once and for all.

"I got you," he told her, but she seemed too shocked to react. He looked over at his mentor's widow, who was now frozen in place, her eyes darting between Rodrigo and Deringer. "You're done, Carmelina."

Seventeen

"What are you doing here?" Rodrigo asked Esmeralda as they made their way out of the room, with Carmelina's shrieks trailing behind them.

"I'm here because this also concerns me, Rodrigo." Esme looked heartbroken, like all of this was beyond what she could bear. "I had a right to know Carmelina was working behind the board's back to sell the company from under me. From under all of us."

He wanted to reach out to her, but he didn't know how she'd react to that. She looked furious and hurt. Octavio came up to them, his expression bleak. "I wish you would've let us know what was happening, Rodrigo, but we're grateful that you put a stop to this. My cousin has always been like this, selfish enough to destroy everything to get what she wants." He shook his head, and it seemed like overnight Octavio had aged a decade. "We're calling an emergency meeting for the day after tomorrow." Octavio turned to Esmeralda then. "I'm sorry to do this, but we'll have to cut your preparation time. You will have to present then." Her face fell, but soon she was nodding.

"I can do that. I'll be ready." His chest swelled with love for her in that moment. His Joya. So strong, always ready to fight, never giving up on her dreams.

"Thank you for understanding and thank you for alerting me to what was going on." Octavio looked at Rodrigo as he spoke. He could see the man was not happy to have been kept in the dark, but Rodrigo had no regrets. If he hadn't talked Perla into selling him the shares without giving Carmelina warning that he was working against her, she would've pulled rank with her younger daughter. At this very moment Carmelina would have been destroying the company.

"Needless to say the board has a lot to consider right now given what has happened." Octavio's gaze was fixed on the door to the conference room where presumably Carmelina was still in a rage. But after a moment the man grinned at Rodrigo, clearly curious. "How did you manage to get Perla to sell you the shares?"

Rodrigo lifted a shoulder and glanced at Esme, who seemed to be waiting for Octavio to be done with him, so she could give him a piece of her mind. It seemed like the initial shock of walking in on Carmelina's fiasco had worn off and she did not seem happy with him at all.

Octavio cleared his throat, still waiting for an answer from Rodrigo, and he did his best to focus. "Perla doesn't trust her mother as much as people thought. A few years ago I helped her hire a financial advisor who was independent from the family. When he told her Carmelina had been trying to gain access to her trust fund, Perla had finally had enough of the scheming. She wanted out." This he directed at Esme. "She's never been keen on the games her mother plays. She's not like Onyx."

"Good for Perla and for you," Octavio said, and with a quick goodbye headed toward the exit of the hotel.

That only left him and Esmeralda.

"I hope you're happy," she said, her arms crossed over her chest. And once again his body reacted in about fifteen conflicting ways to Esmeralda's presence. His heart pounded and his body pulsed with the need to have her against the nearest flat surface, and then take her somewhere he could keep her safe and far away from the likes of Carmelina Sambrano.

"Why are you mad at me? I thought you'd be glad to hear that Carmelina no longer has control of the company." I thought you'd be glad I was able to help you, he almost said. She had to know he'd saved her chance at becoming CEO.

Without saying a word she turned on her heels and walked toward a small room beyond the larger one they'd just exited. He followed her in silence, certain that whatever he was walking into, it would not be pleasant. Once they were inside the room, she turned to face him. Her eyes were furious.

"Why could you let me think for *ten years* that you chose my father over me? How could you, Rodrigo?" He stumbled as what she said sank in. *She knew.*

"Ivelisse was not supposed to say anything." He exclaimed, his mind and body in absolute turmoil. "You were never supposed to know. I was trying to keep you safe. To protect you from all these filthy lies and schemes." He looked up at her and he could tell she saw the brokenness in his eyes, but he didn't have the energy to hide it anymore.

"You really let me believe all this time that when I needed you most you chose *him*? That I wasn't worth anything to you?" She shook her head as tears streamed down her face. God, he had made such a mess of everything.

"I had no choice, Esmeralda," he spat out, now his own anger and resentment coming to the surface. "I'm always the one to fall on the sword. The one to do what needs to be done and then get scorned for making the hard choices. Like everyone else you chose to believe that I'm a cold, selfish bastard."

She flinched at his words, but she regrouped quickly and soon she was on him again. "Maybe we all assume that because you give us nothing, Rodrigo. You love to be the martyr. Acting like no one cares about you. Like it's Rodrigo Almanzar against the world. Maybe people judge you because none of us really *know you*. Because you keep everything so tightly locked inside we can't get close enough. Because you never let anyone in."

"I let *you* in," he said in a voice he could barely recognize.

A sob escaped Esmeralda's throat at his words and when he reached for her she came to him. He pressed his mouth to hers in a frantic kiss. He felt like he was grasping at the last chance he'd ever have to touch her. She opened for him, like she needed him as desperately as he did her. Teeth scraping, hands grabbing, nails scratching. As if they were snatching the last bits of each other they'd get before they lost it forever. But after another moment she pushed him away.

"No." She shook her head. "I can't. I've been doing this

all week. Letting my feelings make me forget how hard it was to lose you. How much it hurt to know my love for you wasn't enough. That it won't ever be enough."

"Esmeralda." It was on the tip of his tongue to say. He needed to say it. "I love you."

She squeezed her eyes shut like she couldn't bear to hear the words at all. "Don't say that. Don't tell me that when you hid the truth from me. When you don't treat me as your equal. Love is not just desire and lust, it's trust, it's a partnership, Rodrigo. My father spent years telling my mother he loved her and when it came down to it, he let her find out he married someone else on the news. Turned his back on her without even so much as an explanation." She swiped at her cheeks where tears were streaming down. "You say you love me, and yet in the past twenty-four hours you let me stay in the dark about a situation that had everything to do with me. That could determine my future." The raw pain in her voice, knowing he was responsible for putting it there, felt like someone was twisting a knife in his chest.

"I didn't want to worry you. Carmelina's a viper and she has no scruples. I wanted to spare you having to deal with her."

She laughed bitterly. "You think I don't know who Carmelina is, Rodrigo? That woman refused to let me come see my father when he was dying in the hospital. If you hadn't made sure my mother heard about it when he passed away, I would've found out he died from an obituary." She looked and sounded exhausted, bone tired.

"I'm not a child, Rodrigo. Do you know why I decided to claim the CEO position?" she asked, and he straightened, dread sitting in his stomach like lead. "It's true that I wanted to claim my place. That I wanted a chance to create my vision. But I also wanted to take something from you."

It hurt to hear it, but in a way he understood. Her face was streaked with tears, misery rolling off her in waves. "I was so hurt. The two men in my life always choosing their damned corner offices over me. So, yeah, I wanted to take it from you."

She sounded small and wounded, and even as her words poked holes in his chest, he ached for her. "My father and his dysfunction, his games, turned everyone in his life into pawns. All of us wondering how we were lacking. Trying to blindly fix ourselves to deserve his love and his regard." Her words almost knocked him to the ground. Because she was right. "But now I realize that he had nothing to give. My father's only love was Sambrano. The thing he built, which in the end he couldn't care for, either. And I'm done thinking there was something in me that wasn't enough. I'm more than enough, and I deserve someone who sees that," she said, pressing a palm to her chest. "I deserve someone who sees me as an equal and continuing to expect it from people who can't give it to me is going to destroy me."

"This job is all I have, Esmeralda," he ground out, even as he saw the last bit of light go out of her eyes.

"Someday you'll figure out that's a lie you've been telling yourself. Too bad that when you do, you'll have pushed everyone who loves you away." And with that she walked out on him without a backward glance.

Eighteen

"**D**id you really think I was just going to let you get away with ignoring my calls?" Marquito asked as he pushed into Rodrigo's office. He'd gone home after the fallout with Esmeralda and had ignored everyone who'd tried to reach out to him. He was wrecked and at a loss of what to do, because she was right about everything.

He'd hoped to figure out how to talk to her, but tell her what? That they could make it work, even as he intended to take the job she was fighting for? He had no clue, but he could not deny the unbearable hollowness he'd been feeling since the moment she'd walked away from him.

And now here he was two days later, still at a loss on how to fix any of it.

"I'm not in the mood, little brother. The meeting with the board is in two hours and I still have no idea what's going to happen. And no matter what, there's no winning. Either I keep the job and she hates me or she gets it and I have to start over."

Marquito made a dismissive sound, which only made Rodrigo's mood darken further. "Starting over owning twenty-five percent of Sambrano is not exactly a bad place, and the board will never let you go. You know that. You own a quarter of this company now, Rodrigo," Marquito said, spreading his arms in the air. "Let that sink in. You had the means and the resources to come up with two hundred million dollars in *a day*. You have a stake in this place. You're no longer an employee, you're part owner of this studio."

He heard the words and still he felt nothing. He'd finally found a way to push out Carmelina, to defuse her power over the future of Sambrano, but he couldn't even enjoy it. Because in the process he'd ruined everything with the woman he loved. He could say that now. He would not hide from the truth now, and his love for Esmeralda was the greatest truth of his life. Just because he'd forced himself to ignore it for ten years didn't make it less of an undeniable fact.

"Esme knows about what went down with her mom ten years ago." Rodrigo knew he sounded wrung out, but there was no helping it. He was really at his wit's end.

"Shit." Marquito whistled. He'd been away at college when all that went down, but over the years his mom had talked about it. "I assume she didn't take it well."

He laughed bitterly at his little brother's understatement and he got up to get a bottle of water from the mini fridge in his office. "You could say that. She accused me of not trusting her, then when I told her I loved her she yelled at me some more. *Then* she told me I didn't treat her as an equal and was going to die alone."

He knew he was being unfair, that it was a hell of a lot more than that, but he was hurt. He felt once again that trying to do the right thing had cost him everything.

"She told me I had a martyr complex," he muttered, then snapped his head up when Marquito choked on the coffee he was drinking.

"You agree with that?" His little brother's cheeks flushed red at the question.

"I mean, she's not *totally* wrong." Marquito at least had the decency of sounding contrite.

"Of course she's not. What *she* are we talking about again?" Jimena's voice resounded in the office as she strode in. Figured that he would have everyone in Manhattan still talking to him here to hand him his ass at his lowest moment.

His brother, the traitor, grinned at his friend's arrival and lifted his coffee cup in Rodrigo's direction. "Esmeralda seems to have regaled my brother with some hard truths before telling him to get his shit together."

"Ah," Jimena responded in a tone that sounded very much like *it was about damn time someone did.*

He ought to throw them both out of his office, but they were the *only* two people left in his corner. "Are you two here to help me or pour salt on my wounds?"

"Did you hear the same thing I heard, Marquito?" Jimena asked, clutching her chest dramatically. "Did Mr. Lobo Solitario just utter the *H*-word?" She actually stage whispered, but he didn't think either of them were funny.

"I ask for help, dammit," Rodrigo said through clenched teeth. "You two think this is a joke? The woman I love thinks I would choose a job over her. Everyone in my life thinks I'm some kind of selfish, power-hungry drone. And I don't even know what all of this has been for," he said, looking out the window that gave him a clear view of Central Park and beyond. One of the most coveted views on earth, and looking at it right now, he felt empty.

"Maybe Carmelina was right, and I did sell my soul for this." He thought of the renovated brownstone that had costs millions, the ranch in Santa Fe with acres of land he'd never even been to, the villa in Punta Cana he rarely ever got to anymore. Money and properties that at one time seemed unattainable. He had so much now. But did he really enjoy any of it? He knew he wouldn't like the answer if he asked it out loud.

"Carmelina is never right," Jimena stated tersely as Marquito nodded in agreement.

But wasn't she? All he did was work and try to prove again and again that he deserved to be where he was. No personal life to speak of. And it *had* made him bitter. It had made him closed off, cold. After Esmeralda and then his mother, he had shut down. Until she'd walked back into his life a week ago and made him question everything.

"Rodrigo, for sixteen years you operated in the shadow of a brilliant but deeply flawed man, who cared for you, yes, but who also tended to treat the people he loved like shit." Jimena's voice was soft, like she didn't want to hurt him, but her gaze didn't waver from his. And he knew he had to hear this. "Which means, one, you need a really good therapist ASAP and two, you have to figure out what it is that *you* want, because news flash, you can do that now. You can walk out of here this minute and you will be doing it as a very wealthy man with a résumé and skill set only a few dozen people on the planet have. I can think of at least five networks who would ask you to name your price if it got out that you're a free agent."

"It's not that simple," he told Jimena, even as her words buzzed in his head.

"It is, though. You, my friend, have arrived at a place in your life where professionally and financially you not only have nothing to worry about, you have *choices*." He knew she was right. But the truth was he didn't want to leave Sambrano. His loyalty to this place was about more than just getting the corner office or the three letters after his name.

"I want to stay at Sambrano. This is finally my moment. After all this time I'm poised to do what I've always wanted to do with the studio." He thought of that old memo Esmeralda had found, the ideas he'd had and never been able to see come to fruition. He thought about the way Esme had clearly gotten his message. How she'd taken the seed of his idea and turned it into a vision for the future of Sambrano. They worked well together. They would make a hell of a team. "I have projects I want to see through. I have things I need to do. *I want to stay.*"

He loved the work he did here. He couldn't let go of the possibility of what the future could hold with him at the helm…and maybe, *maybe* with Esmeralda there, too.

"And what else do you want?" Marquito asked, with a knowing grin on his face.

"I want her by my side." He didn't need to tell them who, they both knew.

"Then go get her, pendejo," Jimena scolded him. "And don't just decide on what you think is a great idea and roll with it without letting her in on it like a jackass. That's what keeps getting you into messes."

"You're really taking advantage of the fact that I'm at a low moment to get all your digs in, aren't you?" he told his friend, who responded with a smart-ass grin. But a plan was already forming in his head. His heart leaped with the possibilities and he smiled as a thought started to form. He might have a solution for how Esmeralda and he could both be at the helm of Sambrano. He just had to convince her that they were better together than they were apart, in business *and* in love.

"Mija, are you hiding from me?" Ivelisse asked Esmeralda as she was sneaking around at the crack of dawn, trying to get out of the apartment before her mother woke up.

"No, Mami," she lied as she leaned in to kiss her mother on the cheek.

"I waited up for you until almost midnight."

"I was just going over my presentation, with the board meeting getting moved up and everything..." she trailed off as her mother studied her, aware that there was a lot more to her late night at the office than the presentation.

"You never told me how things ended. Just a text saying Rodrigo wasn't trying to push you out, and that you were fine. And you were MIA all day yesterday." Her mother reached up to tug gently on the thin hoops Esmeralda was wearing on her ears. The ones made of intertwined rose, yellow and white gold that she always wore for good luck. The ones that Rodrigo had given her for her twenty-first birthday.

"Tell me, mija."

"Rodrigo and I sort of started..." What could she even say? Hooking up like horny teens? That she'd told him she loved him and he'd said it back and then she'd walked out on him?

Her mother's soft laughter brought her out of her highly embarrassing thoughts. "Ay, Mija, even if I hadn't already suspected after you snuck in here almost at dawn after that cocktail party, I would've confirmed it the day he was here." Her mother's smile said *you're an adorable mess.* "You two have always been very bad at hiding the way you feel about each other."

"Well, it's over," she said miserably. She'd left that horrible meeting with Rodrigo and gone straight to her little office share. Had stayed there as much as she could since then. She could've gone home, but she didn't have it in her to answer questions from her mother. And she just could not face anyone at Sambrano. Not after the mess with Carmelina. Especially not when they'd moved her presentation up.

But she was ready, in part thanks to Rodrigo. The footage he'd given her access to and that memo of his she'd found had sparked the idea for her plan, but the conversations they'd had this week had cemented it. Despite the many challenges and disappointments he'd had in his time at Sambrano, Rodrigo still believed in the company. He believed in the mission. And Esmeralda found that she believed in it, too. She could clearly envision a path forward and she hoped she could be a part of making it happen.

And then there were her very complicated feelings for the acting CEO of Sambrano Studios.

It had been almost impossible to walk away from him after he uttered those words she never thought she'd hear again. But Rodrigo could not untangle his sense of obligation and misguided loyalties to her father from what he felt for her. She loved him, but she would not be with a man who could not be vulnerable. A man who didn't trust her, who didn't treat her like an equal partner. She deserved someone who could see in her the person who complemented them, who thought of her as essential to their life.

Her father had turned his back on her because she didn't fit into the image of the family he wanted to show the world. Rodrigo had walked away from her because he'd been ensnared by terrible choices. And even if she understood his reasons now, he could've told her the truth. He could've trusted that she was strong enough to bear it. But instead, he'd pushed her out of his life.

That was her, the person who never quite fit. The easiest one to crop out. The one whose absence wouldn't alter the outcome. And she was done with that. She wanted someone to whom she was essential, someone who not only saw her as part of the picture, but who believed there was no picture without her. She deserved that.

"Of course it isn't over." Her mother's voice pulled her back from her musings, and Esme had to smile at her determined expression. "You two are crazy about each other." Her mother clicked her tongue and pulled her by the hand to the corner of the apartment that held their kitchen. "Ven, te preparé un desayunito."

"Mami, I don't have time for breakfast. I need to get this presentation perfect. These people are just looking for an excuse to push me out. I'm not going to give it to them by showing up late."

"You have to eat, Esmeralda," her mother declared as she puttered around. "And you have to stop this thinking like you don't already belong there. Your father—"

Her mother closed her eyes, trailing off from what she was about to say. Esme had always wondered what her mother thought of whenever she recalled her relationship with Patricio. They'd been together for almost five years when he left her for Carmelina and in the years since, her mother rarely mentioned her time with him. It was like Esmeralda and that Cartier watch were the only proof there had been anything between her mother and Patricio Sambrano. Esme couldn't even recall ever seeing them in the same room together. When her father was done with Ivelisse it was like she'd ceased to exist. Esmeralda had never been able to wrap her head around how she'd coped with that kind of rejection. And still her mother had maintained her goodness, and raised her in a home full of love and optimism.

"Your father…" Her mother's voice cracked like thunder in their quiet kitchen. "Was a man who never learned to love himself. Even with all he achieved. Patricio built an empire from nothing. His mind was a marvel, so fearless, a real visionary. You remind me of him in that way." Her mother's smile was bittersweet. She focused on the window that gave them a view of the river, her eyes fixed on something in the distance. "But he never could shake off the demons of his past. He never let anyone get close enough. Not me, not his wife, his kids. He was so afraid of losing what he had, he never let himself enjoy it. But that has nothing to do with you and the right you have to be there. Patricio made so many mistakes in his life, but I think what he did with his will was his way of trying to make amends."

Esme shook her head at that. "Except he put me and Rodrigo at odds, and how fair was that for either of us?"

"It forced you to be together," Ivelisse quipped,

and Esmeralda had to take a moment to think that bit through. "Patricio could be a real jerk, cruel even. But he rarely ever made missteps with his business."

"I don't know how this is going to end, Mami," Esmeralda confessed.

"You already belong in that boardroom. You're a Sambrano. Whether they agree or not. You have the means now to forge your own way, mija. If you don't want the shares, sell them. Start your own company. But if you want to stay, don't let anyone take that from you."

Her mother's words buoyed her, but still there was Rodrigo. Her pushing for what she wanted would hurt him, and she hated that her father had put them in this situation. "Me getting the CEO position will oust Rodrigo." That didn't mean he couldn't stay on, but she didn't think he'd want to if it wasn't as CEO.

"That's something you both need to figure out together, how to forge forward."

"I told him it was over."

"Then go back in there and tell him you were wrong," her mother said as she brought her in for a hug. "Tell him you were scared. Tell him you want to try again. Rodrigo's not your father, baby. He's not perfect," Ivelisse conceded. "But that boy is loyal and he doesn't give up on the people he loves. Maybe what he needs to hear is that you'll be there for him, too. But first, breakfast."

Esme sat down with her bowl of oats fragrant with the cinnamon and lime zest her mother put in the milk and decided to maybe take her advice.

Nineteen

"I need to talk to you," they both said in unison when Rodrigo rushed into Esmeralda's office. He'd been waiting for her to get in for almost an hour, practically bursting with anticipation. The meeting with the board was set for noon and since his conversation with Jimena and Marquito he'd done nothing but work out the details of how to keep his job *and* the woman he loved. It was now 11:00 a.m., an hour before both their fates would be decided, and he was pretty certain he'd found the solution.

But of course, the moment he walked into her office, Esme had yanked them off script. He'd expected her to send him packing, so he'd prepared to beg. To his surprise, she seemed as eager to see him as he was her. And it appeared she also had something to say.

"I don't want one of us to lose in this, Rodrigo." She sounded conflicted but determined, and that only increased his hopes that things could work out. He was convinced that what he had in mind was the answer. And if she agreed with him, they could walk into the boardroom as a united front.

"Me, either." He ached to touch her, had to put his hands in his trouser pockets to keep from doing it. "We deserve this chance, both of us do, and I think I have a way to make it work, but first I need to say something." His voice almost gave out with those last words.

"You don't have to, Rodrigo, I—"

"Please, Joya. Let me say this to you," he pleaded. This felt like the most important moment of his life, the weight on his chest cementing that this conversation was the one that he *must* get right. He'd lost too much time by keeping what he felt locked inside. He'd let this woman who meant everything to him think he didn't care for her out of misguided loyalty. At the time he hadn't had many choices, but he had them now. He needed to make sure Esmeralda understood she'd never been anything less than essential. That he'd felt her absence in his life every single day of the past ten years.

"There is something I should've said about what happened at that meeting with Global Networks. What I did, I didn't do that for me, for Sambrano or even just for you. I did it for us. Mi amor."

Those two words, *my love*. They fell from his lips so naturally, as if they had been on the tip of his tongue for years and were now rushing to be spoken. To her.

"In these past few years I lost my passion for the work. I have doggedly stayed on at Sambrano because I couldn't think of what else to do. But in the few days you've been here…" he said, taking her hands in his. Unable to hold back, he clutched them to his chest. "You've reminded me of the reasons I fell in love with this business. Of how even during those times when I wondered if I could continue dealing with the intrigue and the scheming, I couldn't walk away. And now I know why."

"Why?" Esmeralda asked breathlessly, as she pressed herself to him. If she was seeking his closeness then things could not be too far gone. Maybe there really was a chance for them. For a future together.

"I needed a partner. I needed someone who shared my vision of where we can take your father's legacy. Someone who understands what this company can be. I was waiting for *you*." He saw her eyes fill with tears, but there was a smile on her lips and a small ember of hope lit up in his chest. "I think we should both get to run Sambrano Studios." He watched as his words registered, and her smile grew a little bit wider.

"Both of us? But the board said they would pick. That only one person could have the job. How?"

He nodded at her questions, and with every passing second he was further convinced this was the path forward. That this was the only way they could have it all. The only way to ensure that the company was run in a way that honored Patricio's vision while giving their relationship a fighting chance.

"We split the position."

"Split it?" she asked, leaning back but never letting go of his hands.

"Yes." He nodded, hoping she'd agree. "President and CEO could very well be done by two people. The CEO is the person who manages operations, who has a handle on the business. I can do that. I've *been* doing that. But the president is all about vision, about keeping us looking at the bigger picture. That's you, Esmeralda."

Her brows furrowed in concentration, head tilted to the side as she considered his proposal. He knew this would mean asking her to trust him, and he hoped he hadn't shattered that completely. She hummed, and he smiled knowing this was the sound she made when she was lost in thought. She let go of his hands, but her expression wasn't forbidding—she was analyzing.

He felt the urgency under his skin. That electric feeling he only got when he knew he had a winner in his hands. In television these days it seemed like everything had been done. So many networks focusing on reboots and revivals of past hits. But every once in a while, something came across his desk that he knew could change the game. He had that feeling now.

When she finally looked up at him, there was a glint in those beautiful whiskey-colored eyes he hadn't seen in what felt like an eternity. Today she'd forgone the suit for something that was more Esmeralda. A dark green knee-length dress that managed to look professional and also highlight every luscious curve of her body. Her honey curls cascaded over her shoulders and when he looked closely he smiled at the sight of her lucky hoops dangling from her ears.

She stepped up, her eyes boring into him. "Before I agree to anything there are a few things I need to be very clear on, Rodrigo Almanzar. One…" She held up a finger, her other hand on her hip. "I will not be a silent partner. I want us to both have the same authority."

"Of course, I expect you to run this place with me."

"Two. I will have opinions, and I will have plans. Some of those will be different from yours or push against what you're envisioning and we will have to find ways to compromise. To figure out what works best for the company."

"A partnership," he agreed, his heart beating in his chest and a smile already tugging at his lips. He was usually careful, never one to count his eggs before they hatched, but it was hard to hold back when he was so close to getting everything he'd ever wanted.

"I refuse to just be a convenient warm body with the last name Sambrano that you trot out for photo ops." She was trying very hard to sound mad, but her lips were fully pulled up in a hopeful smile he could almost bet was a mirror image of his own.

"I expect you to be at the office across from mine every day and to help me build a network that we can both be proud of," he told her, and he tugged on her hand, bringing her a little closer.

"Are you really willing to take a pay cut?" she probed, this time her expression much more serious. He was. He'd thought about it and the reality was that going from making fifty million to twenty-five was almost an absurd thing to be upset about. And he barely spent on anything. Because he had no life. He'd paid cash for his house and the other properties were investments that essentially paid for themselves. It was a good thing, too, since most of the wealth he'd accumulated had gone into a stake in Sambrano. It had been worth every penny.

"Getting half of what I get now isn't exactly a hardship, mi vida." He was running fast and loose with the endearments, but he couldn't seem to stop himself. She was all that: his love, his life, his jewel. And it was about time he started saying it.

He brought her into his arms and she pressed into him like he was her harbor, her body relaxing against him. Soft and warm…and perfect. He would spend the rest of his life earning the right to be the shoulder she always leaned on. "Can we really do this? What if the board doesn't go for it?"

He pressed kisses into her hair, just because he needed to be as close as possible. "This board is interested in preserving the core values of this company, and once they see your presentation and hear *our* plan they won't be able to deny that this is the most logical path forward."

"But what about Carmelina?" He could not help the growl that rose from his throat at the mention of the woman.

"She's lost her power. Now she needs us to dictate what happens with Sambrano. The two of us together have more power than she does."

Esme looked up at him, her eyes bright with something that looked very much like his future and pushed up until their lips were pressed together. "I want this to work," she confessed against his lips.

"*We* will make it work. Because the most important part of this plan is you and me, and we already have that." They pressed their foreheads together as their mouths met again. Soon he was holding her tight. Deepening the kiss. Every cell in his body attuned to the woman in his arms. The only person on earth who could bring him back to himself. Who was able to remind him who he'd always wanted to be. The woman who brought into perfect clarity for him that success wasn't just about power—it was about turning that power into purpose.

Someone knocked on the glass door to his office, and when Esme went to step away from him he pressed her closer. He would die before hiding what this woman meant to him ever again.

"Sir, the board is ready for you," his assistant informed him and discreetly slipped out again.

"Are you ready for this?" Esmeralda asked as she gripped his hand and headed to the door. He looked down at her, overwhelmed by the rightness of the moment. The certainty in what they were about to do. "It feels like we've been waiting half our lives for this," she said, almost dreamily.

"Our future's waiting, mi amor. Let's go claim it," he said, as he walked out of his office with the love of his life by his side.

Epilogue

One Year Later

"Mmm… I love starting a workweek like this." Esmeralda gasped as Rodrigo trailed kisses down her body, his lips parting so he could lap at her heated skin.

"Technically we're off today, amor. Travel day," he reminded her before sucking one of her hard nipples into his mouth.

"Right," she responded, voice reedy with need. They were supposed to fly to Las Vegas in a few hours. They had a big week ahead of them, which had Esme a bit jittery, but Rodrigo's hands and mouth on her always had the power to make everything else feel inconsequential. Especially when his lips hovered right at her heat. She pulsed with need, desire coiling up inside her tighter and tighter until she was trembling from it.

"Mmm, here it is," he whispered as his fingers explored her. His tongue flicked her clitoris, making her cry out. "I love it when you scream for me, mi vida," he told her, voice low and dirty as he sucked and licked Esmeralda into a frenzy.

"I need you," she pleaded, widening her legs to make room for him, and soon he was sliding up her body, cock in his hand and about to enter her.

"Is this what you want?" he growled against her ear as he pressed the tip into her.

She gasped as pleasure threatened to obliterate her. "All of you, baby, please."

"I love you," he groaned as he pushed in slowly. He was a big man and even when she was burning for him she needed time to accommodate all of him. Sometimes she wanted slow, sweet lovemaking, and Rodrigo would do that. He'd keep her on the brink, pleasuring her again and again for hours, but this morning, she wanted it fast and hard. And he seemed to always know exactly what she wanted. In a couple of thrusts he sheathed himself in her. Filling her to the brim.

"You're perfect," he whispered against her mouth as he started to move. His hips circling in that way that made every nerve inside her spark. The heat of him always managed to melt her.

"We're perfect together." She gasped as she moved to meet him thrust for thrust. They'd come together a year ago and started building the life she'd always wanted and thought she would never be able to have. They were true and equal partners in everything. Even their home. As he moved in her, she pressed kisses to his skin, grateful for this man and this life she now had.

"Where did you go, baby? Am I not keeping your attention?" he teased and a pool of heat spread at her center as he brought his thumb to her mouth. "Get it wet for me, sweetheart." She shuddered out a shaky breath then sucked on it as he asked. Once he was satisfied he brought the pad of his finger down to her engorged clit and circled it exactly how he know she liked. Within seconds a frantic, electric wave of pleasure was crashing into her. He doubled his efforts, pistoning into her ruthlessly, and soon he was stiffening over her in a silent cry as his own climax took him.

He gathered her into his arms, as if she was something precious. As she burrowed into Rodrigo, Esme once again marveled at how different her life was now than it had been a year ago when she'd crashed into the Sambrano boardroom to claim her inheritance. After they'd walked into that meeting together and presented their plan to the board everything had fallen into place, almost as if fate had been waiting for the two of them to finally figure it out.

The board had not only approved splitting the president and CEO position, they thought it was the ideal solution. And once that had been sorted out, Rodrigo and Esme began working on their relationship. And that had been a wonderful adventure, too. Last month they'd moved into their new home—a renovated brownstone in the Upper West Side that they'd bought together. And now she was lying in their master bedroom, which had a gorgeous view of the Hudson. She had everything she'd ever dreamed of. Including the man who had stolen her heart at twenty-one.

A kiss on her temple brought her out of her thoughts and Rodrigo's raspy morning voice in her ear made a shiver run through her. "What are you thinking?"

"That I'm happy, and nervous as hell for this week."

That earned her another kiss, this one deeper and hotter, the kind that made her toes curl and her heart flutter. "We got this, baby," Rodrigo whispered in her ear, as he shifted them so she was lying on top of him.

In her heart she knew they would be fine, but she was still nervous. Today they were headed to the International Broadcasters Trade Show, where Sambrano Studios would be unveiling their newest product: a streaming service package with four new networks solely producing Latinx content. Food and travel, history, music, and film and documentary channels celebrating every Latinx culture from Mexico all the way to Argentina. Rodrigo and the board had let her run with her vision this past year, and now they were ready to make it public. The response from the beta trials had been wildly successful, but now her baby would be out there in the world.

"I hope people like it."

"It's brilliant," he said as he put a hand behind her head and brought her down for a kiss. His handsome, beloved face was open and bright as he smiled up at her—Rodrigo smiled so often now. "*You're* brilliant, and this is going to put the Sambrano brand on another level. You were what we needed. You were what *I* needed. The future is bright, mi cielo. And I can't wait to spend it with you."

"Te amo," Esmeralda said, her eyes filling with happy tears as she let the man she loved wrap her in his arms.

* * * * *

COMING SOON!

LET'S TALK
Romance

For exclusive extracts, competitions
and special offers, find us online:

 facebook.com/millsandboon

🐦 @MillsandBoon

📷 @MillsandBoonUK

Get in touch on 01413 063232

MILLS & BOON

THE HEART OF ROMANCE

A ROMANCE FOR EVERY READER

MODERN

Prepare to be swept off your feet by sophisticated, sexy and seductive heroes, in some of the world's most glamourous and roman locations, where power and passion collide.

HISTORICAL

Escape with historical heroes from time gone by. Whether your passion for wicked Regency Rakes, muscled Vikings or rugged Highlanders, av the romance of the past.

MEDICAL

Set your pulse racing with dedicated, delectable doctors in the high-pre sure world of medicine, where emotions run high and passion, comfor love are the best medicine.

True Love

Celebrate true love with tender stories of heartfelt romance, from the rush of falling in love to the joy a new baby can bring, and a focus on emotional heart of a relationship.

Desire

Indulge in secrets and scandal, intense drama and plenty of sizzling ho action with powerful and passionate heroes who have it all: wealth, stat good looks…everything but the right woman.

HEROES

Experience all the excitement of a gripping thriller, with an intense romance at its heart. Resourceful, true-to-life women and strong, fearless face danger and desire - a killer combination!

To see which titles are coming soon, please visit

millsandboon.co.uk/nextmonth

JOIN US ON SOCIAL MEDIA!

Stay up to date with our latest releases, author news and gossip, special offers and discounts, and all the behind-the-scenes action from Mills & Boon...

 millsandboon

 millsandboonuk

f millsandboon

MILLS & BOON

HEROES

At Your Service

Experience all the excitement of a gripping thriller, with an intense romance at its heart. Resourceful, true-to-life women and strong, fearless men face danger and desire - a killer combination!

MILLS & BOON
True Love
Romance from the Heart

Celebrate true love with tender stories of
heartfelt romance, from the rush of falling
in love to the joy a new baby can bring,
and a focus on the emotional
heart of a relationship.

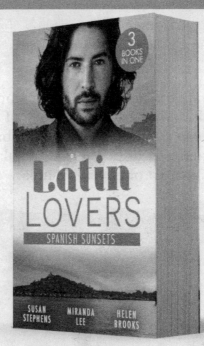